"Starr Ambrose brings forth the perfect combination of humor, heat, and intrigue to entertain for hours."

—Romance Junkies

LIE TO ME

"Likeable characters and an intriguing premise. . . . Sizzles with delicious friction."

—*Publishers Weekly*

"Sassy, sexy, and sensuous. Ambrose adds a welcome, bright new voice to the genre. Her lighthearted repartee imparts a special charm to this novel."

—*Winter Haven News Chief* (FL)

"An excellent debut novel. . . . With this stellar (pun intended) beginning, Starr Ambrose is a name to watch for in the romantic suspense genre."

—Romance Reviews Today

"A truly wonderful read!"

—Wild on Books

"An entertaining read from start to finish. . . . Starr Ambrose has written a great story full of romance, twists, and one very hot accountant."

—Fallen Angel Reviews

"This book really grabs you and doesn't let go. I was hooked from the first page."

—Book Binge

Gold FIRE

STARR AMBROSE

Pocket Books

New York   London   Toronto   Sydney   New Delhi

Pocket Books
A Division of Simon & Schuster, Inc.
1230 Avenue of the Americas, New York, NY 10020

This book is a work of fiction. Names, characters, places, and incidents either are products of the author's imagination or are used fictitiously. Any resemblance to actual events or locales or persons, living or dead, is entirely coincidental.

Copyright © 2012 by Starr Ambrose

First Pocket Books paperback edition December 2012

POCKET and colophon are registered trademarks of Simon & Schuster, Inc.

For information about special discounts for bulk purchases, please contact Simon & Schuster Special Sales at 1-866-506-1949 or business@simonandschuster.com.

The Simon & Schuster Speakers Bureau can bring authors to your live event. For more information or to book an event contact the Simon & Schuster Speakers Bureau at 1-866-248-3049 or visit our website at www.simonspeakers.com.

Manufactured in the United States of America

10 9 8 7 6 5 4 3 2 1

ISBN 978–1–4516–2364–2
ISBN 978–1–4516–2366–6 (ebook)

For Jim

Gold
FIRE

Chapter One

Jase cracked his eyes and peered through the narrow line where the Stetson didn't quite meet his upturned face. A woman in a dark blazer and skirt stood just inside the front door of his saloon.

Hell. Russ must have left the front door unlocked.

Russ could just deal with it, then, because Jase wasn't getting up for anything. He'd celebrated the hell out of his thirty-third birthday last night, and he needed to catch a few z's before the Rusty Wire Saloon opened for business again. The wooden chair he slouched in and the one propping up his feet made a hard bed, but they'd do.

The woman's heels clicked across the dance floor, prompting him to take another peek. Shapely legs with enough feminine sway to put some swing in the skirt moved briskly across his line of vision. Curious despite himself, he lifted a finger to the brim of his hat.

The blazer hid a lot with its generic-uniform look, but he had a feeling the body beneath it was as shapely as the legs. His gaze lingered on a pretty profile, and reddish-blond hair that would have looked great falling to her shoulders, but was inexplicably bound into some kind of grandmotherly bun thing. A waste of good sex appeal.

He concentrated on dozing again as the woman made a beeline for Billy where he was scrubbing down the bar. "We're not open," he heard Billy say before she could dive into her sales spiel. *Good man.*

"I know." Her voice already said it didn't matter, which didn't sound good for Billy. "I'm Zoe Larkin, from the Alpine Sky. I'd like to speak to the owner, please."

Too bad, Jase thought. Billy said it for him. "He doesn't like to be disturbed this time of day. What can I do for you?"

"I'm afraid I can only speak to the owner."

Billy must have hesitated at that, because he heard a glass hit the bar as Russ downed his Alka-Seltzer and cleared his throat. "Can I help you?" Jase silently thanked him. With Russ and Jennifer sitting at the end of the bar and Billy nearby, his nap had a triple line of defense.

Sharp heels clicked closer as she crossed to the end of the bar. "I'm Zoe Larkin, assistant manager of the Alpine Sky. Are you the owner?"

"Next thing to it. Name's Russ Holbrook. I'm the manager, and I'm probably the one you want to talk to if you're from that fancy resort up the road."

Good point. Russ had handled enough past tiffs with the Alpine Sky to head her off at the pass.

"You people got a problem with the Rusty Wire again? Sorry about last night's crowd, but I already told you, I can't keep my customers from moving on to your bar for more partying after they leave here. Long as they leave reasonably sober, we ain't responsible for what they do."

Right. Now show her to the door.

"I'm not here to complain about rowdy customers, Mr. Holbrook."

Undaunted, Russ replied, "Well, if it's the overflow parking, we already put up new signs so's they'd stay off your precious driveway."

"It's not the parking, either. I'm here to propose a business deal, and only the owner can tell me if he's interested."

"What kind of deal?" Russ sounded suspicious.

"The private kind," she said, polite but firm.

"You suing us for something?"

"Mr. Holbrook . . ."

"'Cause if you are, we got lawyers, too, and we don't take to letting the big resorts tell us what we can and can't do."

Jase heard her blow out an impatient breath. "The Alpine Sky is not suing you, Mr. Holbrook. But we *are* interested in talking with the owner. I would appreciate it if one of you would contact him and let him know I'm here."

"One of you" probably included Jennifer, sitting beside Russ at the bar. Jase's mouth twitched with a repressed smile; Jennifer didn't take well to being told what to do.

Zoe Larkin from the Alpine Sky must have seen it, because her voice took on an irritated edge. "Look, it's a simple request. What's so hard about placing a phone call to the owner? Is he out of the country?"

Jase prayed someone would say yes, but they

missed their big opportunity and met her question with stubborn silence. Damn, this nap wasn't going to happen.

He heard an impatient toe tap. "Is he in prison?"

Most times he might have found that sassy attitude amusing. Not today.

"Perhaps I should just take a seat and wait."

Oh, for Christ's sake. "Don't bother," he said, scraping his footrest out of the way and forcing his tired body into a sitting position. He tipped the hat back to meet the lady's surprised brown eyes. Huh, he'd imagined blue, but he liked what he saw. Leaning his forearms on the table, he looked her over with reluctant appreciation. Giving up sleep had some compensations. "I'm the owner, lady. What do you want?"

Zoe shot an irritated glance at the man she'd taken to be a drunk sleeping off an early buzz. With the hat no longer hiding his features, she could see the hard lines of a strong face beneath at least a day's worth of stubble. His clear gaze caused her to do a mental stumble; the lazy sexuality in his eyes belonged more to a bedroom than a bar. Not that it mattered. His good looks were offset by a put-upon frown that said forcing his body into an erect posture was more work than he'd intended to do all day.

She approached slowly, taking in the wrinkled shirt, faded jeans, and worn boots. The man was as shabby as his saloon, which helped squelch her brief twinge of interest. "You're Jason Garrett?"

"It's just Jase."

She stuck out her hand. "Hello, Mr. Garrett. I'm Zoe—"

"I heard. Zoe Larkin, assistant manager from the Alpine Sky." His interested gaze drank her in again, lingering in a couple of places and setting off a squirmy feeling deep inside her that she dismissed with irritation. "You wanted the owner, you got him. What do you need?"

She took a deep breath, forcing herself not to glare. It didn't matter that he was rude, only that he accept her offer. She was fairly certain that hearing it would wipe that smug look right off his face.

"I'm here to make you an offer on behalf of Ruth Ann Flemming, the owner of the Alpine Sky." She paused a couple of seconds for dramatic effect. "Mrs. Flemming would like to buy the Rusty Wire Saloon."

Behind her, a glass thunked onto the bar. The rhythmic sound of the scrub brush stopped. Jase Garrett didn't move, not even the flicker of an eyelid. His gaze was steady on hers for several long seconds, while she tried not to fidget. "Is that so," he finally said.

Since he hadn't made it a question, she didn't answer. She wished he'd ask one, though, because his thoughtful stare made her nervous.

"What does the exalted Alpine Sky want with my saloon?"

"We would like to expand our business."

His gaze took a slow trip up and down her suit. "A honky-tonk doesn't seem like your style, Miss Larkin."

"Thank you, it isn't. But the Alpine Sky doesn't actually want your saloon, Mr. Garrett. We want your land. As you know, our resort is a popular winter destination for skiers. We would like to offer summer activities, too, which means building a golf course. For that we need more land. A semiflat piece, like the one your saloon sits on."

The stillness at the bar behind her was palpable, as if all three people were holding their breath. Jase's shadowed eyes gave nothing away. "You want to tear down the Rusty Wire?"

"I imagine if the building is in good condition, it might be used for something else." She gave the room a quick glance, deciding not to tell him the chances of that were next to zero. "The town's records show that the lot size, including parking, is two acres. You also own the fifty behind it. Those acres adjoin the Alpine Sky, and they would be ideal for an eighteen-hole course."

"That land is untouched wilderness."

She raised an eyebrow. "Mr. Garrett, the Rocky Mountains are full of untouched wilderness. You can buy as much as you want. The only thing special about *your* piece of wilderness is that it adjoins our resort."

"And it's flat."

"Yes, relatively."

His expressionless gaze held hers for a long time. A bar stool squeaked behind her, but she didn't turn.

"The Rusty Wire's not for sale."

She smiled. "You haven't heard our offer yet, Mr. Garrett. It's more than generous."

"Doesn't matter."

"Two point five million."

Zoe heard the woman suck in her breath. She tried not to look smug as she waited for Jase Garrett's eyes to widen and his mouth to drop open in shock. It didn't happen. Nothing happened.

"No thanks." He all but yawned.

No thanks, that was it? It wasn't a deal breaker, but she would have bet everything she had that he'd snap it up, and probably order a beer to celebrate. Irritation prickled just under her skin, making it hard to keep up an appearance of calm. "Mr. Garrett, perhaps you should take some time to explore the price of real estate around Barringer's Pass. Two and a half million is an incredibly high price for fifty-two acres of mostly undeveloped land."

Finally, his expression changed. His eyebrows drew together and a muscle clenched along his firm jaw. "I said no, Miss Larkin. That's my answer. Go make your pitch to whoever owns the land on the other side of the Alpine Sky."

It was wordier than his other responses, but just as negative. It also revealed their weakest bargaining point. She pressed her mouth together, reluctant to admit what she had to say. "The other side is federal land. They aren't open to an offer."

"Neither am I."

She closed her eyes and sighed, making a big deal out of her reluctance to give in. Let him think he'd made a crafty bargain. She dropped her voice. "I'm not authorized to offer more money, Mr. Garrett, but just between the two of us, if you gave me a counteroffer of three million, I might be able to convince Mrs. Flemming to pay it."

He actually scowled. "Miss Larkin, I appreciate your dedication to your job, but I've given my answer. Now run along." Tugging a chair closer, he propped his feet up, slouched down, and dropped the hat back over his eyes.

She stared. A show of resistance wouldn't have surprised her, but she hadn't been prepared for a flat rejection. Who turned down three million dollars for a crappy saloon and a few acres of trees? She was missing something here, and she wasn't leaving until she figured out what it was.

Jase waited for the click of heels across the dance floor, interested enough to take one more look at the resort lady's legs as she left. For one of the infamous Larkin girls, she wasn't what he'd expected. But then, rumors were often wrong.

He didn't hear retreating footsteps. He poked a cautious finger at his hat brim and lifted it an inch. She was still standing there, her pretty lips pulled into a tight line and her irritated gaze boring into him. A no-nonsense look that went well with her severe hairstyle.

Her body language intrigued him, but he had no interest in her offer. He pushed the hat up a couple more inches. "Miss Larkin, I can't help but notice you're still here."

"Nothing gets past you, does it, Mr. Garrett?"

"What else do you want?"

"I want an explanation. I offered you far more than this old place and that undeveloped land are worth. In fact, my guess is that the Rusty Wire is aptly named, and that rust isn't even the worst of your problems in a building this old." She looked around the saloon, taking in the century-old bar along with the new light fixtures and new windows. "You've probably had to dump a ton of cash into plumbing and electrical updates, just to mention the obvious. I think it's safe to assume it takes most of your profits to keep this place up to code."

That was accurate enough to raise her a notch in his estimation; she wasn't just some corporate lackey delivering a message. Assistant manager, she'd said. She probably knew a lot about running an establishment that served the public. Not that it would help her argument any. "What's your point?"

"My point is that I just offered you the equivalent of a winning lottery ticket, and you turned it down without a thought."

"I thought about it. Maybe I just think faster than you."

She ignored the jab. "Why would you turn down a small fortune when keeping the Rusty Wire open will eventually *cost* you a small fortune?"

He flashed a cocky smile to go with his bluff so she wouldn't guess how little he knew about his own saloon's finances.

"Keeping the Rusty Wire open *doesn't* cost me a small fortune, Miss Larkin. If you work up the hill, I'm sure you've seen how busy this place is on a Friday or Saturday night. We turn a nice profit. But thanks for your concern."

Her frown said she wasn't buying it, and he didn't want to argue the details, since he didn't know them. He kicked the chair aside again and got to his feet, walking around the table to place a guiding hand on her elbow. It would have been a nice bonus if his six-foot-three height intimidated her, but she looked to be at least five six, and her high heels narrowed the difference even more. Besides, he doubted assistant manager Zoe Larkin was easily intimidated, even in bare feet.

"Not that it's any of your business, Miss Larkin, but you might say I've already won the lottery. I don't need your three million."

Her gaze narrowed as she tried to figure it out. While she thought, he opened the door and escorted her through the small entry space and out the second door.

She stopped dead in the parking lot as soon as he took his hand off her elbow. "What does that mean? Are you saying you have so much money you can afford to throw some away on a run-down saloon?"

"I'm saying you can't buy me, Miss Larkin. You run back up to that fancy palace on the hill and tell that to the lady who sent you here. Have a nice day now, you hear?" Before she could argue that with him, too, he turned and walked back inside, locking the door behind him.

They were all watching him. Russ and Jennifer had swiveled their stools toward the door, and Billy seemed to have forgotten the scrub brush in his hand. They waited for him to say something.

"Leave it locked until we open." He walked back to his chair and settled in again. With luck, he'd get a couple hours' sleep before they opened at three.

"Jase!"

Billy's yell would have knocked him off his chair if he hadn't been half expecting it. With a sigh, he sat up and faced the three people at the bar. "What?"

"Didn't you hear what she said? Three million dollars!" His eyes nearly popped out.

"Yeah, I heard."

"Are you crazy? Who turns down three million dollars?"

"Someone who doesn't want to sell."

Billy's mouth opened, but he simply stared. Russ took up the slack. "You think this place is really worth that much?"

"Nah, not even with the land."

"Might be worth more than you think," he insisted.

"Trust me, it's not. They must be in a hurry to turn it into a golf course and pull in more business. They'd make up the cost in no time."

"So why'd you say no?"

"Because I don't want to sell, simple as that. I like it here. And I prefer looking at the trees on Two Bears Mountain instead of a golf course. The resorts have already swallowed up enough of B-Pass." He looked at Jennifer. As usual, he couldn't read her calm gaze. "You think I'm crazy, too?"

"No. I think owning the Rusty Wire suits you. What else would you do?"

"Exactly. Thank you. Now, if you all don't mind, I'm going to take a nap."

No one said anything, so he settled back, propped his boots on a chair, and put the hat over his face. Sleep wasn't going to be possible—he could still feel their stares on him. But as long as he faked it, he wouldn't have to answer more questions.

Dodging the truth wasn't easy. Telling it would have been even harder, requiring him to face the unsettling suspicion that the Rusty Wire was the only thing that held him together these days. If he didn't say it aloud, he could pretend it wasn't true.

Maybe Jennifer knew him better than he'd thought.

• • •

Zoe fumed as she drove the half mile up the mountain to the Alpine Sky Village. She was a professional, presenting a major business deal. Or trying to. He might as well have patted her on the head and told her to run along. He *had* told her to run along, the patronizing jerk.

He was a lazy slob, too, if he could sit there and nap while his saloon needed cleaning. She'd spent some time hanging out with people like him and recognized the type. Party all night, sleep all day, and never do a bit of work you don't have to. She'd narrowly escaped getting sucked into that mire herself, and would prefer to stay away from it. People in Barringer's Pass had long memories.

Jase Garrett obviously didn't know her—she wasn't a quitter. She was going to do some homework on him, and hope like hell he was too lazy to do any on her. Next time she went to the Rusty Wire, she'd know everything there was to know about both Jase and his saloon, including what might tempt him to sell.

Reaching the landscaped streets of the luxury resort community eased her irritation. In contrast to the Rusty Wire, everything about the Alpine Sky screamed class and dignity—the stone-and-timber theme of the main lodge and its related condos, the cute gift shops and ski stores across from the lodge, even the quaint stone bridge over the rushing gorge of Elkhorn Creek. Their narrow valley didn't allow them to spread out like Aspen or Vail, but they had the best ski slopes around, and their little community was charming as all get-out.

For service, accommodations, and grandeur, the

place was perfection. All except for the manager, her boss. If she was lucky, she could slip inside without encountering him.

It wasn't going to happen. Crossing the marble floor of the lobby, she saw David behind the admissions desk. Their new clerk appeared to be hanging on his every instruction, already captivated by her boss's handsome face and air of authority. It didn't matter that David was twenty years older than the desk clerk, with hair gone prematurely silver-gray. It never did. They always fell for his sophisticated look and charm, and the cool way he passed all the problems on to Zoe, as if they were no more than minor blips on his radar screen. If James Bond had gone into hotel management and been merely passably good at his job, he would have been David Brand.

Zoe seemed to be the only one who found him condescending and arrogant. His feelings for her weren't any warmer.

They both knew she'd be a better manager than David. Buck Flemming, the original owner of the Alpine Sky, preferred keeping women where he insisted they belonged—beneath men—so David had skated by while she did all the work. Then Buck had died. Ruth Ann took a couple of minutes to play the grieving widow before freeing up her social calendar by making her son, Matt, the new general manager. Zoe hadn't met him, but David had. He didn't give her the details of the meeting, but his irritation made it obvious; finally, someone else had not been charmed by David Brand.

Matt had given her the golf course deal without even meeting her. She and David both knew her success might result in a shake-up in management.

Gloves off, game on. David wanted nothing more than for her to fail. Hearing him gloat had zero appeal, so she tried to sneak past the front desk. He looked up and caught her eye with a cool smile. "Excuse me, Victoria," he told the starry-eyed clerk. "I need to talk to Zoe, but I'm confident you can handle things on your own. You're doing beautifully." She beamed, but he didn't see it as he intercepted Zoe at the back hallway.

"I'm just here to pick up my laptop," she told him.

His smile almost looked sincere. "Let's take a minute to chat in my office, shall we?"

She tried not to roll her eyes. "Let's chat" meant *Let me find something to criticize about the way you handled things so I can enjoy how bad you'll look when Mrs. Flemming hears about it*. It killed her that she was about to make his day.

He closed his office door and sat behind the desk before giving her an expectant look. "I heard your car was at the Rusty Wire."

Crap, he had snitches. "I stopped by to meet the owner."

"Oh, let's not be coy. We both know why you were there. So how good are you at high-level negotiations? Did he go for your lowball price?"

She felt her whole body tighten, and told herself he'd find out soon, anyway, being her supervisor. "No."

"That's too bad." He clicked his tongue in mock disappointment. "It would have looked good if you could have brought this deal in under budget. But I suppose Ruth Ann and Matt won't be *too* disappointed with three."

They wouldn't have had she managed it. She clenched her teeth and made herself say it. "He didn't go for three, either."

"Really?" He savored it, a smile playing at the side of his mouth as he tried to look concerned. "How disappointing for you. How much does he want?"

"He says he won't sell at any price." David nearly lit up, and she rushed to squash his hopes. "I haven't given up. I'll get to him, I just haven't found his weak spot yet."

David's smile was serene. "Maybe he doesn't have one. It would be awful to disappoint the Flemmings, though. I heard Ruth Ann put Matt in charge of the whole expansion project, and you know how she is about her baby boy. He's not the person you want to piss off." He looked positively thrilled that she might.

"He won't be disappointed."

He punched the air like a cheerleader. "That's the spirit."

She looked around, wondering if there was anything she could accidentally bash his teeth in with. Her gaze fell on a large box in the corner. Beneath packing labels and tape, the box bore the distinctive double-E logo of Everton Equipment.

She frowned. As far as she knew, Everton didn't make ski equipment. But they did make an exclusive line of clothing and equipment for golf. She gave David a puzzled look. "Are we already ordering for a golf line? They don't even know if the project is a go."

"More pressure on you, huh?" He enjoyed it for a moment before nodding at the box. "Those are sample shirts direct from the factory. Naturally, if the Alpine Sky builds the golf course, we'll carry only the best brand in our pro shop. I imagine Everton heard rumors and decided to do some early lobbying for their brand."

Really early; she was surprised they even knew about it. That meant Ruth Ann and Matt must be operating on the assumption that buying the Rusty Wire was a done deal. Zoe had to convince Jase Garrett to sell—and fast.

David went to the box and lifted the flaps. "Here, take one." He pulled out a dark blue polo shirt and tossed it to her. "Wear it to the Rusty Wire; maybe it'll help." For some reason that made him grin.

She'd had enough of David's encouragement. Clutching the shirt, she stood. "I'm not giving up, you know. I'll find a way to convince him to sell."

He smirked. "Good luck."

She wasn't stupid enough to count on luck. This required research. She had several hours before her shift started to find out everything she could about Jase Garrett.

It didn't take long. Not many people lit up a Google search like Jase did.

At first she thought she had the wrong Jase Garrett as she scanned all sorts of hits on downhill skiing events and websites. Then she saw the photos. A younger version, but unmistakably the chiseled face of the man she'd talked to at the Rusty Wire.

And the accolades. She lost count of the titles and trophies.

And, oh my God, the *medals*. She'd hit on them right away and nearly fell off her chair. Olympic medals, flashing in the winter sunlight—three gold and one silver. Jase grinned in the picture like the winner he was, holding them up for the camera.

On the cover of *Time* magazine.

Zoe stared at the picture for a long time. The red, white, and blue parka, the confidence in his squared shoulders and raised chin, the glint of victory in his eyes. And the words beside the picture: "Jase Garrett Shines for America."

He'd been famous. Probably had endorsement deals with major companies, which explained why her offer hadn't tempted him. She was not the first person to offer him millions of dollars.

Why hadn't she known? Her eyes strayed to the date—ten years ago. She'd been in her first year of college. Well, that explained it; she'd barely noticed the world beyond campus during those years, being much too busy trashing her future. But he was only a few years older than she was, which meant he would still have been young and strong enough to compete in the next winter Olympics. She quickly searched the U.S. ski team four years later, but couldn't find his name. An injury could have kept him out; it happened all the time. No matter, nothing could take away from the four medals he'd earned that one year. And if he'd ever been injured, he seemed fine now. She hadn't noticed so much as a limp.

He might no longer compete, but Jase hadn't retired to a tropical island or gone off to mingle with the jet set. He lived in tiny Barringer's Pass, where he had access to the best ski slopes this side of the Alps. She'd bet anything he still skied. That sort of dedication to a sport didn't just fade away.

A slow smile crossed her face as she realized how she could use that.

Closing the laptop, her eyes fell on the polo shirt she'd tossed on her desk. Size large. On impulse, she folded it and tucked it into her shoulder bag. A little reminder of the marketing powerhouse backing up her idea might be the perfect way to make her point.

Chapter Two

By 9 p.m. the next evening the Rusty Wire was in full Friday night swing. Since most of their customers were local, their business didn't suffer in the off-season. From the look of the parking lot, tonight was no exception.

The double-door entry with an air lock between the two doors was an excellent sound barrier in addition to keeping out the winter's cold. From outside she heard only the dull thump of a bass line. Inside, music and laughter hit her like a wave, rolling over and around her. The air was warm with the heat of a few dozen bodies, half of them crowding the dance floor as they stomped, clapped, and sang along while doing a line dance. From the level of excitement, she guessed more beer would be hitting the floor tonight.

Zoe skirted the dancers, letting her gaze sweep the tables. Several groups of people laughed and talked loudly. One table full of women dug into a deep-dish pizza, and she inhaled appreciatively as she passed. A harried-looking waitress in jeans and a white T-shirt carried a tray laden with nachos and beers. There was no sign of Jase.

Reaching the crowded bar, she walked down its length, checking out customers and the two bartenders. Still no Jase, but she recognized the woman pulling beers as the one who'd been there yesterday. Zoe found an open stool and caught her attention.

The woman finished drawing a beer, then approached Zoe slowly, her eyes giving Zoe's neatly tailored suit a disdainful once-over. "Miss Larkin. What can I get you?"

"Do you know where I can find Mr. Garrett?"

She took her time deciding whether to release the top-secret information, then nodded to a spot over her shoulder. "Back there."

Zoe hadn't noticed the room that extended off one side of the saloon. Through the wide doorway she could see poker and pool tables, all in use. The walls were decorated with poster-size pictures of gunslingers and cowboys, and framed collections of barbed wire. Zoe gave the closest display a puzzled glance. Who knew there were so many types of fence wire? And who cared?

From the line of chairs along the wall, several people watched the pool players. Jase was one of them.

Strictly speaking, he wasn't watching the game. His attention—and his smile—were focused on the young woman sitting close beside him. As Zoe watched, the girl tossed her mane of blond hair and leaned close to his ear to say something. His smile widened to a grin.

Something like irritation hit Zoe in the chest, except

it couldn't be that because she didn't care what in the hell Jase Garrett did or who he did it with. Muttering a thank-you to the bartender, she tugged firmly on her fitted blazer and strode into the back room. A few pairs of eyes followed her, but Jase didn't look up until she stopped right in front of him. His smile faded as his gaze ran down her official dark-blue Alpine Sky blazer and skirt all the way to her sensible heels, then back up again.

"Miss Larkin," he drawled. "Fancy seeing you here. Just knocking off work?"

"I'm *at* work, Mr. Garrett."

He sighed and sent the girl a disappointed look. "Sorry, looks like I need to take care of some business."

"No prob." The girl planted a kiss on his cheek and stood, pausing to give Zoe a curious look. Zoe took her first good look at the cute little blonde. My God, she couldn't be over eighteen. From her Internet research, she knew Jase was thirty-three. The letch.

"I'll see you later, sweetheart," Jase said, giving the girl a farewell wink. Zoe's mouth tightened with disapproval, which didn't seem to bother him in the least. He hooked his hands behind the chair, his knees nearly bumping hers as he slid into a relaxed slouch. "Have a seat."

Her gaze fell to his invitingly open lap. For one second a warm tingle spread through her at the idea of snuggling against his firm chest and being held by his strong arms. She squashed it and stiffened. "I don't conduct business while seated on someone's lap."

He raised an amused eyebrow. "I meant the chair." He cast a pointed look at the chair next to his. "But if you'd prefer my lap, you're more than welcome."

She sat on the chair, flushing with embarrassment and wondering if his body language had deliberately led her to misunderstand or if her mind had gone there on its own. Either way, she resented him for it. She couldn't afford to let a man sneak around her carefully constructed image of professionalism and polish. Especially a man who so clearly embodied everything she hated.

Overcompensating, she held her knees primly together and placed her shoulder bag on her lap, folding her hands over it. Shields up.

"Mr. Garrett, I came to discuss the Alpine Sky's offer to buy the Rusty Wire."

"I guessed." His gaze took a leisurely trip down her body and back up again. She figured it was meant to unnerve her and forced herself not to squirm.

"I brought something for you." She pulled the polo shirt out of her bag and handed it to him.

"You're bribing me with a shirt?" He looked at it. "Good brand." One eyebrow lifted in surprise as he held it against his chest. "Fits, too. Well, damn, I think you've swayed me, Miss Larkin. Now that you've thrown in this nice shirt, I'll be glad to sell you the Rusty Wire."

She gave him a tolerant smile, trying not to notice how the dark-blue shirt only deepened the blue of his eyes. "The shirt is simply to remind you that the Alpine Sky stands for quality. Quality accommodations, quality equipment, and quality services. I want you to remember that when you consider our offer."

"I already declined your offer. Do I have to give back the shirt?"

"I believe I can sweeten the deal for you."

"I don't know, three million and a shirt is already pretty sweet."

His sly smile put tiny crinkles beside his eyes and caused a sudden skip in her heartbeat. She caught her breath, annoyed by her reaction, and at the same time wondering what it would be like to be the focus of that dazzling *Time* magazine cover grin. It was probably best if she never found out.

She wished he'd stop looking at her hair. She'd deliberately pulled it back and up to make it less noticeable. Strawberry blond was a distracting color. Frivolous. She never wanted to be taken for frivolous again.

"The shirt and the three million are not the whole deal. I believe the Alpine Sky can offer you something that might change your mind."

His look of secret amusement disappeared. "Really?" he asked in a flat, dry tone.

His direct gaze was more unsettling than she'd expected. She swallowed and pushed on. "You're a skier."

She had the impression walls had suddenly gone up between them. "Around here that's hardly unusual," he told her. Even his voice was guarded.

"An *Olympic* skier. A gold medal winner. That's beyond the usual, even in this town."

Lines appeared around his mouth now, and he clenched his jaw. "That was a long time ago."

"You were famous. Respected."

"Fame is fleeting."

"No, Mr. Garrett, it isn't. Not that kind of fame. An Olympic medal is highly regarded by every skier I know. You have four." He kept his stony gaze on her, saying nothing. "Do you still ski?"

"I don't compete." The words were harsh and clipped.

"The knowledge doesn't go away. Have you ever thought of doing something with that experience, Mr. Garrett? Sharing it with talented young skiers who may have achieved some measure of success but strive for more?"

His brow lowered over his eyes. "Just say what you came to say, Miss Larkin."

"The Alpine Sky is willing to offer you that opportunity. A position as a ski instructor." She felt confident Ruth Ann would go along with the plan. Anything to get Jase Garrett to sell.

He pushed the shirt back into her hands. "I don't want to be your ski pro. Good-bye."

"Not our ski pro," she said, ignoring the shirt and letting it fall between them. "We already have one. I'm talking about a position above that level. You would only instruct advanced students, young athletes who come to sharpen their skills and get pointers from the best in their field. Athletes who have a passion for the sport equal to your own."

She watched him closely. Anyone who made it to the Olympic level in his sport had to have an enormous amount of drive and determination. That might not show when it came to running a saloon, but it had to be there still. Sure enough, interest flickered deep in his eyes, and she went after it. "You could select the students yourself. Handpicked, top-rated skiers. You would have full control of the program, and I promise the salary would be generous."

She held her breath. His piercing glare softened and something wavered behind it, temptation edging its way through that hard shell. For a moment she was sure she had him.

Then it was gone. The shutters were back in place as his mouth pressed into a firm line. "No."

Again with the flat no. It couldn't be that quick, that absolute. Not after the way he'd hesitated—she hadn't imagined that. "What do you mean, no?"

"No, thank you. *Nein, non, nyet.* See ya around."

She frowned. "Why?"

He gave her a look of disbelief. "Do you always have to know why? You must have been one of those kids who drive their mothers crazy, asking why all the time."

"I was, so you might as well answer or I'll have to keep asking. How can I convince you to sell if I don't know what you want?"

He leaned forward and she didn't dare back off, even though he was so close she smelled the spicy fragrance of his soap. So close she could have counted the individual eyelashes that lowered, narrowing his gaze to a tight beam. Uncomfortably close, and unnervingly *male.* "Listen carefully, Miss Larkin," he rumbled, and she imagined she could feel the vibration of his words in the air. "You can't."

She blinked and gathered her thoughts. He was wrong. He had to be. What she couldn't do was take no for an answer. Her job and her future depended on closing this deal and proving her value to the company. If she blew it, David would see that she never got another chance.

Begging wasn't in her nature. Fighting for what she wanted was, and she was just exasperated enough to challenge him. "Tell me one thing. How does an Olympic medalist lose all desire to achieve anything? Are you telling me sitting around day after day in a run-down honky-tonk is a fulfilling life?"

Silence hung between them as he stared at her. Damn! She'd crossed a line, but it was too late to take it back even if she'd wanted to. Beneath his scowl, Jase's face was tight and dark. "That's right, you've nailed it. I'm a washed-up loser and this is all I want from life, so you can't tempt me."

Heat rose in her cheeks. "I didn't mean . . ." *To speak the truth? To piss you off? Well, hell.*

She sighed and got to her feet, facing him. "Yes, I did mean it. I'm not going to pretend I didn't. You were a competitor, Jase." His first name just slipped out. She'd wanted to keep it strictly professional, but what the hell, this was about to get personal. "You had ambition, the kind that won't let you quit. And talent, more than anyone else in your field. It's not in you to quit. And believe it or not, I understand that kind of drive. I don't have any Olympic medals to prove it, but I know what it means to try your best, and when that's not enough, to dig down deep and try even harder."

He still watched her closely, but the anger had left his face. He nodded. "I believe you do know."

"You do?" Agreeing with her had been the last thing she'd expected.

"I've lived in Barringer's Pass for ten years, and I skied here for years before that. There aren't many secrets in a small town, Zoe Larkin."

The tiny pause before her name gave it all the impact it needed to remind her that the two older Larkin sisters had a reputation in this town, one Zoe was beginning to think they might never live down. "You recognized my name," she said, her voice strained despite her carefully blank face.

He didn't answer. He didn't have to.

"What you heard . . . it hasn't been true for a long time."

"You mean you're not the person you were ten years ago."

She squinted her eyes at him. Clever. She got the comparison, but it wasn't the same thing. "I'm not the same person, but I have the same determination. I might have put a lot of energy into raising hell years ago, but I put even more into changing people's perception of me. Ten years ago I was good at being bad. Now I'm good at being capable and responsible. It's just a matter of what I've tried to achieve." She held her chin up and didn't care if she looked defensive. "What have *you* managed to achieve during the past ten years?"

"Anonymity," he growled. "And you're trying to ruin it." He stood, obviously a signal that they were done talking.

For a moment she was done thinking, too. Seated, Jase's athletic body had a lazy sort of grace that made it easy to understand why that young woman had been interested in him. Standing in front of her, his effect was strangely multiplied. She blinked, unable to grasp a single thought as she noticed the way his T-shirt stretched over well-defined chest muscles, and the strength in his biceps as he crossed his arms. She sucked her lower lip between her teeth as she raised her gaze to his, trying to ignore the strange flutter in her stomach. What had she been saying?

He didn't give her a clue, just stared at her with a funny look on his face, probably wondering if she was altogether sane. She wondered the same thing. Men never shook her control, not years ago when she had used them to rebel, and not now when she kept them at a safe emotional distance. Who was this Jase Garrett . . . Oh, *that* was what they'd been talking about.

"Why do you want to be anonymous?" She ignored the sardonic lift of his eyebrow at another *why*. "Who wouldn't want people to remember an accomplishment like winning an Olympic medal? Most people probably wouldn't shut up about it, and you want to hide from it?"

She wished she could read his hooded gaze. "Do you remind people about your past, Zoe Larkin?"

She felt heat rise to her cheeks, and was glad he'd had the decency to keep his voice low enough that no one else heard. Between gritted teeth, she hissed, "It's not the same. I'm not proud of it."

"Then maybe we're more similar than you know." Before she could figure that out, he added, "I don't see how this has anything to do with your company's offer to buy the Rusty Wire."

It didn't. She was just curious about him, damn it. The fact that she shouldn't be irritated her even more.

She thrust the shirt back at him. "Here, keep it. Think about the offer." The Alpine Sky shirt might remind him of the offer to coach top skiers, the only thing she'd said so far that had tweaked his interest. She turned to leave.

"Wait a minute." He grabbed her arm. She stopped, far too aware of his hand on her blazer as he stepped around to face her. She tried not to wonder what it would feel like to have his hand on her bare skin.

Below his furrowed brow, his eyes searched hers. "My turn to ask why. Why are you so determined to get me to sell?"

"I told you, the Alpine Sky needs your land if it's going to have a golf course."

"And I told you to kiss that idea good-bye, but you won't, and I want to know why it bothers you so much." She started to deny it, but he cocked his head in a warning look.

She pressed her lips together. "I'm doing my job. Is that a foreign concept to you?"

He studied her. "And you might lose your job if you don't get me to sell?"

"I won't lose it." She'd just never advance. Never get out from under David's thumb.

"There are other places to work, you know."

"Not many. Only two other big resorts in Barringer's Pass, both fully staffed. I'd have to leave B-Pass." Something that would never happen, not as long as this town still remembered the Larkin name with disdain. Leaving town might make things easier for her, but it wouldn't stop the whispers that plagued her two sisters and broke her grandmother's heart. Only she could do that, by sticking to her plan and proving she was trustworthy and honorable.

And it was none of Jase Garrett's business.

"I can take care of myself, and my job," Zoe continued. "Unless you'd care to sell out of pity? I can play the victim if you're one of those types who simply have to rescue damsels in distress."

The corner of his lip twitched upward. "Zoe Larkin, assistant manager, playing a damsel in distress? Tempting, but I'm afraid I'm not that type."

"I didn't think so. See you later." She pushed past him and made her way back through the tables to the door, feeling his eyes on her all the way.

She'd almost reached the door when an excited laugh on the dance floor drew her attention. The girl was young, with long brown hair that looked just like . . . Zoe gaped. "Sophie?"

Her sister turned, still caught in the arms of a gorgeous hunk of cowboy. "Zoe!" she laughed with delight. "What are you doing here?"

"I could ask you the same."

"Are you kidding? I love this place, come here all the time. But I didn't think it was your style." Her amused glance took in Zoe's skirt and blazer as her partner pulled her closer, still swaying to the lively country music. Sophie moved back into the rhythm. "Talk to you after this dance?"

"I'm leaving."

Sophie accepted the news with a shrug. "'K, catch you later." She wiggled a couple of fingers that peeked above the cowboy's hand, then laughed as he whirled her away in a fast two-step.

Zoe blinked. Somehow she hadn't pictured her doctoral candidate little sister kicking up her heels at a cowboy bar.

The Rusty Wire was just full of surprises, none of them good. Her cultured, brainy little sister had gone country. The saloon wasn't operating on the edge of insolvency, like Ruth Ann had thought. Worst of all, its owner was a stubborn jerk with a distracting smile that did funny things to the pit of her stomach and made her wonder what it would be like to get up close and personal with that mouth.

God, it was warm in here.

Zoe hurried outside and stood in the relative quiet of the parking lot, inhaling deeply. Jase Garrett had monopolized all her senses and gotten under her skin in a way that made her want to squirm deep inside. It was pathetic. Also highly inappropriate for a business relationship. She flapped the deep V-neck of her blazer, letting the cool night air touch her skin as she pulled out her phone with the other hand and tried to remember where she'd parked.

Jase stood watching the door even after she'd gone. Her offer to buy the Rusty Wire annoyed him, but her persistence worried him. He didn't need to explain his career choice to anyone, especially some corporate lackey who only wanted to use him to further her own career. Even an admittedly sexy lackey. Zoe Larkin was on the verge of bringing up a part of his past he'd finally stopped reliving every day. He should be glad to see her go. Still, he couldn't escape the feeling that he'd left something unfinished when she walked away.

It wasn't concern for her job—he didn't give a rat's ass for the big resorts and their employees. He didn't know why he'd even asked if his refusal to sell might impact her job. It was just that he'd been caught up in the surprise of her rich brown eyes, which he'd expected to be blue, when he'd noticed the nervous tic beside her left eye. She was more tense than she let on. A little desperate, too, if she thought throwing in a free shirt meant he'd suddenly decide to coach young skiers to Olympic gold.

"Uncle Jase!"

He turned to find his niece standing beside him, her long blond hair now pulled into a ponytail and two pool sticks planted beside her, one in each hand. "You promised to teach me how to make the cue ball jump another ball, remember?"

How could he forget? She'd sat down next to him, batting her big blue eyes the way she'd been doing since she could toddle, begging to learn the trick shots that would undoubtedly turn her into the sharpest pool hustler in the state. His sister would kill him.

"Sure, Hailey." It might help take his mind off Zoe Larkin.

"You gonna do something with that?"

He followed her gaze to the shirt in his hands. Damn it, he didn't want the thing. It would only remind him of her offer to disrupt his peaceful life and throw him back into a world he'd deliberately shut out.

"Give me a minute, honey, I'll be right back."

Suddenly motivated, he wove his way across the dance floor and strode out the door. If he hurried, he could catch her before she drove back up the hill to Camelot.

He did a quick scan along the front row of cars, then worked his way farther back until he'd almost reached the most distant corner, where employees parked. There. He'd recognize that purposeful stride anywhere. The faint snatch of her voice confirmed it as she said something into her phone, then slipped it into her purse. He trotted across the asphalt, but not too quickly; he saw no reason to interrupt the fluid swing of her hips before he absolutely had to.

Unfortunately, boots weren't made for stealth—she heard him coming. He was still twenty feet away when she whipped around, one hand holding her shoulder bag in place while the other clenched into a fist at stomach level, a key poking out between her fingers.

He slowed and held up his free hand even as she recognized him and lowered her fisted keys. It didn't improve the sour look she gave him. "Change your mind?"

"Yeah, you can keep the shirt." He tossed it at her from three feet away, and she made an awkward catch with the hand holding the keys.

He thought she'd give him an argument since she always seemed to have one ready, but she simply shook her head in disgust. No words were necessary—her look clearly said he was a jackass.

He'd planned to be coolly polite, but that look ticked him off. "Wouldn't want you to have to make another trip back to the slums to retrieve it."

Real mature. Now he sounded like a jackass even to himself.

"It was a gift," she said, her words frosting the air between them. "But God forbid you feel obligated to do something out of character, like say thank you."

Every response that came to mind sounded even more infantile than the last, so he clenched his jaw and said nothing. She narrowed her eyes in one final glare, then turned to go.

He was reaching out to touch her arm with some

lame explanation for his attitude when a crash split the night, followed by the sound of shattering glass. Zoe flinched and ducked. Before she could react further, he threw himself forward, wrapping his arms around her and forcing her down, shielding her with his body. More glass exploded, shards rattling against metal as they landed, but not near enough to touch them.

"Stay here!" he ordered. He took off at a run.

Chapter
Three

He didn't look to see if she'd obeyed. Racing to the end of the lot where the employees parked, he paused and scanned the vehicles. A group of five cars ended with a little red Chevy that had squeezed in next to the Dumpsters. The sound had come from that direction. No one was around, confirming his fears that someone hadn't been throwing glass into the metal bins. Whoever had caused the noise had cut and run.

Cursing under his breath, he walked around the Chevy, checking the taillights, windows, and headlights. The light from the pole beside the Dumpsters bathed the car in yellow, showing that everything was intact. But tiny chips of glass sparkled on the asphalt between the Chevy and the black pickup next to it. Already knowing what he'd find, he walked to the front of the pickup.

"Son of a bitch."

"What happened?" Zoe stood by the back of the truck. Of course; why would she do what he'd told her to do?

She didn't wait for his answer, striding between the vehicles to join him. She stared at the shattered glass and plastic of the headlight and the caved-in safety glass of the driver's window. Most of the spiderwebbed window glass still hung in place, but showed a deep indentation from what he guessed was a baseball bat or golf club.

"Oh my God," she breathed.

Much stronger phrases ran through his head.

She looked around. "Who did this? Where'd they go?"

"That way, I imagine." He nodded behind them where twenty feet away aspen and ponderosa pines crowded together in a forest blacker than the night at the edge of his fifty acres.

She took in the cluster of vehicles that huddled near the back entrance of the Wire. "This truck belongs to one of your employees, doesn't it?"

"You might say that." The words grated like gravel in his throat. "It's mine."

"Yours!" Her gaze whipped toward him. When he didn't say anything, she studied the vehicles again. The red Chevy on the end, the gray Honda that had nosed onto the grass on the other side of his truck. He saw the slight stiffening in her back when she finally realized what he'd known right away. "It wasn't random," she said, her words slow and careful. "The cars on either side would have been easier to reach. Easier targets."

"They wanted to send a message."

"They who? What message?"

He steeled himself to meet her puzzled look, disliking the idea that it might all be an act. "Don't you think it's obvious?"

Her expression gradually closed. One hand went to her hip. "You think someone from the Alpine Sky did this?"

"Who else?" It was more a grim statement than a question.

"You're crazy."

He barked out a bitter laugh. "I'd be crazy *not* to believe it."

"It serves no purpose. How would a broken window and headlight convince you to sell when three million dollars didn't?"

"Intimidation. It means worse could happen if they don't get what they want."

She shook her head, not accepting his answer, frowning at the dark parking lot as if a clue might be out there. A few seconds later her eyes sparked with triumph. "How would anyone from the Alpine Sky know that you hadn't changed your mind? There's no point to this if you'd already agreed to sell, and they couldn't know what you'd said to me in there."

"Good point," he allowed. "No one could know I was able to resist your tantalizing offer of a free polo shirt."

"You're such a jerk," she muttered.

"Unless you already told them."

She crossed her arms. "Which I didn't."

He tried to read her stubborn glare, wishing he believed her denial, but unwilling to be that naive. He reminded himself that he wasn't dealing with the pretty girl who worked up the road, he was dealing with the representative of a large resort, a business used to getting what it wanted in this tourist-oriented town. And an employee eager to deliver.

"You spoke to someone on the way out."

"Yeah, my obviously deranged sister. I was surprised to see her."

"And when I came out here, you were talking on the phone."

"So?" Her eyes went wide with shock. "You think I was setting up some kind of hit?" She stared, openmouthed. Searching for a good explanation? Wondering if she'd been used? He couldn't tell the difference. "I wasn't talking about the Rusty Wire," she finally said through clenched teeth.

"So you say." Her eyes were hot, and he was sure she was trying to incinerate him where he stood. "It doesn't matter. Tell them it won't work." He pushed his face close to hers, aware that even though she tensed, she didn't back down an inch. "I'll never sell."

All she could do was fume as Jase marched back inside, leaving her in front of his battered truck. He thought she'd caused this. Conspired to vandalize his truck. The idea was even more offensive than his rude attitude, especially when there was probably a long list of people tempted to bash in his headlights, and more.

The man was a prick. A bastard. She called him every name she could think of as she stomped to her car and headed up the mountain to the Alpine Sky. He was subhuman scum, and talking to him had ruined her perfectly good evening.

It was ludicrous to think the resort would operate like a common thug, resorting to intimidation and violence to get its way. The business world was much more subtle. Still, a small corner of Zoe's mind whispered that what Jase had accused her of wasn't impossible. She *had* been on the phone with someone from the Alpine Sky—Geoff, at the front desk, who'd called about a reservation mix-up. When he apologized for interrupting, she'd told him it was okay, she wasn't making any progress here anyway. He could have passed that information on to anyone. Could someone have been at the Rusty Wire, ready to act on that information? A quick phone call was all it would take.

It was so unlikely she snorted aloud. She was letting Jase's paranoia rub off on her. It seemed far more likely that some ex-girlfriend had been royally pissed off, probably over that little blond cutie, and took it out on his truck. He probably had plenty of exes, and she could easily imagine that they all hated his guts. He was just that kind of guy. Trying to blame it on the Alpine Sky was another example of his abrasive personality.

She felt a little better by the time she parked at the main lodge, but not enough. She needed to be sure.

Using the main entrance, she stopped at the front desk. Geoff was there, talking with a guest. She waited for him to finish, then motioned him over. "Hi, Geoff. I know this sounds stupid, but when we talked on the phone was there anyone else around who might have overheard you and realized that the owner of the Rusty Wire had turned down our offer?"

The young man looked confused, but gave it some thought. "I guess. Mike and Gretchen were going over someone's charges, and David called right after that and mentioned your meeting, so I told him it didn't go well." He swallowed. "Was it supposed to be a secret?"

"No, don't worry about it." Crap. She still didn't buy it, but couldn't prove it wasn't true. She gave

Geoff a reassuring smile. "I'll be in my office for the next hour, but please don't interrupt unless it's an emergency."

"I wasn't going to. How'd you find out so fast?"

She was already walking away, and paused to turn back. "Find out what?"

"About Mr. Flemming."

An ominous prickling danced across the back of her neck. "What about him?"

"He's waiting in your office."

"He's . . . What? *Matt* Flemming?" The owner's son, and president of Alpine Resorts, Inc. When Geoff nodded, she swallowed and struggled to look composed. "When did he get here?"

"This morning, I guess. He bought lunch at the downstairs café and went out for supper with David. Now he's waiting to see you. Um, didn't you know?"

"No." She'd heard from her staff in tedious detail about less important matters, but nothing about Ruth Ann's golden-boy son coming to visit her.

She'd had all of two days to convince Jase Garrett to sell. If Matt Flemming was inserting himself in the process this soon, he must be pretty damn desperate to close the deal. And he probably already sensed failure in her efforts.

She added sniveling snitch to David's less-than-fine qualities.

Matt Flemming wasn't just waiting in her office, he was rearranging it.

He stood with his back to her, addressing two men from maintenance. "Put it up against the other desk," he directed. The men swung a large desk into place, snuggling it against hers so that the two people sitting at them would face each other. She'd always been uncomfortable with that arrangement.

"What's going on?"

Matt turned and broke into a smile that nearly made her take a step back. She blinked to make sure she'd only imagined a digitally inserted twinkle. His blue eyes crinkled with pleasure, and one closed in a quick wink, as if they shared a secret. "Hello! You must be Zoe." He strode forward, shaking her hand while his gaze darted over her, taking in her hair, her face, and her clothes in one frankly admiring glance. The twinkle sparked again. "I'm Matt Flemming. I'll try not to be in your way, but it looks like we have to share an office for a while. It was either you or David, and since we've never met, I wanted an opportunity to get to know you. I hope you don't mind sharing." He cocked his head with a look of concern.

"Uh, no." As if she'd say anything else.

And why would she want to? She did her own quick assessment, from his dark blond hair to the manicured hand that held hers in a firm grip. Strong jaw, easy smile, eyes that shone with intelligence as they held her own captive . . . the man oozed charisma, a nice complement to his polished executive look. She warmed, indulging in a quick fantasy of sharing more than her office.

She cleared her throat and pulled her hand back. "May I ask why?"

He laughed as if she'd said something clever. "Of course. I'm here to help with the land acquisition for the golf course, and I was told it might take some time. I understand there have been a few problems?"

She flushed, inwardly cursing David Brand. "One problem, really. The owner doesn't want to sell, and I'm afraid he's quite stubborn on the point. Not that I've given up," she rushed to assure him.

"Excellent. I'm sure we can speed things up if we combine forces."

He gave her that disarming grin again, making her wonder if he was flirting or if it was just her. Maybe her sex switch had gotten flipped on, then stuck in a permanent state of lust. For someone who never let men throw her off her stride, she was batting an embarrassing zero for two this week.

Zoe busied herself answering e-mails about the resort's upcoming Beer and Bratwurst Festival while Matt directed the men about phone and fax connections. When they finally left, he tested out his new chair, leaning back and swiveling, making sure his keyboard and phone were within comfortable reach.

He caught her watching. "Sorry, I imagine it's distracting to have someone else in your office."

Very. But possibly not in a bad way. "Do you usually work the evening shift?" She glanced at her watch—11 p.m., not the usual hour to encounter upper management.

"You mean, will I always be underfoot?" He chuckled at her blush. "I set my own hours, but no, I don't usually work at night. Although maybe I should; apparently I've missed meeting one of our finest assets."

She gave the subtle come-on a polite smile and let relief soak in. Maybe the Flemmings still hadn't crossed her off the promotion list for good.

"Besides, I understand meeting with the owner of the Rusty Wire is best accomplished at night." At her look of surprise, he added, "I called the saloon. The manager said if I wanted to see the owner, I'd have to come by during business hours."

"I think he's drilled that into them."

"No problem. We can meet him on his own ground. What do you say you and I go to the Rusty Wire tomorrow night at nine? We can get something to eat, and I can meet Jason Garrett."

She couldn't say anything. Did he think he'd be a more capable negotiator? Or did he just want to watch while she beat her head against the wall one more time? Either way she'd come off looking bad.

It didn't help that he'd made it sound sort of like a date. She didn't think dating her boss was smart, even though the idea of going out with rich, clean-cut, handsome Matt Flemming had definite appeal.

She forced a nervous smile. "Sure."

Jase pulled into the parking lot of the Rusty Wire later than usual, noting that Russ's and Billy's cars were already there. So was another car he didn't recognize. Parked across the lot from the others, a man and a woman stood outside an idling silver Jaguar, scanning the fifty acres of trees and meadowland behind the saloon.

Jase's first thought was that it was a stupid car for the mountains. It would be in storage most of the year if they lived in Barringer's Pass, which made him think they weren't local. They could be tourists admiring the scenery; he'd often seen elk come right up to the parking lot from that patch of wilderness. But someone with money taking an interest in his fifty acres was too much of a coincidence to ignore. He turned his borrowed SUV toward the Jag.

The woman saw him coming. She said something to the man, then hurried around to the driver's side while he got in the car. By the time Jase reached them, they were cruising toward the exit. The woman waved and smiled as if she knew him. He searched his memory for an elegant-looking blonde, age somewhere around forty, and came up blank. As they passed, he glanced at the Colorado license plate: RUTHANN. He frowned; he'd heard that name before.

Jase parked and entered the saloon through the back door. No one was in the small kitchen yet, but Russ was sitting at the desk in the back office. Jase paused outside the open door.

"Hey, Russ, does the name Ruth Ann ring a bell? Pretty, blond, fortyish maybe? Drives a Jag."

Russ thought a moment. "That's the name of Buck Flemming's widow, ain't it?"

"No idea." It had probably been in the papers a few months ago when old Buck had keeled over from a heart attack. The local real estate tycoon had been in his eighties and fat as a toad, so no one was surprised when he'd dropped dead over lunch. Jase only remembered because the Alpine Sky had been one of Buck's properties. In Jase's mind he'd been a decent neighbor, catering to his high-class crowd and leaving the Rusty Wire alone. Relations had developed a considerable amount of friction since the wife had inherited the resort.

"You sure Ruth Ann isn't his daughter?"

"Buck didn't have a daughter, just a stepson. Slick kid with an ivy-league MBA. He runs the resort for Mommy." Russ's lip curled, indicating what he thought of the kid's management style.

The blonde was Mommy? She wouldn't be the first woman to marry a fat old man forty years her senior, and he doubted it was Buck's charm that had won her over. He didn't care, either. If she was still lusting after his land, she needed to learn that not everyone gives Ruth Ann what she wants.

The older man's obvious distaste made Jase wonder if Russ was worried about the offer, and that Jase might change his mind. It was hard to know; Russ had never been big on sharing his feelings. Jase propped a shoulder against the doorjamb as he regarded his business manager. "You never said anything about the offer. You think I should sell?"

Russ lifted a shoulder. "Not my call."

"You must have an opinion. Selling would put you out of a job."

"Worse things have happened. I'll survive."

Worse things, like Jase causing Russ's son's death in a stupid downhill race that went out of control. Russ had survived the grief and agony of Adam's death. The loss of an only child. And for Jennifer, the loss of a husband. They'd lost *everything* that day. Adam never had the chance to reap the benefits of fame that Jase had won—the lucrative endorsement deals would have meant a lot to his financially strapped family.

Jase cleared the gravelly tightness in his throat. "Just so you know, you have a job here as long as you want it," he said, leaving before Russ felt obligated to thank him. The last thing he wanted was Russ's thanks. The man had always kept his feelings to himself, but since Adam's death he'd been so withdrawn Jase wondered if he even had feelings anymore. Jennifer, too. Nine years gone, and she hardly ever laughed, not like she used to, with a bright laugh that carried a jolt of electricity. Losing Adam had left them all a little dead inside.

As if on cue, Jennifer came in the back door, stopping in Russ's office to drop off her purse before heading for the front of the saloon. She threw Jase a distracted hello and he followed her to the bar. He watched from the customer's side, propping a foot on the brass rail as she pulled out her inventory log behind the bar. No other bartender was more meticulous about the daily accounting, noting how much was on hand and what needed to be replenished before opening. It had always seemed like tedious work to Jase, but Jennifer claimed to like it, preferring the orderly, logical work of stocking the bar and measuring out drinks to actually mingling with the customers. She wasn't shy but, like her father-in-law, she'd put up a wall nine years ago and never stepped out from behind it.

She'd set her logbook down and was scooping her brown hair into a ponytail when she noticed him watching her. "Hot today," she said, snapping the rubber band in place and tugging the hair taut. "We might be wishing for air-conditioning by this afternoon."

It was a friendly and persistent disagreement between them. She knew he wouldn't make any more changes than necessary, maintaining the historic integrity of the saloon. "The roof fans will have it cooled down by evening." He gave his automatic reply, his mind elsewhere.

It must have shown on his face. Jennifer paused. "Is there a problem?" As she said it, her brow creased with a new thought. "Did you hear from Marty? Is it my transmission? Am I going to need to replace it after all?"

"No, no." He waved her concern aside. "Nothing like that. Marty said he just had to replace a gasket. Don't worry about it." At least, that's all she'd ever see on her copy of the bill. As long as she was too stubborn to accept his financial help, he had to do it behind her back. It was another long-standing argument between them, and it wasn't worth reopening now.

"Well, something's wrong."

"I was just thinking." He might as well ask, since she knew he had something on his mind. "You didn't say much about the offer from the Alpine Sky."

She shrugged. "It's not my decision."

"I'd like your opinion."

She studied him for a moment, her expression unreadable. "I thought you'd made up your mind about keeping the Rusty Wire. You seemed pretty sure about your answer to that Larkin woman."

So she'd zeroed in on the name, too, finding Zoe's old reputation a stronger identifying factor than her current job at the Alpine Sky. He hadn't realized how much Zoe had to fight against that, or how long people's memories were. He should have, especially for the bad stuff. No one ever forgot that.

"She's the assistant manager," he said, feeling he should do some small part in focusing on her present, since he expected the same from her. "I gave her an automatic answer at the time, pure impulse. Now I'm trying to be rational, take everything into account. So what do you think?"

"I told you, I can't imagine you doing anything else. I thought you were happy running the Rusty Wire."

She watched him as if his answer really mattered. He hadn't expected that, putting his feelings ahead of the logical considerations of money and economic impact. Maybe the old Jennifer was still alive under that hard shell.

"I *am* happy here," he told her. It might not be the whole truth, but it wasn't a lie. He'd shut down other parts of himself nine years ago, the parts that pursued challenges with abandon, and set meaningful goals. The parts he'd once thought would be his whole life. It hadn't mattered—nothing had meaning after Adam died. Life since then had more or less drifted by in a pleasant blur, maybe not as fulfilling as he'd planned, but not without happiness. That part wasn't a lie, so he repeated it. "I'd miss the saloon if I sold."

She squinted at him, as if she might be missing something. "Why are you asking? Is there something you'd rather be doing?"

Thoughts prodded the back of his mind, trying to pierce the barrier—the Olympic games he'd missed, the business he'd started with his buddy Brandon then practically abandoned. He shoved them back. "No."

She seemed to relax. "Then there's your answer."

He nodded. No need to reassure her that her job was secure when it appeared she was more concerned with *his* life, and whether he was happy. He was glad he'd asked, glad to know some part of Jennifer cared about him. If she'd wanted his life to be pure misery, he wouldn't have blamed her.

Any doubts about his answer were settled. Russ and Jennifer were behind him on this. He wouldn't sell.

Zoe stared at the computer screen and the nine-year-old obituary displayed there. Adam Holbrook, age twenty-three, killed in a skiing accident. The details had been harder to find than Jase's Olympic fame, but were far more revealing. Adam, a top-rated skier, had been practicing downhill runs with his best friend, Olympic champion Jase Garrett. Adam tried to pass Jase by cutting through a small stand of pines. He'd hit a tree, sustaining fatal head injuries. He was resuscitated at the scene but remained unconscious, and died two days later in the hospital. Zoe didn't need a news report to figure out what hadn't been reported—two days of agonizing hope and indecision before the family decided to take him off life support.

The family—that was another surprise. Adam's father, Russ Holbrook, was the man who'd introduced himself as the manager of the Rusty Wire. Adam's mother was deceased and his sister lived in Phoenix, but the young widow, Jennifer, looked too much like the woman tending bar to be a coincidence. Zoe already knew that Jase had bought the saloon eight years ago, which meant it was a year after Adam's death. The fact that he'd hired Russ and Jennifer had to mean something, but she wasn't sure what.

Jase had dropped out of the sport after Adam's death. Annual competitions he'd previously entered never listed his name again. On a hunch, she searched for combinations of Jase's name with Nike, the largest company offering an endorsement contract after his Olympic victory. She viewed copies of old ads, noting the dates. The most recent one had run two years after Adam's death. Nothing since. She imagined that Nike had been patient in waiting that long to pull their support and find a new champion. Other sponsors undoubtedly did the same. Four Olympic medals only pay off for a limited time once the athlete quits the sport.

Zoe rocked back in her chair, pondering the information. The Rusty Wire had become Jase's sole focus after Adam's death. But it wasn't like he'd thrown himself into the work, not if he'd hired Russ to manage the place. He seemed more like what she'd taken him for at first, a regular patron who showed up to socialize. Adam's death seemed to have reshaped the entire course of Jase Garrett's life.

"What are you up to?"

Zoe jumped at Matt's voice, and closed the screen. "Nothing important." For some reason she didn't bother to examine, the information felt too personal to allow Matt to include it in his strategy to make Jase sell. Although she was certain it figured prominently in Jase's flat-out refusal.

"Good, then we can go check out the Rusty Wire. It's nearly nine, so we should be able to get a good idea of what Jason Garrett does there that keeps him so tied to the place."

Very little, she thought but didn't say. It wasn't the business itself that kept Jase tied to the saloon. It was a dead man. She'd find out how and why. Then maybe she'd tell Matt.

Chapter Four

M att held the passenger door open for her, just like a date. Too much like a date. It felt old-fashioned, which was both awkward and good at the same time.

He got behind the wheel for the short drive down the mountain and gave her a curious glance. "Aren't you hot in your jacket?"

She was. But she was also acutely conscious of the need to look professional, and not like the good-time girl she once was. That kind of reputation died hard. Besides, his shirt alone looked like it cost more than her entire outfit—heck, so did his haircut—and she needed every advantage if she was going to stand next to the glow of perfection. "I only wore a sleeveless shell underneath," she told him. "Not professional enough for a business meeting."

He chuckled. "I'd hardly call an evening at a decrepit old saloon a business meeting. Sleeveless is fine."

"It's not really decrepit, you know. He's kept it up well."

His glance seemed to question whose side she was on, so she showed her loyalty by doing as he suggested and shrugging out of her blazer. He looked at the white scoop-necked shell, his gaze lingering appreciatively, and smiled. "Much better."

Definitely like a date.

So was the hand he placed on her back when they entered the Rusty Wire, guiding her to a table near the dance floor. Zoe decided to go with the feeling. If a rich, handsome man came on to her, a man with a likable personality and the right career goals, she'd be a fool to turn him down just because he happened to work with her. Above her, technically. But it wasn't as if Matt got involved in the day-to-day running of the resort. He didn't even live in Barringer's Pass.

At least, she didn't think so. It was as good a conversation starter as any. "Do you live around here?" she asked.

"Sometimes. I have one of the condos in the Pine Hollows unit," he said, naming a luxury condo complex for singles owned by the Alpine Sky but detached from the main lodge. He gave her an odd look. "You must have known that."

"I knew Mr. Flemming had one," she said, slightly flustered. "I mean, your stepfather."

"It's mine now." He smiled and cocked his head as if suddenly struck by an idea. "You'll have to come see it sometime. I could use some female input on redecorating."

He made it sound harmless, but who knew? He was too damn good with those lingering looks, the kind that made a woman think there was nothing in his world at that moment but her.

Or perhaps her and the waitress. Matt's gaze snapped to the young blonde walking by in what seemed to be the Rusty Wire uniform: white T-shirt, blue jeans, and a short black apron to hold her order tablet and pen. He motioned the young woman over, flashing the same attentive smile.

"Miss, could you take our order?" he asked. He slung an arm over the back of his chair, and turned to face her. His change in focus was subtle but clear, and the waitress seemed to pick up on it.

She looked him over and grinned back. "Sure. What'll it be?" she said, without bothering to take out the order pad.

"Two Coors." He let his gaze slide to another table and gave a short nod in that direction. "And that pizza sure looks good. Could you bring us a small pepperoni? I've never been here before and I'd like to try it."

She gave an approving nod. "Good choice. We have the best pizza in town."

"Really? I'm not from around here, so I'll have to take your word on that."

It might not be much of a line, but it got the waitress's attention. She gave Zoe a glance, as if wondering whether he was here because of her or if the new guy in town was up for grabs. She must have decided to go for it, because she gave Matt a wink. "Trust me on this one. The Rusty Wire only does nachos and pizza, but they're fantastic."

Matt laughed. "Fantastic, huh? That's quite a promise." They exchanged smiles for a couple of seconds while Zoe wondered if he could possibly not realize he was flirting, and decided he couldn't. Her expectations cooled several degrees.

"You must like working here," Matt said, oblivious to Zoe's unamused stare.

"I do," the waitress agreed.

"It's nice to hear someone say that. So the management is as good as the food?"

"The owner's a great guy," she assured him.

Matt shook his head. "Lucky you. Wish I could say the same about the guy I work for."

Zoe studied him as the two shared a laugh. Matt gave the waitress one last grin and turned as she left, aiming his sparkling gaze back at her.

"What was that about?" she asked, all resentment gone.

"Just checking to see how well liked Garrett is. It's good to know everything you can about someone if you're doing any kind of business with them. Don't you think so?"

She nodded, reassessing Matt. She'd never thought to do that when she approached Jase with her offer to buy his saloon. Matt Flemming could probably teach her a lot more about management than she'd learned on her own.

She was still absorbing that when he spoke again. "Do you always wear your hair up?" he asked.

She gave a startled blink. "Usually." It went with her straight-laced professional look. Long reddish-blond waves didn't.

"You should take it down."

She didn't change her fashion or grooming styles just because a man asked her to. In fact, that was usually a good reason *not* to do it. But Matt was doing that intense thing again with his eyes that made her want to please him. Made her want to keep him looking at her like that, and not at another woman.

It would have been a good place to draw the line, letting him know that their relationship was strictly business and was going to stay that way. Maybe it was a test, designed to learn her boundaries.

She unfastened the clip and shook out her hair.

Jase frowned at Zoe, then dodged a waitress who ducked past him in the hallway that led to the kitchen and restrooms. He'd been frozen there ever since he spotted Zoe sliding her delectable ass onto one of the saloon chairs.

She looked different without her official blazer. More approachable. Her date must have thought so, too, leaning in close when he talked to her. Jase didn't know what the guy had said that made her let her hair down, but he instantly resented him for it. The man was trespassing on his fantasy—he'd had the thought first, when she'd sashayed into the Rusty Wire in her prim business suit and with her take-charge attitude. He hadn't put words to the feeling then, but he did now; *he* should have been the one she unclipped her hair for. He narrowed his eyes as she shook her head, sending long reddish-blond waves cascading over her shoulders like some sexy-librarian wet dream come to life, then smiled at her pretty-boy date. Who in the hell was this guy?

He kept his eyes on them as he wove his way around the dance floor, pausing to talk to friends as he made his way to their table. Zoe was laughing at something her date had said as he got there, head thrown back in apparent delight. Jase rested a hand on the back of her chair, making her jump as her head brushed against his arm. She lifted startled brown eyes to his.

"Jase!"

Her cheeks had a pretty pink flush. "Hello, Zoe. Nice to see you enjoying the humble atmosphere of the Rusty Wire. I didn't think it was your style."

"It's not. I mean, I wasn't . . ."

"And you brought a date."

"He's not . . ." She stopped in mid-denial, looking uncertain. "Jase Garrett, meet Matt Flemming, the president of Alpine Resorts, Inc."

Ah, the enemy. And possibly Zoe's date—the enemy twofold. He showed his teeth and stuck out his hand. "Nice to meet you. I didn't know there was more than one resort."

"There isn't. Yet." Matt smiled easily and took Jase's hand, a firm clasp, radiating sincerity. "Nice place you have here."

Sure, that's why he wanted to tear it down. He bet the guy was one hell of a bullshitter. "Glad you like it. Come back anytime, we're not going anywhere."

Matt chuckled, a rich laugh filled with camaraderie that made Jase feel like he was buying a used car. "A direct man—I admire that. I think I'll enjoy negotiating with you, Jase."

"Hate to disappoint you, Matt, but you won't get the chance."

"Don't be so sure. I can make you a very tempting offer, maybe add a few perks you haven't even thought to ask for. We've given this a lot of thought, and want to make it beneficial for both sides."

"We, meaning you and your mother?"

"It was an expression. She's the owner, but I run the business. I'm afraid my mother never took an interest in Buck's holdings."

"She was interested enough to check out my fifty acres earlier today."

The news didn't seem to have an impact. "We talked about it, of course. She probably wanted to see what we'll be buying."

He had the same problem as his mother—the confidence that he could get whatever he wanted. "Wanting isn't the same as having. The land isn't for sale."

He didn't look worried about it. Flashing whiter-than-white teeth, Matt said, "We'll see. It's early yet, and it's been my experience that people sometimes change their minds."

Jase gave him a tight smile. He figured his first impression was a fair one—the man was a prick. Every instinct said things were going to get messy. He wanted to think better of Zoe, but working for a man like Matt Flemming, and possibly dating him, might say a lot about her willingness to go along with some underhanded tactics, like bashing in car windows and headlights. Matt didn't seem like the type to flinch at that, or more. Maybe that stunt was why she seemed a little nervous right now.

He looked down at her. She wouldn't meet his eyes, and had scooted forward so she wouldn't accidentally touch his hand where it rested on her chair. It was obvious he made her uncomfortable.

Guilt would do that. He couldn't explain why he felt disappointed in her. If she was helping Matt Flemming, she wasn't worth his attention.

"You kids have a good time," he told them, his heartiness as fake as Matt Flemming's geniality. He left with a last lingering look at Zoe and the tumble of hair she'd finger-combed into a semblance of neatness. It looked like she'd just gotten out of bed. No wonder she kept it in such a severe style at work—when he looked at that untamed fall of hair framing doe eyes and a softly curved mouth, work was the furthest thing from his mind.

He was lost in the image as he entered the back room and nearly walked right past his best friend.

"Hey, Jase. What's the problem?"

Brandon Myers gripped an upright pool cue as he gave Jase a curious look. Jase shook his head. "Nothing, just preoccupied." He looked at the young man with Brandon who was taking his shot at the balls, figuring him for a college student on summer break. Probably too green to be playing Brandon. "You taking advantage of this boy? Don't let him hustle you, kid, he's not as bad as he claims."

"Neither am I." The kid made an easy shot, sinking the ball.

"Don't ruin my fun," Brandon said. "Who's that chick you were talking to?"

"What chick?" He said it just to give himself a couple of seconds to focus as the seductive image of Zoe slammed back in place.

"The hot redhead. She looks familiar."

"Just someone who works up at the Alpine Sky. Name's Zoe Larkin."

Brandon's eyebrow went up and he glanced in Zoe's direction. "That's why she looks familiar. I went to school with her older sister, Maggie."

"Shit," the kid muttered, stepping back with a sour expression. "Your turn."

Brandon stepped to the table and looked over the scattered balls. Singling one out, he sighted along his cue stick. "You ever heard about the Larkin sisters, Jase?" He smacked the cue ball and watched it ricochet before clipping the four and knocking it in.

"Yeah." Jase looked back at Zoe just as Matt leaned close and made Zoe laugh. His stomach tied itself in a tight knot. He turned to see Brandon studying him. "What?"

"Nothing." He lined up his shot and gave the cue ball a hard tap. It smacked two other balls, sinking them both. The kid lost his confident look as Brandon prowled the table, considering the layout as he talked. "You got time to do some trout fishing tomorrow?"

"Sure." Forgetting about the saloon for a few hours sounded fine.

"Good." He leaned over the table, then gave Jase a hard look. "'Cause you and me gotta have us a talk."

Matt's gaze kept drifting back to Jase where he stood in the back room. "He doesn't talk much."

He didn't have to—he got his point across. "Are you going to make him a new offer?" Zoe asked. If so, she was dying to know what he thought would tempt Jase.

"Not tonight. Tonight we're just getting the feel of the place, trying to figure out what's so special about the Rusty Wire that Garrett doesn't want to sell." His gaze slid to the dancers as the music changed from a rollicking, shout-along country tune to a much slower pop ballad. "Come on, let's try out the dance floor while we're waiting for our food."

Before she could answer, he jumped up and took her hand, leading the way to a clear spot on the floor.

She stepped hesitantly into position, left hand on his shoulder and right one waiting to clasp his. He took the hand she offered, sliding his other arm around her back and pulling her close. Her left arm folded awkwardly between them, and she moved it to the only comfortable position, draping it around his neck.

Her boss was coming on to her. Zoe couldn't pretend that he wasn't and couldn't decide how she felt about it. By any objective standards, she shouldn't be slow dancing with Matt Flemming, but it was hard to be objective about a man who looked good enough to lick, and who looked at her like she was the most fascinating person he'd ever met. Those rapt gazes were more than flattering. If she had placed an order for the perfect man—sophisticated, ambitious, smart, and handsome—the universe would have stuck a bow on Matt Flemming and left him on her doorstep. Minus the bow, that was practically what had happened.

Still, what must he think of her, a junior executive who falls into his arms at the first opportunity? She worked hard to be taken seriously, to be seen as a professional. Letting down her hair and slow dancing with her boss wasn't part of that picture. Suddenly uncomfortable, she stiffened and pulled back.

"I'm sorry." Matt's words made her look up. He smiled apologetically and shook his head. "I'm making you uncomfortable." She started to deny it, a stupid, knee-jerk reaction to placate her boss, but he didn't let her. "Yes, I am." He stopped dancing and held her at arm's length. "I've put you in an awkward position and we barely know each other. It's wrong. Call me overeager to get to know my staff." He laughed and shook his head.

She smiled back, relieved when she caught sight of their waitress heading their way. "That's our order. Thanks goodness, I'm so hungry!"

"So am I." His eyes were boring into hers again, leaving Zoe with little doubt as to what he meant.

She had the presence of mind not to say anything. But there was no question in her mind about her willingness to see what exactly the picture-perfect man would want with her.

The pizza was gooey with cheese over globs of tasty sauce, and loaded with pepperoni. Zoe was in love. Matt was nearly forgotten through her first two pieces. By the third piece she'd slowed down enough to notice that Matt's attention kept drifting to the bar.

She turned her head to see what was so interesting. Several people sat on the stools that had obviously been a recent addition to the original bar. At the far end Jase stood talking to the woman Zoe had determined was Jennifer, the wife of his dead friend. Jennifer said nothing, just wiped down some beer spigots as she listened, nodding occasionally.

She turned back to Matt, and found him still watching. "Her name's Jennifer. She's known Jase a long time, probably longer than most people here."

He flashed a smile that made her feel as if she'd just received an A from her favorite teacher. "You read my mind." His gaze followed Jase as he walked away from the bar. "I think I'll go get another beer. You want one?"

"No thanks."

She used the time to go to the restroom and run a comb through her hair. When she returned to the table,

Matt was still at the bar, leaning on his arms as he coaxed a few smiles from Jennifer.

If anyone could break through her reserve, it would be Matt. People warmed to him fast. Zoe had to admit it raised a few caution flags. She wasn't immune to the effect, although he'd counteracted it nicely. He'd been straightforward about his feelings, at the same time acknowledging the touchy situation it put them in. Direct and honest—what more could she expect?

The chair across from her scraped as someone sat down, and she jerked her attention away from the bar.

"Your boyfriend likes to flirt," Jase said. He leaned forward across the small table, his face less than two feet from hers. She noted the soft curve of his upper lip, the line of his nose, the straight brows. If she touched his cheek, she knew, his whiskers would feel like the fine side of an emery board, barely scratchy . . .

She gave herself a mental shake and managed a disinterested look. "He's not my boyfriend."

"Your date, then."

"My boss." She knocked their relationship back a step without thinking. It didn't feel right to let Jase know she was interested in her boss.

"Friendly management style he has there."

She arched an eyebrow. "Don't you have anything better to do than watch us?"

"I always keep an eye on suspicious customers."

"Then you're wasting your time, because we're about as unsuspicious as you can get. We're here during business hours, not sneaking around behind your back, bashing in headlights. The Alpine Sky is a class act, and so are the Flemmings."

He studied her. "You really believe that?"

Beneath his scowl, his blue eyes were piercing, searching hers for the answer. It took her by surprise— he was serious. He obviously saw something in Matt that she didn't see. Or he imagined it; he was good at that, judging by how quickly he'd accused her of helping whoever had taken a few swings at his truck.

"I've worked for the Flemmings for years," she told him, exaggerating the relationship to include the whole family. "They've never been anything but generous and fair." Except for Buck's demeaning view of women, but that was in the past.

As she spoke, he glanced toward the bar and stood up. She knew without looking that Matt was on his way back.

Jase passed beside her as he left, leaning close to her ear. He let several strands of red hair slide through his fingers. "I like it better down," he said, his voice a low rumble that raised goose bumps along her arm.

She shivered and rubbed them away self-consciously. It didn't help. She could still feel the whisper of his breath tingling against her scalp, and the tug of his fingers on her hair. Goose bumps popped out all over again.

Whatever it was he did to her, she was going to have to get over it. Fast.

Fishing had been a terrific idea. In spite of whatever motive Brandon had for getting him out here, forgetting the saloon for a few hours felt good.

Jase cast his lure, the zing of the line breaking the clear air over Killdeer Creek with a high-pitched whine. As soon as the feathery lure hit the surface he began reeling it in again, almost hoping a fish didn't take it. The constant repetition of casting and reeling in had become soothing in its monotony.

"We should have come earlier," Brandon called out as he stepped from around a boulder fifty feet downstream. He splashed his way toward Jase through the knee-deep water, his steps slow in the clumsy hip waders and strong current.

"You didn't catch any?" Jase asked when he got closer.

"No, how about you?"

"Just one. A big guy, probably as big as that one you got at Deadwood last summer."

"Huh. Did you take a picture?"

"No."

"Then he was smaller."

Jase laughed and finished reeling in the line, securing the lure to the pole. "You ready for lunch?"

"Past ready. You think I invited you fishing just to let the trout laugh at me? I want one of those sandwiches your new cook makes. You should sell them."

"And here I thought you liked my company." He waded toward the bank as Brandon followed.

"Nah, I'm just using you for food." He splashed ashore and started removing his waders. "Plus, I asked you so I could make sure you know what the hell you're doing before you get involved with one of the Larkin girls."

Jase stopped, the wader's shoulder straps hanging at his waist. "Jesus, Brandon. Do you really intend to pull some Dr. Phil shtick on me?"

"It's for your own good, boy-o. I wouldn't be a friend if I didn't let you know what you're getting involved in."

Jase pulled the waders off. "First, I'm not getting *involved* in anything. Our relationship is purely business. And second"—he scowled and emphasized his words—"*I'm not getting involved.*"

Brandon regarded him mildly. "Pretty passionate about that, aren't you?"

Jase reached into a canvas bag and tossed Brandon a tightly wrapped sandwich. "Screw you."

"My, my, we're touchy."

Brandon hoisted himself onto their usual lunch spot, a flat-topped boulder by the creek. Jase gave him a warning stare, then climbed up beside him. For a couple of minutes they both concentrated on the thick buns stuffed with meat and cheese, and oozing with sauce.

Brandon finally swallowed and smiled with utter contentment. "Heaven."

"Amen," Jase agreed. He took another bite, relishing the perfection of his world—the best scenery, the best food, and his best friend.

"It's been a long time since you looked at a woman like that."

"Oh, for Christ's sake." Jase lowered his sandwich. "You're not going to leave it alone, are you?" At Brandon's bland look, he ripped off a bite and spoke around it. "Fine, get it out of your system. What's the problem with Zoe Larkin?"

"Nothing. I don't even know her. Might be a wonderful person."

"So?"

"So she and her older sister, Maggie, had a hell of a reputation in this town when they were teenagers. They grew up at some hippie commune in the mountains and didn't exactly make a smooth adjustment to town life. Wild parties. Easy sex, if you believe the stories."

"I've heard the rumors. What's the point?"

"*That's* the point. By the time you quit skiing and started noticing the rest of the world, they'd both done a total one-eighty. But you heard about them. You'd *still* hear about them if you asked around. That kind of reputation takes a long time to die."

"Sucks for them. But it doesn't affect me."

"It might if you start something with Zoe."

Jase gave him a hard look. "I guess you didn't hear me the first three times."

"Didn't have to hear you. I saw you looking at her all night long."

Jase shifted uncomfortably and knew he couldn't deny it. No matter how hard he tried, he hadn't been able to get Zoe Larkin out of his mind.

He stared at the swirling water for several seconds. A similar churning sensation ran through the depths of his mind. "The Alpine Sky wants to buy the saloon," he finally said. "Zoe's the negotiator."

Brandon lowered his sandwich. "Holy shit!"

"My reaction exactly."

"Are you thinking of selling?"

"Hell, no."

"Good." Reassured, Brandon took a bite and chewed thoughtfully. "Why do they want the saloon— tired of the competition?"

"Hardly. We don't have the same customers. They want to tear it down and put a golf course on my fifty acres."

"Damn! I like that land." He frowned thought-fully. "Like golf, too. And I can see how it makes good business sense for the resort." The creases deepened on his forehead. "B-Pass probably wouldn't mind the extra taxes and tourist money, either. Bet they'd rezone quick enough. But—" He shook his head. "Hell, we've got enough development on the slopes. Too much. I like your land the way it is."

"So do I." He liked his life the way it was, too, without worries or responsibilities. The thought of losing that made him even more uncomfortable than losing out to a golf course.

They ate in silence for a while. Finally, Brandon said, "So if you told them no deal, why is Zoe still coming around?"

"Did you see the guy with Zoe? That's the owner's son. He says, and I quote, '*People sometimes change their minds.*'"

Brandon looked at him, his expression gradually turning cold as he followed the implications. "Is that what happened to your truck?"

"I'd put money on it."

Bandon narrowed his eyes. "Is Zoe Larkin in on it?"

The three-million-dollar question. "I wish I knew."

They pondered it for a minute before Brandon asked, "What else can they do to pressure you?"

Jase shrugged. "I don't know. But I'll bet you a day's pay I'm going to find out soon."

"A day's pay ain't shit, lately, especially with our little company. Orders are down. We could use something new to grab the customers' attention."

He knew it, and had been resisting Brandon's hints to come up with a product for the winter sports equipment company they'd started years ago. "I did the snowboard redesign."

"And I think it's gonna do well. But we need more to go with it."

That was the problem with owning a business—it needed to make money. It was probably a good thing Brandon cared about that, because ambition was something Jase avoided.

"I'll think about it," he said. "Later."

Brandon dropped Jase at Cliff's Auto Center where he picked up his newly repaired truck and drove to the Rusty Wire. The charred smell hit him even before he saw the fire truck in the parking lot. From behind the saloon, an acrid, gray cloud sent a lazy column of smoke into the sky. He hit the gas, speeding around the building just as a long tongue of flames leapt skyward through the smoke.

The Rusty Wire was on fire.

Chapter Five

Jase screeched to a stop near the fire truck, taking in the scene as he jumped out. A shed at the back of the saloon was engulfed in flames, and the fire had taken a strong foothold on the back entrance.

Adrenaline seized him. He'd run past two firemen before a third grabbed his arm and yanked him back. "You can't go in there." The tone was firm, from someone used to giving orders.

"I'm the owner!" To his right, a jet of water burst from the thick fire hose and began doing battle with the flames. He struggled against the man's grip on his arm. "Let me go! Someone might be in there!"

"No one's inside. There were only two employees. They're both standing over there."

Jase followed his nod and saw Jennifer and Billy behind their cars, frightened gazes fixed on the saloon. He yelled Jennifer's name, but the sound was lost in a sudden bang as a window burst. Jase ducked. The fireman let go, racing to help with the hose.

Fresh flames poured from the broken window.

Russ's office, he realized, automatically tabulating the amount of flammable items inside. A lot. The arc of water moved over it, drowning the flames at the window and soaking the roof above.

Jase watched for what might have been seconds or minutes. The fire department must have arrived quickly, but the flames had taken a firm hold, and were seeringly bright. Hundred-year-old wood, he thought, watching the vigorous blaze. And all those files in the back office. When he finally turned away, his eyes stung, as if he'd been looking directly into the sun.

Feeling numb and useless, Jase walked over to Jennifer and Billy. Billy blinked at him, as if in a stupor. Jennifer was more collected and stoic. She pressed her mouth into a tight line, and shook her head as she anticipated his question. "I don't know what happened. I smelled smoke and opened the back door, and the shed was on fire. It had already spread to the saloon's roof. I yelled for Billy, we got out, and I called the fire department."

He touched her shoulder, realizing as he did it that he'd avoided touching her for years, as if she embodied some sacred essence of her dead husband. He cringed inwardly, hoping she didn't resent him for it. "Thanks, Jen, you did the right thing. I'm just glad you're both safe."

He looked at the shed, already burned to a blackened, smoking ruin. It was more accurately a lean-to, butting up against the back wall of the saloon. The structure was as old as the main building, probably built to store cords of firewood when woodstoves had been the only source of heat. Jase used it to store extra tables and chairs. There'd been no gasoline cans or piles of dirty rags that might easily combust, although the shed itself was probably a tinderbox. Decades of paint hadn't kept the wood from drying and cracking. It wouldn't have taken much to send those boards up in flames.

Still, wood didn't catch fire by itself. A hard lump formed in his gut. "Jennifer, did you see anyone hanging around before you smelled smoke?"

"That Larkin woman stopped by to see you, but I told her you weren't here."

He tensed at the unexpected news. "What did she want?"

"She didn't say."

He didn't want to ask the rest. "When was that?"

"Not long before I discovered the fire. I talked to her when she pulled into the parking lot, then I went inside." She slid a meaningful glance at him.

He looked away, irritated by the sudden ominous prickle along his scalp. If there was anything to it, he'd find out, but he couldn't prejudge Zoe based on Jennifer's statement alone. He had a feeling she didn't care much for Zoe. "How about you, Billy?"

The kid tore his eyes from the fire with a dazed look. "Huh?"

"Did you see anyone else here earlier today?"

He thought about it, brow furrowed. "No, why?"

"Just wondering." Wondering how the arsonist had approached. He had no doubt it had been deliberate. The saloon had one security camera near the front door, focused on the front lot. He'd check it later, especially to see when Zoe had been there, but he knew it was probably futile. Zoe wasn't stupid. There were other ways to approach the shed if someone wanted to be sneaky.

The fire was nearly out. The fire hose moved over it like a hungry predator, chasing down spurts of flame as soon as they popped up, soaking the charred skeleton that had been the Rusty Wire's back hallway and office. It could have been far worse.

A light breeze came up, blowing a fine mist of water from the hose. It filled the air, catching a rainbow that arched above the smoldering debris. An optimistic person might see it as a sign and take hope from it.

Jase was currently sour on hope.

Zoe saw David change course as he crossed the lobby, going out of his way to intersect her path. She could tell from looking at the nasty sneer he already wore that she wasn't going to like the conversation.

"Putting in extra time these days, I see," he said.

Damn his lousy spies. They must have seen her car when she'd driven to the Rusty Wire earlier that afternoon. She didn't care to explain to David what she'd been doing. As she scrambled for a plausible lie, he added, "Your shift doesn't start for half an hour yet. Couldn't wait to suck up to Matt, eh?"

She frowned. "What are you talking about?"

"Your new attitude. Playing the eager employee and throwing yourself at him in hopes of getting ahead."

The only thing that helped her keep her temper was knowing he'd like her to lose it. "I came in early so I could talk with the head of housekeeping before she leaves. I'm *not* throwing myself at Matt Flemming."

"No? What do you call going out for drinks with your boss?"

"A business dinner. I hear you had one with him, too." Although she was pretty sure they didn't slow dance.

"Right, I'm sure it was the same thing." His lip turned up on one side. "Did he take you out to discuss your new position in the company?"

"What new position?"

"I didn't think so. So it wasn't exactly the same. Well, let me save you the effort—you're already in line for the job."

"I don't understand; did Matt say you weren't going to be the manager of the Alpine Sky?" She tried not to look too pleased about it.

"He needs one of us to manage the golf course. He calls it a promotion."

"That's a lateral move." With less authority, leaving the manager's job wide open if David got the new position. Her hopes could be realized . . . but only if Jase would sell and let them build the damn golf course. She was beginning to believe that wasn't going to happen.

"It's a demotion, no matter how he spins it," David said. "I'm not surprised that someone like you would sleep her way into the top spot in the company. It may even be working. I think he's already on your side."

If they weren't in the lobby, in full view of the front desk and concierge, she'd be tempted to push him into the rock pool. Stepping closer and speaking between gritted teeth, she said, "I'm not sleeping with Matt Flemming. I prefer to rise on my own merits. If he's looking to dump you, it might have something to do with performance."

He snorted. "I can see you're all concerned, but don't worry," David told her. "I can look out for myself. Two can play that game." He arched one eyebrow, making it look like a challenge.

She had no doubt he'd suck up to Matt—that was how David operated. She'd opened her mouth to deliver a nasty response when David's gaze flicked past her and he broke into a huge smile. "Ruth Ann! Don't you look gorgeous!"

Zoe turned to see a middle-aged blonde walking toward them, her long, swinging strides bringing to mind the runways where she used to model. She'd never seen Buck's wife in person before, as Ruth Ann had had little interest in the resort before inheriting it. Apparently that had changed.

Zoe automatically did a typical female assessment— expensive haircut, fashionable clothes, and shoes that probably cost as much as Zoe's monthly rent. Her complexion was suspiciously taut and wrinkle free for a woman old enough to be Matt's mother, not to mention her breasts, which were as plump and perky as a twenty-year-old's.

Zoe couldn't manage a single snarky thought. The cosmetic magic worked; Ruth Ann, who had to be fifty-five if she was a day, looked no more than forty. A hot forty.

She walked straight to David and accepted his polite kiss on the cheek. "David, darling, I'm starving. Can we leave now?"

"Of course." He gave Zoe a condescending smile. "I'm sure Zoe can handle whatever minor problems might pop up during the evening. Ruth Ann, have you met Zoe Larkin? She's my assistant manager."

Not yours, Zoe thought, gritting her teeth.

"Oh, you're the girl Matt told me about!" Ruth Ann offered her hand in a limp shake while looking her up and down.

"It's nice to meet you." Zoe was curious to know what Matt had said about her, and whether it was personal or professional, but couldn't think of a polite way to ask.

David didn't look at all pleased that Zoe had been a topic of discussion between Matt and his mother. He put an arm around Ruth Ann's shoulder and turned her away, sending two signals at once—*We have better things to do than talk to you*, and more significant, *I'm allowed to do this*.

And possibly allowed to do more. Buck's estate had probably left Ruth Ann set for life in everything but male companionship. If she was in the market for young, handsome, and ingratiating, David fit the job requirements.

"We're going to check out the B-Pass nightlife," he said over his shoulder. "Hold down the fort, would you? I left a to-do list on your desk." He waved a dismissive hand. Ruth Ann didn't look back.

A to-do list? Zoe ground her teeth. If there really was one, it was going straight into the shredder. David hadn't needed to tell her what to do from the moment Buck hired him, and he wasn't going to start now.

She almost wished there would be a major crisis just so she could efficiently handle it on her own. A broken water main, a collapsed retaining wall, a lightning strike . . . something. But everything ran smoothly and the sky remained clear, leaving her with little to do besides paperwork.

Even Matt was busy at his computer, clicking away at the keys. That was fine, the man had a business to run. But she was restless. Maybe if she ran her new idea past Matt and he approved, she'd be able to approach Jase with an offer he might find more appealing.

She cleared her throat, flashing a smile when Matt looked up. "Can you take a minute to talk?"

"Sure." He pushed away from the keyboard without hesitation, which was encouraging. This was the man she had to impress, and the ease with which he passed out approving looks was almost too good to be true. "What do you want to talk about? If it's dinner, I thought we might eat here tonight. If you'll join me, that is." He grinned.

She'd have to be crazy not to. She hoped her fair skin wasn't betraying her by flushing with pleasure. "Actually, after I tell you what I've been thinking, you may want to go to the Rusty Wire instead. I have an idea that might make Jase change his mind about selling."

"Great! But I think it will have to wait a while. He's probably a bit preoccupied right now, and I like to have someone's full attention when I deal with them."

It was hard to imagine anyone not giving Matt their full attention. Being the focus of that direct eye contact was riveting. She'd also noticed the subtle way he leaned toward her when he spoke, probably something he wasn't even conscious of, but that she found extremely flattering.

The rest of Matt's statement puzzled her. "Why would Jase be preoccupied?"

"I imagine he'll have his hands full getting the place repaired after that fire. Kind of useless, too, since we're just going to tear it down once we buy it."

He presumed a lot, but it barely registered. "What fire?" The place had looked fine when she'd stopped by around two o'clock.

"You didn't hear? The fire department had to put out a blaze at the back of the building this afternoon. Fortunately, it was confined to the office and some little outbuilding, but there's bound to be smoke damage to the rest of the building. Garrett won't want to be closed longer than necessary, so he's probably trying to get repairs started."

Matt made it sound trivial, but a cold shiver passed through her. "There was a fire at the Rusty Wire?"

"Just a small one. One fire truck had it out in an hour."

"An hour! Was anyone hurt?"

"No, it was just property damage."

Property damage to the office area. "That could be disastrous if accounting and inventory files were destroyed."

He nodded, as if pleased that she'd sorted out the most important issue. "You're right. Garrett didn't strike me as the type to keep backup files, either." He shook his head and made a clicking sound with his tongue. "Too bad. This could be a real mess for him."

For *any* business owner, backup files or not. She would have thought Matt would be more concerned, if only for selfish reasons. "Couldn't this delay a sale?"

"To tell the truth, I hadn't considered approaching him again until he got things straightened out. I wouldn't kick a man when he's down, Zoe. We'll back off on the offer until we see where he stands."

"Of course." She felt slightly embarrassed for assuming he might try to push ahead with the sale. His stance was admirable. And her idea could wait.

Matt stood. "I nearly forgot, I need to meet with a potential investor. It shouldn't take long; how about if I find you later for dinner?"

She smiled. "Great."

He winked as he left. The man had business savvy and ambition, yet obviously didn't let it override his humanity. Matt Flemming seemed more and more like everything she'd always wanted in a man. It was amazing she felt so at ease with him. Maybe it was a mark of maturity that she didn't get all weak-kneed and nervous around him like she did with Jase. Maybe this was how mature love developed, as an easy, natural growth from friendship and respect.

She should ask Maggie. Zoe picked up a pen, rolling it between her fingers as she thought. Her older sister had fallen suddenly and blissfully in love last year, and was now happily married. Her husband, Cal, seemed equally smitten. That was the kind of relationship Zoe wanted. They might have had a rocky beginning, but Maggie had obviously found everything she'd wanted in Cal Drummond.

Before she could change her mind, she picked up the phone and dialed. Maggie answered right away. "Hi, Zoe, what's up?"

"Do you have a few minutes?"

"Yeah, we just finished clearing the supper dishes."

"Great, I have a question about . . ." Damn, she should have thought this through. If Maggie knew who this was about, she'd be up here to check out Matt before the night was through. It was too soon to drag a matchmaking sister into this relationship. If it even *was* a relationship. She clicked the pen, thinking. "It's a hypothetical question. About falling in love." God, that was weak.

There was a long pause. She could imagine Maggie's eyebrows shooting up and her lips twitching with repressed questions. "Uh-huh, okay. Hypothetical question."

"Really."

"I believe you."

Liar. But she was committed now. "When you first met Cal . . ." A light began blinking on the phone and she glanced at the readout—the front desk. She couldn't ignore it. "Hang on, Maggie." She changed lines, tapping the pen impatiently on the desk. "Zoe."

"Zoe, it's Geoff. There's a man here who would like to see you. A Mr. Jase Garrett."

The pen hit the desk. She sat up straight, thoughts racing. Was it possible Jase was throwing in the towel? Maybe the fire damage was worse than Matt knew, was too extensive to make it worth repairing the old saloon. She'd hate to see him give in that way, but a victory was a victory. This could be her big moment. "Show him back here, Geoff." She punched line four. "Maggie, I have to handle this. I'll get back to you."

"Yes, you will," Maggie said forcefully. "If you don't, *I'll* be calling *you*."

Terrific, she'd left her sister on full alert. She hung up and took a few seconds to straighten her desk and close the document on her computer. She was standing to adjust her blazer just as Geoff rapped his knuckles on the open door.

Jase walked past Geoff, then closed the door on the desk clerk's surprised expression. He stopped a few steps away, arms folded and biceps bulging just enough to be sexy as he regarded her. Some purely female part of her went gooey, and she gave herself a hard mental slap, taking note of the more relevant information—he didn't look happy.

"I just heard about the fire," she told him. "I'm sorry. Would you like to sit down?" She gestured at a chair, but he ignored it.

His gaze drifted to Matt's desk, then fastened back on her. "I only saw one name on the door."

"That desk is temporary. Matt Flemming is sharing my office while he's here. Would you like to speak with him, too?"

"No. I came to see you."

Her pulse quickened—for purely business reasons, she told herself, the anticipation that she was about to close the deal on her own. She waited as he looked around her rather ordinary office. He showed no inclination to sit down, and she'd be darned if she'd sit while he stood. They were on her turf, and she wasn't going to concede the psychological advantage by letting him tower over her. She might not be as experienced in management techniques as Matt, but she knew that much.

He studied her for several seconds before he finally spoke. "I've just been talking with the fire marshal."

"Oh?" she said in polite response. She would have expected that he'd be talking to his insurance agent. "Was there much damage to the saloon?"

"No, just the back hallway and office. A good wash and a fresh coat of paint will take care of the rest of the place. We'll probably be able to open again in three days."

"Oh." Then he wasn't here to strike a deal after all. Since he almost certainly heard the disappointment in her voice, she tried to be more upbeat. "That's good news."

"Yes, it is. But that's not why the fire marshal was talking to me. He wanted me to know that the fire was arson."

"Arson!" Her stomach clenched, realizing where his suspicion would fall. "Is he sure?"

His lip twitched in what was almost a sneer. "They're very good at that sort of thing."

His attitude scraped against her temper. "If you came to imply that the Alpine Sky had anything to do with it, you're wrong."

"That's not why I'm here."

"Oh." She wrinkled her brow in puzzlement. "Why *are* you here?"

His stony stare didn't waver. "They know it was started in the shed by the back door, using a gasoline-based propellant and a large amount of paper, probably newspaper."

"That's good." He cocked an eyebrow, and she rushed to correct herself. "I don't mean good that it's arson. I mean it's good they can tell that much about how it started. Gasoline and newspaper. I didn't know they could be that exact." She felt as if she was babbling, so she shut up. It was his fault. Something about the way he looked at her always made her feel jumpy inside.

"That's not all they know. From the way it burned, and from talking to the two employees who were inside, they know when the fire was set. It was sometime between two and two-thirty."

"Amazing. Maybe it will help them catch whoever set it."

A small tic narrowed his eyes for a second. "Yes, especially combined with the other piece of evidence I have."

"There's more? Lucky for you, you have a careless arsonist."

"Or stupid. Apparently the arsonist didn't know I have a security camera in the parking lot."

"You caught him in the act?"

"Unfortunately, no." Bitter disappointment tightened the muscles along his jaw. "It doesn't show the back of the building, just the front entrance and parking lot. But that was enough." She waited expectantly, and he moved a step closer. "Only one car pulled into the lot during that time period—a red Ford Escort."

Her eyes widened in sudden shock. "My car!"

"Your car."

She stared as the full implication soaked in, finally understanding the reason for his icy, closed expression. "You think *I* set the fire."

"With that video, I think I can prove it."

The hell with appearances. Zoe dropped into her chair, stunned by the mix of emotions swirling inside her. Anger. Fear. Confusion. She looked up, fighting back trembling, to emphasize the one fact she knew. "I didn't do it."

"Right." His look of disgust hurt more than it should have. "Are you going to try to make me believe it was someone else in that car? Because it's not going to work."

"No, it was me." It sounded weak, even to her. "But I swear I didn't set the fire."

"Then you better have a damn good alibi, because that video is going to the police. Arson is a crime, and whoever set that fire is going to prison."

Chapter Six

Jase fought against the instinct to take pity on her. Just because she suddenly looked small and vulnerable was no reason to go easy on her.

Bashing in headlights had been over the line, but could still be called petty vandalism. He'd been willing to overlook it if it had stopped there. He wouldn't overlook setting the Rusty Wire on fire. People could have died. If Zoe did it, she deserved every bit of his wrath, along with a stiff prison sentence.

Steeling himself against the naked worry in her eyes, he said, "If you didn't intend to burn down the Rusty Wire, why were you there?"

"I had an idea, something I thought might change your mind about selling."

"Even though I told you that won't happen."

A small spark of defiance lit her eyes. "You think that's a reason to not do my job? Unlike you, I have a career plan and goals I want to achieve. If I quit trying every time someone told me no, I'd still be working the front desk."

He wanted to ask if one of those goals involved marrying her boss. But that wasn't the topic. "You stopped by to see me, but didn't go inside?" He stepped closer. "Come on, you can do better than that, Zoe. You'll need a better alibi when the police question you."

She reacted to his looming presence as he'd known she would, edging back in her chair, intimidated. She immediately covered it with anger. "I didn't go in because I didn't have to," she snapped. "You weren't there."

Her white-knuckled grip on the chair arms was the only evidence of fear. It was clear she didn't like to show weakness, or give in to fear in the face of over-whelming odds. He knew that feeling well, and under-stood it more than most—it had taken him all the way to the Olympics. He just hadn't expected to see it in Zoe. He'd expected tears, and pleas that she'd simply been following orders. He had to admire a never-say-die attitude.

It didn't make her innocent. "You couldn't know I wasn't there. My truck was still at the repair shop." He knew that hadn't mattered, that Jennifer had told her he was gone, but he wanted to hear Zoe's version. The time line mattered.

"I didn't need to see your truck." She looked dis-gusted, as if he should have known this. "Your bar-tender was taking out trash when I pulled in, and came over to the car. She told me you'd gone fishing and she didn't know when you'd be back, so I left."

"That's it? That was the whole conversation?"

"Of course not," she said crossly. "I left out the *hi, how are you* stuff, *nice weather,* and *that's a cute blouse, where'd you get it and when is the sale over,* and *have a nice day.* Stuff like that." It was clear his stupidity tried her patience. "Sorry, I didn't think you cared about the sale at Marlene's Boutique."

But he did. It meant the conversation had taken longer than Jennifer said. "How long did you talk to her?"

"I don't know, a few minutes. What difference does it make?"

Even though she'd been visibly shaken by his accusation, this didn't seem like a bluff. Her big brown eyes hadn't once broken contact with his. A sliver of doubt crept into his mind. "You talked for several minutes?"

"What's the matter, doesn't that show on your security tape?"

"No." But it might explain the amount of time it took for her car to leave.

"Well, I'm not lying. Ask Jennifer."

He had, but he'd ask again. Maybe Jennifer had underestimated the time. Or maybe Zoe was lying to save her skin. If it came down to believing one or the other, there was no contest. Jennifer had been his best friend's wife. He'd known her for ten years, employed her for eight. She had nothing to gain by lying.

Zoe did. In addition to wanting to keep her job, she'd just been threatened with prison. He hadn't been kidding.

He placed his hands on the arms of her chair, leaning in close enough to catch the flowery scent of her hair. She pushed back, stiff and wary, with no place to go as a blush rose to her neck.

"I'll check with Jennifer." He ground out each word through clenched jaws. "If I find out you're lying, that security video goes straight to the cops. And if you did lie, you'd better alert your boyfriend, because you'll be under arrest before your shift is over."

She tightened her mouth, her eyes locked with his in a hard stare. "I'm not lying."

If she was, she was damn good at it. The spark in her eyes looked more like hate than fear, a silent message that he'd pushed her as far as she would allow. Anger hovered between them, hot and palpable.

So did something else. It snapped and crackled like the fire that had devoured the shed, heating the space between them. Pulling him closer. For several long seconds he hung captive, memorizing the gold flecks in her eyes, the dusting of freckles across her cheekbones, the curve of her lips. His gaze lingered as her lips parted slightly, the full pink swell of them drawing him closer . . .

Jase jerked backward, releasing her chair as if he'd been burned. Jesus, had he really been thinking about kissing her? The woman who'd probably set his saloon on fire? He needed to get out of here before his warped judgment led him to act on any more dangerous impulses, like unpinning that hair. He didn't even like red hair. There was just something about the texture and the blond highlights that made him want to run his fingers through it.

Without another word, he turned his back and left. Let her wonder what in the hell was wrong with him. He wondered, too.

Zoe stared at the open doorway, dazed, until she finally realized the desk phone was ringing. Without looking, she picked it up. "Zoe."

"You didn't call me back." Maggie's accusation

snapped her fully into the present. "You can't ask about love and some hypothetical guy, then abruptly hang up. Unless that was Mr. Hypothetical you left me for?"

She sighed. "I knew you'd jump to conclusions. And no, that was the guy who intends to charge me with arson."

"Arson! What the hell?"

"There was a fire today at the Rusty Wire, and the owner thinks I set it."

"That's the most ridiculous thing I've ever heard."

It was nice to have someone jump to her defense without question, but the truth was, the charge wasn't so ridiculous. Jase's security video could go a long way toward proving her guilty, something she didn't want to think about right now. "You're right. Forget him. He's not the one I was thinking of when I called you."

Maggie harrumphed again over the arson charge, but apparently couldn't ignore her curiosity about Zoe's possible love life. "Okay, so ask me about falling in love with this other guy."

The topic had lost its appeal, but Maggie wouldn't be put off. Zoe sighed as she paused to gather her spinning thoughts. "First, let's be clear—there's nothing going on. He hasn't even kissed me. We've danced together, that's it. But he's so . . . I mean, it's possible he might . . ."

"He has potential?"

"Yes," she said, relieved. "At least, I think he does." She hesitated, then decided to go with the truth. "Frankly, he seems like the perfect guy."

"Mmm," Maggie hummed appreciatively. "Good start."

"I know. He meets all the qualifications on the list, so I wondered if that was how you knew Cal was the right one for you, because he fit into your life so easily."

"Whoa, back up. Qualifications? I know you like your life to be organized, but you don't actually have a *list*, do you?"

"Well, not on paper." At least, not as long as she didn't print out the Word document on her computer.

"Zoe! Love doesn't come with a checklist!"

"I know that." No one understood her compulsion for organization. "But at some point you had to realize that Cal was the right man for you, and that you belonged together."

"Well, sure . . ."

"How did you know that? Was it because he matched every important quality you ever wanted in a man? Like the two of you seemed to just . . . fit?"

Maggie's laugh verged on hysteria. "Are you kidding? Cal didn't match *anything* I thought I wanted in a partner."

Zoe sighed in frustration. This was hard to put into words, and Maggie wasn't making it any easier. She never should have brought it up in the first place, but it was too late to back out now. "Look, I know it was rocky for you guys at first, but after that mess with the tabloids was over, when it came down to just the two of you, did it seem like things fell into place? As if you suddenly realized Cal was the one you'd been looking for?"

Maggie choked back another laugh. "Zoe, *nothing* fell into place. Cal lived and worked in another state. He had a messed-up family life, a lot of old baggage from a previous marriage, and a teenage sister who came along as part of a package deal. One who clashed with him on every issue, I might add. None of that would have been on my man-I-want-to-marry list."

She must not be saying it right. "But you must have known you shared the same values and priorities."

"Well, sure."

"See? *That's* what I'm talking about. That kind of list."

"That's not enough."

Her sister's flat statement slapped her satisfied smile into a scowl. "Why not?"

"Because it doesn't help when you hit the rough patches, and every couple does sooner or later. Shared priorities are too easy to walk away from. You need tingles to make it work."

Zoe took a second to frown at the phone. "You want to be more specific?"

"Tingles. You know, that funny feeling you get every time you're together. Like . . ." Maggie searched for the right words. "Like a fluttery feeling in your chest when he touches you. Or a rush to your head when he whispers in your ear. Or a disoriented feeling when he walks into the room, like the world just moved under your feet."

Zoe relaxed. Maggie was getting ahead of things. "I told you, he hasn't even kissed me. We're a long way from feeling the earth move."

"No you aren't," Maggie said. Zoe wished she would stop making annoying presumptions. "I'm talking about something that happens right from the beginning. Maybe right from the moment you see him.

I'm not sure about that because I was pretty pissed off the first time I saw Cal, but certainly from the moment you start having rational conversations."

Zoe frowned. She'd had a few rational conversations with Matt, but couldn't recall any tingling.

"Are you sure this happens to everyone?"

"No," Maggie admitted. "But you asked about me. Let's say the two of you are talking, and you notice how nice-looking he is. Or smart."

Now, *that* she could relate to.

"It's more than that," Maggie continued, squashing her hopes. "You also notice little details that you don't see in other people—the way his lips curve when he smiles, a tiny scar on his chin, the way he smells. It's like your senses can't get enough of this guy, and they register everything. And your body goes on overload, and your skin prickles all over, and you feel all squirmy inside." She sighed happily. "You know what I mean?"

Zoe blinked without seeing. "Maybe." Oh, yes. She'd felt exactly like that not ten minutes ago. But there was obviously another reason for it. Didn't they say hate was the emotion most similar to love? Apparently hating someone caused the same sensory overload. And it was getting in the way of her plans for love.

Maybe she should do something about it, something that would let her move past her annoying interest in Jase so she could concentrate on Matt. No half measures, either; total immersion was the only way, until all the tingles were gone.

She reached for the mouse pad as she thought, opening the document titled LIFE PLAN. Scanning the to-do list, she idly typed in *Jase Garrett*, then hesitated, reluctant to write the words that burned in her mind. Chickening out, she put in a question mark.

"I hope that helps," Maggie said. Hinting for more.

"Yes, thanks," Zoe told her, jerking back to the present. It hadn't helped at all. Obviously love was different for different people. With tingles or without, Jase Garrett didn't trust her farther than a fish could fly, and intended to have her arrested. Matt Flemming had truly admirable qualities, and was attracted to her. It wasn't even a contest.

She could forgo tingles.

Jase drove directly from the Alpine Sky to Jennifer's house, but she wasn't home. It looked like Zoe would get a day's reprieve before he confirmed that she'd been alone in the parking lot for several minutes. He felt strangely relieved, which just pissed him off. He shouldn't hesitate to turn in a criminal, especially one whose acts could easily have included murder. His libido wasn't a reliable indicator of good character.

Maybe he just needed to get laid. He hadn't had sex since his brief fling with Carla, which had been . . . shit, way too long ago. As soon as the saloon opened again, he'd start paying closer attention to the customers. Surely there were plenty of attractive women who were both sexy and free of criminal tendencies.

It was as good a reason as any to get moving on the repairs.

Jennifer and Russ showed up at the Rusty Wire the following morning to help assess damage and start the cleanup. Jase waited until Jennifer took a break to approach her, following her when she stepped outside the temporary door in the boarded-over back hallway.

She stood with hands in her pockets, contemplating the blackened timbers that had once been Russ's office. Half the room had been destroyed. The other half was scorched and water damaged, but standing. It would get ripped down later today when the reconstruction began.

"Depressing, isn't it?" Jase said, standing beside her.

She wrinkled her nose. "It stinks."

He nodded; the acrid stench of wet ash made him want to sneeze. "The fire would have been a lot worse if you hadn't discovered it so soon. Thanks, Jen. I owe you for that one."

She turned a contemplative gaze on him. For a moment he thought she was going to suggest a way to repay her, but she turned away. He could never tell what she was thinking. "Thank the fire department," she said. "If they hadn't been on their way back from a car fire, they might not have gotten here in time."

It was true; five more minutes and the old timbers of the main building would have gone up like matchsticks. They'd been lucky.

"I wanted to ask you about something, Jen. Remember when you said you saw Zoe Larkin shortly before the fire?"

"Yeah. I guess you saw her car on the security tape, huh?"

He nodded. "She was here right when you said. You must have talked to her for a few minutes."

"Not really. I just answered her question, and went back inside."

The unexpected reply made him stop breathing. A

cold feeling of dread slithered through his chest as he realized how much he'd wanted to believe Zoe. "Are you sure you didn't talk to her longer than that, maybe chat about the weather or something?"

"I *know* I didn't. I didn't see any reason to be friendly with someone who wants to tear down the Rusty Wire." Jennifer slid a cautious look his way. "You mean she didn't leave after I went inside?"

"I don't know," he said, because he didn't want to say she'd stayed in the parking lot alone for several minutes, doing who knew what.

He didn't have to say it. "She set the fire, didn't she?" Jennifer asked.

Shit. He didn't want to think it, but her words buzzed like hornets in his ears, insisting he pay attention. If Jennifer was telling the truth, Zoe couldn't have been talking to her the whole time she'd been out of view. He'd replayed the security video and noted how much time had elapsed between her car driving in and leaving—nearly six minutes. Plenty of time to talk about a sale at Marlene's. Or to open the shed, douse some newspapers with gasoline, and strike a match.

If it hadn't been her, then someone had used a different approach. "Someone could have sneaked in from the woods without being seen," he theorized aloud.

Jennifer looked doubtful. "Who?"

Anyone. Just so he didn't have to feel this gut-twisting resignation that said Zoe had committed arson.

"They'd get pretty scratched up that way," Jennifer mused. "And they'd have to leave their car on the road where everyone could see it while they hiked in and out. If it was me, I'd just drive right in. Like Zoe did."

"If she did it." He didn't like hearing it stated as a certainty.

Jennifer sighed with obvious impatience. "What's that thing Russ always says about a razor?"

Hell. "Occam's razor. The simplest explanation is usually the right one." He frowned in annoyance, and not just at her conclusion. It hadn't taken Jennifer long to accept the idea that Zoe had started the fire. "You don't like her much, do you?"

She shrugged. "I don't know her. That makes it easy to be objective."

Implying that he wasn't? "I'm objective," he said, annoyed.

Jennifer broke off a piece of charred drywall, rolling it in her hand and avoiding his gaze. "You seem distracted around her. Maybe she's hitting on you."

He snorted. "Trust me, she's not."

"She came here to see you, didn't she?"

"She's trying to persuade me to sell."

"Maybe she's doing that by pretending to be attracted to you."

"She hates me, no pretending about it."

She was quiet for a moment, then tossed the fragment of drywall into the soggy ashes. "I don't know, Jase, I get a funny feeling from her. Like she's up to something. Something secretive."

He got a funny feeling from her, too, but he was pretty sure it wasn't the same one Jennifer got. "She's up to something, but it's no secret. She wants me to sell."

Jennifer tilted her head, watching him. "Or she just wants you, period."

Hot pressure settled in his groin at the thought of

Zoe wanting him. He dismissed it with a touch of irritation. But this was a first—in all the years she'd worked for him, Jennifer never had a word to say about his love life. Admittedly, Zoe was pretty, and had a certain something that he found attractive—hell, nearly irresistible—but why Jennifer would care was beyond him. It wasn't like . . .

The thought that had sneaked into his brain tingled across his scalp, raising the fine hairs on his neck. He gave Jennifer a sidelong glance. Could she be jealous of Zoe?

The idea made him so uncomfortable he turned away, looking at anything but her. Not Adam's wife. Not the woman he'd known as a friend ever since Adam started dating her. The woman who'd been inconsolable at Adam's death, and locked in a shell ever since. He knew how deeply she'd been hurt.

With a small jolt he realized what he had no desire to acknowledge. If she were finally coming out of that self-imposed isolation, putting her wounded heart on the line, he would be the man most likely to understand her loss. The safest choice and the easiest to trust.

Jase shuffled his feet nervously, kicking up unpleasant odors from the ash. It was possible in a sad, bittersweet way. Jennifer had never shown a hint of romantic interest in men since Adam's death. She'd never shown any interest in Jase's love life, either, never mentioning the women who had briefly become his lovers. Maybe that reserve had finally cracked, with her first, cautious feelings directed toward him.

If so, he would have to be very careful. He cared very much about Jennifer, but not in a romantic way.

He didn't want to see her fragile feelings damaged. Fortunately, she didn't have anything to worry about when it came to Zoe Larkin.

"Whatever Zoe might have pretended to feel for me won't matter after today. Not if I turn that video over to the police."

She nodded. "Good."

He would worry later about what to do if Jennifer decided to take it to the next level and make a move on him. He'd have to find a way to let her down easy without damaging her confidence. And then he had to do something about getting himself a normal love life, because fending off his dead friend's widow and having hot fantasies about a possible arsonist weren't working for him.

The string of touristy shops flanking the Alpine Sky resort resembled nothing more than a small Bavarian village. It was a design they were putting to good use. Zoe stood at the center of the stone-cobbled public square, supervising the erection of a band shell for the upcoming Beer and Brats Festival. Preparations for the event were on schedule, but she still didn't welcome interruptions from the front desk.

"Run the electric cables behind those trees," she called out to one of the workers before speaking into her phone. "Geoff, can you ask Mark to handle whatever you need? I've got a lot going on here." As she spoke, she gestured at a stand of pine trees for the benefit of the sound guy.

"Um, I don't think so." Geoff's voice sounded tentative in her ear. "There are two police officers here, and they asked to see you."

She stilled, slowly lowering her arm. The police could be there for any number of reasons—problems with a guest; an ordinance violation; they'd even shown up once to euthanize a wounded elk. But her thoughts flew to Jase's accusation of arson, sending a chill through her body, and she had to make a conscious effort to keep her voice steady. "Of course, I'll be right there."

She saw them as she crossed the lobby from the terrace entrance, a young man and a middle-aged woman in the brown uniforms of the Barringer's Pass police force. They stood by the front desk, hands resting on the heavily equipped belts that made them intimidating in a larger-than-life way. Geoff hovered nearby. Belatedly, she wished she'd told him to have them wait in her office, where they wouldn't attract the stares of curious guests.

She was grateful for the sharp click of her heels on the marble floor. The sound always made her feel professional and in control. She stopped in front of them, a polite expression pasted on her face. "May I help you?"

The man straightened to an imposing height, putting both hands on his hips. "Are you Zoe Larkin?"

"Yes. I'm the manager on duty. How may I help you?"

"I'm afraid you'll have to come with us, ma'am."

Her heart fluttered and fell. "What?"

He didn't move, didn't even blink. "We need to take you in for questioning regarding the fire at the Rusty Wire Saloon."

The clipped words made it clear he meant *right this second*. Zoe's eyes darted to the female officer, but her gaze was as flat and hard as her partner's. "I, uh, really shouldn't leave. Could we talk in my office?"

"I'm afraid not." It might have sounded kind, almost apologetic, if he hadn't looked like he was facing down a murder suspect. His finger twitched slightly at his belt and she had sudden fantasies of him whipping out the cuffs.

When he reached into his breast pocket, she flinched, then relaxed when he produced a folded piece of paper. He thrust it at her. "We also have a warrant to search your car."

She felt suddenly light-headed. "M-my car?"

"Yes, ma'am." It was the female officer. "We'll need your keys, and you can show us where it's parked."

She stared, openmouthed. My God, they seriously suspected her of arson! Jase hadn't wasted any time. The consequence he'd threatened slammed back into her mind: prison.

Zoe put a hand on the counter for support, trying to make it look casual, while her head buzzed with static. She had to pull herself together. She wouldn't fall apart, not in front of her staff. Image mattered. The whole town had taught her that lesson when they'd refused to forget her rebellious youth. She'd spent years repairing her reputation, working hard, gaining credibility and respect. Now it was about to vanish in a matter of seconds. All because Jase didn't believe her.

She turned to Geoff, struggling to keep her voice calm. "Geoff, could you call Bill and ask him to cover for me until I get back?"

"Sure, uh, when, I mean how long . . . ?"

"Not long." She hoped. She wouldn't even consider

the possibility that she wouldn't be coming back. The police might suspect her, but she was innocent. They couldn't possibly have evidence against her. They wouldn't find any in her car, either. They were just trying to intimidate her.

They were doing a good job of it.

"Car keys?" the female officer reminded her.

She swallowed hard. "They're in my office." The woman followed her, as if she might make a break for it. She took the keys, then stood aside to follow Zoe back to the lobby. Zoe walked outside without a backward glance, not wanting to see the shock on Geoff's face. At the curb she paused beside the two police cars, pointing to the employee lot. "It's around the corner, the red Ford Escort."

"You're going to have to take us there, ma'am."

Great. She walked halfway around the main building, drawing attention with her armed, uniformed escort, then walked back again with the serious young cop who seemed a little too satisfied with his role. He helped her into the backseat, then got behind the wheel.

He was silent through the ten-minute ride, never acknowledging her on the other side of the glass divider. If it was a deliberate attempt at dehumanizing her, it was effective. So was the condition of the car. She wrinkled her nose and looked around the stripped-down backseat. Scratches marred the back of the hard plastic seat, probably from handcuffs, and an unpleasant odor emanated from the floor. She sat forward, hands locked on her knees to keep the trembling inside her from shaking her whole body.

She'd never imagined herself in the backseat of a

police car, and could barely grasp the reality. She was a suspect.

Fear shook her clear to the bone, but hate kept her focused. Jase Garrett would pay for this. Accusing her of arson was bad enough, but she'd been sure nothing would come of his threat after he talked to Jennifer. She had a witness, for heaven's sake! But he'd turned it into an investigation anyway.

She hated him. It was time to stop being decent with him.

Zoe was starting to sweat under her arms. She was pretty sure it wasn't the temperature of the room, since Officer Carlson looked cool as a cucumber. It was her temper, which she'd rediscovered twenty minutes into the repetitive, detailed questioning, and which was seriously ramping up.

She'd been patient the first time through the story, describing her reason for going to the Rusty Wire, her conversation with Jennifer, then how she'd taken another minute to check her phone messages before driving home. She'd even filled the whole page provided for the written version of the story, writing until her hand cramped. She hadn't used that much longhand since high school.

But Carlson was pushing her to her limit, going back over different points in her story and getting the same responses. Yes, Jennifer had told her Jase wasn't there. No, she hadn't left a message for him. No, she hadn't seen anyone else. Really, how much could she say about five uneventful minutes of her life? If he expected her to break under the unbearable boredom, it just might happen. But he wouldn't get a confession.

What he'd get was a lecture on police harassment and a threat to call her attorney, who she was going to look into retaining as soon as Carlson let her out of here.

Carlson leaned forward. "Let's go back to the point where you had just pulled around the building and spotted Jennifer."

"Why?"

He didn't like that. "I don't need to give you a reason, Miss Larkin. I need you to answer the question. Now—"

He broke off as the door opened. Zoe looked up, eyes going wide with surprise. "Cal!"

"Hi, Zoe." Maggie's husband gave her a quick smile before he turned a tight expression on Carlson. "I need to see you a minute, Carlson."

"I have a couple more—"

"Now." Even in jeans and a T-shirt, Cal's voice had the same authority it had when he was in his police uniform. Carlson responded to it, abruptly leaving and closing the door behind him.

Zoe waited. It took less than a minute. Cal opened the door, shaking his head in disgust. "Come on, you're done. I'll give you a ride back to work."

She didn't ask questions, gratefully following Cal's long strides to his pickup. Night had fallen while she was inside, leaving the parking lot bathed in bluish-white halogen lights. She climbed into the truck and turned to him as he pulled out of the lot. "How did you know I was here?"

"Heard it on the police scanner at home. Sorry I didn't get to you sooner, but I had to see that security tape first, to see if they really had a case against you."

She almost didn't want to ask. "Do they?"

He blew out a long breath. "Maybe. But you have one big thing in your favor—an employee at the Rusty Wire confirmed your story. The only part in question is how long she talked to you. A prosecutor could build a case on it, but it's not enough. It'll all hinge on whether they find evidence in your car. Gasoline, specifically. If there's even a drop on the carpet, it will look suspicious. Have you ever had an emergency gas can in there?"

She shook her head. "No."

"Good." Cal gave her a long look. "I don't want you to worry. They aren't ready to bring charges, and I don't see that changing."

As long as they found nothing in her car. For a brief moment she recalled stories of police corruption and planted evidence, then shook it off. Not the Barringer's Pass police department. Her own brother-in-law was a cop here, and he'd know if there'd ever been the slightest hint of dishonesty on the force.

"Zoe." She didn't like the cautious way he glanced at her. "This will get out."

Oh, crap. He was right. The police reports were a popular item in the local paper. She swallowed around the tightness in her throat and said, "I'm just glad you came, Cal. How'd you get that guy to let me go?"

"He didn't have to take you there in the first place. He was just trying to intimidate you into saying something he could use to arrest you."

"Is that legal?"

"Yeah, but I'd call it overkill in this case. Carlson claims he got a tip. Someone implied that he could uncover new facts if he leaned on you hard enough." He gave her a sharp glance. "Someone's trying to cause problems for you, Zoe."

Jase. Zoe scowled out the window without seeing the tourists still shopping in the downtown stores. "Can they? Do I have to worry about being sent to prison?"

"No." But she didn't like the grim look on his face. He was quiet for several seconds, his hands tight on the wheel. "But if it did happen—and it won't—I know a good trial lawyer. They'd never get a conviction."

Her mouth went dry. A jury trial. She imagined trying to defend her character in Barringer's Pass, where too many people remembered the wild Larkin girls. Take any dare, break every rule. She jammed her fingers under her thighs to hide their trembling.

Jase might get his wish to see her in prison. But she wouldn't go without a fight.

Chapter
Seven

Jase toweled off after his shower, gave his hair a cursory rub, and went in search of clean clothes. They were becoming scarce; he'd spent most of the day painting and swabbing floors at the Rusty Wire, sweating through a couple of changes of clothes. It was boring labor, mopping floors and rolling paint on every inch of wall and ceiling until his shoulders ached. The amazing part was how satisfying it was. He hadn't felt this fond of the old saloon, this *connected* to it, since he'd first bought the place.

Maybe Russ and Jennifer felt the same way. They'd helped with the long hours of cleanup, accompanied by ripping and banging sounds as the burned debris outside was torn down and hauled away. He tried not to think about how many times he'd looked up and found Jennifer watching him.

They'd caught a break that the fire had stopped short of the restrooms; rebuilding them could have kept him closed for weeks. Now, with the last of the paint drying and a new back office and hallway under construction, the Rusty Wire was ready to open for business. He anticipated a crowd, too. He was still proud of his idea to call the feature writer from the local newspaper to come out and cover their renovation. The story would be out Wednesday, in time to pull in their regular Friday night customers and anyone else who wanted a look at the scene of the crime. There were always plenty of those.

Jase pulled on his last clean pair of jeans and gathered an armload of dirty clothes for the washing machine. He had just finished stuffing them in when the doorbell rang. He glanced at his wrist, but his watch was still in the bedroom along with the shirt he hadn't put on. Still, it had to be past nine o'clock—late for visitors, especially after the long day he'd just put in. Whoever it was, they weren't getting invited in. All he wanted tonight was a quiet hour or two to make a dent in his backlog of dirty laundry, then crawl into bed.

Pouring detergent, he started the machine and went to answer the door.

He glanced out the window on the way and did a double take. No mistake—that was red hair glowing beneath the overhead porch light. A jolt of energy zapped through his body.

Zoe. Curiosity woke every tired nerve ending. She would never come here to make another offer; being at his house took her out of her professional comfort zone. It had to be something else. This was going to be interesting.

He pulled the door open. An evening rainstorm had drenched the upper slopes, leaving the air heavy with the fragrance of pine and earth. The smell swept inside with the opening door, along with something flowery that must have come from her. He inhaled deeply, drinking in a dose of summer and Zoe as he appreciated the view. Her light red hair shone like polished gold in the light, creating a shimmering halo atop her head. Pretty. She might have looked angelic if not for the way her eyes narrowed and her pink lips drew into a tight pucker when she looked at him.

He smiled anyway. "Hello, Zoe."

"You rotten son of a bitch."

He'd been right about the interesting part. He looked over her official blue blazer and skirt. "Aren't you supposed to be at work?"

"Yes. I had to take the rest of the night off because you decided to be an asshole."

And she was going to ream him a new one. Oddly, he didn't care. He liked the idea of having her in his house, even spitting mad. "Would you care to come inside and elaborate?"

"I can say what I need to say in less than a minute." But she stepped inside, probably because he'd stepped back, widening the gap between them. She obviously intended to keep this an in-your-face encounter. "If you wanted a fight, Garrett, you've got it. And I don't give up easily."

"I believe you. What are we fighting about?"

"As if you didn't know. No matter how dirty you play, you won't make me go whimpering back to my boss in defeat. If you want to complicate things with false accusations, bring it on. I can handle it. But don't stand there and play innocent when we both know the truth." Her lip curled in disgust and her eyes narrowed to slits. "You are the lowest form of slime on the planet. An oozing pustule on the ass of humanity. A pathetic, lying, soulless coward."

Jase raised his eyebrows, hardly knowing what to respond to first. He gave her tirade an A for creativity and for rousing his curiosity, but the last accusation rankled. He didn't see how it could apply. "I'm a coward?"

She took an angry swipe at a stray lock of hair, and he felt a twinge of disappointment. He'd kind of liked the way it curled on her cheek.

"Only a coward sends someone else to do his dirty work, then hides behind a legal smoke screen, leaving the police and public opinion to torment his victim."

"The police?" Any trace of amusement fled. This was more serious than he'd thought. "Who's being tormented?"

"You know damn well who!" She poked him in the chest for emphasis, then faltered, as if realizing for the first time that he wasn't fully dressed. Her gaze lowered to his bare feet, then rose again to linger on his bare chest. Just as his groin tightened in response, she blinked and fury hardened her features again. "Don't pretend it's all about justice, because I know you *enjoy* it." Her hands formed fists at her sides, and he wondered if it was to keep from touching him. "You sent the police to drag me in and humiliate me in front of my coworkers, just for your own sick amusement. Well, laugh all you want because I've lived through public humiliation before, and—" Her breath hitched the tiniest bit before she glared even harder. "I can do it again. Just watch me."

This kept getting more and more confusing, and he had a feeling he was missing some vital clue. He held out his palms. "Zoe, wait. Hold it a second. How did the police get involved?"

"That's rich. How do you think?" She stepped forward, raising her face to lecture him at close range, a tactical mistake, since it just made him think about lowering his head to kiss her. She seemed oblivious, anger putting an attractive flush on her cheeks. "They got involved when you gave them your security video, just like you knew they would. And they took me in for questioning, exactly as you planned. Are you really going to stand there and play dumb on top of it? You threatened to do it, and you did. There's no point in denying—"

"Hold on!" He placed his hands on her shoulders to cut off her lecture. She was close, and his gaze dropped inadvertently to the V-neck of her blouse. A scattering of freckles disappeared beneath it and for a second he imagined where they might end. His jeans grew even snugger. He swore beneath his breath and took a step back.

Zoe crossed her arms and clenched her jaw, clearly annoyed at being stopped in mid-tirade, but giving him a turn to speak. She played fair even when she was mad. In the back of his mind, he thought that mattered. Fair-minded people probably didn't sneak around setting fires.

He tried to make sense of her accusations. "The police took you to the station to question you about the fire?"

"As if you didn't know."

"I didn't."

The line of her mouth tightened as she took a deep breath. "Yes, the police questioned me. Do you get an extra kick out of hearing me say it? You really are a sick bastard, aren't you?"

He frowned. "Zoe, stop passing judgment for a minute. Are you telling me the police have my security video?"

"Of course they do. It's the main piece of evidence in their investigation. You should have made a copy if you wanted to play it over and over for entertainment purposes. Not that it shows anything incriminating—"

"I didn't give them that video."

"Yeah, right. Are we going to play semantics? You put it down and they picked it up?"

He ran a hand through his still-damp hair. "Look, I need to understand this." He closed the door and gestured at the living room. "Sit down and start from the beginning, slowly."

She stiffened, looking suddenly wary. "No thanks, I don't care to hear more of your lies. I've heard quite enough already."

He put his hands on her shoulders again, deliberately keeping his eyes away from those freckles. "Zoe, listen to me. I'm not lying. I didn't do it."

His words finally resonated with her, probably recalling her own claim of innocence. She stared for several seconds as the tension eased from her jaw and her brow creased. "You didn't turn me in?"

"No, I didn't. And I'm not even sure what happened, so will you please explain it to me?" When she hesitated, frustration got the better of him. He grabbed her hand and marched the ten steps to the couch, surprised when she followed without protest. "Sit."

She eased gingerly onto the edge of the couch. He sat at the opposite end to keep her from bolting.

"Start at the beginning," he encouraged in a gentler voice.

She studied him, licking her lips slowly. He followed the motion with interest, consciously resisting the urge to move closer. "Two officers came to the resort. One had a warrant to search my car. They took it away, I don't know where. I had to borrow one from my sister. The other cop took me to the station to go over the five minutes I spent in your parking lot. In tedious detail. Twice. Not to mention my required essay on the subject." She gave him a hard look, as if still reserving suspicion about his complicity.

"They specifically said they had the security video?"

"Yes, with ominous overtones. My brother-in-law even watched it. He's a cop."

He rubbed a spot in the center of his forehead, hating the layers he was beginning to sense here. Someone was trying to hurt Zoe, which was more reason to suspect she was innocent.

"I'd like to know how they got it. After Jennifer told me she'd talked to you, and I realized she might have something against you, I decided to hold on to it. I thought it was possible you were telling the truth."

"Gee, thanks."

He didn't like the snarky tone, but he understood her frustration. She'd never tried to deny being in that car, had just possibly told the truth about what happened in the parking lot, and for her trouble she'd been hauled down to the police station and questioned like a suspect. He'd be more than snarky. "I'm sorry for what you went through."

She didn't look mollified. "Who gave it to them if you didn't?"

He winced. That was the part that was causing the throbbing behind his forehead. Only one other person had known about that video, and known how incriminating it might be for Zoe. "One of my employees."

"Who?" she demanded.

"It doesn't matter who."

"It does to me. I take criminal accusations seriously."

He couldn't disagree. He also couldn't let her turn it into a personal war. Pressing his lips into a grim line, he said nothing.

Irritation flashed in her eyes. "You just left it lying around for anyone to take?"

"No, I burned it to a disc and locked it up. Our office was destroyed in the fire, but we have a small safe behind the bar that we use for cash overflow during the evening." A safe only two other people could open. And Russ hadn't known about the video.

It took her only a few seconds to figure it out. "Jennifer."

"I didn't say—"

"She manages the bar, doesn't she? She must have access to the money. Even if she saw the DVD and didn't know what it was, I imagine she would have been curious enough to check it out. All she had to do was pop it in a computer and play it." Her reasoning was dead-on, so he winced, knowing what was coming next. She bit her lip and frowned over it. "The question is why? Is it because I've been trying to get you to sell the saloon?"

Jase sighed and shook his head. "I don't think so. I think she's jealous."

"That doesn't make sense. She doesn't know

anything about me, so why would she be . . . Oh! You mean over you?"

He might not be as good-looking as that rich ass-hole she was dating, but he wasn't bad. He arched an eyebrow. "Is it that hard to believe?"

She hesitated, then flushed so deeply he wondered what had gone through her mind. "I don't understand why she'd see me as a threat," she said, stumbling over her words a bit.

He'd wondered about that, too, and decided it was probably for the same reason Brandon had confronted him during their fishing trip. He'd been paying a lot of attention to Zoe when she and Matt Flemming had come to the Rusty Wire. They had both come to the conclusion that he was hot for Zoe—and because there was an uncomfortable element of truth to it, there was no way he was going to tell her that.

"Jennifer and I have been friends for a long time. It's possible she feels more for me than I realized. I'm afraid she's decided it's time to make her move, and she sees you as a threat and wants you out of the way."

"That's ridiculous."

She was still a little pink, making him wonder what she found ridiculous—that Jennifer would be jealous or that she might actually have a reason to be. The thought was too distracting. "I don't have a better answer, Zoe. And in case it's true, I have to ask you for a favor. Please don't say anything to her; let me handle it. Our history is a bit . . . sensitive, and I don't want you to accidentally stir up some unpleas-ant memories."

Her gaze was unwavering as she nodded slightly. "Because of Adam."

Surprise hit him, followed immediately by resentment. "You've been researching my past."

She wasn't the least bit embarrassed. "Of course I have. I told you, I take my job seriously."

He knew a portion of his life, both good and bad, had been news, but it made him uncomfortable to have someone snooping through the worst tragedy of his life so many years later. He bit back the anger, settling for a terse "Newspapers don't tell the whole story."

"They never do." She tilted her head and gave him a long look. "Neither do rumors."

She didn't mean about him. She meant the rumors about her. Fair point. "Whatever you did in the past isn't relevant," he told her.

She opened her mouth to speak, then closed it, apparently deciding to leave well enough alone. Which was exactly how he felt about Adam. "So you'll let me handle Jennifer?"

She nodded grudgingly. "But if you're wrong, and she says she didn't do it . . ."

"I'll tell you, and we'll figure out who did."

"Okay." He thought she'd get up to leave, but she didn't appear to be finished. Shifting uncomfortably, she said, "If the police accept that I didn't set the fire, how will they find out who did?"

He gave her a bitter smile. "That's up to the police. I don't need their help, I already know who did it if it wasn't you."

"Who?"

"Your boyfriend."

"Boss," she corrected, obviously annoyed.

"Tricky combination."

"It's none of your business. Anyway, you're wrong. Matt wouldn't go sneaking around, setting fires."

"No, that's not his style. He'd hire someone to do it. Same thing."

She couldn't deny it, so she settled for a nasty scowl. "You're wrong about him. He wouldn't even let me present my new idea out of respect for your situation, you having so much to deal with after the fire."

No, he'd rather let all the problems he'd caused embed themselves under Jase's skin, irritating him so much he'd be begging Matt to buy the saloon. It would never happen. But she'd made him curious. "What new idea?"

"I just told you I'm not supposed to discuss it."

"Trust me, I won't feel disrespected, or whatever the hell your boyfriend-boss told you I'd feel. Come on, lay it on me." It was more than curiosity. He'd jump at any opportunity to move past the upsetting police incident.

She stood stiffly. "I don't think your mood is conducive to giving it a fair hearing. I'll come by the Rusty Wire when you're open for business again."

He stood, too, moving a step closer as he did. "Then I'll see you Friday when we reopen."

"Fine." She marched to the door and pulled it open before he could do it for her. The damp pine scent blew in again as she stepped onto the porch, then hesitated. She turned toward him, seeming to wage some inner battle before finally clearing her throat. "I apologize for jumping all over you like that. I thought you—" She cut off the excuse and grumbled, "Sorry."

"It was entertaining."

He was afraid it might make her mad, but one side

of her mouth twitched upward. "I rehearsed it all the way over here. It was sincere."

"I could tell." He let her take three steps down before adding, "An oozing pustule on the ass of humanity?"

She paused, biting her lip to hold back a smile. "That one was spontaneous."

He watched her drive away before closing the door. He wasn't tired anymore. In fact, he hadn't felt this energized in a long time. Zoe would come see him Friday to offer another sweet deal, and he'd turn her down flat. He couldn't wait.

By Wednesday, Zoe's anger had defused. She shifted on the hard bench of the picnic table and watched a group of tourists pause on the bridge that spanned Elkhorn Creek. The wooden bridge with its decorative iron trim divided the public parking lot from the downtown shops, and it seemed like every group of visitors to Barringer's Pass took turns posing there. It was the second-favorite photo op in town, ranking right below random celebrity sightings.

She ignored the tourists and concentrated on the soothing rush of water as the creek tumbled down Two Bears Mountain. The narrow strip of park along the creek was picturesque and rustic, making it perfect for a midday lunch with her sisters.

Maybe a bit too rustic. "Why did we have to eat here instead of in a restaurant with a nice, padded, bug-free booth?" Zoe complained, brushing a spider off the picnic table. She took a close look at her cottage cheese and peaches to make sure the spider hadn't brought a friend.

"Because Sophie dresses like a lumberjack and no decent restaurant would let her in the door." Maggie threw a pointed glance at the red-checked wool shirt tied around their younger sister's waist, dividing her faded T-shirt from her ripped jeans.

"No choice," Sophie said, reaching for one of Maggie's french fries. "Those old mines are dirty and cold." She popped the fry in her mouth and told Zoe, "Spiders aren't bugs. They're arachnids."

Zoe rolled her eyes at her younger sister's passion for creepy crawlies. "Good to know."

Maggie slid her fries out of Sophie's reach. "Is that bug study you're doing a paying job or another crazy internship?"

"*Paid* internship," Sophie said. "Documenting insect life in abandoned mines is real work."

"Right." Maggie peered at Sophie's braided hair. "Something's moving in there."

Sophie grabbed her long brown braid as Zoe chuckled. "Can we talk about something else, please?"

"Sure. How did Grandma take the news about your trip to the police station?"

"Better than I did." Trying to head off rumors made her too aware of the days when the rumors had been true and her relationship with her grandmother had been strained to the breaking point. "I don't want to talk about that, either."

"Okay." Maggie smiled. "Tell us about your hypothetical love interest."

She'd forgotten all about questioning whether Matt might be the right man. She'd nearly forgotten about Matt himself. Ever since last night, her thoughts kept returning to Jase. The way he'd faced down her accusations with casual good humor, the way he'd been uneasy at the idea that Jennifer wanted him, the way his bare chest had shown the firm lines and hard bulges of well-developed muscles. Jase was . . . distracting.

Sophie stopped shaking her disheveled braid to look at Zoe. "Are you seeing someone special? Do I know him?"

"No." That phone call to Maggie had been a huge mistake.

Undeterred, her younger sister turned to Maggie. "Who is he?"

"She won't say." Maggie looked smug as she bit into her burger and chewed. "But he could possibly be The One, so I think we should at least get to meet him."

"Oooh!" Sophie's eyes sparkled.

Zoe stabbed her fork into a peach slice. "Right, 'cause being grilled by my sisters is the perfect way to convince him to get serious about me."

"So he's not serious yet?" Sophie asked.

"She only danced with him," Maggie told her.

Blabbermouth, Zoe thought.

Sophie sucked in a breath. "Is that what you were doing when I saw you at the Rusty Wire? I thought you were there alone." She turned to Maggie. "She *left* alone."

Maggie scrunched up her brow. "You went dancing at the Rusty Wire?" As if she just couldn't imagine it. "Does that have something to do with the owner accusing you of arson?"

Sophie gasped. "Arson?"

"He realized he was wrong," Zoe said. At least, she was pretty sure Jase had realized he'd been wrong.

"And I wasn't dancing, I went to see him about selling his saloon to the Alpine Sky."

Sophie looked concerned for her favorite nightspot. "What does your resort want with the Rusty Wire?"

"They want to tear it down and build a golf course."

"No!"

"Don't start. I'm sure there are other bars where you can rub up against your favorite cowboy."

"But the Rusty Wire has character. Isn't it historic or something? No one should be allowed to tear it down."

Zoe gave her a sour look. "You'll be glad to know the owner agrees."

"Good." Sophie chewed her apple thoughtfully. "Hey, is he your hypothetical love interest? I've seen him, he's pretty hot."

Zoe scowled. "No."

Sophie ignored her, turning to Maggie. "Have you seen him? Totally buff. Fun guy, great sense of humor."

"Why don't *you* date him?" Zoe muttered, although the idea of Sophie and Jase together grated on her brain cells like gravel against tender flesh, scraping her nerves raw.

"Nah." Sophie dismissed the idea. "He's too old for me. Probably has a girlfriend, anyway. Or five. Seems like there're always girls hanging around him."

She'd noticed that, too. Women liked Jase. Not for the same reason they liked Matt; Jase didn't have that polished look of success that hung on Matt as if he'd been born with it. Jase was rougher around the edges, outspoken, and blatantly physical. The kind of guy she could imagine spending his days outdoors, bare-chested, doing something sweaty—if only he had that much ambition. It was an important point. The fact that she responded to him on some basic level irritated her more than she cared to admit.

She huffed and looked away. Her gaze drifted, taking in a couple carrying shopping bags and a group of teenagers loitering around the bike rack. A familiar laugh drew her attention. Two men and a woman crossed the bridge, heading toward the Silver Nugget, the pricey restaurant overlooking Elkhorn Creek and the slopes of Tappit's Peak beyond it. She sat up straighter, recognizing David first, then Ruth Ann. Her movement must have caught David's attention because he raised his eyes to look directly at her.

His grin grew broader as he gave a cheery wave, which was enough to send warning flags shooting up in her mind. David being friendly couldn't mean anything good. He hooked his arm possessively through Ruth Ann's, steering her toward the restaurant and giving Zoe a look at the other man. He turned her way, absently following the direction of David's wave. Her mouth fell open as she found herself staring at Matt.

She took it in quickly—her immediate boss, the resort owner, and the president of the company all going to lunch together. Without her. Her shift at the resort didn't start until 5 p.m., but they knew darn well her job required that she be available for business meetings before then. It might just be a friendly lunch, but the predatory gleam in David's eyes said he was moving in on her territory and there wasn't a damn thing she could do about it.

Unless Matt invited her to join them.

Matt grinned at her, said something to his mother, then started toward her. Zoe sat up straighter.

Both of her sisters turned to follow her gaze. "Who's that?" Maggie asked.

"Yummy," Sophie murmured. "Is that an actor? I don't recognize him."

"That's my boss."

Sophie frowned. "I don't remember David looking that good. Or that young."

"He's David's boss, too. He's the owner's son, Matt."

"Ah." Sophie contemplated Matt as he cut across the grass. "Money, power, and looks all in one package," she murmured. "Nice combo."

"I had a Ken doll that looked just like him," Maggie mused, then widened her eyes. "That's him, isn't it?" she whispered excitedly.

"Shhh," Zoe hissed, glad Matt was so close she didn't have to answer. Ever since her older sister had fallen madly in love she'd developed radar for spotting it in others. There went Matt's hypothetical status. She should have let them think her potential The One was Jase.

Zoe stayed seated but beamed at Matt as he stopped beside her. "Hi!"

"Hi, yourself. I didn't know you had sisters, but you three gorgeous ladies have to be related."

Zoe opened her mouth, but her older sister was faster. "I'm Maggie," she said, introducing herself with a handshake. "And this is Sophie." Sophie stuck her hand across the table, appraising him a bit too frankly as he took it.

He gave each one the full force of his direct gaze

and perfect smile. "Matt Flemming. I'm pleased to meet you." He turned to Zoe, letting his hand rest lightly on her shoulder. "We're having an impromptu lunch. Would you care to join us? That is, if your sisters don't mind me stealing you away." He flashed his smile again, and they mirrored it with twin grins. Zoe gave her sisters a cautious glance. Speculation had to be zipping around like fireworks behind those polite looks.

"I'd love to, but I don't think I'm dressed for it," she told Matt, glancing pointedly at her knit top and jeans.

"You make blue jeans look like the latest fashion statement," Matt said. "No one will say anything."

He'd asked; that was all that mattered. She smiled and shook her head with sincere regret. "I wouldn't be comfortable in that restaurant dressed like this," she insisted. Appearances counted, especially when people expected the worst from you, but he probably didn't know about that and she wasn't going to explain it. "Go enjoy your lunch. Their crab salad is great."

He cocked his head. "You're sure? It'd be more fun with you there."

"Positive."

"Okay then, I'll see you later." He gave her shoulder a slight squeeze, said good-bye to Maggie and Sophie, and cut back across the grass toward the Silver Nugget. Zoe waited through ten seconds of nail-biting silence.

They looked at each other. Sophie wiggled her eyebrows. "Nice," she said, drawing it out.

"He touched you," Maggie said, going straight for the jugular. "Bosses don't do that."

That thought had been screaming in Zoe's mind,

too, but she pushed it aside. "I'm sure you've touched Holly while you were working in the store."

Maggie gave her a don't-be-stupid look.

"He *kept* touching you," Sophie added. "He likes you, and not in a give-you-a-raise way."

Zoe pretended disinterest. "I wouldn't mind a raise."

"This is going somewhere," Sophie declared with conviction. "The question is, how far do you want it to go?"

Both of her sisters waited expectantly, and Zoe's nerves got the best of her. She laid her fork down, twisting her napkin while giving the question some honest thought. "I'm not sure. I like him, and he does meet all the criteria, with room to spare."

"What criteria?" Sophie asked Maggie.

Maggie rolled her eyes. "You know how methodical she is."

Zoe smiled, making her decision. "I think it's worth finding out."

She expected cheers or high-fives—something other than the scoffing noise Maggie made. "Figured it out logically, did you? How exciting. Maybe you and Matt could each pull out your lists and compare attributes."

Shoot, the matchmaker hadn't seen a spark between them. It was more irritating than it should have been. "There's nothing wrong with a cool head. It's better than a broken heart."

Sophie smirked. "I think I read that on a fortune cookie. And what's with the list? You used to date without a checklist."

"I used to do a lot of things I wouldn't want to re-peat."

Maggie sighed and reached out to take her hand. "Sweetie, do it however you'd like. We both want you to make the right decision. If that means using a check-list, then go for it. Right, Soph?"

"Right. Who knows? Maybe he really is The One."

"You think so?" she asked, but looked at Maggie.

"It's too soon to tell," Maggie said with a reassuring smile. "You haven't even kissed him yet."

She was right. A kiss would definitely cross the line from employee to romantic interest. She could already feel pleasant prickles of anticipation.

Sophie held her hand out as if bestowing a blessing. "Go. Kiss. Then report back. You have one week."

"Deal," Zoe said.

Chapter Eight

Jase hoped questioning Jennifer didn't require delicacy, because he wasn't in the mood for it. He stopped her as soon as she came in, while she was still kneeling behind the bar, pulling out her ledger. "Did you give that DVD of the security tape to the police?"

She straightened, facing him calmly. "Yes. That's what you intended to do, isn't it?"

"No, actually. I'd decided not to."

"Oh." She blinked a couple of times, then shrugged carelessly. "Sorry."

She didn't seem to get how important the issue was to him. "Jennifer," he said, his voice harsh enough to widen her eyes. "It wasn't your decision to make."

She studied him for a long moment, her expression gradually turning into a cold mask. She folded her arms tightly across her chest. "I see. And how was I supposed to know you decided to hide evidence from the police?"

The accusation took him by surprise, and he scowled. "I'm not hiding evidence. The tape doesn't show anything."

Her stare was icy enough to frost the beer mugs. "It shows your new friend from the Alpine Sky driving over here just before the fire started. If that's not evidence, it's a pretty strange coincidence."

He bit back a denial, realizing she was right. He'd simply chosen not to see it that way. But turning it in without his knowledge was out of line. "So you went out of your way to make sure the police knew about it."

"It wasn't out of my way. One of the city cops came by while you were out. He said he was investigating the fire, so I gave him the DVD." Her eyes turned to slits as she stared him down. "I didn't know it was a *secret*." She emphasized the last word with a sarcastic lift of her eyebrows.

He clenched his jaw, wondering how this had turned around, putting him on the defensive. Her aggressive response was unexpected, and more evidence of how much she disliked Zoe.

"Your job is to take care of the money, Jennifer. Anything else in that safe is not your concern."

Her mouth tightened. "Fine."

Jase felt as tightly wound as Jennifer looked. They'd disagreed before, but he'd never had to confront her about anything she'd done. It left him feeling sick to his stomach and glad it was over.

"What's going on?"

Russ stood at the end of the bar, giving each of them a piercing look. Jase's stomach clenched a little more as he wondered if Adam's father would automatically rise to his daughter-in-law's defense. Russ and Jennifer had been almost like family to him—emotionally damaged and distant, but still family. The last thing he wanted was an angry split in their ranks. "We had a disagreement over procedure," he told Russ. "We settled it."

Russ looked at Jennifer. "Seemed more serious than that."

Jennifer's face had shuttered and closed, a look he'd seen too often during the past week. "Everything's fine," she snapped. It was clearly a lie, and just as clear that she wasn't going to discuss it. Grabbing her ledger, she stalked toward the kitchen.

Russ's gaze settled on him. Jase shook his head, cutting off questions. "I didn't agree with something she did, but it's over. Just let it go."

He couldn't read the older man's expression, but caught his almost imperceptible nod. The knot in his stomach loosened. Russ turned to leave, tilting his head toward the kitchen as he did. "You think *she'll* let it go?" he asked.

Jase stared at Russ as he left, then at the closed door to the kitchen.

Tension pulled at his gut again, tightening the knots. Jennifer wasn't good at letting things go.

Zoe's plan to kiss Matt wasn't going to happen at work. That much became clear Friday when a popular professional football star checked into the resort with his girlfriend of the moment, who just happened to be starring in a hit TV sitcom. Paparazzi and reporters descended like locusts, and she was kept busy soothing the complaints of other guests while herding photographers out of stairwells. She barely had a chance to say hello to Matt.

Friday was better. The celebrity couple accepted an invitation to a party at the private residence of some local producer, and the media herd followed. All the resort had to do was make sure no enterprising reporter broke into their suite while they were gone. Security had it under control.

Matt walked in at eight, sat on the corner of her desk, and announced, "The Rusty Wire is open for business."

She leaned back in her chair and smiled. "I know." And she was ready, wearing a more feminine blouse this time, one that wouldn't look out of place in the saloon when she took her jacket off. Her hair was down, its waves falling just past her shoulders.

"You still want to hit Garrett with that new proposal?"

"Yes, but you haven't even heard it yet."

"I trust your judgment, and you can fill me in on the way over. It's time for a scouting trip." He grinned engagingly and gave her that long, direct look that said it was really a date and he couldn't wait to go.

She smiled to herself. One scorching-hot kiss, coming right up.

Jase saw her as soon as she walked in, her plain skirt and heels showing off her long legs better than jeans could have. Her top was clingy enough to actually draw his attention away from her legs. Very nice. She was here with her offer, as promised.

The slick weasel from the Alpine Sky followed her in. Shit.

"Now you can quit watching the door," Brandon said. "She's here."

"I wasn't watching the door."

"I've been here for two hours. You look that way

every time it opens, and it's putting you off your game. Take your shot so I can beat you again."

Jase lined up the shot, glanced up to see where Zoe sat, then knocked the cue ball. It hit the side, grazing the twelve ball enough to make it move an inch.

"Pitiful," Brandon said. "Stand aside."

He half-watched while Brandon cleared the table. He also watched Zoe lean close to Matt, then laugh at whatever smooth pickup line he'd fed her. From the way the guy touched her all the time, he was sure Matt was ramping up his moves.

Brandon pulled the stick out of his hand. "Christ, Jase. Just go talk to her. I'm gonna find Hailey—I need some decent competition."

Jase nodded and walked toward the front room where most of the noise and action were. Where Zoe was. He wouldn't go talk to her yet, though. He wanted to watch them for a while, see how much the boyfriend-boss status had shifted.

A while turned out to be eight minutes. That's all he could take of Matt Flemming leaning close to her ear as he put his hand over hers on the table, twining their fingers together. Jase could feel the hairs on the back of his neck bristle. If she couldn't see what a sleaze the guy was, he needed to show her.

He paused at several tables on the way to theirs, saying hello to regulars and thanking them for coming to their reopening. Chatting up the customers. Just following his normal routine.

He gave Matt a surprised look. "Howdy, neighbors. Another date? Nice of you to help celebrate my reopening." He grabbed a chair from a nearby table and wedged it between Zoe and Matt, straddling it.

Arms folded across the top, he gave them a friendly smile.

"Hi." Zoe pulled her hands off the table, looking self-conscious.

He'd bet Matt had to reach deep to find that untroubled look. "Hello, Garrett. Actually, we came on business."

"Oh?"

"We'd like to talk with you if you have some time."

"I'd take you back to my office, but I'm temporarily without one. But we can talk right here. What is it, another offer, with yet more money?"

"Sorry." Matt gave him a condescending smile. "The last offer was generous enough. But I'd like to add something to it that might be just as valuable to a conscientious businessman like yourself, one who cares about his employees."

"Am I conscientious?" He turned to Zoe, giving Matt the back of his head. Matt might be presenting it as his own idea, but Jase knew it came from Zoe. He'd rather hear her list his attributes.

"I believe you are," she said calmly. "I believe you feel some responsibility for the people you employ, and you wouldn't want to see them lose their jobs if you sell the saloon." She paused. "Especially Adam's wife and his father."

Her research hadn't turned up everything, not yet, but this she'd gotten right. She'd obviously done more than read news articles if she'd learned about the debts Adam had left behind—the coaching bills, the loans that paid for travel to various competitions. Russ and Jennifer had never talked about it, and their financial situation wouldn't have been in the news reports. But it was there if someone could read between the lines. Zoe had been clever enough to figure it out.

"You're right," he told her quietly. "I won't sacrifice a couple dozen jobs for a pile of money I don't need."

"Everyone needs money," Matt said. "And more is better than less."

"Some of us are satisfied with enough. I have enough."

"So I heard." Matt looked slightly puzzled, but amused. "That's why I'm not offering more money. I'm offering jobs."

The way he'd appropriated Zoe's idea irritated Jase, even if Zoe didn't seem to mind. "I thought this was Zoe's idea."

"What made you think that?"

Zoe sat perfectly still beside him, but he felt a sudden kick on his ankle. She didn't want her boyfriend-boss to know she'd mentioned it to him. Why? Because she would have talked to him without telling Matt? He liked the thought of Matt knowing that. Or maybe she was simply willing to let her boss take the credit for it. That chapped his ass. But he wouldn't get her in trouble.

"I just assumed, since she was sent here to offer the first deal," he answered, looking Matt in the eye. "But it doesn't matter. Go ahead and tell me about these jobs you're offering. Are you planning to promise jobs to my whole staff in a burst of generosity?"

"That's up to you. What I'm offering is a position doing what you're doing now—running a bar."

"The Rusty Wire is more than a bar."

Matt smiled. "My mistake. I'm sure you're familiar with the nineteenth hole on golf courses. Our clubhouse will have a bar, and we'll need someone to run it. We hire you, and you hire whoever you need. Jobs saved."

Jase didn't say anything for several seconds. He had to give Zoe credit, it wasn't a bad idea. Russ and Jennifer would still have secure positions, along with the kitchen and waitstaff. If he'd been debating selling, it might have been the deciding factor. Big if.

"Nice solution," he told Matt. "I have to hand it to you, you know how to make an offer hard to resist."

"Just trying to address all your concerns," Matt said, still leaving Zoe out of it. Jase hoped to hell she was offended. "I can have a contract drawn up and delivered to your lawyer's office tomorrow morning. You'll be three million richer before lunch."

"No thanks."

Matt couldn't quite hide his annoyance, giving Jase a brief feel-good moment. "I thought the jobs were important to you."

"They *have* jobs."

"They could have better ones. I'm willing to bet we offer a more comprehensive benefits package than you do."

He wasn't so sure about that. Not that it mattered. "What about that year or more in between tearing this place down and building the new clubhouse? Unemployment doesn't cover all the bills."

Matt still looked annoyed, but some of the stiffness left his body. "Is that all you're worried about? We can add a stipend in the contract, enough to get them through."

"Generous of you." He let Matt look satisfied for several seconds. "But I'm not interested." He stood while Matt gave him a calculating look, which Jase thought was pretty restrained considering the way he'd played him. "Nice talking with you, though."

He finally looked at Zoe, who was biting her lip and scowling. Probably holding back one of those "why" questions. "You two have a nice night." He should have smiled when he said it, but couldn't, and it came out sounding more like a dare. One he hoped she was going to lose.

Zoe kept her mouth shut as Jase walked away. She hadn't wanted to correct Matt in front of Jase, and it didn't matter who'd come up with the idea as long as Jase accepted it. But he'd known it was her idea, and knew it made Matt look bad to pretend it wasn't. She didn't know who she was most mad at—Matt for not giving her credit, or Jase for secretly enjoying making Matt look arrogant.

Since Jase was gone, she chose Matt. He'd seemed so honest and decent she hadn't expected this from him.

She opened her mouth to tell him how insulted she felt when his gaze shifted from Jase's retreating back to her, and his features softened with concern. "I'm sorry, Zoe, I didn't mean to be rude to you." He reached across the table to grasp her hands, encasing them in his own. "You must think I'm a complete chauvinist and a bastard for cutting you out like that."

Her anger faltered. She couldn't have said it better. "Why did you?"

He gave her an embarrassed smile. "I thought *he* might be a chauvinist bastard. I wondered if one of the reasons Garrett was putting us off was because he didn't take you seriously. He didn't say anything to make me think that, but you can't always tell. Some of these local cowboys have old-fashioned ideas about a woman's place, and they resent having to deal with them as professionals. If Garrett was like that, I thought he might prefer an offer that came from me." He shrugged. "I guess that isn't his problem."

She could have told him that. Jase might be stubborn and annoying and frustrating as hell, but he'd never given her reason to think he didn't respect her ability to do her job. He simply didn't care for what she had to say.

In fact, she didn't know any man who would turn down a three-million-dollar deal just because it was offered by a woman. That attitude belonged to another generation. The only man she'd ever met who'd been that closed-minded and pigheaded was Buck Flemming.

Suddenly, she got it. Buck had been Matt's stepfather. The one who had given Matt his start in the business world, and probably been his mentor. Matt had seen that prejudice on a daily basis at work, and almost certainly at home, putting women on a pedestal and keeping them there, out of touch with any important dealings. It was to Matt's credit that he rejected that bias so soundly himself.

The hard shell around her heart crumbled. She slipped her hands free so she could grasp his. "I understand," she told him. "But most men aren't like Buck." Matt's skill at reading people had obviously slipped with Jase.

He gave her a pained smile that pulled at her heart. "I couldn't be sure until I tried. I felt lousy doing it. But I guess in the long run it doesn't matter who came up with the idea, does it? Not to Garrett. He doesn't want to budge on this."

She was forced to agree. She didn't understand why, but Jase seemed determined to resist the most lucrative offer he'd ever get for this place.

Strangely, Matt didn't seem upset. In fact, he looked like he was trying to find a way to improve her spirits. He gave her fingers an encouraging squeeze. "Forget about Garrett, Zoe. Don't let him spoil your mood."

"But he's ruining your plans for a golf course! How can you not be upset?"

"That's business, honey. Sometimes things don't work out." A sly smile touched his mouth. "But don't throw in the towel yet. Give Garrett a few weeks to think about what he turned down. Let him deal with the hassle of repairs and constant maintenance while he remembers that three million dollars could buy him a house on a tropical beach. With that money and his low expectations, he could spend the rest of his life with a beer in his hand, watching girls in bikinis play volleyball. Instead, he has nine months of winter, girls in cowboy boots, and the occasional drunken fight in the parking lot. I have a feeling he'll come around. And he knows where to find us when he does."

She still wasn't sure he was reading Jase correctly—he'd had all that for eight years and didn't seem tired of it. But she smiled as she shook her head. "You're the boss."

"Not for the next hour. I think we deserve some time off." He cocked his head with a playful grin. "And I deserve a dance with a pretty girl. What do you say?"

There probably wasn't a girl in the place who would have said no to that smile. She let him guide her to the dance floor where everyone had fallen into rows as they line-danced to an old Brooks & Dunn song.

"Do you know how to do this?" Matt asked uncertainly.

"Sure, I'll show you. It's easy." Maybe not so easy in heels, but no harder than doing it half drunk, which was how she'd usually done it years ago, back when her fake ID and the clothes she'd changed into after leaving her grandma's house had been her idea of fun.

They joined the end of one row and Zoe took him through the steps in slow motion until he caught on to the pattern. By the second dance he was stepping and turning like . . . well, not a pro, but at least like someone who'd done it before. No one would ever mistake him for a cowboy in his tailored slacks and white dress shirt, but he kept up with the group.

She didn't have to tell him what to do when the music changed to a slow tune. He pulled her into his arms, flashing another grin that told her this was the part he'd been waiting for. A smile crept onto her lips as he settled her against his chest. Any thought of him being her boss was long gone. She caught envious glances from a couple of women nearby, and couldn't dampen a spark of pride that she was the one in his arms.

They danced without talking, even slower than the rhythm of the song. The music soothed her into a dreamy state. Matt paused as the song ended, still holding her, looking at her as they waited for the next one to start. His gaze roamed her face and hair, even dipping briefly to the V-neck of her blouse. She smiled nervously, wondering what he was thinking. He didn't say anything, and then another song started and they were swaying again. She closed her eyes and concentrated on the sensations, like Maggie had said—the scent of his cologne, the softness of his hand around hers, the smooth warmth of his shirt against her cheek. She sighed with contentment. Everything about Matt was perfect. His easy temperament. His confidence and good looks. Even the professional way he'd dealt with Jase. She'd almost taken offense when he'd appropriated her idea, but really, how could he know Jase wasn't as closed-minded as Buck had been? It was an angle she hadn't even considered, another reminder that she could learn a lot from him.

The song ended. Zoe's daydream dissolved with it as conversation and laughter filled the dead air between songs. Matt released her hand and she felt a tug of disappointment that they'd finished dancing. She knew she should be working; they'd already danced to three songs and she should get back to the resort. But the mood had been so intimate, she could almost imagine what it would be like to . . .

His hand cupped her chin, lifting it upward as he leaned down and kissed her. For one startled second she thought it was her imagination, then realized that the soft lips pressing against her own were as real as the hand beneath her chin and the other one holding her securely against him. She kissed him back, enjoying the gentle but persistent kiss that lingered just long enough to let her know it was more than a friendly first-date kiss. It was an I-intend-to-do-this-again kiss, and if she couldn't tell that from his lips, she could see it in his eyes when he lifted his head and gave her an approving smile. She smiled back, composed and steady despite the little pulse of excitement that fluttered in her chest.

Without words, Matt had made it clear that their relationship was more than professional. A perfect kiss for the start of what she suspected would be the perfect romance. She tried to memorize the moment—how he'd looked, the song they'd danced to, the first thing he would say after kissing her.

"Let's get something to eat before we head back."

A completely ordinary sentence. Somehow it felt right for the easy way Matt was falling into her life, barely creating a ripple. Because they fit together so well.

She smiled, nodding in agreement, still amazed that it was all happening so naturally. No ringing bells, no ground moving under her feet. Just a feeling that all was right with the world. Which made sense, when you found the right guy.

Jase slammed the mug down on the bar. Beer slopped over the side in a wave of sticky foam.

"Hey!" Jennifer shoved him aside and snatched up the mug. "If that's what you call helping, I don't need it."

"Sorry," he muttered, not even looking at the small lake of beer she mopped up. He kept staring at the far end of the dance floor where Zoe stood smiling at Matt.

He'd kissed her! Fuck! The slimy SOB was her boss; he had no right putting his hands on her, much less his lips.

And it sure as hell looked like she'd kissed him back. Not that he gave a damn what Zoe did and who she did it with, but he was starting to believe Zoe was a decent person. Unfortunately, she worked for a guy who wouldn't know decent from dirt.

"You plan to help or just get in the way?" Jennifer said. He moved aside as she followed his gaze. Her mouth thinned into a tight line. "What's *she* doing here?"

"Still making offers to buy."

"You still refusing?"

"I told you I'm not going to sell."

Jennifer slid a drink down the bar to a customer, and gave Zoe a dark look. "But she keeps coming back." Her gaze returned to him and narrowed with speculation. "And you keep watching her."

"Maybe she likes it here." He didn't want to discuss Zoe with anyone, least of all another woman who might be edging toward a full-blown territorial catfight. "I think I'll get out of here for a while."

"Good," she muttered.

He couldn't leave fast enough. Passing the kitchen and restrooms, he unlocked the temporary back door and slipped through, closing it on the noise behind him.

The framing boards of new construction rose around him, ghostly pale from the solitary light by the Dumpster. He inhaled deeply, letting the smell of sawdust replace the clinging aroma of pizza and beer. It didn't help clear his mind. His head had been clogged for days with thoughts of Zoe, and seeing her kissing Matt had the same effect as dragging a stick through a mud puddle, swirling thoughts and feelings into one big, murky mess. He needed to sort them out.

He stepped through the framework of walls and into the night. Noises from the saloon were subdued here, but still loud enough to remind him that he was only a hundred feet away from dozens of people.

Happy, noisy people. The noise could make it hard to think, but most of the time that was what he wanted. For eight years those people had helped keep him sane, or at least kept him from driving himself crazy.

When he'd bought the Rusty Wire, he'd been in danger of losing himself, of no longer being Jase Garrett, the man who'd won four Olympic medals. He was Jase Garrett, the man who'd killed his best friend. His life had crashed down around him. He didn't even care, he just waited for it to bury him and end his suffering. Then the Rusty Wire had gone up for sale, and he'd suddenly found a distraction from the pain in his heart.

The saloon was his escape. Nothing to win other than a pile of poker chips. No competition more serious than a game of pool. No way to let the drive to win blind you to everything else until you killed the man who'd been your best friend for the past five years. He'd settled into the Rusty Wire, content to hide from the pain of life. He'd done a good job of it for eight uneventful years. He didn't even have to compete for women, finding that when one left another always came along. Life was blissfully bland . . . until Zoe.

He wasn't sure what she had done. It wasn't the offer to buy the saloon that had unsettled his world. Refusing that hadn't required any thought on his part. But something about her stuck in his mind and he couldn't let it go. Something about the way she wouldn't give up, wouldn't stop digging for reasons, wouldn't stop asking those goddamn questions why. Her drive to succeed was too familiar—she'd been right about that. They were alike. She'd known that he'd buried a part of himself, and couldn't understand why. That damn favorite question of hers.

She confused him. Muddied the waters. He couldn't help admiring her gutsy determination to achieve her goal, but at the same time, he hated it. Hated that her ambition reminded him of himself and the life he'd run away from. He'd had good reason to run, too. To insulate himself so his selfish goals could never ruin another life. He didn't want to be tempted out of his safe retreat by some sexy woman chasing her own success story, along with the wrong man. He just wanted to hang on to the Rusty Wire.

He also didn't want to watch Zoe give herself to that asshole boss of hers. That *really* disturbed him.

The best thing to do was avoid her. Out of sight, out of mind—he hoped to hell that saying was true. He would stop thinking about her, starting now.

The decision made the turmoil in his mind ease a bit. He looked at the arc of sky above him, sprinkled with thousands of stars, and drew in a deep breath. Fresh night air filled his lungs. Pine-scented air. It reminded him of Zoe standing on his front porch, hair glowing in the lamplight, pursed lips temptingly kissable.

Fuck! It had taken all of two seconds before she'd invaded his thoughts again. He might as well go back inside where the music and conversation might wipe everything else from his mind.

He retraced his path through the unfinished construction and opened the back door. Immersion was immediate as the familiar noise of his saloon washed over him. Music pounded into the hallway, a song by Linkin Park; the rockers outnumbered the cowboys tonight. On his right a metallic crash came from the kitchen, followed by laughter. He hoped it had been an empty tray and not someone's order. On his left female laughter filled the air as someone opened the ladies' room door and stepped into the hall.

Zoe.

He stopped. The pulsing music faded to nothing more than a muffled beat in his head.

She turned, a casual glance over her shoulder that changed abruptly as her eyes met his. She stared, indecision evident in every muscle of her body. The kitchen door swung open between them but she didn't move, forcing a waitress to hug the wall as she scooted past.

Jase watched her weigh her choices, knowing he should make it for her. They were casual friends, at most. More like acquaintances. He should just nod and walk by.

What he should do and what he wanted to do were two very different things. A magnet embedded in his chest couldn't exert a stronger pull, and he knew if he tried to walk past her at that moment, he wouldn't be able to stop himself from touching her. It didn't matter that they'd never had a conversation in which she didn't irritate him. She also attracted him. It probably wasn't a good combination.

Her few seconds of indecision seemed to last an hour, then she bit her lip and walked toward him. He didn't move, letting her come all the way to the back door, wondering if she felt the pull, too. That might explain the wariness in her eyes.

She stopped, close enough to touch. He stuck his hands in his pockets.

"I just wanted to say thanks," she said.

"For what?"

"For not telling Matt I was at your house. Not telling him I'd already mentioned a new proposal."

He shrugged. "If you want to let your boyfriend walk all over you, that's your business."

"He's not walking all over me," she snapped.

She was supposed to add that he wasn't her boyfriend. He waited, but she didn't say it. Shit.

"For your information, he intentionally presented the offer as his idea, just in case you turned me down because you didn't like dealing with a woman. It was a legitimate strategy."

He couldn't help it, he laughed. "You believe that?"

Her chin came up in that defiant look he was getting used to seeing. "Of course I do. He had a good reason."

"If you say so."

She pressed her lips together and huffed out a sigh as she prepared to educate him. "Did you know Buck Flemming?"

"Never met him."

"I worked for him. That man could have kept the ACLU in business all by himself. Every woman he employed probably could have had a lawsuit against him for discrimination or harassment. *That's* the business model Matt had when he went to work for his stepdad."

He snorted another laugh. "You don't think he knew Buck was a walking anachronism? You're trying too hard, Zoe."

"To do what?"

"To excuse Matt Flemming's behavior. You need to convince yourself he's someone he isn't so you can justify falling for him."

She stiffened, scowling hard. "You have no idea what you're talking about."

He wished he didn't, but he could see her hands clench at her sides and was certain he'd scored a direct hit. She wanted a relationship with Matt. It pissed him off big-time. Not because he found her attractive—that was beside the point since he didn't intend to act on it. It was because she wanted Matt for all the wrong reasons.

He smiled, letting his cynicism show. "I'll bet he fits right into that neat little career plan of yours."

She looked outraged. "You think I'd date my boss just so I could get a promotion?"

"No, I think you'd date him because he's the safe choice for a girl still haunted by a bad reputation."

If she'd been angry before, she was on overload now. Her cheeks blazed with color as she stepped closer. "My past has nothing to do with Matt," she hissed between clenched teeth.

"Bullshit. It has everything to do with him." A rational corner of his brain told him to shut up, but it was overruled by his careening ego, which insisted he point out everything that was wrong about Matt. "You're all about image, with your tailored suits and your hair pinned up as tight as your attitude. Good job, there's not a trace of the Larkin sisters left for people to see."

"You're an ass," she whispered.

"In fact, I wonder if you even know who Zoe Larkin is anymore, or what she wants."

"I know better than *you* do."

"No you don't, because I'm damn sure it's not that calculating, manipulative, piece-of-shit boss of yours."

She raised her chin, toe to toe with him. "You don't know a damn thing about what I want, Jase Garrett."

Maybe he didn't. But he knew what she *should* want—someone who respected her enough to let her take the credit for her own ideas.

And he knew what *he* wanted.

He didn't think about it—he'd done enough thinking where Zoe was concerned. He acted on impulse. Sliding his hand down the back of her head, through that hair that had been tormenting him, to the nape of her neck, he pulled her the rest of the way to him and locked his mouth to hers.

Beneath his hands, her body went rigid and she slapped her palms against his chest, pushing away. Her lips were unyielding, but it didn't matter. Her startled gasp gave him the opportunity he needed. He swiped his tongue across hers, tasting her, learning her, demanding more.

She went straight to his head—her scent, her flavor, the heat of her body against his. He inhaled a light, flowery fragrance at the same time he tasted the lingering spiciness of pizza. Her breasts pressed against him, igniting a fire on his skin. His mind spun with desire.

It took a few seconds to realize that she wasn't moving, was in fact resisting him. He was forcing himself on her. His exhilaration hit a wall. As intoxicating as it was to lose himself in her, he didn't want to do it this way.

Reluctantly, he softened the pressure on her mouth, lifting his lips from hers, missing them as soon as he did. A tiny sound made him pause. A whimper deep in her throat, small and desperate. Needy. Her hands stopped pushing against him as they crept upward toward his neck. Her mouth came back to his, seeking. She parted her lips and kissed him.

He responded roughly, pressing his mouth to hers, matching her eagerness as he pushed her against the wall, pinning her. He thought she might tense again, but beneath his hands, she melted, molding herself to his body. Her hands clung to his neck, possessive and demanding. Her leg bent and slid between his, intimate and warm. And her mouth . . . He ran his fingers beneath her hair as he held her head steady, delving into her, tongue seeking, lips melding perfectly with hers, over and over again.

For a long moment he forgot where he was, exploring the newness of Zoe's mouth and responding with his whole body. Pressed against him, she had to feel his erection, had to know he'd been instantly aroused by her response. It only made her push into him harder, until he could feel the heat burning between her legs where she straddled his thigh. He let his hand slide down her back to grip the soft curve of her ass. Another whimper escaped her throat, driving him crazy.

A second crash from the kitchen jolted him back to reality. It must have done the same to her, as her lips suddenly stopped moving beneath his and pulled away. Her breath came fast, fanning him as he opened his eyes. Inches away, her eyes fluttered open and focused on his face, growing wider as awareness seeped in.

She didn't have to speak—he could see the thoughts swimming in those golden-brown eyes. *That was what a kiss should be.* She hadn't looked like that, all dazed and surprised, when Matt kissed her. It was enormously satisfying.

He stepped back, reluctantly dropping his hands.

She licked her lips, drawing his gaze downward, mesmerizing him with the urge to kiss her again. He knew her kiss was an addiction that wouldn't be easily satisfied. Knew, too, that the caution he saw on her face was due to the stark heat she saw on his. That was probably a good thing. She'd better be aware of the lust that had raged to the forefront when she'd kissed him back, because it wasn't going away anytime soon.

She edged sideways, still watching him, ready to take off. He took another step back, letting her go. He'd made his point, emphatically. There was nothing else to say.

She turned and took a quick step toward the saloon. And stopped dead.

He followed her openmouthed stare down the hall to the figure standing at the other end. Matt stood perfectly still, arms folded, cool gaze moving between them.

Well, shit. The bastard had a way of ruining everything.

Chapter Nine

Zoe's mind stripped a few gears as it tried to keep up. She was staggered by Jase's kiss—my God, that kiss!—and had to blink hard at Matt before she was sure he wasn't a figment of her imagination. He was real, all right. Shit.

Her hot flush was replaced by a cold sweat, the kind produced by sudden fear. Her underarms were probably staining her blouse at this very moment. It irritated her enough to bring her to her senses.

She refused to be embarrassed. She'd done far worse in her life than kiss two men in one night. It wasn't like she and Matt were dating, or had even talked about it, despite what his kiss may have implied. Nothing had been said, no promises made. They were here during work hours, on business, not as a couple, regardless of how he chose to bend the rules. She could justify what she'd done.

Unfortunately, he probably wouldn't see it that way. She realized with a sinking feeling that she might have damaged whatever chance she had with him.

Behind her, Jase strode confidently toward the noisy saloon, passing Matt with a quick nod and a genial "Flemming." He disappeared into the crowd, leaving her to face Matt.

He didn't move. She swallowed and walked toward him, hoping she looked as nonchalant as Jase. She wasn't sure what she'd say, but knew it wouldn't be an apology. Anyone who apologized for a toe-curling kiss like that had to be a complete idiot.

She stopped in front of Matt, mimicking his blank stare and saying nothing. It wasn't easy; the tic beside his eye was probably from anger. Part of her wanted to act contrite and wallow in guilt—the stupid part. Thankfully, the larger part had more dignity.

Finally, he cocked his head with a questioning look that managed to remain cool. "Should I be worried about the competition?"

She let her breath ease out with relief. He wasn't going to be furious or unreasonable. There was still a chance for them. "No," she said.

He nodded thoughtfully. "Good." No smile, just the same calm expression. His lack of emotion was probably a good thing, although it was a little creepy. "I think we should get back to work now."

"Good idea." The sooner she got out of the Rusty Wire, the better. Her head was still spinning and her lips felt raw from that kiss, and she couldn't think while Matt was standing beside her and Jase was shooting glances at her from across the room.

They rode in silence back to the Alpine Sky. Matt looked like he had questions, but he didn't ask them. She decided it was part of the careful, logical way he analyzed a situation before deciding what to do. She respected that. He probably made lists, too.

He pulled up the curving drive to the main entrance, waving off the doorman. Leaving the car running, he turned to her. "I have to go meet someone. I won't see you until tomorrow."

"Oh. Okay." It seemed like a weak excuse, but she couldn't blame him. She reached for the door handle.

"Hey." That one word, barely above a whisper, turned his smile sexy. "I really do have to go. And I'm looking forward to seeing you tomorrow." He reached across the console for her hand. "You need to know something about me, Zoe. I don't give up easily."

She smiled back. He was still interested! Her relief lasted all of two seconds, when the memory of kissing Jase tore back into her mind, hot and wild, shredding her contentment as easily as it overrode the pleasant sensation of Matt's hand on hers. Blood rushed to her face. She sent Matt a panicked glance, knowing he couldn't miss that blush against her fair complexion.

Matt's expression oozed confidence. Thank God for the male ego—he probably assumed his interest had flattered her speechless. That was better than the truth. Fingers trembling, she got out as quickly as possible, slammed the door, and waved. Then walked briskly to her office.

The shaking started again as she sank into her chair. This was all wrong! Matt Flemming was the one who was supposed to make her weak with desire. He was perfect for her. A good kisser, too. She remembered the warm feeling she'd had after their first kiss, thinking that it felt *just right*. Who wouldn't be thrilled by that?

Apparently *she* wouldn't. Matt's kisses disappeared like vapor the second she thought of the inferno she'd felt with Jase. He'd touched something deep inside her, something strong and vibrant, and coaxed it to the surface. She'd been energized and dizzy at the same time, and desperate for more. In countless kisses with countless men, no one had done that to her before. Even after it ended, the flame he'd ignited still burned, so strong she would have sworn it showed on the outside. She felt *sparkly*, for God's sake.

Zoe groaned aloud and dropped her head to the desk, banging her forehead several times, muttering, "No, no, no." This couldn't happen. First Jase Garrett had ruined her best shot at a promotion, and now he was messing up her relationship with the best man to come along in years. Hell, the best man ever.

It had to be his bad-boy appeal. She thought she'd exhausted the urge to throw her life away with the wrong man, but apparently there was still some insanity left, a wild spark that hadn't burned out yet. That didn't mean she had to indulge it. She'd been down that road before. Shit, she'd taken a five-year detour down that road, from age fifteen to age twenty, nearly steering her life into a ditch for good. She wouldn't do it again.

She could be completely content kissing Matt for the rest of her life. His kiss was certainly competent. She flinched at the word and searched for a better one. *Skilled*—that worked. It was not only accurate, but flattering. She bet if he put his mind to it he could be downright incendiary.

Zoe groaned aloud. Life had been so much easier when Jase thought she was a lying, cheating arsonist.

She dropped her forehead to the desk again and left it there.

Jase propped his feet on the porch rail and watched the old pickup negotiate his curving driveway, rolling to a stop where the hillside began its steep upward slope. Brandon jumped out with more energy than usual, taking the ten curving stone steps up to the porch two at a time.

"Hey, man." He high-fived Jase before pulling up a chair and settling his feet beside Jase's on the rail. "Nice day to watch the weather."

Jase lifted an eyebrow. "You're pretty damn happy for someone who's not getting any. I thought Megan was out of town this weekend."

"Out of town and out of my life."

"Oh. Sorry."

"It's been coming. But get this." He leaned forward, dismissing the split with his girlfriend. "We just picked up a contract from Nike for the new snowboard line."

Jase glanced over in surprise. "Someone there remembered me?"

"Nah. The marketing people didn't give a damn about using your name, said you're ancient history, but they loved both the body design and the graphics."

Jase cared more about his design work than his former glory anyway. "Nice. Good money?"

"I won't know the exact net until I talk with the manufacturing side, but enough that neither one of us will have to worry about next year's income."

Jase smiled at his friend's excitement. Brandon's graphics had been carrying their company, and he deserved to reap some rewards. "You'll finally be able to get a new truck."

"Whoa! Never. And don't say that so loudly, she might hear you." He looked over the rail and raised his voice. "He's just kidding, baby." He gave Jase a mock glare. "If I get stranded ten miles from nowhere, you're the one I'm calling for a ride."

"Uh-huh. You know that truck's not a sentient being, right?"

"Shows what you know. That truck loves me. We've been together sixteen years. That's about fifteen more than any girlfriend I've had." He sighed happily. "There's nothing like the love of a good truck."

Jase snorted. "Cynical, but simple. You might be on to something."

A cautious look crossed Brandon's face. "Woman problems?"

He'd opened his mouth without thinking, and tried to blow it off. "Same old shit. Can't figure 'em out."

"That's my line. You've always been pretty good at it." Brandon gave him a shrewd look. "Are you still obsessing about Zoe Larkin after Uncle Brandon told you not to?"

He scowled. "I'm not obsessing."

"Whatever you call thinking about her all the time and following every move she makes."

He couldn't deny thinking about her. Hell, he hadn't been able to think about anything else. "Something like that," he muttered.

"Huh." Brandon tilted his chair back, giving it some thought. "I thought you suspected she was part of that truck-bashing incident."

"I did, but now I'm not so sure. Same with the fire."

"They have another suspect?"

"Not that I know of." His gut told him Matt

Flemming was a more likely suspect, but the police had found no evidence that he'd hired someone to do it. "I'm just starting to think she doesn't have it in her."

"Hmm." It sounded doubtful. "Is she still looking to buy the Rusty Wire? It's not a good idea to mix business and pleasure."

"I'm not doing business with her." He couldn't deny the pleasure part.

Brandon was quiet for several seconds as he weighed the facts. "Well, obviously you're not going to take my wise advice about leaving her alone."

"Guess not."

"So quit fartin' around like you're twelve years old, and make your move. Talk to her."

"Did that."

"Ah, I get it. She shut you down." He nodded sagely. "Might be for the best. Like I said, getting involved with one of the Larkin girls could be messy."

Jase felt a prick of annoyance. He might have brought up Zoe's past, but he didn't like to hear others do it. "She didn't shut me down. We argued."

"Not the best start," Brandon agreed. "Women do tend to hold a grudge. But don't worry, if it wasn't personal, she'll get over it."

Jase clenched his jaw and stared at a stand of pine trees as his words replayed in his head. "I might have mentioned her past," he admitted. "And the way she lets her boss walk all over her. Then I told her she didn't know what she wanted from life."

Brandon looked at him in disbelief. "Smooth move, Romeo."

"Yeah." He might as well finish it. "Then I kissed her."

"Jesus!" Brandon laughed and shook his head.

"You're not too smart, but you've sure got balls. That is, if she didn't knee them halfway up your throat."

Jase tapped his fingers in a nervous beat against the arm of the chair. "I thought she was going to, but then she kissed me back."

"No way!" When Jase slid an affirming glance at him, Brandon eyed him as if he'd suddenly grown gills. "Someday you'll have to tell me how you did that."

"Hell, I don't know myself." Maybe saying it out loud would help him make sense of it. "I was insulting her, and I swear she was mad enough to gut and fillet me on the spot. Then the next thing I know, I'm kissing her, and she doesn't want me to, but then suddenly she's kissing me back, and . . ." And desire had hit him like a freight train, with a throbbing erection like he hadn't had since he was eighteen. He'd had to fight the urge to strip her bare and take her right there against the wall. Incredibly, he was pretty sure she felt the same way.

He couldn't say that. "Fuck if I know what happened." He slid lower in his chair, staring at the trees while musing over the kiss. There was only one thing to do. "But I'm damn well going to make sure it happens again."

Brandon gave him a suspicious glance, then looked away again. "Doesn't sound like you. You're the lucky son of a bitch who sits back and lets the ladies come to him."

It was true; Jase couldn't remember the last time he'd actually gone out of his way to have a relationship with a woman. If one wasn't interested, another one would come along soon enough.

But Zoe wouldn't be one of those women. She had

a plan for her life, and a casual affair with a saloon owner wasn't part of it. Matt Flemming was. The guy might genuinely like her, but he couldn't make her happy, and the possessive way he touched her raised Jase's hackles.

"Zoe's different," he told Brandon. "She'd sooner run in the other direction."

"Smart girl."

Jase ignored him. "I'll find a way to change her mind."

Brandon put his hands behind his head as he stared at the treetops. "Huh. That's interesting."

Jase waited for more, but it didn't come. Impatience finally won out. "Why is it interesting?"

"Because I haven't seen you do that in, oh, years and years. Go after something you want, I mean. That would require . . ." He frowned at the sky in exaggerated puzzlement and snapped his fingers. "What's that word? That thing you don't have? It's been so long I can't remember. Oh, yeah. Initiative."

"Very funny."

"Very true."

Jase bit back the retort he'd been about to make. Brandon looked serious.

He frowned. It wasn't as if he hadn't done anything the past nine years. He'd provided some designs for their snowboards and skis, even if it had been Brandon's new graphics that carried the business lately. And he may have been hiding from the rat race, but running a saloon wasn't exactly nothing. Of course, Russ and Jennifer did most of the actual running. Only the money decisions fell to Jase, and they hadn't been a challenge.

Still, what was wrong with that? Avoiding challenges

didn't mean his life had been empty and meaningless. It had been a *good* life. Shooting pool and going fishing whenever he wanted. Skiing for fun instead of to win. Enjoying the customers who came to the Rusty Wire.

Maybe it was a little routine, one day blurring into another, one girlfriend blurring into another . . .

And no real accomplishments to show for almost a decade of his life. Jase winced. Damn, Brandon was right. He'd lain back and let life happen around him without making a move to participate. Avoiding the need to win had taken him out of the game completely. He was a loser, something he'd never been able to accept graciously.

He looked at Brandon. "Guess you're right. I haven't accomplished anything in the past nine years."

"Not a lot. Caught some big fish, though."

Brandon didn't look disturbed by the lack of anything larger. And why should he? It wasn't his life being wasted. "I think it's time to change that, go after what I want."

"Zoe Larkin?"

He puzzled over it. "I don't know." He needed to get this right, to make sure he didn't waste his time chasing after the wrong thing. Start with the basics. "I want the Rusty Wire. I'll do whatever it takes to keep it out of Flemming's hands." He paused. "I still don't know what I want with Zoe Larkin."

He just knew he wanted something, beginning with another one of those mind-numbing kisses. If it had the same electric kick as the last one, he'd take it from there.

Matt had called her at home. Zoe hoped it was for a real date, something where she could forget that he was in a position of power over her. That had to be what had tempered her reaction to his kisses. It was probably also why kissing Jase had been so explosive—it was all about power. She was the one offering three million dollars for his saloon. The fact that he didn't want it was irrelevant, money was power. It was simple psychology.

But Matt hadn't called to ask her out. He wanted her to come in early for a meeting. She sat at the conference table, unnerved before he even started talking. Any meeting Matt called with just her and David had to be about their future positions with the company. David had to know it, too. He sat across from her, looking too damn smug for comfort.

"I'll make this brief," Matt said from the head of the table. "You both know we've been planning some changes in management for the Alpine Sky. Since Buck passed away, I've taken a larger role in management, and I will continue to do so. We simply don't need two managers at your salary levels. One of you will stay on as general manager, while the other will run the new golf course and clubhouse once it's built. Unfortunately, the new position doesn't pay as much, but your experience with the company makes either of you the top choice for—" He raised an amused eyebrow at the hand she shot into the air. "You have a question, Zoe?"

"Yes." Hell, yes. "I thought we'd shelved the golf course plan for now, but you're talking about it as if it's a done deal. Did I miss something? Did Jase change his mind overnight?"

Matt smiled. "No, he didn't. But I'm confident in your ability to persuade him to sell, and I want us all to be prepared when it happens."

He'd said it without a hint of snarkiness, which was

reassuring, but it was still a hell of a lot of confidence. Seriously misplaced, too, if you believed Jase Garrett. She did. "I don't think he needs the money, Matt. He got all sorts of product endorsement deals after his Olympic wins—not as much as the professional sports stars, maybe, but enough to keep him comfortable."

"And those contracts were yanked a year later after it became evident he had no intention of returning to competition. When you're in violation of contracts, you don't get to keep the money."

She should have thought of that, but hadn't really considered how much he'd lost when he quit competing. Probably because Jase had led her to believe he had enough money. She should have questioned what he meant by *enough*. It still didn't explain why Matt thought the money mattered.

"Speaking of major sports stars," Matt went on, "I assume you're familiar with the name Kyle Russerman?"

"The pro golfer," David said. He was nodding and smiling, as if he already knew where this was going. Zoe narrowed her eyes suspiciously.

"Kyle's been elusive about putting his name on products, but my mother has had several meetings with him and taken him to see the property. Yesterday she finalized a deal that will make him the official partner in our golf course. That pretty much guarantees its success."

"Already?" Zoe stared at him.

David chuckled to himself. "If anyone could persuade him, it would be Ruth Ann."

"True." Matt nodded. "And it gets better. With the money from the Russerman deal to front us, we will be expanding Alpine Resorts, Inc., with a new resort on the island of Aruba. Buck was always reluctant to expand, but now that he's gone, my mother and I have decided to take the company in a new direction."

Zoe blinked, unable to find words for all the thoughts that popped into her mind. She'd be working in a management position for an international corporation, which put a nice shine on her already polished résumé. Also, Matt was more ambitious than she'd realized, possibly building a huge financial empire. And more willing to take risks with the company.

He seemed to be waiting for her response. David also watched her expectantly from across the table, clearly unsurprised by the news. The arrogant bastard.

She cleared her throat. "Um, I assume you're talking about several years from now . . ."

"Actually, my mother is flying to Aruba today to arrange financing and look at some promising property. She's already put the house in B-Pass up for sale, since she would prefer to live in the Caribbean."

David seemed strangely unmoved by the news that his meal ticket was leaving the country. "The house will sell quickly," he assured Matt. He turned a smile on Zoe. "The view from the great room is amazing, and the multihead shower in the master bath feels better than a visit to our spa."

She had to give him credit for packing so much information into one sentence. He'd been in Ruth Ann's house. He'd used her shower. In other words, he'd slept with Ruth Ann. And he wasn't perturbed about her leaving, which meant he had reason to believe the position of general manager was a lock.

She wasn't as surprised by what he'd said as by the

fact that he'd said it in front of Matt. Her gaze flew to Ruth Ann's son. He was checking e-mails on his phone, seemingly unconcerned. Either Ruth Ann used men like candy and sleeping with David meant nothing, or it meant everything and Matt would do whatever she said, in which case Zoe had just been royally screwed over.

She stood to leave.

Matt looked up from his phone. "Zoe, please stay a minute. I'd like to go over your next meeting with Jase Garrett."

She lowered herself back down, a sick lump congealing in her stomach. This couldn't be good. David wiggled his fingers at her as he left the room.

As soon as the door clicked shut, Matt laid his phone on the desk and propped his hip beside it. He contemplated Zoe for several nerve-wracking seconds. "You have the next two days off," he finally said. "I'd like to see you tomorrow night."

His eyes pinned her with a meaningful stare. Her mouth parted with a soft "Oh" as his intention sank in. This had nothing to do with Jase. It had to do with Matt making his bid to force Jase out of the picture.

She liked that idea. The sooner she got Jase Garrett off her mind, the sooner she could concentrate on the man she'd been waiting for. Except his intense gaze looked a bit heated, and she didn't want any misunderstandings.

"I'm not like David."

A smile played at the corner of his mouth. "I'm not asking David out."

"That's not what I meant."

"I know what you meant." The smile was gone.

"You're not offering sex in exchange for a job. Did I get it right?"

"Yes."

"Asking you out has nothing to do with the Alpine Sky, Zoe. This is me and you." He paused, letting it sink in. "Okay?"

She breathed out a sigh. "Okay."

"So is that a yes?"

"Yes."

His eyes crinkled with pleasure. "Good. I'll pick you up at seven."

"Let me give you my address."

He held up a hand as she reached for a pen. "Don't bother, I know where you live." When she glanced up in surprise he flashed a grin. "Personnel files."

She laughed and stood. The meeting hadn't turned out so badly after all. He wanted to kiss her when she left, she was sure of it, but it didn't prevent him from keeping his word. Their private life would stay outside the office.

It was all about professional ethics; Jase Garrett could stand having a lesson.

Jase folded his forearms on the high counter, nice and friendlylike. The lady on the other side looked up from her desk and smiled. "May I help you?"

"Yes, ma'am. I have some questions about city zoning laws."

"Bill!" she yelled, turning slightly toward the adjoining room without taking her eyes off Jase. "Man here to see you!" Smiling sweetly, she said, "Bill's chairman of the planning board. You're lucky you caught him here on a Saturday."

A middle-aged man appeared, brushing crumbs off his fingers and onto his potbelly. "Bill Rutter," he said, offering a reasonably clean hand. "What can I do for you?"

Jase shook the offered hand, surreptitiously wiping a crumb off on the counter. "My name's Jase Garrett. I own the Rusty Wire Saloon out on Evans Road."

Bill's face lit up. "Sure, I know where that is. Glad to meet you. Boy, you've had a lot of action up your way lately."

"You mean the fire? Yes, we did, but we're back in business."

"Good, good, glad to hear it." He leaned closer. "I heard it was arson. A woman, yet. That was a surprise, wasn't it, Lilly?" He looked at the woman behind the desk who'd made no pretense of getting back to work.

Lilly shook her head sadly. "Not really. It's a shame, though. Those Larkin girls never did have much use for rules."

They'd heard about Zoe? The shock of it was followed by such a strong jolt of anger he had to swallow back a handful of swear words. Zoe hadn't even been arrested, but this woman had already accepted her guilt. No wonder Zoe was so defensive concerning rumors about her past.

"You heard wrong," he said, emphasizing the last word. "Zoe Larkin didn't have anything to do with it."

Bill cocked his head. "You sure? Bernie Kohn at the police station said they brought her in for questioning the very next day. They had a videotape of her setting the fire and everything."

Jase ground his teeth. His hands ached to grab Bill by his dirty shirt and yank him against the counter, the better to scream in his face. Maybe break his nose while he was at it. That would feel better than swallowing his anger while keeping his face carefully neutral. "I guess your friend Bernie didn't know the whole story," he said. "Zoe had information. I talked to her myself, and, confidentially, what she said should be very useful to the police." He didn't hesitate to spin the facts in her favor; if Zoe was right, it took a lot of good deeds to counteract one bad rumor. "And the tape was from my security camera, so I know for sure it didn't show a darn thing."

"Huh," Bill said, digesting the news with an amazed look. "Funny how stories get twisted around, isn't it?"

Yeah, real funny. He hoped Zoe never heard this one. "Glad I could give you the facts. But that's not what I came in for today. I wanted to ask about the parcel of land I own behind the saloon. It's that wooded strip you see when you drive into town from the north, fifty acres lying just below and south of the Alpine Sky."

"Gotcha!" Bill pointed a finger at him and made a clicking sound. "You're wondering about getting it rezoned so you can sell, right?"

He frowned. "Sort of." More like hoping the city might oppose rezoning it, and oppose the golf course. It would be the easiest way to get Matt Flemming off his back. But he had a bad feeling that Matt was a step ahead of him. "Have you heard something about me selling that land?"

"Sure. And you don't have to worry about it at all. We assured the buyer he wouldn't have any problem getting that land rezoned for a golf course. In fact, we're more than eager to help facilitate the sale." He grinned. "A golf course is just what this town needs!"

Chapter Ten

Jase stared at Bill as questions flooded his mind. So many questions, his mind had gone numb with them. He winced and rubbed a spot in the center of his forehead, giving Bill a cautious look. "Are you saying someone from the Alpine Sky already talked to you about getting my land rezoned?"

"Talked to the whole planning board except for Barb, who's out of town. Not an official session, of course. Just an informal meeting to feel us out on the idea. That guy from the resort is pretty sharp." He swiveled his head. "Wouldn't you say so, Lilly? Had all his ducks in a row."

"Sure did," Lilly agreed.

Jase squinted to compensate for the nerve that had started jumping beside his left eye. "Would that be Matt Flemming?"

"That's the guy. Had a lawyer with him, too, but Matt seemed to know his stuff."

Jase ground his molars. "They asked about rezoning my land?"

"Just making sure the city wouldn't have any objections. They were prepared, with all the plans, too. Here, let me show you." Bill walked to a metal filing cabinet and opened a long, shallow drawer. Jase glimpsed a stack of large maps lying flat in the drawer as Bill pulled one off the top of the pile and brought it to the counter.

"They left this copy so we could show Barb. Have you seen this yet?"

"No," Jase choked out as he stared at the professionally drawn topography map. The Alpine Sky resort and its little village of shops lay at the top. Near the bottom where the Rusty Wire should be, he saw the footprint of a large building with a swimming pool and a parking lot. In between lay a parkland of fairways, water hazards, and sand traps, dotted with small stands of trees. His forest was gone.

"See, here's where your saloon used to be," Bill said, circling the clubhouse with his finger. It might as well have been a knife stabbing Jase in the heart. "This squiggly line here is a road they'll put in directly from the resort, which will keep extra traffic off Evans Road. And these are the proposed lakes, right along the line of natural drainage for minimum impact on the environment. Impressive, isn't it?"

Jase just looked at him. *Impressive* was certainly an appropriate word for the forethought and planning that had gone into the map. Also presumptuous and arrogant. He could have come up with some more unpleasant words if he took a second.

"The city doesn't care if they level a swath of forest?"

"Well, they didn't exactly level it," Bill said with a chuckle. If he didn't stop using the past tense for Matt

Flemming's rape-and-pillage plan, Jase would rethink that broken nose. "They left a few clumps here and there. But you can't have a golf course without lots of open land, can you?"

"No, you can't." He watched Bill steadily. This was what he'd come to find out. "And the planning board thinks Barringer's Pass needs a golf course?"

"Hell, yes! Excuse me, Lilly, heck yes. It's been a long time since we've had any major construction here, and the town could use the jobs. Builders, landscapers . . . and just think of all those golfers who will probably eat at our restaurants and shop in our stores. It's a bonanza!"

Jase's anger faltered. The jobs saved at the Rusty Wire didn't compare to the number of jobs that would be added at the golf course. Or the increased business downtown. For the first time, he wondered if he was doing the right thing by opposing the sale.

"I didn't know our unemployment rate was that high," he murmured.

"Oh, it's not, but more jobs being available means more people moving here, which means a demand for more rental units, which means . . ." Bill grinned and spread his arms. "More building! It's a circle of prosperity that could bring a couple thousand people here, easy. Everyone wins."

Jase frowned. Not everyone. He wasn't exactly a tree hugger, but he appreciated Barringer's Pass for the same reason many tourists did—the quaint little town was surrounded by thousands of acres of wilderness, ideal for skiing, hiking, fishing, hunting, horseback riding, photography, fall color tours . . . he couldn't name all the reasons people came here to enjoy the natural beauty. Fifty acres of trees wouldn't change that one way or another. A couple thousand more people would.

"What about the impact on schools and city services?"

Bill grinned. "Exactly—more teachers, police, fire-fighters, the whole deal. The city council will love this idea!"

The city council was more growth-minded than he'd known. He suddenly regretted keeping his head in the sand for the past nine years. "It's a small valley, Bill. Where do you plan to put all these people?"

"Trust me, they'll fit," Bill assured him. "We might have to rezone some of the older homes to enlarge the commercial district, but they aren't helping the tax base as much as shops and restaurants will. Commercial development equals progress. B-Pass will thrive."

"B-Pass will be crowded. You know all those movie stars and producers and other celebrities who build their fancy homes around here? They're looking for peace and quiet. They might just take their money and move to Montana."

"They might." Bill shrugged. "But they'll sell to people who prefer a thriving city to a wilderness retreat. No loss."

Jase frowned. There were two things wrong with that. One, most of Barringer's Pass figured anyone who wanted a thriving city could move to Denver. And two, celebrity sightings were part of the local atmosphere. For years the residents of Barringer's Pass had enjoyed their private slice of Hollywood, grateful for the money the celebrities pumped into the economy, and tolerant of their occasional excesses. No one wanted to see them leave.

Except, apparently, the planning board and the city council.

Jase straightened. "Well, thanks, Bill. That tells me what I needed to know."

"No problem. You're about to help start some very exciting times for our town."

Not likely. Not unless Bill found excitement in pissing off the Flemming family, in which case things were going to get downright entertaining. And possibly dangerous.

Zoe knew she should have driven her own car as soon as Cal pulled into the Rusty Wire parking lot. She could have made a sharp U-turn instead of being held hostage in a honky-tonk, and risk running into Jase. "Why are we coming here?" she complained from the backseat.

"Because Sophie said it was fun." Maggie's tone said that was reason enough. "Don't you want to see what it's like when you aren't here on business? Besides, Cal and I have never been here."

"I was content to leave it that way," Cal grumbled. "You know I'm not much for dancing."

Maggie patted his shoulder. "Poor baby." She turned toward Zoe. "Let's face it, you and I have been snobs for too long. We restrict ourselves to the classy clubs, and bars at the resort, and we never mingle with the hometown crowd."

"With good reason," Zoe reminded her. Restoring their reputation meant only being seen at classier places. It also didn't hurt that the resort visitors had never heard of the Larkin girls. Deflecting old rumors wore on the nerves.

Maggie gave her a determined look. "I'm through trying to prove to this town that I'm respectable, and you should be, too. If they can't see it by now, then forget them."

That was easy for Maggie to say; her husband was a cop in Barringer's Pass. Even after last year's scandal, people were more apt to accept her and consider her a solid citizen. Zoe didn't have that advantage. "I already narrowly missed being accused of arson just because I was seen at the Rusty Wire; I don't want to risk being involved in another incident."

"There's no risk." Maggie barely waited for Cal to park the car before hopping out and opening the back door. "Come on. Nothing's going to happen when you're with a cop. Just loosen up and have a good time."

It wasn't as if she had much choice. She let them lead the way inside, trailing along like a reluctant kid while scanning the room for Jase. If she was lucky, he'd have the night off and be home with his feet up, watching TV. He seemed like the sedentary type.

"Pool tables!" Cal turned to Maggie with a happy grin and slung an arm over her shoulder as they made their way toward the back room. "Why didn't Sophie mention that?"

Zoe glanced past Cal, then ducked back behind him. Damn it! Jase was there. He was bent over a pool table with his arm reaching around a girl to guide her shot. Zoe heard her squeal with delight and took another peek. It was the cute little blond thing from her previous visit, the one who looked like she should be home working on her cheerleading flips instead of hanging out at a saloon with a guy twice her age.

An experienced guy. A guy who kissed with enough passion to cause an internal meltdown. The feeling came flooding back, leaving Zoe weak-kneed and flushed.

"I think I'll stop at the bar and get a drink. You guys go try out the pool tables."

She veered off before Maggie could object, taking an open stool at the far end of the bar where she wouldn't be tempted to peek around the corner and accidentally see Jase pull his perky girlfriend against his chest and kiss the last bit of innocence out of her. He could do it, easily. It fogged her mind just thinking about it.

"Looking for Jase?"

Zoe blinked, bringing Jennifer's face into focus. Her first thought was that the woman had no clue about serving the public; that tight expression couldn't be helping business. Her dark hair was clipped at the nape of her neck tonight, making her features look even more drawn. She'd almost believe the woman never smiled, except she'd watched Matt coax a smile out of her and knew it could be done.

"No," Zoe said. "I'm here with my sister and brother-in-law. I'd like a glass of white wine, please."

Wordlessly, Jennifer filled a glass and set it in front of her. She met Zoe's eyes with a cool gaze. If Zoe hadn't watched her take out the glass and pour, she would have wondered if she'd spit into it first.

"Seven dollars."

Zoe pulled out a ten. "Keep the change. It would cost me even more than that at the Alpine Sky."

Jennifer pocketed the money without a thank-you. "That's because we don't have to charge extra for a pretentious atmosphere."

Zoe lifted an eyebrow, taking her measure. "No, there's nothing pretentious here." Including the bartender, who seemed to value the stark truth. "You don't like me much, do you, Jennifer?"

"Not really."

Honesty wasn't always an attractive quality. "You don't even know me."

Jennifer shrugged. "Don't have to. I know you offered Jase a ton of money so you could tear this place down. And even though he said no, you keep sniffing around here, looking for him."

"I'm not sniffing after Jase." She'd snapped it out, frowning at the unpleasant image. "We aren't even friends." They weren't enemies, either, since an enemy didn't kiss you into a delirious puddle of goo. They were *something*—was there a term for someone who knew how to push all your buttons, both good and bad? She didn't want to think about it because she could already feel the heat rising to her cheeks and knew the sharp-eyed bartender couldn't miss it.

Jennifer smiled disbelievingly at her denial. "Right."

It seemed her nasty mood was contagious. "Look, I already have a boyfriend," Zoe told her. Sort of. Close enough to stretch the truth. "I'm not interested in Jase."

"You shouldn't be. He's not your type."

She paused. "What's my type?"

Jennifer gave her a condescending once-over. "Ambitious. Successful. Sophisticated."

Matt. She couldn't have described him better, and Zoe was annoyed that Jennifer made it sound like second place. "You're absolutely right. You can have Jase all to yourself."

The cynical look fell from Jennifer's face, replaced by surprise. "Me?"

It was a good fake; she must have thought no one knew. "You act like I'm moving in on your territory. I'm not."

Jennifer stared in disbelief for a moment, then apparently gave up the act. "Fine. Then stay away from Jase."

"Believe me, I intend to, except to discuss business."

"He won't change his mind."

"Neither will my boss, so I'll just keep doing my job and looking for a way to convince him to sell." Jennifer was clearly unhappy with that answer, enough so that Zoe added, "I told you, we aren't in competition. If you want Jase, go for it."

"*Want* him?" Jennifer gave one short laugh and turned away. End of conversation. Zoe watched her move down the bar, frowning after her. *What was that about?*

Zoe swirled her drink. Jase had told her Jennifer was jealous, and she'd certainly sounded like it to Zoe. She didn't like Zoe hanging around Jase, and she'd tried to implicate her in the fire. Could Jennifer be so deep in denial that she didn't know how she felt about Jase? Falling for your boss could be confusing; Zoe knew about that. Falling for Jase probably compounded it. She could understand Jennifer thinking, *I can't possibly be drawn to this man*. Boy, could she ever.

She sipped her wine, thinking it over. Confusion might be a common reaction to Jase. He had that strong, silent thing going for him and those incredible kisses, but he also sat around a saloon doing nothing with his life. He was a tempting loser, the kind of man you wanted in bed, but not in the rest of your life. It was enough to send any woman's mind reeling.

Except for the cheerleader in the other room, stroking her cue stick over Jase's balls. She didn't look in the least confused.

Zoe caught a man looking her over as he walked toward the restrooms. She deliberately looked away, staring pensively at the Coors sign behind the bar. She probably looked available, sitting at the bar alone. The last thing she wanted was some guy hitting on her, but there was no way she was going in the other room, not while Jase was bending some sweet young thing over a pool table.

No wonder Jennifer felt grumpy about the competition if they all looked like that.

She was ready to leave anytime. Unfortunately, since they'd spotted those pool tables, she probably had a long wait for Cal and Maggie. When she finished her wine she should order another glass and ask Jennifer to join her. They could amuse themselves by listing all the ways in which Jase Garrett was a loser and a jerk.

Jase had mistaken the redhead at the pool table for Zoe before realizing she was a little taller, and her hair was a little darker. Also, she had a touching-hugging-kissing relationship with a man who was not Matt Flemming.

Curious to meet the woman who was obviously Zoe's sister, he made introductions and invited them to switch partners, giving him time to talk to Maggie and giving Cal the opportunity to play a stronger opponent. After one game, he and Maggie quit to watch the show at the next table. Cal was currently barely holding his own against Hailey.

"Stop going easy on her, Cal," he advised from the sidelines. "She needs to get her butt kicked."

"I wish I *was* going easy on her," Cal grumbled. "I think I just got suckered by a high school student."

"College," Hailey sniffed. "I graduated from high school last month."

"You can take her, honey!" Maggie called as he lined up a shot. "Show that little girl who's boss!" Stepping close to Hailey, she confided, "If you attack their manliness, it totally screws up their thinking."

Hailey nodded. "So does cleavage." Catching Jase's narrowed eyes, she added innocently, "So I hear."

Eyeing his niece suspiciously, he leaned toward Maggie. "Please don't give her any more advantages over the rest of us. I already owe her enough to cover her first semester at Colorado State."

Cal missed his shot, but brightened as he stepped back. "Gambling without a license? That's illegal. I could arrest her." He gave Hailey a speculative look. "Unless, of course, she wants to throw the game."

Hailey smiled sweetly as she stepped up to take her turn. "That would be dishonest. Of course, if that's the only way your fragile ego will survive getting beaten by a girl . . ."

Maggie laughed.

"Cute," Cal told her. "I've got a little sister a lot like you. I'd introduce you, but we keep her chained in the garage."

Hailey nodded sympathetically. "Too much for you to handle, huh?" She smacked the cue ball, banking off the side to sink the five.

Cal arched an amused brow and turned to Jase. "I almost feel sorry for the boys at Colorado State. But I wouldn't mind watching her beat them, either."

Jase smiled. He liked Cal Drummond. Maggie, too, who seemed like Zoe but less complex. He was willing to bet that what you saw with Maggie was what you got—she was uninhibited, with her emotions right there at the surface. Zoe was more restrained and cautious about revealing herself, but boiling with emotion deep inside. She would probably need to feel completely safe before showing the kind of social abandon her sister displayed.

He smiled to himself—he could help her with that. Once Zoe let her guard down, he had a feeling she would be explosive. He'd seen a glimpse of it when he kissed her, as if an outer shell had melted away beneath his hands, freeing something colorful and wild. The power of it had stunned him, and left him wanting more. But she'd shut down, closing him out.

He wasn't discouraged. She'd felt it, too—he'd seen the amazement in her eyes. The attraction, too. If he could get her to trust him again, they could see just how explosive that passion could be.

Jase started at a sound, jerking his wandering mind back to reality. For a second he thought someone must have called his name, then realized that what he'd heard was a loud, angry voice from the tables out front.

A drunk with a temper. It happened occasionally, and all he could do with drunks was get them outside, then confiscate their keys until they sobered up. If they agreed to play nice, they could come back inside, but they were done drinking. So was anyone who sat with them, because he wouldn't have their buddies slipping them drinks.

"Excuse me a minute," he said. The man was getting more belligerent and his bouncer probably needed help. He didn't want any of the waitresses trying to deal with a belligerent drunk.

He saw the guy right away—all he had to do was follow the stares. The guy stood beside a table on the other side of the dance floor, a body double for Conan the Barbarian, gesturing and yelling at a cowed waitress about a dirty glass.

Damn, it was one of the new girls, too. She looked scared to death.

Jase strode up to the table, stepping in front of the waitress. At six foot three he could almost meet the guy eye to eye, but figured he was outweighed by about seventy pounds. He held up both palms in a peaceful gesture. "Hey, buddy, take it easy. Let's not scare the ladies. If you've got a problem, I'll be glad to take care of it."

The guy scraped a withering gaze over him. "You the manager?"

Close enough. "That's right."

"Then I've got a problem, all right. You're serving drinks in dirty glasses." His voice was remarkably unaffected as he held up a drink that looked like whiskey on the rocks. Maybe anger had cleared his head.

Jase looked. Sure enough, a greasy smudge crossed the lip of the glass. "I ain't drinking out of a glass that hasn't been washed." He slammed the glass on the table. "You got anybody back there doing dishes, or are you just wiping 'em with a rag and refilling them?"

Jase didn't have to check, he knew Joe never let a glass leave the kitchen unless it was spotless. But mistakes happened, especially when the place was this busy. Plus, the customer was always right, especially when he was stinking drunk, the way this guy sounded. He spoke over his shoulder without taking his eyes off the angry hulk. "April, get the man a new drink. No charge."

"I already did," April said, fear quivering in her voice.

"That's the *second* dirty glass she brought me!" the man yelled.

Now he knew for sure the Rusty Wire wasn't to blame; Jennifer and April both would have double-checked that second drink. But behind the drunk he saw a few customers glance at their drinks. He cursed under his breath; once the idea was planted, they'd have a rash of customers with dirty glasses. It wouldn't matter that they were most likely streaked by their own greasy fingers and lips, they'd still expect a free replacement. He could accept that relatively minor loss, but hated knowing that some of them would leave here believing the Rusty Wire really had been using dirty glasses. He needed to get this guy settled down or out of here, and quickly.

"I apologize, sir. If you don't want a replacement, we'll give you a full refund, no problem. Come with me." The apology really irked him, knowing it wasn't deserved, but sometimes it helped, getting grudging co-operation. This wasn't going to be one of those times.

"Come where? Back there by the kitchen? I ain't setting foot in that rodent-infested place. When I used the john, I saw a mouse run under a wall. Probably on his way to the kitchen."

The place seemed to go silent, even though Shania Twain still sang about feeling like a woman. The couples on the dance floor stood still, watching the confrontation. At the tables, no one spoke.

Jase set his jaw, fury rising inside him. The guy was flat-out lying, and doing more damage every second. It didn't matter that not one of those customers had ever seen a mouse in here; half of them undoubtedly wondered if they'd just seen one scuttle under the bar. The guy might just be spewing alcohol-fueled rage, but it had to stop. Now.

"Sir, I have to ask you to leave." He closed the distance between them, encouraging him to step toward the door. Where the hell was his bouncer?

"I ain't going nowhere. I'm calling the health inspector. They're gonna shut this dump down."

"You do that. From the parking lot."

A chair scraped behind him. "Who you ordering around?"

Jase turned. A second man, as burly as the first, stood at the next table. In the back of his mind, it registered as odd. Another hulk, at the next table? Siding with the first? But he had no time to think about it. Two men threatened him, from either side. He was in good shape and had some experience grappling with mean drunks, but not two jumbo-size drunks at the same time. And not with a bug-eyed waitress frozen at his side.

"April!" He saw her blink. "Get out of here. Now."

April looked at him, mouth open, eyes wide with fear. He wasn't sure she even understood what he'd said. Shit.

He was reaching to shove her forcibly out of the way when she suddenly jerked backward, propelled by a hard yank on her arm. He glanced past her to see who'd had the presence of mind to rescue her, and stared in surprise. Zoe?

He didn't have time to wonder where she'd come from, or how long she'd been there. A movement at the corner of his eye warned him that the first pissed-off giant drunk had decided to take advantage of the distraction and start a fight. He barely avoided the man's fist as it plowed through the air beside his head.

He preferred to back off if he could avoid a fight, but the man behind him was no doubt winding up his own punch in drunken support. He took the only option available. Grabbing the man's wrist before he could pull it back again, he yanked forward as he stepped aside, sending one giant crashing into the other. While both of them staggered, he twisted the man's arm behind his back and pushed him face forward across a table.

A roar of pain and profanity told him he had the arm just high enough to wrench some tendons without dislocating the shoulder. Drunk Number One was furious, but subdued, and smart enough not to move.

He couldn't say the same for Drunk Number Two.

The impact with his friend had sent him staggering backward, but that only bought Jase a few seconds. One more, and the guy would be on his back. Now would be a good time for that bouncer to show up.

He didn't. Behind him, the second drunk bellowed with rage. Jase couldn't let go of Drunk Number One, so he half-turned, hoping to lessen the hurt Drunk Number Two was about to lay on him. He tensed, legs braced. When nothing happened, he turned to look. The man's angry bellow turned into something more like pain as he fell to the ground, clawing at his face. Instantly, Cal was on him, flipping him to his stomach and sitting on his thighs as he writhed and yelled.

As Jase watched, Cal tossed something to Maggie with a "Thanks, babe," and caught the zip cuff she tossed in return. Seconds later, Drunk Number Two lay cuffed and cursing on the floor.

"Mitch!" Drunk Number One yelled at his friend and lifted his head, trying to see. He squirmed beneath Jase's hold. "Hey, dickhead, what'd you do to him? You can't get away with that. I'm gonna call the police. Then I'm gonna call the health department. They're gonna close you down, you motherfucking prick."

Jase used his free hand to grab the guy by the collar and pull him upright. "Let me save you some trouble. Meet the police." He turned him to face Cal.

Cal gave Drunk Number One a cold look. "At your service." He grabbed the guy's wrist and slipped it into another cuff. All the fight suddenly went out of the man and he stood stoically as Jase guided his other hand through the cuff and Cal pulled it tight.

"Thanks," Jase said. He nodded toward Drunk

Number Two where he still lay moaning on the floor. "What did you do to him?"

Cal grinned. "Pepper spray. Maggie carries it in her purse. I grabbed it, then sent her out to the car for the cuffs. She called it in, too. A squad car should be here soon."

Jase grunted approval. "You ever want to moon-light as a bouncer, you're both hired. I seem to have an opening." He scanned the room for the burly man whose presence alone usually stopped fights. The man was gone. "Let's take these two outside to wait for their ride."

Cal hauled the other guy to his feet and they left. Jase heard a smattering of applause and glanced back to see who'd started it. Zoe and Maggie. It caught on as they went out the door, followed by the rising sound of voices as the saloon returned to normal.

The two drunks stood quietly beside the building as they waited. Jase looked them over. Drunk Number One was clear-eyed and strangely removed, as if his rage had never happened. Drunk Number Two sent Jase a deadly stare from eyes still streaming with tears.

A bad feeling took hold in his gut. "They don't look drunk," he told Cal.

Cal gave them a thoughtful look. "No, they don't." When Jase didn't add anything, he asked, "You think-ing they just wanted a fight?"

Jase remembered his bouncer's unexplained ab-sence and suspected the man had been bribed to disappear. The fake drunks had had a mission, and they hadn't wanted it interrupted. "I'm thinking they wanted more than that," he said. The accusations the first man had yelled echoed grimly in his mind. The whole room had heard them. "And I'm afraid they may have accomplished it."

Zoe toyed with her glass as she sat at the bar, waiting for the inevitable. She was going to have to talk to Jase. He was with Cal, so she couldn't avoid him. It shouldn't make her nervous; it wasn't as if she'd been hiding from him. Not as far as he knew, anyway. She was just having a drink. Alone. For half an hour, while her sister and brother-in-law were in the next room. Yeah, that looked good.

"That was so cool," Maggie said for about the fifth time. "I've never seen Cal arrest anyone before."

"You told me."

"I know, I'm sorry, I just can't get over it. It was so . . . manly. I feel a little giddy." She paused, looking worried. "God, am I sick? Why do I like to see my husband get aggressive with someone?"

"You don't, you like the idea of him protecting you." She knew because she'd felt the same way watching Jase take charge of the situation that had started uncomfortably close to her. Her heart had thundered in her chest, and not out of fear.

"Right," Maggie said with obvious relief. "It's a genetically ingrained response. Survival of the species, and all that. I'm *supposed to be* impressed when my man saves me." She grinned slyly. "Boy, am I ever. I can't wait to get him home and show him exactly how impressed I am."

Zoe flushed with heat, unable to stop herself from imagining doing the same with Jase. Damn it! She had to keep that guy out of her head.

"Zoe."

Jase's voice, close behind her, sent goose bumps dancing across her shoulders. She composed herself before turning around. "Hi."

Beside her, Maggie whipped around, hopped off her chair, and plastered herself to Cal. "You were awesome," she told him in a low, breathy voice.

Cal drew his head back to see her better. "Um, thanks, but it was really nothing."

"Oh, trust me, it was something."

Cal gave his wife a puzzled look, then smiled in sudden understanding. "You're right, I was incredibly brave."

"I'm ready to go home. Are you?"

"I need to stop at the station . . ." He watched his wife slowly lick her lower lip, then bite it. "But it can wait. Let's go."

They started to walk off, Maggie snuggled inside Cal's arm. Zoe cleared her throat. "Uh, guys . . ."

They turned. Maggie looked puzzled, then embarrassed. "I forgot! Come on, Zoe, we'll drop you off."

Zoe could imagine how fast she was going to get kicked out of their car. She stood, but Jase put a hand on her arm.

"You two go ahead," he told Maggie and Cal. "I'll make sure Zoe gets home. I want to talk to her."

Zoe opened her mouth to protest, but Maggie and Cal were already heading for the door. No one had even consulted her. Zoe frowned in annoyance, but didn't call them back. From the look on her sister's face, they'd be lucky to make it out of the parking lot without pulling off their clothes. Three would obviously be a crowd.

That didn't mean Jase could take control of her life.

She faced him, hands on hips. "Who said I wanted to stay?"

"We need to talk, Zoe," he repeated in a low voice.

She started to argue, but paused at the serious look on his face. Whatever this was about, it had nothing to do with her avoiding him by hiding out at the bar. It also had nothing to do with the brief surge of lust she'd felt a minute ago. Her annoyance gradually changed to concern. "What's wrong?"

"Not here." His jaw twitched as a muscle tensed. "And I'm warning you, you're not going to like it."

Chapter Eleven

He surprised her by going past the restrooms, out the back door, and straight through the construction at the back of the building. Seconds later, she stood in the dark on the grassy strip next to the Rusty Wire, looking around uneasily. The log wall of the saloon blocked most of the light from the parking area, and the wall of trees fifty feet away absorbed any light from town. It was a sheltered enclave, dark and intimate.

Or ominous. She wasn't sure which feeling to go with.

"Why do we need to be out here?" She tried not to be nervous, but the pitch-black forest was creepy. And Jase was . . . close.

"I don't want to take a chance on anyone hearing what I have to say. It's about those two guys we turned over to the police. I'm pretty sure they weren't drunk. They wanted to start a fight any way they could, and they nearly succeeded. If your brother-in-law hadn't been there to help, it could have been ugly."

That cleared up any doubt that he might not have known who Cal and Maggie were. He knew, just like he knew Zoe had come with them and tried to avoid him. She'd feel embarrassed about it except for the fact that he obviously had a bigger issue on his mind. "Why would they want to start a fight? Do you know them?"

"Never saw them before. But that whole thing was staged; I'd bet my life on it."

It took only a second for the awful implications to sink in. "Then all those things they said . . ."

"You got it. They were meant to cause problems for the Rusty Wire."

She swallowed hard. "Jase, they really will, fight or not. Those accusations will be in the police report, and lots of people heard them. Dirty glasses, a mouse . . ." Her stomach churned at the thought of having to deal with something like that at the Alpine Sky. "Rumors about unsanitary conditions can kill a business as fast as a fire."

"That's right."

He was waiting for her to connect the rest of the dots, and it didn't take long. A cold, hard knot formed in her chest because she knew the conclusion he'd reached made sense. "You think someone from the Alpine Sky paid them to do it."

"Yes." His gaze, dark and fierce, bored into hers. "Don't you?"

She didn't want to, but she was running out of explanations for the things that kept happening at the Rusty Wire. Vandalism, fire, claims about unsanitary conditions, all coming right when the Alpine Sky was pressuring him to sell. It had to be more than coincidence.

But she narrowed her gaze, suspecting his thoughts had gone a step further. "You think *I* had something to do with it, don't you? That's why you brought me out here." Anger burned through her, consuming any fluttery feelings she might have had about Jase. "You know, I'm getting pretty damn tired of being the focus of your suspicions. You've already decided I'm the one responsible, so why don't you just call the cops and get it over with."

"Zoe . . ."

"No." She swatted aside the hand he held up. "Don't try giving me any lame excuses. Just get it over with. They won't be able to prove anything, but you'll point enough suspicion my way to make everyone think I'm involved. That's how it works, isn't it? Go ahead, what are you waiting for?"

"I'm not trying to blame it on you."

"Sure you are. You're taking advantage of my reputation in this town to make me a convenient scapegoat. And you know what? That makes you a fucking asshole." The anger felt cleansing, which was good, because she was just getting started. "You think just because I kissed you that I'll stand by meekly while you use me for—"

His scowl deepened. "Damn it, Zoe, just shut up for a minute." When she glared back, mouth pressed into a tight line, he let out a long sigh. "I don't think you had anything to do with it."

"Right," she said, full of sarcasm. When he simply stared her down, a hint of doubt crept in. "You don't?"

"No."

She frowned. Just when she thought she understood him, he turned everything upside down again. "Why not?"

He gave a bitter laugh and rubbed his forehead. "'Why' again. Hell, I don't know. Maybe I'm crazy. Something about you scrambles my brain. Maybe it *is* because you kissed me, because for a second there I saw the real you without your guard up." He cocked his head, looking her up and down as if they'd just met. "You'd make a lousy poker player, Zoe. Or a liar. You're not good at hiding your feelings once you let them see daylight, are you?"

Heat rushed to her cheeks and she hoped he couldn't see it in the dark. The feelings unleashed by that kiss had centered around lust, hot and out of control. She wasn't about to discuss it. Covering her embarrassment, she tossed her head and stuck her hand on her hip. "Is that supposed to be a compliment, that I'm not a good liar?"

"It's supposed to mean I don't think you're part of a conspiracy to destroy me. You're not cold and ruthless enough for it."

No, she was hot and dangerously weak, at least where Jase was concerned. Thankfully, he was more interested in talking about the Alpine Sky trying to ruin his business. "If this is the same old accusation that Matt is behind everything that's happened, you're wrong." Matt's approach had been nothing but ethical. Underhanded and illegal was more David's style.

The thought startled her, jolting her off track. How far would David go to prove his worth to Ruth Ann? And how far would Ruth Ann go to get what she wanted? Her mind raced, following new lines of suspicion.

Jase wasn't as easily distracted. "I'm not going to argue with you about it, Zoe. You don't have to agree, you just have to stay away from this fight. Their tactics are dirty, and they're bound to get worse. I want you out of the line of fire, and away from all of the finger-pointing that's going to follow."

He was trying to protect her? She wasn't even going to try to wrap her mind around that one, because what he was suggesting wasn't possible. "Getting you to sell is my project. What do you expect me to do, quit my job?"

"Quit, go on vacation, take an extended leave of absence—whatever it takes to get away from the Alpine Sky. It would be even better if you could get out of Barringer's Pass entirely."

Did he really have no clue about the realities of running a business that did more than serve up beer and music? "I think you've been hiding out in this saloon for too long. I can't just leave my job at a moment's notice. And I certainly wouldn't leave when they need me most. If someone is doing these things to convince you to sell—and I admit that's what it looks like—then I think I should try to find out who it is."

"No," he said forcefully. "You shouldn't. You should stay out of it."

"You don't get to tell me what to do, Jase."

"I'm trying to *help* you."

"How, by getting me fired for walking away from my job? How would that look?"

"Jesus, Zoe!" His explosive response startled her, and she stared as he raked a hand through his hair in exasperation. "Forget for one fucking minute about how something will make you look! You're so concerned with your professional image that you can't see you're walking straight into another scandal. Don't you get it? You need to get far away from this before you get labeled and branded all over again."

Branded. She went still, finally registering his distress. It was real to him, as if he'd seen it happen. She stared at him as a familiar fear crept out from the corners of her mind, spreading over it like a black cloud. Swallowing against the sudden tightness in her throat, she said, "It's started again, hasn't it?" Her voice was barely above a whisper. "People are talking about me, saying I set the fire, aren't they?"

His eyes clouded with anger, answering her question even before he spoke. "I made it clear you weren't involved, Zoe." His voice was gravelly, holding back emotion. "I'll repeat it to the whole town if I have to. But I can't stop it from happening again. The Alpine Sky is determined to get what they want—they already have plans in place with the zoning board. They don't care who gets hurt, or who gets blamed, even if it's one of their own." His eyes glittered in the faint light, as intense as his voice. "Get out, Zoe. Don't let them hurt you again."

She stared for several seconds, too numb to respond. This couldn't happen! Not when it wasn't her fault. She'd followed all the rules, outshone every shining example. Her wild past was just that—the past. Yet when something happened and they needed someone to blame, there she was, one of the Larkin girls conveniently in the middle of things. Suddenly, all those years of being a model citizen counted for nothing.

Tears burned behind her eyelids, but she blinked them away furiously. She wouldn't cry. Feeling sorry for herself would just turn her into the victim they wanted her to be. She wasn't the town's wild child anymore, and she wasn't anyone's victim.

She was a fighter. She wouldn't let them do this to her again.

Vulnerability showed in her eyes, raw and painful. Jase had seen it. A second later it was gone, hidden behind that ever-present wall of determination. But it was too late for her to pretend the gossip and rumors hadn't cut her to the bone.

"They can't hurt me," she muttered aloud as she lifted her chin. "I won't let them."

"It doesn't matter how tough you are," he said quietly. Gently, because he'd glimpsed that fragile side underneath. "Gossip and speculation hurt."

She studied him for several seconds. "Is that what happened to you when Adam died—people jumped to their own conclusions?"

A twinge of the old pain stabbed his chest. He hadn't expected her thoughts to go that way, but he wouldn't back away from it. "No. There were no rumors about me, Zoe. Just facts. I goaded Adam into a stupid race, dared him to reach beyond his ability. He couldn't. The accident was my fault." He reached out, smoothing the hair away from her face, running his thumb along the line of her jaw. "It's not the same, Zoe. You haven't done anything wrong, but you're going to get blamed if you're connected in any way. You're too convenient. I don't want that to happen."

"You want me to run away from a fight."

He frowned, stopping short of running his thumb across her lower lip, the temptation almost overwhelming. He hadn't realized how determined she was to salvage her reputation in Barringer's Pass. "It's not running away when it's not your fight to begin with, Zoe."

"Whoever set that fire *made it* my fight."

"If you leave and the incidents continue, like we both know they will, people will realize you weren't involved."

Her mouth pursed into a stubborn pucker. "If I leave, I'll look like I'm guilty, and hiding from the police." The imaginary criticism stiffened her back. "I don't run and hide, and I don't quit just because things get tough."

Her accusing look stabbed clean through him and made the unspoken part as obvious as if she'd said it aloud. "Like I did?"

She didn't hesitate. "Didn't you?"

His concern for her feelings obviously wasn't reciprocated. That brief flash of vulnerability was buried so deeply now that he wondered if he'd imagined it. Maybe he'd tried to see softness where there was only cold, hard determination.

"I wasn't hiding," he ground out. "I was avoiding causing any more deaths."

"If you believe that, you're the only one who does. Why won't you give Adam his share of the blame?"

He nearly rocked from the blow. She wasn't just cold, she was out of line. "You don't know anything about it," he said, the menace in his voice obvious even to him.

She didn't appear to be fazed. "I know Adam wasn't stupid. He knew what he was doing, and he knew the risks. You hid from life, Jase. But life includes mistakes. Everyone makes them. You, Adam, me. I don't know about you, but I'm going to overcome mine. I'll convince people that I've changed. If I have to be even more straightlaced and proper to do it, then I will."

"*More* straightlaced?" He barked out a laugh in disbelief, using it to cover the irritation he felt when she'd brought up Adam's death. "Hell, Zoe, you're already so straight you're as rigid as a steel rod. I suggest you learn how to bend a little before you break."

He'd never torn into a woman like that, and he wasn't proud that he'd done it now. But holy Christ, Zoe could press his buttons! And she'd needed to hear it. Not that she'd appreciate it—most women would probably slap his face and break into tears. He didn't think Zoe would.

He was right, the glint in her eyes was pure hatred. "Thank you so much for pointing out my faults when you can't even deal with your own. You're a great example of how to overcome emotional problems."

He gave her a level look. If he expected her to believe anything he said, he had to concede the truth. "You're right. I've been avoiding life for too long. And that's going to change. But you're hiding behind your proper, professional image as much as I've been hiding inside this saloon."

Criticizing her image would have been more effective if she'd been wearing her ubiquitous blue suit and sensible shoes. But for once she wasn't dressed for work. Her skimpy top tied in front, leaving several inches of skin between it and her low-slung jeans. If he didn't dislike her so intensely he would be tempted to rest his hands on her bare skin just above the curve of her hips and pull her against him, then mold his palms against the curve of her ass . . .

God, he was sick. Imagining foreplay at the same time he was verbally tearing her to shreds.

She didn't look like she cared to speak another word to him, but she managed to bite out, "I want to go home now."

"Fine." Which meant he had to drive her. Shit. Well, the sooner he got her out of his hair, the better. "Let's go," he muttered.

The truck keys were in his pocket, so he led her around the Rusty Wire to the parking lot. He wanted to take her hand, but was sure she'd punch him if he tried. She followed without a word, getting in and staring straight ahead into the night. She'd probably be happy to go the rest of her life without speaking to him. He started the truck and backed out, speaking without looking at her. "Where am I going?"

"Eighty-four eleven Larkspur."

The town was small enough that he didn't have to ask where Larkspur was. Neither of them said a word as he drove through the well-lit downtown, still busy with the Saturday-night restaurant crowd, then up the darker residential streets where houses huddled on the wooded slopes above Barringer's Pass. She sat in stony silence, letting him navigate on his own. He spotted her house easily when he saw her red Escape parked under the sketchy shelter of a carport. He pulled up behind it. The house was small, easily eighty years old, and the carport wouldn't be much protection against the snowdrifts of winter. He didn't know what kind of money Zoe made, but it obviously wasn't affording her a luxurious lifestyle.

She was out of the truck without a thank-you or a good-bye, which he figured proved how furious she was. Proper behavior was so ingrained in everything she did, the snub had to be deliberate.

He met her in front of the truck. She raised her cool stare to him. "I didn't invite you in."

"I'm walking you to your door."

"Thank you, but I know the way."

He stared back in reply and held his arm out toward the house. She narrowed her eyes in a final glare and walked past him. He followed. A pissy attitude wouldn't stop him from seeing a woman to her door when he brought her home alone at night.

Her house was on a more level patch of ground than his, with only a small step up to the cracked slab of cement that passed for a front porch. He stood right behind her while she turned her key in the lock, questioning his own wisdom of being so close to her. He could have watched her enter from inside the truck if he was concerned about her safety. But no, he had to torture himself with the light, airy scent she wore and watch the porch light cast a shimmer of gold over her red hair.

This was crazy. He wanted her. Zoe was obstinate, contrary, and perpetually irritating, yet he burned with the need to strip her naked and make her scream with desire. If she tugged him close right now and, with a husky whisper, invited him to her bedroom, he'd gladly go.

She pushed the door open and turned to face him. He watched her hesitate the tiniest bit, her brows together and lower lip between her teeth, and his fantasies went on high alert. Then she stepped inside and slammed the door in his face.

He walked back to the truck and backed out of the

driveway, taking one last look at Zoe's house. A flicker caught his eye. In the living room, a curtain peeked open, then whipped back in place.

Despite his annoyance, a slow smile spread across his face. Something impossible to ignore lay between them, just below the surface, and he'd bet anything she felt it, too.

Zoe barely had time to stomp to the bedroom and throw her boots at the shoe rack when the phone rang. She snatched it up without even checking the caller ID, snapping out, "Hello."

"Hi, you got a minute?"

Sophie. She sat on the bed. "Sure, what's up?"

"You can't tell Mom we talked about this."

A prickle of concern slipped across the back of her neck; it had been too long since she'd been to the commune. "Why, is something wrong with her?"

"No, nothing like that," Sophie reassured her. "It's kind of about you."

A sinking feeling hit her stomach. "She heard I was questioned by the police, didn't she? Who told her?"

"She was in town yesterday, at Maggie's store. They went out to lunch, said hi to a few friends, the usual. It came up once or twice. Or more."

Great, now her mother would think her daughter had taken a dive off the deep end again. "I'll call her first thing tomorrow. She needs to know I didn't have anything to do with the fire."

"Don't be silly, she knows that. But that's the problem, she thinks someone needs to defend you against the establishment pigs."

"Oh, crap." Her mother's outrage was nothing to be

taken lightly; no one could rally around a social injustice like a commune full of old hippies. "She'll just call more attention to it."

"I think that's the point. She wants people to realize you're being unjustly persecuted, and you'd never do a single thing to hurt others."

"It's a hard sell. I wasn't exactly a Girl Scout, Soph. People remember."

"Then they don't know you. All your rebellious acts were self-destructive. You'd never target someone else."

Zoe blinked at the insight. Drinking too much, sleeping around, skipping school . . . it had all been part of her personal war against rules, aimed at hurting all the authority figures in her life. In the end she'd hurt no one but herself.

"You're pretty smart, you know that?"

She snorted. "Mom's the one who said it. I think she'd like to say it to everyone in town, starting with the chief of police."

Zoe groaned. "I don't want that kind of attention. If we leave it alone, it'll blow over." She wasn't so sure about that, but knew it didn't stand a chance of blowing over if the commune got involved. "I'll call her tomorrow. Thanks for letting me know."

She hung up, pondering how she could keep her commune family out of it.

The sudden chime of the doorbell jerked her out of her thoughts. Zoe's gaze flew to the clock beside the bed—after 11, too late for anyone to be at her front door. Unless it was an emergency.

Or unless Jase had come back.

She jumped up and rushed down the hall, not daring to admit that she was hoping to see Jase's slow smile and muscular body standing outside her door. She turned the lock and peered outside. No one.

Opening the door wider, she stepped onto the porch. A prank? Lame, but there were a few kids down the road who might be bored enough to—

She sucked in a gasp as she turned toward the side of the house. Flames leapt high into the night sky, coming from a large object in back of her car, just outside the carport. Acting on instinct, she ran across the grass in her bare feet, twisted on the faucet at the side of the house, and aimed the garden hose at the fire.

A stream of water hit the fire with little effect. It pushed the flames aside enough for her to see the source of the pyre—one of her large plastic garbage cans blazed like a dry tree in a forest fire, tongues of flame licking higher than the roof of the carport. Even as she sprayed it with water she smelled the gasoline and knew water would be useless. Twisting the water off, she watched, waiting for the fire to burn itself out. Already the fuel was nearly gone, and the stench of burning plastic filled her nostrils. When she couldn't take the noxious fumes any longer, she went in the side door, found the fire extinguisher under the kitchen sink, and took it outside, spraying the melted wreckage of her trash can. It hissed out under a blanket of white foam. A hunched mound of melted plastic remained, dark brown topped with fluffy white foam, listing like a melted cupcake. She'd need a trash can for her trash can.

Belatedly, she looked around. The nighttime neighborhood was quiet; even her brief inferno hadn't drawn anyone's attention. If anyone watched, it was from deep in the shadows of a neighbor's yard. She suspected they did; kids would stick around to appreciate their handiwork. She didn't discount that it could be connected to the fire and vandalism at the Rusty Wire, but if it was, she didn't understand the message. She worked for the Alpine Sky, not the saloon. If someone thought she was too friendly with Jase Garrett, they really weren't paying attention.

Disgusted, she picked up the fire extinguisher and headed toward the front door. She wasn't sure she'd closed it behind her in her initial panic.

She had. But she hadn't been looking at it when she slammed it behind her, or she would have stopped right there. Even in the faint glow from the streetlight down the block, black letters stood out against the faded white paint of the door. The fresh spray paint still dripped and ran, giving the words an eerie look, like the title of a horror movie.

ONCE TRASH, ALWAYS TRASH

Zoe's chest constricted painfully, shallow breaths scraping her throat. She glanced at the ruined hulk of the trash can in her driveway, then back at the message on her door as she swallowed against the hard lump in her throat.

Now she got it.

Chapter Twelve

Jase browsed through the new fishing lures at Marshall's Hardware, selecting one called a Silver Flashing Wiggler. Dangling the bit of metal and plastic to catch the sunlight, he considered the likelihood of a trout mistaking it for a bug. Not much, he decided. Too much flash and not enough wiggle. Trout were selective, and it took just the right combination to catch their attention.

A streak of red-gold touched the corner of his gaze, and he looked up to see a bouncy red ponytail cross the end of the aisle. His eyebrows shot up. Zoe?

He walked to the end of the aisle and looked toward the front of the store. It *was* Zoe, heading for the check-out counter, hair swinging in rhythm with her hips. He turned quickly, looking past the bait and tackle aisle to make sure Marshall's hadn't added a cosmetics section between electrical and paint. They hadn't. Since a hardware store was the last place he expected to see Zoe early on a Sunday morning, he followed her.

He was no more than twenty feet behind her and about to call her name when she spotted a large, hairy man coming through the front door of the store. She stopped dead, staring. Jase winced, and hoped she didn't make her revulsion obvious. The man's ZZ Top beard and long gray ponytail looked clean, but decidedly unkempt, matching his ripped jeans and worn sandals, not up to snooty Alpine Sky standards, he was sure. Neither was the tie-dyed bandanna wrapped around the man's head like a sweatband. He didn't blame her for staring, but felt slightly embarrassed that she didn't move politely aside. He had started forward to take her arm and forcibly move her out of her shocked stare when she gave a delighted squeal of "Pete!" and threw herself into the man's arms.

Zoe clung to the big man's neck as he spun her in a circle, then set her down, both of them laughing. Jase watched, mesmerized, as they exchanged greetings like long-lost relatives. "Long lost" was an apt description for the hairy man, who looked like he might have been wandering the mountains for the past couple of years.

He didn't realize he was staring until Zoe saw him and stared in return. "Jase!"

"Hi," he said, his gaze moving from one to the other.

She looked more off balance than he felt, so he stepped forward and held out his hand to the large man. "Jase Garrett. I'm a friend of Zoe's."

"Far out." The man gave him an engaging grin and shook his hand. "Pete Parnelli. I'm part of Zoe's family."

It seemed like an odd way to say it, rather than Uncle Pete or Cousin Pete. Zoe must have sensed his confusion. "I grew up on a commune. Pete's practically like a dad."

If the rest of the commune members looked like Pete, he imagined proper, well-dressed Zoe was the black sheep of the family. The idea amused him so much he had to bite back a grin. "I'd heard there was a commune up on Two Bears," he told Pete. "Been there a long time, hasn't it?" Stuck in a time warp from 1970, obviously.

"That's us. The People's Free Earth Commune," Pete said proudly. He nodded at Jase's hand. "You fly-fish?"

Jase realized he was still holding the Silver Flashing Wiggler. "When I can."

"Outasight. Ever tie your own lures?"

Jase let the grin through, enjoying Pete's open friendliness. "Wouldn't be a true fisherman if I didn't try. I'm not very good at it, though. You?"

"I've had some luck with a few I made."

"Some luck?" Zoe gave his shoulder a friendly shove. "Aren't you the modest one." From the way she said it, Jase suspected the guy was a master.

"You should have Zoe bring you up sometime. I'll show you the secret to making a lure they can't resist. Then we can try it out."

"Far out!" Jase purposely repeated the outdated slang while raising an amused eyebrow at Zoe. "Why don't we do that, Zoe?"

Zoe's enthusiasm backed down a notch. "Um, work's pretty hectic lately, but I'll try to get up there soon," she told Pete. Grabbing her shopping basket, she moved to the checkout. "Gotta run now, but it was great to see you. Tell Mom I said hi."

Pete flashed a peace sign, told Jase, "Later, man,"

and sauntered off. Jase fell in behind Zoe as she handed a can to the clerk.

"What are you doing, following me?" she hissed. "And quit sucking up to my family."

He smiled. "Rein in that ego, honey. It's not all about you. I come here all the time." He tried to see what she was buying, but the clerk was too fast getting it in a bag. It looked like turpentine. He tried to picture her in paint-stained clothes, brushing a new coat of latex on the walls, but couldn't see it. "Pete seems like an interesting guy. I wouldn't mind going up there to see how he makes his lures."

She scowled at the counter and didn't respond. She was probably still mad from last night, but he suspected it was the invitation to visit the commune that really pissed her off. She stayed at a low boil as she swiped her credit card and signed, then grabbed the bag from the clerk. "See you around."

He watched her leave. The clerk looked at him, then pointedly at his hand. "You buying that?"

Jase held up the Silver Flashing Wiggler, giving it one last consideration. "If you were a trout, would you eat that?"

The kid gave him a bored look. Probably only responded to a Big Mac set directly in front of him. "Never mind, I don't want it." He set the lure aside. "Can you tell me what you just rang up for that lady?"

The kid hesitated, as if trying to decide whether there was a reason not to do it. "Why?"

"Because we were talking and she recommended the product, but I forgot the name."

"Oh. Mason and Hewett painter's solvent."

"Huh. I wonder why she thought I needed that,"

he mused out loud. When the kid didn't respond, Jase gave him a helpless look to kick-start some customer service instincts.

He shrugged with disinterest. "Most people use it to take off spray paint."

Jase frowned, not sure why she'd need that, but getting a bad feeling about it. Spray paint that had to be removed was generally where it shouldn't be. Like graffiti. "I'll have to come back later," he told the clerk.

"Whatever."

He didn't see her car in the parking lot, but that didn't matter now that he knew where she lived. Ten minutes later he pulled into the driveway of 8411 Larkspur just as she was dragging a new plastic garbage can out of the back of the Escort. He took it from her and set it inside the carport next to a blackened, half-melted piece of plastic. He studied the twisted mass. "You're hard on garbage cans."

She shrugged and looked away. He took another look at the melted mass, sniffing. Then looked around. In front of his truck on the gravel drive he saw a large black smudge with a light center. He gave her a puzzled look. "You set it on fire?"

"It's none of your business."

He didn't buy it. Zoe had a temper, but it wasn't like her to pull something so irresponsible. He strolled over to the blackened stones, pondering them as she retrieved her bag from the Escort. What had happened here? Spray paint remover, he remembered, and his gaze automatically went to the house. The pale yellow aluminum siding was faded, but clean. In fact, the whole front of the house was tidy and free of graffiti, which made the front door stand out—the center was covered with a large piece of cardboard. It hadn't been there last night. Dread settled in his gut as he strode to the front door.

She slammed the hatchback. "Hey! If you want to help, you could carry this for me." When he didn't stop, she ran around the corner of the house to intercept him. He was already ripping off the duct tape that held the cardboard to the door. "Jase, leave that alone. I told you, this is none of your business."

But the cardboard was already off.

ONCE TRASH, ALWAYS TRASH. He'd known he wouldn't like what he found, but the lurid letters were a kick in the gut. He could only imagine how they'd made her feel. Heart pounding with sudden fury, he turned. "Why didn't you tell me about this?" he demanded.

She stood straight, pale and tight lipped. "Because it's none—"

"It *is* my business, goddamnit! It's because of me that someone did this to you, and you know it. I told you to get out because it was going to get rough, and now someone else is telling you, too. When are you going to listen?"

"Never." She hadn't flinched when he yelled, and, tilting her chin up the way she did when her stubborn streak kicked in, she held her ground as he stepped close. "I make my own choices, and I fight my own battles. Besides, it's just stupid graffiti."

"And a burning garbage can that could have set your house on fire."

She met his hard stare. "Big deal."

"Don't play dumb, Zoe, it doesn't look good on you."

He knew adding insult to injury wouldn't help, but

damn it, she made him furious. Apparently, it was mutual. "Leave," she ordered through gritted teeth.

Instead, he snatched the bag she held in her hand and pulled out the paint solvent. "Get me a rag," he snapped.

"I certainly will not. This isn't about you."

He already knew arguing with her was futile. He dug his keys out of his pocket, using one to pry the metal lid off the can of solvent.

"Jase, I mean it."

He set the can aside and pulled his cotton T-shirt over his head. Wadding it into a ball, he picked up the can.

"Jase, stop!" She made a desperate grab for the shirt, but he held on. Her expression crumpled with defeat. "Don't ruin your shirt." Frustration kept the edge in her voice, but he knew he'd won when she sighed deeply. "I'll get a rag."

"Thank you." He meant it; he really liked the T-shirt.

She disappeared inside, leaving him on the porch. Two minutes later she came out with two rags. He took them both.

"One is for me," she said, reaching for it.

He jammed the extra rag into his waistband, out of her reach. "No, it isn't. Zoe, look at me." He waited until she huffed out an impatient breath, folded her arms, and met his eyes. "Listen to me carefully, because this is nonnegotiable. There's no way in hell I'm going to let you debase yourself by kneeling out here where all your neighbors and anyone driving by can see you while you scrub this filth off your door. I'm doing it, and you're going in the house. If anyone sees it before

I get it off, at least they'll know someone's got your back. Is that clear?"

Her eyes were suddenly overly bright. She blinked and swallowed hard, then turned without a word and went inside. He let out a relieved breath. Then tried not to be furious at the world that Zoe was so unaccustomed to having someone take her side.

Picking up the can, he set to work.

Zoe spent the next hour peeking out the living room window. He'd put his shirt back on—she tried not to be disappointed—and she could see small sweat stains under his arms. When she could tell he was finishing up, she poured two glasses of lemonade and went outside.

He gave her an appreciative smile as he took the glass. "Thanks."

An hour had given her plenty of time to feel guilty . . . and grateful. She sat on the edge of the porch, bare feet planted on the sidewalk as she made her confession. "I'm the one who should thank you."

He settled beside her and took a long drink, downing nearly half the glass. She watched his throat move as he swallowed, noticed the thin sheen of sweat on his neck, the bulge of muscles in his upper arm. Realizing she was staring, she looked away before he noticed. If he weren't so physically distracting, it would be easier to say this. Feeling awkward, she rubbed her toe across the rough cement surface of the walk, then glanced at him and spit it out. "I'm sorry I was so bitchy. I'm not used to people taking my side."

"I gathered that." She noticed he didn't deny the bitchy part, but he smiled at her, a slow smile that gradually widened to a grin.

Responding to his smile was automatic. For a moment she was caught by the warmth in his eyes, her heart tripping as her mind went blank. As infuriating as the man was, he had a physical attraction she couldn't deny. She liked looking at him. Liked remembering what it had felt like when he'd held her close and . . .

Damn it! She blinked and frowned, irritated that she could lose herself in a simple gaze. She kept her eyes on the sidewalk. "Jase, I appreciate what you did, but . . ."

"But you still won't do what I asked. You won't walk away."

"I can't. But I can do something else." She met his expectant gaze. "I have an idea who might be behind everything that's been happening to you."

"So do I—Matt Flemming."

"No." She glared, indignant. "You keep accusing him when he's been nothing but considerate of you."

"Uh-huh."

It seemed the only way to convince him was to prove him wrong, which she intended to do. "Someone else has a lot to gain if you sell, and he's totally without scruples. He could easily have done everything that's happened, or arranged to have it done."

"Who?"

She paused, remembering how he hadn't wanted to rat out Jennifer. But he'd had years of loyalty to base that on; she had no reason to protect David. "My direct supervisor. David's doing anything he can to suck up to Ruth Ann Flemming and get me out of his way. Matt doesn't think highly of him, but if he can get you to sell, Ruth Ann would probably give him whatever he wants."

"You work with a fun bunch of people."

She drank her lemonade and stared morosely at the sidewalk. "Tell me about it."

They sat in silence for a few minutes. Finally, Jase said, "I like your friend Pete."

She glanced over to see if he was being sarcastic, and was pleased that he wasn't. "He's a great guy. A lot of people think he's weird, though. You know, the beard and ponytail and all. I've seen some townies point and snicker behind his back."

He laughed softly. "I'm a townie, huh?"

She smiled at it herself; it had been a long time since she'd used the term, since before she'd become a townie herself. "The commune is another world. When we went into town we looked different, so it became an us-and-them mentality. Hippies and townies."

He grinned. "I can't see you as a hippie."

"Picture hair down to here." She indicated a line a few inches above her waist. "Ripped jeans, several woven leather bracelets, and beads."

He cocked his head, giving her a long look. "I'll bet that side of you is still there. I'd like to see it."

She didn't know what to say to that, and looked away, uncomfortable. She knew he was talking about more than her clothes; it was the rigid behavior they'd argued about last night. His judgmental words still hurt, mostly because she knew they were true. She *had* become rigid, with all the lack of fun that implied. It had felt necessary in order to redeem her reputation in the eyes of those despised townies, but she was starting to wonder if it was worth it. Some of them would never believe she was anything but a wild child at heart.

"So that's the reason for your big teenage rebellion?"

He must have wanted to steer away from another argument. Relieved, because she did, too, she nodded. "Basically. We had a lot of freedom at the commune, which is why our grandmother insisted we stay with her during the school year instead of being home-schooled. She wanted us to learn how to fit in, but it backfired. Maggie and I handled it okay until high school, when the rules started feeling oppressive. We weren't used to so much structure. We rebelled in the only way we could, by breaking the rules."

"*All* the rules?"

"Every one we could. Skipping school, failing classes, smoking pot . . ." She hesitated to admit it, but it was suddenly important that Jase know the real Zoe Larkin. "And sleeping around. For a few years I was what you'd call easy. I did whatever would shock my mother and grandmother."

"Sounds like you did a good job of it."

"My grandmother was humiliated." She felt her cheeks blush just thinking about it. "I owe her a lot for not kicking me out and washing her hands of me."

"How about your mom?"

She shook her head, amused by the memory. "I don't know if anything shocks Mom, short of polluting the planet, which will send her into orbit. Let me warn you now, never toss a gum wrapper on the ground in front of anyone from the People's Free Earth Commune. But improper social behavior . . ." She sighed. "Before she went AWOL from society, my mom earned a doctorate in psychology at Berkeley. Just my luck, huh? She explained in clinical terms exactly why

I was acting out, and told me to do whatever I had to in order to find my place in the world, and to remember that she'd never stop loving me."

He burst out laughing. "I'll bet that took the wind out of your sails."

"Well, I didn't feel quite so radical after that, but it still took me a while to figure out that I didn't do well in an unstructured environment. I needed boundaries and goals. So I set up my own rules, and made a list of the things I wanted to accomplish."

"You have a list?" A spark of interest flashed through his amusement. "Out of curiosity, how does one go about getting on it?"

She felt herself color so fast that she looked away, hoping he hadn't notice. She recalled typing his name on her list, with a question mark, and her cursor hovering behind it, leaving her intentions open.

He could come off it just as easily. One moment of insanity wasn't a commitment to anything.

"One doesn't. It's just for abstract goals."

"I see. Very anal." When she shot him a dirty look, he held his hands up in surrender. "Not criticizing, just saying. And I think your mom's a pretty smart lady."

"She is. She's just . . . different. They all are. It's a true commune, you know. Shared work, shared profits, and as environmentally friendly as they can get without giving up their cell phones."

"Modern hippies." He nodded happily. "I like it. Will you take me up there sometime?" When she blinked with surprise, he reminded her, "Pete invited me."

"I know, but . . ." She scrunched up her eyebrows. "Most people don't want anything to do with them."

"Why?"

"Because they look like 1970, and except for phones, they live like 1870. They grow most of their own food and keep goats for milk and cheese. They don't watch TV and they homeschool their kids. They don't much care for the government, and they're good at skirting laws they don't like. They're . . . different."

He leaned back on his elbows. "I don't want to watch TV with them or have a political debate, I want to see Pete's fishing lures." He looked suddenly pained, as if he'd just realized she had a fatal disease. "Oh my God, you don't fish, do you? If you did, you'd understand how monumental it is that he's willing to show me his lure-making secrets."

She found it hard to act concerned. "Is it a serious flaw in my character?"

"Tragic." He shook his head sadly. "But you're pretty and otherwise smart, so we can still be friends."

The word sank in slowly. *Friends.* She swiveled on her butt so she could look him directly in the eyes. "Are we friends?"

His grin was wicked. "I hope so, because I intend for us to have another of those flaming-hot kisses, then see where things go if you don't run away afterward."

The fire in his eyes nearly stopped her heart.

Her head swam as heat raced to her cheeks at the memory of that kiss. A completely different sort of heat flared between her thighs. The response was so sharp it unnerved her. Lust was fine, but she didn't care for feeling out of control, which was how she'd felt kissing Jase. She didn't have to do it again to know where it would go, and that she wouldn't be able to stop it.

It would never happen. But just because she

wouldn't give up control, it didn't mean she was afraid. She drew a steadying breath and lifted her chin. "I didn't run away."

He grinned. "No, you didn't. We were interrupted."

The fire in his eyes burned hotter. He still leaned back on his elbows, making no move to touch her, but he felt closer. For a panicked moment she realized she had inched closer, drawn like a magnet. His grin dared her to go all the way. Part of her was ready to fall on him right there on her front porch, and she knew he wouldn't do a thing to stop her. Taking a shaky breath, she threw up the only obstacle she could think of. "I don't think your girlfriend would care for you kissing me."

"What girlfriend?"

"The little blonde who flutters her eyes adoringly at you."

He wrinkled his brow, then burst out laughing. "My niece, Hailey. She's been sucking up big-time, trying to get me to teach her every last thing I know about pool."

Her cheeks flooded with color again, and this time she couldn't hide from his amused look, which made it even worse. She'd give anything to take it back, but could only manage a lame "Oh."

The laughter in his eyes was gradually replaced by something far more intense, pinning her in place. "Hailey doesn't give a damn who my friends are. Or who I kiss."

Great, nothing to stop him. Or to stop her from throwing her reputation away with a do-nothing saloon owner. She drew on every rigid, straightlaced impulse she could find. "That's not the sort of activity I normally engage in with my friends." You couldn't get more prudish than that.

"Okay, then I guess we can't be friends." He got to his feet suddenly, and she stared up at him. Leaning down, he cupped her chin, sending her heart on a mad gallop. "Because we are definitely going to do that again," he said, his voice low and certain. Then his lips found hers with a quick, teasing taste of what he had promised.

He pulled back, his direct gaze as dizzying as his kiss. She barely had time to blink before he turned and left.

She watched him walk to his truck, too stunned to move. He backed out, sent her a casual smile and a wave, and drove off. She watched until the black tailgate was out of sight, then sagged. She was so screwed.

Lying back on the warm cement porch, she stared blankly at the puffy white clouds drifting over Tappit's Peak, trying to wrap her mind around the shocking realization. Despite her ability to arouse the interest of checklist-perfect Matt Flemming, the man she wanted was Jase Garrett.

By the time Matt picked her up Sunday evening, she'd analyzed it to death. She'd finally decided she knew what made Jase so irresistible—he accepted her, hippie commune, wild past, and all. The whole package. Matt only knew the present-day Zoe Larkin, the one who wore suits and gave 100 percent to her job. If he could still accept her once she told him about her past, she figured it would be an instant aphrodisiac. He'd be beyond perfect, and she'd be so hot for him that her feelings for Jase would fizzle like an ember hitting a bucket of water.

Theoretically. She meant to test that theory tonight.

The bouquet Matt handed her at the door was gorgeous. He kissed her cheek, then stood back to look her over from head to toe with a big smile. "You're stunning, Zoe. I hope our reservation at the Peak measures up to the standard you set."

The Peak. The nicest restaurant in a town that prided itself on its four- and five-star resorts and restaurants. She smiled nervously. If he was going to be uncomfortable about dating a Larkin girl, the Peak was the last place he'd want to be seen with her.

She plucked at the bouquet. "Matt, before we go out there's something we need to talk about."

"That sounds serious." He smiled, as if nothing could be that wrong between them. If only that was true.

"Matt, you didn't grow up in Barringer's Pass, and I know you haven't lived here long. We might get high-profile visitors, but we're a small town, with a small-town mentality."

"Are you trying to tell me the nightlife is limited? Because I already know that. I'm okay with flying to L.A. or New York for a weekend every now and then."

He said it as casually as someone else might suggest driving to Denver. He not only met all the qualifications for the perfect man, he went above and beyond them.

Don't get distracted.

"Uh, no, that's not what I was getting at. I'm talking about how everyone knows everyone else, and how gossip gets around."

"I've heard that. Do you want to get a vase for those? You're going to turn your fingers green if you keep picking at those leaves."

"In a minute." She laid the flowers on the closest living room chair and clasped her hands together to keep her fingers still. "Matt, I'm trying to tell you that if you'd been around ten years ago, you would have heard people talking about me and my older sister. The Larkin girls had a reputation." She looked down at her hands, too nervous to look him in the eye. "It wasn't a good one. In fact, it was pretty bad. If you ask around town, you'll still hear about it."

"I know."

She jerked her head up. "You *know*?" My God, he'd been here barely a week, and he'd spent most of his time at the resort. Was she that infamous?

"Zoe, I told you, I have confidence in your ability. I didn't come to that opinion without something to base it on. I had extensive background searches done on both you and David before I ever came to the resort. I learned about your outstanding performance at the Alpine Sky, and yes, I learned about the way you and Maggie tore a swath through this town when you were teenagers." He raised an eyebrow. "Mostly through the men."

She would have blushed if she wasn't so stunned. Her handsome, rich boss had known about her wild child reputation when he'd kissed her and when he'd let her know he wasn't giving up on winning her affections. Maybe she *would* blush.

"Did you think that would stop me from going out with you?"

"Well, uh, yes."

"I'll try not to be hurt that you thought I was so shallow."

Now she *did* blush. "I didn't. I thought you might

be justifiably concerned about your image, especially since people around here don't know you yet."

He chuckled softly, pulled her close, and kissed her. "I'm pleased to be seen with you, and I'm sorry you were worried. Okay?"

She smiled. It was more than okay. Now she had absolutely no reason not to get all tingly over Matt's kisses and feel hopeful about their possible future together.

She wasn't tingling yet, but that last kiss hadn't counted. She'd still been in shock. Next time she'd be ready for it.

Dinner was pleasant. Being with Matt was pleasant. With Jase she always felt like a tightly strung instrument, vibrating at every word or touch, but Matt made her feel relaxed. Even afterward, riding in his sporty Mercedes with the top down, she leaned her head back and closed her eyes in contentment, enjoying the warm night air. The soft purr of the engine and the breeze playing with her hair lulled her as Matt shifted gears with smooth efficiency on the steep mountain roads. She didn't even open her eyes to see where they were until they came to a stop and the engine was silent.

She turned her head, taking in the artfully placed boulders near the entrance to a modern condominium. Pine and aspen trees crowded close, giving the unit the sense of seclusion that made the Pine Hollows unit popular with their single guests. Surprised, she looked at Matt. "This is your place."

"I thought you might like to see it."

Even if she'd been naive enough to take that at face value, the steady burn in his gaze would have told her he'd brought her here for more than a tour of his new condo. He waited quietly as she considered the implications of taking their relationship to a new level. For such an important turning point, her decision felt deceptively anticlimactic. "I'd like that."

He smiled and reached out to tuck a strand of hair behind her ear. She waited for the expected shiver of delight from his touch, but felt only a sense of satisfaction at her decision.

That had to be a good thing. They'd gone right past the shivery, tingling phase to a sense that intimacy was the next logical step. It was a sign of maturity that she wasn't dizzy with passion. She wasn't a kid bent on proving something, and this wasn't a wild impulse.

She was going to have sex with Matt Flemming. It was possibly the smartest decision of her life.

Chapter Thirteen

She was glad he didn't go through the pretense of showing her every room. He walked directly to the living room bar and said, "Look around if you want to. Would you like something to drink?"

"No thanks." She'd had wine at dinner, and any more alcohol might dull her senses. She wasn't going to make love with the perfect man and remember part of it as a pleasant blur.

Matt drank from his glass, then set it down on the coffee table and joined her by the French doors. "Nice view," he murmured, not looking outside. Taking her chin in his hand, he tilted her face up and kissed her. She relaxed into it, parting her lips and tasting whiskey as his tongue slipped across hers in a sensual dance. His mouth moved from her lips as he kissed her cheek, nibbled her earlobe, then swiped his tongue inside her ear.

Goose bumps raced across her shoulders. They might actually qualify as tingles, if that's what she was looking for. She wasn't. She'd decided that was for unexpected passion, the kind that sneaked up on you when you didn't expect it. She *expected* passion tonight. The hell with Maggie's tingles.

She ran her hands over Matt's chest, then slipped her arms around him as he kissed her again. His hands found her hair. "I'm glad you wore it down," he said, letting the strands slip through his fingers the same way her stylist did when contemplating layers. "It's sexy."

She almost told him that down seemed to be the consensus, then realized she was picturing Jase touching her hair as he left her table, his voice low and intimate as he told her that he liked it down. She didn't want Matt to ask who else had told her that. She didn't want to think about Jase at all.

To distract herself, and because she hadn't done it before, she ran her hand through his hair and watched it fall back with barely a strand out of place. Jeez, even his hair was perfect. Medium length, with several shades of blond. With his mother's background in modeling, she wondered how he'd escaped the runways. He would have been ideal for it. Maggie's comparison to a Ken doll had been apt—well-dressed, handsome, and . . . plastic?

No! Not Ken at all. Matt was real and warm, with desires that would never have occurred to Maggie's Ken doll when she'd made him kiss her Barbie.

Desires Matt wasn't shy about expressing. His hand slid down her back to caress her butt, giving it a firm squeeze. "You have such a great ass," he growled in her ear, and used his grip on it to pull her closer. His other hand slid down, too, both of them pressing her into the erection that snuggled against her lower abdomen. He moved back and forth, his heavy-lidded eyes watching her as he moved suggestively. There was no doubt he was aroused by her, and couldn't wait to do something about it.

She might be far from inexperienced, but she couldn't go from zero to oh-baby in one minute flat. "Matt, what's your hurry?" she asked, smiling to take the edge off and at the same time wondering if it might be better to let him see her discomfort. She'd expected him to be a little smooth and more subtle.

To her surprise, he chuckled in her ear, immediately slipping his hands around to frame her hips as he stepped back, separating their bodies. "You're right, I'm sorry. I've just wanted you since I first saw you. And I want to make it last. I want to savor every inch of you."

Perfect might be an inadequate word for this guy.

He leaned close and nibbled at her ear again. "You know you want me, too," he whispered.

In theory. Which made it all the more puzzling that the circles his thumbs were making over her nipples weren't doing a thing for her. There was no reason why a gorgeous hunk of man who was admittedly hot for her couldn't coax her into arousal.

She was concentrating on feeling some excitement stir in her breasts when one of Matt's hands dropped to her thigh and found its way under her dress. It rose fast, his goal clear, and without thinking she pressed her lower body against his so he was forced to detour to her butt. He squeezed hard as he rubbed against her, and the feeling that tightened her stomach and twisted in her gut had nothing to do with arousal.

Matt's thumb stopped moving and his hand

dropped from her backside. He gave her an impatient look. "What's wrong, Zoe?"

"I don't know." She tried smiling but doubted it came off well. She wasn't good at faking emotion. "I guess I'm nervous."

"You don't look nervous. You look scared." And he looked annoyed.

"Don't be silly, I'm not afraid of . . . you." She was going to say sex, but suddenly she didn't feel comfortable thinking about being naked in bed with Matt.

Which was ridiculous. They'd be great together. He respected her mind. Wanted her body. He was gorgeous. Handsome. She swallowed hard and looked down. Impressively aroused.

Her stomach did an unpleasant flip.

She took another step back, and wiped her palms against her dress. "Look, I don't think I can do this, Matt. I'm sorry." His face hardened into an expressionless mask. "I don't feel well," she added weakly. It wasn't a lie. In fact, she felt more upset every second.

His brows pulled together. "You don't look well. Maybe it was something you ate."

"I think it was." Now, *that* was a lie. The Peak would just have to take one for the team, because she wasn't about to tell Matt that he was the one turning her stomach. More precisely, it was the thought of him putting his hands all over her. Her reaction was confusing and annoying, but she knew it was true. She had to get out of here before she demonstrated just how sick she felt all over his carpet.

It must have been obvious. "Are you going to throw up? The bathroom is down the hall."

"I think you should just take me home." Her voice even had a convincing quiver.

He grabbed his keys and ushered her out of the condo, keeping a wary arm's length away as he helped her into the car. She was already starting to feel better now that sex was off the table, but she playacted all the way home, holding her stomach and offering a sickly smile when he looked her way. When that made her feel too guilty, she leaned against the door and closed her eyes, withdrawing into her pretend sickness so she wouldn't have to meet those beautiful blue eyes and wonder what the hell she was doing.

The perfect man and the perfect opportunity—how often did that come along? Maybe never again. But apparently she wasn't meant to have perfection, because she knew without a doubt she would never be getting into Matt Flemming's bed.

She let him help her to her door, and slipped inside with a mumbled good night. He caught the door before she could close it. "Are you sure you'll be okay? I could stay awhile."

If her sickness looked convincing, it was from mounting guilt. "I'll be fine. If I need anything my sister and brother-in-law are just a mile away."

He looked doubtful, and part of her wondered if she'd lost her mind, throwing away such a good guy. At the same time her hands trembled with the urgent need to get him out of there. "I'm sorry," she said again, and pushed the door shut.

She leaned against it until her hands stopped shaking and her stomach settled down. Then she took a long shower and tried to wipe away the fantasy playing in her head of a man's hands caressing her as his mouth savored every inch of her body, because the hands and mouth she pictured didn't belong to Matt Flemming.

Jase rarely heard from Jennifer outside of work, so when she called, he knew it was a come-fix-it call. A closet door this time. The kind of thing she would have asked her husband to fix if he'd been alive. That was exactly why Jase needed to be her landlord.

Convincing Jennifer to rent the house he'd bought as an "investment property" was his only successful attempt to help Adam's widow. It probably said more about the shortage of cheap rental properties in Barringer's Pass than about Jennifer's willingness to accept help. She'd been so stubborn about not taking a thing from him that he'd assumed it was because she held him responsible for her husband's death. Not that he'd blame her. But she'd relented on the small house, and he'd been able to make sure the rent was in line with her income.

She answered the door with a tissue in one hand, and he couldn't miss the redness in her eyes. He was suddenly nervous, not used to seeing emotionless Jennifer looking vulnerable. "Are you all right?"

"Fine." She sniffed and wiped at her nose. "Just a cold. Come on in. It's the closet in my bedroom."

He followed her to the back of the house, stopping at the bedroom doorway to stare. He'd been in every room of the house before, and seen all the modest, nondescript furnishings. The bedroom had changed. The bed looked like something out of a catalog, the mattress framed by a new brass headboard, and the puffy quilt piled invitingly with pillows. The dressers were new, too. Lacy curtains moved in the breeze, also new.

Jennifer never bought new things. Even though he thought she deserved them, seeing her bedroom transformed made him uncomfortable. The bed she'd shared with Adam was gone.

He cleared his throat. "You changed things."

"Oh. Yeah. That bed was pretty old, and the new one made the old furniture look even worse, so I ended up replacing everything. You know how it goes."

It might go that way for some people, but not Jennifer. He'd never met a more frugal person, denying herself luxuries to the point that Jase had wondered if she thought she didn't deserve them. Apparently he'd been wrong. She had to have been saving for years to buy all this.

"This is it," Jennifer said.

The bifold closet door was completely off its track and propped against the wall. "What happened?"

"I was trying to reach something on the shelf and I fell backward into the door. I guess I knocked it off the track. I tried to put it back, but it's too big and awkward." She sniffed again and blinked several times.

He looked at her closely, wondering if she was covering up an injury. "Are you sure you didn't hurt yourself when you fell?"

She looked away. "No, I told you, it's just a cold."

He frowned, then looked at the closet, trying to figure out what she'd done. Removing a door like that from its track required folding and lifting it, an odd thing to have happened if she fell against it. He couldn't imagine it happening any way but on purpose, yet couldn't argue with the fact that the door was off the track. With a mental shrug, he set the door in position and lifted it, locking it back in its track.

Jennifer gave a couple more sniffs and smiled weakly. "Thank you. I feel stupid making you come out here just for that. I probably shouldn't have been digging into that stuff anyway."

"Why don't you give it to me while I'm here, and I'll put it back up there for you." He was probably eight or nine inches taller than she was; she wouldn't be able to do it without standing on a chair.

She hesitated, glancing at what looked like two photo albums on the nightstand, then gave a trembling sigh. "Okay." Picking the albums up as if they were fragile, she handed them to Jase.

He couldn't miss the silver script across the padded white cover: OUR WEDDING. He knew without looking that the second album was pictures from their honeymoon in Jamaica.

Shit. She *had* been crying. Nine years, and the pain was still fresh. She clung to the memories, even though he wasn't sure why she'd decided to reminisce today.

Oh, hell. Yes, he did. This was July. They'd been married in July.

His eyes met her reddened gaze. "Was it today?" he asked softly.

She nodded, then lowered her gaze as if embarrassed to be caught reminiscing. "I don't think about him most of the time," she whispered. "Really, I don't. But today would have been our tenth anniversary. I had to see the pictures."

Ten years. It stabbed deeply, and twisted. They'd been married only one year when Adam died. He knew in Jennifer's mind they were still married. He didn't want to forget his friend, but dwelling on his loss wasn't healthy. Lately he'd realized just how unhealthy, keeping him stagnating for nearly a decade.

Jase, Russ, and Jennifer all had to move on, but of the three of them, Jennifer was the least able. She'd been the type to build her world around a man, too clingy for Jase's taste, but apparently fine with Adam. It hadn't ended just because he was gone. Whenever she asked Jase to fix something that Adam would have done himself, it was like ripping off a barely healed scab, allowing the wound to bleed again. Every single time. She couldn't hide it.

He knew from experience that she didn't want his sympathy, didn't want to be held so she could cry it out. Didn't want to be touched at all. All he could do was watch helplessly, knowing that if he hadn't challenged Adam to that last race he'd be here today and Jennifer would be the happy young woman she used to be.

Jase laid the photo albums carefully on the closet shelf and shut the door. The instinct to comfort her was strong and he stuck his hands in his pockets to keep from reaching out to her. "I'm sorry, Jen."

She nodded and wiped at her eyes with the backs of her hands. "I'm okay." She took another dramatic, trembling sigh and lifted her chin. Her mouth firmed, a fraction of her strength returning. "I'll be fine, Jase. Don't worry. I know I need to let it go, and I will. I'm making changes, getting rid of the stuff I kept just because it was ours. Like the bedding and the dressers." She allowed a tiny smile as she gestured around them at the room. "See? This time it only reflects me. Not flowery and delicate, but still feminine."

It was a good description of the light pinewood and the brass bed frame. He gave her an encouraging smile. "I like it."

She looked suddenly shy and hopeful. "Do you?"

It wasn't like Jennifer to ask his opinion. To ask *anyone's* opinion. If she'd asked him whether she should buy a Ford or a Honda, he would have been stunned. Asking whether he liked her new bedroom furniture sent a bolt of panic shooting down his spine. He was suddenly reminded of her resentful attitude toward Zoe, and his feeling that she might be jealous. That he might be her first romantic interest since losing Adam.

And that they were standing in her bedroom.

Jesus, it was like a perfect storm. The wedding album, the redecorated bedroom, and the door coming off its track, all reminding him of what she'd lost and the obligation he had to take care of her. If she'd wanted to drive home that point, she couldn't have planned it better.

The realization, unlikely as it was, gave him a chill. "Sure, it's nice," he said, suddenly anxious to get out of there. "Well, if you don't need anything else, I have some, uh, some fish I need to clean." He edged toward the door. "I left them on ice when you called, so I need to get back there now."

She gave him a bemused look. "Okay. Thanks for fixing the closet."

"No problem." He got to the door as fast as he could without actually running, then trotted to the truck as if his imaginary fish might spoil if he lingered another thirty seconds.

He breathed easier once he drove away, but knew

he wasn't entirely safe. They saw each other at the Rusty Wire nearly every evening. He'd have to be on his guard, making sure they were never alone before opening and after closing. He didn't know what might make him less desirable in her eyes if she hadn't already been turned off by his lazy do-nothing lifestyle, but he could at least be less available. Maybe she'd look elsewhere if he made it clear he was interested in another woman.

And it just so happened that he was. Not that he needed an excuse to go after another of those scorching-hot kisses from Zoe. He'd told her what he wanted. She hadn't raised any objections, and Zoe was good at objecting. If he could just get her to stop thinking and listen to her body, he could make her forget all about Matt Flemming.

Zoe could hardly concentrate at work. It was obvious that she felt better, and she knew Matt took note of it as soon as she came in Monday evening. He also couldn't miss the fact that her hair was pulled back in a twist, as unsexy as she could make it. She did her best to avoid talking to him, and a few demanding guests made it easy. Some computer whiz kid celebrating his twenty-first birthday wanted his hot tub filled with champagne, a request David cheerfully dumped in her lap as he left. After a lengthy discussion with their sommelier and a very brief discussion with the kid's credit card company, she approved it. Handling that was easier than dealing with the actress who wanted an extra queen-size bed for her two attack-trained Rottweilers, along with an in-room dog sitter while she went out for the evening. A volunteer for that one was hard to find, but the actress finally flashed enough hundred-dollar bills to convince a young man from security to expand his job description to include dog sitter. Zoe left him with a walkie-talkie in hand, just in case.

The distractions were welcome. She would have to face Matt eventually, though, and she rehearsed a speech all the way to work on Tuesday about taking things slower. She didn't have to give it. He wasn't there, and didn't show up all evening.

It was only a reprieve. But it gave her time to think, and it wasn't Matt on her mind. Figuring out what she felt for Matt was easy—she felt nothing, no matter how hard she tried. But Jase Garrett stirred a cyclone of feelings—frustration; irritation; confusion; and over all of it, an earthy, panty-melting lust. She couldn't deny it, she just didn't know what to do about it.

The obvious answer shouted in the back of her mind and throbbed between her legs. Sleep with him.

In an odd way, it might help. Maybe her confused lust for Jase was holding her back from Matt. And maybe if she slept with Jase, she'd work him out of her system so she could get on with her life plan, Matt included. Jase would probably be a letdown as a lover, anyway, too selfish and lazy to think of anything but his own needs. This could work.

Hoping the night air would clear her mind, she rolled down her windows for the drive home. Fifty degrees could be bracing, waking up tired brain cells.

The cool wind carried the smells of earth and pine, and sent shivers over her exposed neck as she drove down the mountain. Passing the Rusty Wire, she glanced at the building, expecting it to be dark at two-thirty in the morning. It wasn't. She slowed. In the floodlight over the front door, two men appeared to be having an argument. She didn't want to get involved, but she hated that excuse from so-called concerned citizens. What if it turned violent and one of them needed help?

She idled at the entrance. Loud swearing from one man was answered by a curt word from the other. One word was all it took. Recognizing Jase's voice, she turned into the parking lot. A disagreement with an angry customer in the middle of the night couldn't be good. She had no idea how she could help, but some backup had to be better than none. She stopped several yards from the men and stepped out of her car, not sure which man she'd be backing up.

A furious middle-aged man snatched something from Jase's hand. "Thanks a lot, you just wrecked my marriage," he said bitterly.

Zoe's stomach clenched. It looked like she wouldn't be taking Jase's side.

"Your wife'll probably thank me," Jase assured him, far less perturbed.

"Bullshit! You don't know how she gets. I was supposed to be there two hours ago." He pulled out a cell phone as he talked, his demeanor suddenly changing. "Hi, baby. I'm sorry, I know I'm late, but I swear I wasn't with Becky." He winced at the answer. "Honest, baby, you can believe me. I was with Stan at the Rusty Wire." He looked around helplessly. "No, he already left. But you can call him tomorrow—"

"Give me that," Jase said, grabbing the phone from the man's hands. Zoe took a step forward, as indignant as the man. She knew Jase had seen her, but he ignored them both, speaking into the phone. "Ma'am? This is

Jase Garrett at the Rusty Wire Saloon. I'm afraid I'm the reason your husband is late. He had too much to drink, and fell asleep on the table. I took his car keys and let him sleep it off. I woke him up a few minutes ago, and he's leaving for home now. If you'd like, you can stop in here tomorrow evening. I have several employees who can verify that your husband was here, drunk and snoring most of the night."

Zoe bit back a grin. The man watched, frozen with fear.

"Yes, ma'am. Good night," Jase said. He handed the phone back. "I explained why you're late. You'll have to explain why you were too drunk to drive. Good luck."

The man pocketed his phone and turned, swearing under his breath as he walked to a pickup truck. They watched wordlessly as he drove off.

As the sound of the pickup died away, Jase turned to her. He looked her over from twenty feet away, then walked closer, each booted step echoing loudly across the empty parking lot. Her heart sped up, as if there was something exciting about being close to him. And damn it, there was. He'd done a lot to piss her off, but lately he seemed to do everything right.

He stopped in front of her, thumbs hooked in his pockets. "What are you doing here?"

She smiled, enjoying the little rush of adrenaline she got from looking at him. There was nothing wrong with looking. "Coming to your rescue. Or his, I wasn't sure."

"His?"

She shrugged. It really was odd, the way she reacted to him, as if she could already feel his hands encircling her body, pulling her against him. She didn't have to check for tingles, her body fairly vibrated with them, the nape of her neck alive with an electric current that raised the tiny hairs to attention. It was beyond analyzing, beyond the need for long-range plans. It required action.

In the back of her mind something clicked into place so firmly she wondered if it had been audible.

He obviously hadn't heard it. "I suppose you thought that was the rational thing to do, step into the middle of an argument in the deserted parking lot of a saloon at two-thirty in the morning?"

Well, if he was going to put it that way . . . "I didn't really think it through. I just acted on impulse."

A spark of interest lit his eyes, igniting an answering flare below her stomach, because she knew full well which impulses he was remembering. "In different circumstances, I'd approve." He cleared his throat. "But I think you should have listened to logic on this one. A dark parking lot, two strange men arguing . . ."

"I knew it was you." Was he really telling her to be more rational? "I'm not afraid of you."

The flashback was almost a physical thing. She'd said the same words to Matt. Then, she'd been unable to stomach the idea of having sex. This didn't feel at all the same.

She watched Jase reassess the situation, amused that she'd thrown him off his stride. It was a nice feeling. Powerful.

His gaze took in her Alpine Sky blazer and skirt, lingering a little too long on her breasts and legs. "On your way home from work?"

"Mm-hmm." She made no move to leave, doing a little body scanning herself. Lingering here and there.

"You have crappy hours."

"Same as yours," she said, unperturbed. She ran her eyes over the breadth of his shoulders, the corded muscles in his arms. She'd looked before, but not as openly. His T-shirt did nothing to hide a well-defined chest, and his jeans tightened around the strong muscles in his thighs. He probably didn't even need a bouncer—he looked capable of handling anything. Or anyone.

Her, for instance.

She sucked her lower lip in at the thought, letting it slip slowly beneath her teeth as she raised her eyes to his.

His gaze was stuck on her mouth, his eyes slightly narrowed. When he finally looked up, he no longer seemed off his stride. In fact, he looked pretty decisive.

"How about a drink before you go home?"

No wild, impulsive choices, she reminded herself. Just well-thought-out, sensible decisions, with a definite goal in mind.

She smiled serenely. "I thought you'd never ask."

Chapter Fourteen

He was still locking the door as she crossed the empty dance floor to the bar, her heels making a hollow sound in the deserted room. The saloon looked different in the half-light of the fluorescent tubes behind the bar. Chairs were turned upside down on tables, and the back room was a shadowy cave. She ran her hand along the edge of the bar as she walked its length, considering what it had seen in more than a hundred years of use. And not just drinking. With no carpet on the floor, she guessed more than one naked backside had been pressed against the bar top after hours.

My goodness, she thought, amused by how quickly her mind had adjusted to the new program.

She turned to Jase, who was doing something behind the bar. "Are we alone?"

"Yes. Watch what you touch, the bar only got a quick wipe before I sent everyone home." He opened two beer bottles, holding one toward her. "Beer?"

"Thanks." She took a sip as Jase came around the bar.

If possible, he seemed even more laid back after hours. He tipped his bottle up, looking her over, his gaze slow and deliberate as he drank. "You surprised me, Zoe. I didn't think you were the type to impulsively accept an invitation this time of night."

"I'm usually not." She looked at the beer bottle in her hand, then set it aside. Beer wasn't what she really wanted. "But I've had this small problem lately, and it's affecting my usual sensible choices."

"Oh?"

"Yes. It seems I'm attracted to you."

He hid a smile with a casual sip from his bottle. "Interesting problem."

"Yes, because giving into an urge like that is something I don't do. As you said, I make sensible decisions. And you and I . . . well, that's far from sensible, what with your lack of ambition and my well-thought-out career goals."

"Hmmm."

"Obviously, I need to get over it. Get you out of my system."

He nodded.

She waited for him to ask how she planned to do it, but he just took another slow drink, watching her as he did. For a person with little ambition, he had an intense focus. Pleasant shivers crossed her shoulders. He might be letting her lead, but there was no doubt he knew where they were going.

And there was no turning back. Now that she'd decided to satisfy her curiosity, her body quivered, anticipating his touch. He would mold her against him, stroke her, kiss her in that mind-reeling way that both staggered and aroused her. Just imagining it drove her crazy in a delicious, electrifying way.

Beneath prickles of excitement, the relief almost made her laugh—*this* was how it was supposed to feel. No suggestive language or groping required. Matt could have tried all night and never gotten it right, but all it took with Jase was a look. She was steaming from it, while doing her best to look as calm and collected as he did.

She let the certainty of what she was doing sweep through her, thrilling at the new sensation. She doubted he felt it; he was too absorbed in watching. She didn't know if he was undressing her with his gaze, but it sure as hell made *her* think about undressing.

"Hot in here," she said, reaching for the buttons on her blazer.

His eyes followed her hands as she undid the jacket, then slipped it off and draped it over a bar stool. A smile played at the corner of his mouth, causing a flock of butterflies to take wing in her stomach. Humor flashed in his eyes. "I don't know. I'm starting to get into that proper look of yours, Miss Larkin. It's like a hard shell covering a soft, creamy center."

She arched an eyebrow, congratulating herself on looking cool while seriously overheating. "As I remember it, you called my look stiff."

"Did I?" He considered it, raking another hot gaze over her body. "Right word. Wrong person."

Oh, my. Her gaze dropped to his jeans. Better lighting would have helped her appreciate that more. She gave him a heavy-lidded smile as she reached for the buttons on her blouse and undid two.

Jase exhaled a long, appreciative breath.

If he loved seeing the evidence of restraint in her come undone, he wasn't the only one affected. Each move seemed to free something in herself. It uncoiled in sinuous slow motion, her tightly wound control letting go. It was a new feeling. In her wild days she might have acted uninhibited, but it was just that, an act. It had required effort to overcome good sense, along with copious amounts of alcohol. The only effort involved here was in not rushing the process.

With deliberate slowness, she toed off each shoe. He watched, then lifted his eyes. There was nothing cool about that look.

Her heart pounded, a ridiculous level of excitement for merely baring her arms and feet. Licking her lips felt downright dangerous. She did it, just to watch his eyes blaze with interest.

She paused long enough for him to wonder what she'd do next. She hadn't planned this, and thinking was becoming difficult, but the next move seemed obvious. Miss Larkin needed to shed every bit of her stuffy image.

Placing a foot on the lower rung of a bar stool, she slid her skirt up just far enough to expose the top of her thigh-high nylon. Then pushed the stocking down, slowly. She didn't have to look to know he followed every motion. With deliberate care she draped the nylon over the stool, then repeated the process with her other leg. Skirt inched up, nylon inched down. Languid movements, while her heart took off at high speed and blood rushed in her ears.

The freshly mopped wood floor was smooth and cool against her feet as she turned to face him.

He lifted an eyebrow. "Better?"

She smiled slyly. "Almost."

How could he look so relaxed? The room was charged with so much electricity it prickled against her skin. Yet he stood there expressionless, feet slightly spread and bottle dangling from his fingers. Watching her. She'd be tempted to check for a pulse if not for the fire in that unwavering stare.

God, that look—it stole her breath and sent heat pulsing downward to throb between her thighs. If he didn't make a move soon, she might just throw herself on him.

Lifting her fingers to her blouse again, she opened the third button. Beneath her hand, her heart banged like a drum against her ribs. The center of her bra and a fair amount of skin had to be showing. She opened one more, watching for a reaction.

He didn't move. She thought it was possible he had gone even more still.

Holding her breath, she reached up and behind her head to unclip her hair.

He set his beer down on a table. "Jesus, Zoe." The breath he took was deep, a man coming up for air. "That's enough."

She stopped, not daring to move as he took three strides forward and covered her hand with his own. He held her gaze as he lowered her hand, eyes hot and steady on hers. "Let me," he said in a low voice that sent electricity skittering down her back and arms.

He reached up slowly, found the clip, and let her hair tumble down. She gave her head a slight shake, knowing the lights behind her sent gold fire shooting through every strand. A satisfied smile touched his mouth before he turned his hot gaze back to her, both of his hands buried in her hair.

She inhaled deeply, eyes locked with his as he took over. She felt his hand move between them and the bottom of her blouse pull from her skirt. Still watching her, he undid the last buttons, letting her blouse fall open. He didn't look.

She searched his face, finding both desire and a control she hadn't expected. She didn't know where he'd found it, because she had lost hers. Was losing more with every second. His fingers had skimmed between her breasts without touching, an oversight that immediately became an obsession in her mind. *Touch me.* Her breasts swelled with it. She bit her lip, wondering if the silent plea showed in her eyes the way it ached in her breasts.

He raised a hand to cup her cheek—not the touch she'd been hoping for, but a good prelude because he turned it into a caress as he leaned in and kissed her. She made an appreciative sound and opened to him, letting the light-headedness sweep over her as he took what she offered. Hands on his shoulders, she clutched fistfuls of his T-shirt and held on. For a moment she swayed between pleasure and desperation as she sank into his kiss, at the same time yearning to feel his hands on her. To touch her, right there where a puff of air slipped inside her open blouse.

And then, oh God, he was doing it. His palm slipped around to cup her breast, exploring the curve of it, fingering the hard bud of her nipple. She whimpered against his mouth and pressed into his hand, out of her mind with wanting him. His touch was bold and sure, and her response to it wiped away any comparison she might have made of him with Matt. With Jase, she couldn't get enough.

He seemed to feel the same way. In one deft move he flicked the bra strap off her shoulder, making room for his hand. His palm was warm, and the callused pads below his fingers mildly abrasive as he rubbed them over her. She trembled, weak-kneed from pleasure. She needed more.

To her annoyance, his hand stopped moving. He smiled and studied her lazily. "You're pretty direct about going after what you want, aren't you?"

"That can't be news to you."

He chuckled low in his throat. "No, and I'm beginning to appreciate it." In one smooth motion he pushed her blouse off her shoulders, letting it drop to the floor. "I've been known to take a single-minded approach to what I want, too." He opened the clasp on her bra and pulled it away. "Right now, I want you."

She closed her eyes blissfully as he kissed each breast. "Finally," she choked out. "We agree on something."

He smiled, then pulled his shirt over his head and tossed it aside. Trapping her against the bar, he placed small kisses along her neck. "There's only one problem."

She didn't see a problem. Physically, he looked as fit as the photos she'd seen of him in *Time* magazine. She ran her hands over the hard lines of his chest, pleased to see that he hadn't let everything go during the past nine years. "What's the problem?"

"If you were hoping I had a couch in my office, I don't. At the moment, I don't even have an office."

She'd realized that, she just hadn't let it stop her.

"You own the place," she said, absorbed in tracing the outline of muscles beneath his thin dusting of chest hair. "What's worked in the past?"

"A house." He licked her bottom lip.

He'd never made love to a woman here—that gave her a whole new thrill. She'd make the first time something neither one of them would forget.

"The bar?" she asked, eager for any solution and stuck on that first fevered thought.

He rubbed against her, the warm skin of his chest against her breasts raising her temperature more than the kisses he placed along her jaw. "No good. Not unless you're into lying on sticky beer."

Not really. She had a hard time thinking while he dropped tender kisses along her shoulders. "Those pool tables in the back room looked pretty sturdy."

He raised his head, pausing to give her a horrified look. "Since we're getting along so well, I'm going to pretend you didn't say that."

"Oh." She bit back a smile. "Sorry. I don't know pool table sex etiquette."

"Now you do. Keep thinking."

But his head dipped back to her breasts and thinking became impossible. She moaned at the pull of his mouth on sensitive flesh. Raw heat streaked downward, and she buried her fingers in his hair and held on. When that still wasn't enough, she reached for the button on his jeans.

He moved her hands aside. "Slow down. We'll get there."

"I'm already there. You need to catch up."

"Trust me, I don't."

She squirmed at the need taking hold inside her, but let him set the pace. He was doing a good job.

His hands had found the zipper at the back of her skirt and pulled. The skirt fell to the floor, followed by her half-slip. His questing mouth moved lower.

She drew in a shaky breath and grabbed the back of the bar stool next to her for support. Seconds later she reached for the stool on her other side, too. Leaning against something would have been better, but the bar was basically a ledge poking uncomfortably against her shoulder blades. She could find a wall, but it was hard to see once her vision blurred and her eyes closed. Hard to do anything but hang on once his fingers slipped inside her. She wouldn't ask him to move, not even if the place caught on fire again. All she could do was ride the waves of pressure as they built and built, until finally she gasped, "Jase!" and the world dissolved into a fall of glittery stars.

She opened her eyes to his lazy smile. "You okay?" he asked as he nibbled at her ear.

"Mmm." She took a few deep breaths and waited for strength to return to her legs before moving. The climax had left her only partially replete and more desperate than ever for what she really wanted—to feel him inside her. To feel him rock into her hard and fast while she watched his eyes glaze over with need. To fill that need the way he filled her.

This time she wasn't taking no for an answer.

She reached for his waistband, unfastening his jeans. He didn't try to stop her, and it took only seconds to unzip, then shove his jeans and underwear down far enough to free his erection. She gripped and stroked.

"Jesus, Zoe," he groaned. "I hope you thought of a place to do this, or we're going down to the floor right now." Without waiting for an answer, he pulled his boots off, then stripped out of the jeans.

She pulled a chair off the closest table. "Sit," she ordered. He did, holding on to her as she straddled his legs and sat on his thighs. She grinned in anticipation. "I always wanted to try this."

"Wait." He nodded at the floor. "Back pocket of my jeans."

Condom. Jeez, good thing one of them had some brain cells left. She retrieved it quickly, getting back in place as he opened it, thinking it was nice he'd had one handy. Thinking, too, that anyone who kept a condom that handy had reason to think he'd need one. Since he'd had no idea she'd show up in his parking lot, she couldn't help feeling a pang of jealousy.

She had no right to feel it. "Lucky you had it," she said, smiling to make herself believe it.

"I keep them behind the bar. Stuck it in my pocket when I got the beers."

She shouldn't feel that rush of relief, either, and covered it by raising her eyebrows. "You stock condoms at the bar?"

"I hand out two or three a week. Sometimes you can see where a spontaneous hookup is headed." He watched her scoot closer, heat blazing in his eyes. "But sometimes they come as a surprise."

"You weren't surprised," she murmured in his ear as she settled over him, holding still while something inside her soared. "You knew I'd end up here."

He kissed her deeply, then gently pulled strands of hair away from her face, tucking them behind her shoulder. "I knew I *wanted* you here," he said, his throaty rumble telling her how much he still wanted.

"I wanted to see you bend a few of your rules, see how well we worked together."

"I didn't bend them. I broke them to pieces."

"Am I that bad?" he asked, smiling.

"No." She wasn't sure what he was, but he was a lot more complex than she'd given him credit for. She sighed. "I think I was that wrong." Closing her eyes, she rocked against him, enjoying the part she finally got right.

She wanted to love the position, to abandon herself to the pleasure, but movement was awkward. He held her waist while she hooked her feet behind the chair but the inability to take him fully and still move was maddening.

She paused, about to suggest they resort to the floor, when he growled with frustration, gripped her tightly, and stood. She clung to his neck with a startled "Eep" as he elbowed chairs aside left and right. They crashed to the floor on each side of her and he laid her back on the cleared tabletop, still joined with her. His eyes flashed with intensity as he gave a satisfied thrust.

Oh, God, yes! Astonishment mixed with a thrilling jolt of lust. *That* was what she'd waited for.

He watched her, gripping her hips and pushing into her again. Jaw set with determination. Arm muscles tight. Holding back, she knew, until he took her over the edge one more time.

Her insides went liquid with need. She arched her head back, lost in the rhythm as it pulsed through her, primitive and strong. Abandoning herself to the pleasure, she wrapped him with her legs as he stroked into her. She would have feared the loss of control with another man, but gave it eagerly to Jase, knowing she could trust him. Knowing he would give as well as take. She let him take her higher and higher until the ecstasy spasmed through her again, hard waves that grabbed him, too. She heard a hissed breath as he went rigid, then finally collapsed on top of her.

She circled him loosely with her arms, feeling the cool sweat on his back, enjoying the weight of him as her breathing returned to normal.

The numbing haze faded from her brain, bringing her back to reality—lying naked on a saloon table beneath Jase Garrett.

She smiled. No regrets. Not for rejecting Matt, and not for having sex with Jase. Her world had flipped radically in the past couple of days, the guidelines she'd set for herself shattered to pieces. She'd rejected a man with every quality she'd ever wanted, and had sex with a man who had none of them. Amazingly, it felt right.

She had a lot to think about.

Later.

Jase propped himself on his forearms, enjoying the sight of Zoe flushed and satisfied beneath him. Knowing exactly how it felt. He'd possibly just had the best sex of his life, and he wasn't ready for it to be over. He'd tried to make it last longer, but seeing prim, proper Zoe turn into a wanton seductress right in front of him had seriously frayed his willpower.

He'd been ready to take her since she showed up in the parking lot wearing that prim and proper Alpine Sky suit that didn't fool him for a second; beneath that suit was a repressed woman waiting to shake off years of self-imposed restrictions. He was more than willing to offer his services.

Which he'd apparently done well, judging by the dazed look in those lovely golden-brown eyes. He was inordinately pleased to have put it there, and strangely possessive about not wanting another man to have a chance to do the same.

He brushed away a few strands of hair that clung to the dampness on her forehead and smiled as the dreamy glaze left her eyes. "Did I ever tell you how much that stuffy business suit turns me on?"

"I think you just did, although I was hoping it was what was under the suit."

"That part was even hotter." He kissed her, a long, slow finish to their lovemaking, before he stood and helped her to her feet. She looked a little wobbly, and he put his arms around her. It seemed like a good excuse to press her naked body against his one more time, and she didn't object, holding him close and laying her cheek against him as she tucked her head just below his chin. It felt so right he just stood there, drinking in the closeness.

"I should go home now."

Funny, that was usually his line. Hearing it from her sent an unpleasant jolt through him. He pulled his head back and looked at her. "So you can draw up a new life plan?"

She gave him a sour smile. "Looks like I have to."

"Don't."

"Well, I can't operate without one, and I really don't think it's your call."

"I mean, don't go home. Come to my house." Her face went blank and her mouth opened in surprise. He understood—he was almost as surprised as she was when it popped out of his mouth, but he knew immediately that he wanted it. Badly.

Since surprise wasn't outright rejection, he tried harder, giving her what worked best, sensible reasons. He wasn't above playing dirty.

"You have to give it a fair shot, Zoe. Have you really worked me out of your system so fast? Because all you've done for me is show me something I hope I can have again. It's not like you to leave a job unfinished."

Gambling on her feeling the same way wasn't too risky, not after the look he'd seen on her face and the response he'd felt in her body. But he backed it up with emotion anyway. "I can't promise one more time will be enough for me, because I'm not just hot for your body. I like you. I like your stubborn dedication to your job, and the way you won't take no for an answer. You're smart, and you're persistent. It's a sexy combination." It was easy to look sincere when he meant every word.

Her steady look was hard to read. "You said I was irritating."

He grinned. "You are. Doesn't change the rest." Running a hand under her hair, he caressed the back of her head, watching her eyes close as he tugged gently, then sifted it through his fingers. "What do you say?" he murmured, sneaking in a kiss. "It's one night. You can draw up your new life plans later, and add amendments and corollaries to your heart's content. The ones that exclude worthless bums like me."

She was thinking, which was better than saying no.

Despite what she thought, when he did something, he did a thorough job, which meant he couldn't hit her with logic and emotion without throwing in the physical aspect. With a suggestive smile and lift of his eyebrow, he ran two fingers down her cheek, down her neck, down her fair, freckled skin to her bare breast. She looked down, as he'd hoped she would, following his fingers as he traced a path over her breast, beneath it, across the nipple. Her eyes closed. He played there lightly, teasing, holding back a smile as goose bumps ran down her arms. Leaning close, he whispered, "I'm not done with you, Zoe. Come home with me. Stay the night."

She sighed, a long breath of resignation, and he knew he had her before she opened her eyes. "You're right. I don't think we're done. And I really do want to forget about you."

"Thatta girl."

Zoe followed him in her car, wondering the whole time if she'd lost her mind. Saloon sex was one thing. Spending the night at Jase Garrett's house, even when that night was already closer to dawn, was another entirely. It was deliberate and no longer private, not with her car sitting in his driveway for anyone to see. Definitely not in line with her responsible, conservative image. It was more like something she would have done ten years ago.

Except back then she would have done it for the shock value. Now she didn't want anyone to know. Not the nosy residents of B-Pass, who were apparently eager to see a Larkin girl go bad, and not her sisters, who knew her cautious dating life didn't include men like Jase Garrett. She preferred to keep this to herself, at least until she understood it.

Thankfully, his house was secluded. Maybe no one would notice the red Escort parked beside his truck. Then Maggie and Sophie wouldn't get the chance to ask what she was thinking when she dropped Matt Flemming in favor of a hot fling with his polar opposite.

She didn't have an answer. She *hadn't been* thinking. She'd been acting on instinct, something she hadn't trusted herself to do in her entire adult life. And because it had been so right, she'd followed her instincts again, trailing him along the dark roads to his house.

She wasn't done with him any more than he was done with her. And she didn't understand him. Jase was more than he appeared to be. More motivated to get what he wanted in life, and more caring about people outside his own little world.

She'd misread him. What else had she missed?

For starters, his financial situation. The house she walked through wasn't the home of a lazy saloon owner with no other discernible income. Trees and darkness had hidden part of the house when she'd been there before, and with her rage in full bloom, the living room hadn't registered. It did now, from the huge stone fireplace to the expensive furniture. So did the large, tiled kitchen she passed, and the study that looked like it functioned as his main living space. The dining room and two bedrooms were bare. He'd put a lot of money into building the house, but stopped halfway through furnishing it. Out of money? Or out of interest?

At least the spacious master bedroom was furnished, including a chair on the adjoining deck. Even in the dark she knew it would have a spectacular view of Tappit's Peak. Views were what people paid for in Barringer's Pass, and they didn't come cheap.

They'd obviously miscalculated. Matt had dismissed

Jase's claim of having "enough" money by saying that his endorsement deals would have been yanked. If they had, he obviously had another source of income. The Rusty Wire didn't pay for homes like this. Just one clue that she didn't know Jase nearly as well as she'd thought.

"You're staring." Jase came up behind her, laying his hands on her shoulders. "Don't tell me you're having second thoughts."

"No, it's just that it's all so lovely."

"It is?" He looked around the room, obviously worried. "I wasn't going for lovely."

"Don't worry, your manhood is intact. I just meant you have a beautiful home."

"It's just a house." He massaged the muscles beneath his hands with surprising skill. She relaxed into it, rolling her head. He lowered his head, kissed her ear. "Tell me more about my manhood."

She laughed, doubting he needed reassurance. It felt good to have a relaxed relationship with him, teasing and bantering without the pressure to persuade and close the deal.

"I love it when you laugh." His soft comment got her attention better than any teasing remark he could have made. He loved something about her. She was surprised by how good it made her feel. "It sounds like the real you. You never laugh when you're working."

God, was that true? For a second, she blinked in concern, then realized why he was wrong. "That's because you only see me at my most annoying times, when I'm trying to convince my bullheaded neighbor to sell his saloon."

"True." He smiled. "Do you laugh a lot at the Alpine Sky? Maybe I should visit you there again."

She sobered quickly at the thought of working with David and Matt, her daily problems with spoiled movie stars, and worries over the aggressive expansion plans. "No, I guess I don't. But it's not that kind of job."

"You mean it's not fun."

She frowned. "Most jobs aren't."

"Some are. Mine is."

She started to say that was because he didn't really work, he socialized. But she'd seen how people responded to him; he was a one-man public relations department, working the room, keeping people happy. Doing what an owner should.

He was a people person who obviously loved his job, while under her efficient, competent facade she didn't love hers. And he'd zeroed in on it.

Thinking about work was spoiling her good mood. She turned to face him as he dropped his hands down to circle her waist, keeping her close. "I didn't come here to talk about work."

"Direct, as usual." He kissed her, unbuttoning her blouse as he did. "Not a problem. We can save the getting-to-know-you for later."

She responded to his kiss hungrily, rubbing against the erection that was already straining the front of his jeans. "You already know me," she murmured into his ear. Far too well. If he was going to be so damn perceptive, she'd give him something else to concentrate on.

Luckily, when he did something, he gave it his full attention. It wasn't possible to complain about a man who could bring her to the brink of ecstasy time and again without allowing her that final release, but lying in his bed she decided it was entirely possible to go mad from it. The only consolation was that he was as tortured as she was.

He hovered above her, placing delicate kisses on her eyes, forehead, and cheeks, and she couldn't care less. Her attention was centered on the wonderful yearning that pulsed between her legs, and the teasing erection that brushed all the right places without giving either of them satisfaction. She clutched the firm muscles of his ass to hold him in place while she thrust upward, but he moved enough to miss the target and give them both a searing, hot jolt of pleasure as he slid over her.

He hissed in a breath, then smiled. "Vixen." He kissed her nose.

"Beast." He rocked slightly, sending another delicious shock wave rushing through her. She laughed, a combination of delight and exasperation. "Jase, I'm suffering here."

"So am I. You drive me crazy." He nipped at her lower lip. "Some of us don't get two orgasms every time. I want to make this last."

"I sympathize with your deficiencies, truly." She grinned at his evil look. "But I assure you the second is needed just as desperately as the first."

"Show-off."

"Did you know it's possible to die from unrequited lust?"

"You made that up." She wiggled against him, and he groaned, letting it turn into a chuckle. "But I think you're right."

When she reached between them he didn't stop her.

She guided him into her, nearly shaking from the tiny explosion of pleasure as their bodies joined.

He sank in, moaning happily. His first movements were agonizingly slow, drawing out every incredible sensation. She sucked in a breath and dug her fingernails into his back, riding every cresting wave, gasping as they came faster and faster, harder and harder. When she finally lost herself in the shattering end she clung to his shoulders, crying out his name and taking him with her.

He collapsed on top of her, breathing hard. She heard a mumbled curse, a harsh word so filled with awe it sounded reverent, and she melted a little more inside. Getting enough of this man wasn't going to be as simple as she'd thought.

Her well-planned life was going to hell. She probably should be upset.

Maybe tomorrow, when she wasn't so exhausted.

He slid off her, bringing a shiver as air touched sweat-slicked skin. A moment later he'd pulled the covers over them both and she snuggled her back against the firm wall of his chest.

She felt the rise and fall of each breath as it slowed to normal, along with the steady beating of his heart. Her own still pounded, and she wondered if he felt it, and if he knew it was because of the way he wrapped her in his arms, as if he never wanted to let go.

"Zoe?" His voice rumbled close to her ear.

"Hmm."

"I feel it's only fair to tell you. I think your plan is stupid."

Her heart surged back to a pounding gallop, and she squeezed her eyes shut. She knew what he meant—he didn't think he'd get tired of having sex with her. She was more pleased than she should have been.

It was a sweet thought, but she couldn't afford to be wrong. That would screw things up even more than they already were.

She said nothing and pretended to drift off to sleep, then really did.

Zoe opened her eyes and squinted at the clock on the nightstand. Twelve o'clock. From the brilliant sunlight pouring through the French doors, that had to mean twelve noon. She sat up, stretched out her legs, and winced at the pull on her inner thighs. Last night had given her muscles a more vigorous workout than they'd seen in some time.

Which, after all, had been her intent. Satisfy the cravings for the sex her body had missed so she could forget it and get on with her real life. Spending the night hadn't been the plan, but her body had craved more than she'd realized. Jase had satisfied her wonderfully.

Now it was time for the perfunctory thank-you and good-bye.

She looked down at Jase. He slept with one arm thrown over his head, quilt kicked down to his waist. His face was strong, even in sleep, jaw shadowed with dark whiskers. The firmly muscled chest was already familiar to her, and if she was honest, still tempting. Nothing wrong with admiring a well-built man. Last night proved she could keep the fantasy separate from the practical reality of her life. But it was over, and there was no sense in pushing her luck. She resisted the temptation to lay her head on the soft hairs covering the center of his chest and curl into the warmth of his side.

As she watched, he opened his eyes. His unfocused gaze landed on her, and he blinked sleepily and smiled. "Morning."

Smiling back was automatic. "Good morning."

"What time is it?"

"Noon."

"Guess we were really tired." His smile quirked on one side, remembering the reason, and her heart skipped a beat. Jase's eyes roamed lazily over her face and hair for several seconds, his expression turning thoughtful. "Jesus, you're pretty in the morning."

She uttered a sharp, nervous laugh. "Lucky for me you still can't see straight." But she felt a warm flush creep up to her cheeks at the way he'd said it, without thought, as if stating a simple fact. It was probably a residual sexual pull left between them that caused a fluttering in her chest. "I need a shower before you get the sleep out of your eyes."

"I'd better come with you, make sure all the pretty doesn't wash off."

She made a sound of disgust and tossed her pillow at his head. "Moron." Nonsensical sweet talk had never made her go all mushy. Still, the way he'd said it tickled her deep inside, as if he knew she hated corny lines and just wanted to get a rise out of her.

"A moron who's smart enough to wake up with you in my bed." She yelped as he grabbed her around the waist and pulled her down for a good morning kiss.

She kissed him back, digging one hand in his tousled hair while the other smoothed over the strong muscles of his back.

He crossed one leg over hers, his morning arousal evident even through the layer of quilt caught between them. His kiss ended with soft nuzzling beside her ear. "So, am I out of your system yet?"

"I don't know." Which was an outright lie.

"Well, I don't think we should take any chances. Maybe a shower will wash me out." He slid a hand down her side and over her hip, sending shivers along the same path.

She sighed happily. "It's worth a try."

Jase's phone rang while they were still toweling off. She was relieved to have him step away for a few minutes. It was hard to think past the feel-good fuzzies that had become a permanent state when she was with him, and she needed to do some serious thinking. Having sex with him was supposed to help her stop thinking about having sex with him. Where in hell did she get that stupid idea? Having sex with him only made her want more sex.

With him.

That was the unsettling realization she kept coming back to. That, and the even scarier realization that they weren't just having sex, they were making love. It was hard to keep things impersonal when he got *extremely* personal with his mouth, not to mention those penetrating gazes.

And he made her laugh. She liked being with him. Damn it.

Being in a relationship with the man who was screwing up her professional life was even worse than lusting after him. She didn't know how to get out of it. She didn't *want* to get out of it.

Damn it!

She sighed at her reflection in the mirror. It looked awfully smug and satisfied to be the face of defeat.

She was baring her teeth at the mirror, wondering if he had an extra toothbrush, when Jase walked back into the bathroom, his angry, brooding face appearing behind her in the mirror. She forgot about toothbrushes. "What's wrong?"

"That was my friend Brandon." His jaw rippled with the tension of clenched muscles as he gave her a long look. "How do you feel about Matt Flemming?"

Shit, whoever Brandon was, he must have ratted her out. He'd told Jase she'd gone to Matt's condo and of course Jase had leapt to the wrong conclusion. Not that it was any of his business . . . although it sort of was if she was sleeping with him.

She faced him. "We're just friends." Because she hadn't expected Jase to turn suddenly possessive, she couldn't hide her annoyance when she added, "Did you think I'd be here if we were anything more than that?"

"No. I just wondered how hard it was going to be if you had to choose sides."

Confusion mixed with tiny prickles of dread. "Why would I have to do that?"

"Because I think he might finally have found the way to defeat me."

Chapter Fifteen

She hurried into her blouse and skirt while Jase got the *Echo*—the twice-weekly paper delivered free to every house in Barringer's Pass—from his mailbox. He laid it on the kitchen table so they could both see it. They didn't have to open it.

Right below the front-page banner of the *Echo*, large bold type proclaimed, "Rusty Wire Investigated for Health Code Violations."

"Oh, shit," Zoe said. Then started reading.

Minutes later, she looked at Jase. Anger was there, but also a deep, restless worry that left lines beside his eyes. "You were right," she told him. "Someone put them up to it. Those two guys were supposed to start a fight just so they could do this." She gestured at the paper. "But it won't work, Jase. They won't find anything because there's nothing to find."

"It doesn't matter. The damage is already done. You said it yourself—they planted doubts in people's minds. A clean inspection won't make any difference."

She didn't want to believe it, but she had no choice.

Just by raising the question, the association was planted in people's minds. The Rusty Wire was infested with mice. Dishes were reused without being properly washed. Employees tried to hide it, and were rude and abusive to customers who questioned their practices.

She knew how the reasoning would go: With so many claims, there must be something behind it. Two customers had been upset enough to get themselves arrested, and the health department had been called in. It must be true.

Jase's phone rang again, and he checked the caller ID before answering with "I just heard, Jennifer." He listened, his expression growing darker by the second. "No, stay there. I'll be right over."

He pocketed the phone and looked at Zoe. "The health department inspector says they're close to closing me down."

She blinked, a moment of shock stealing her words. "How can they do that? You're not even open! They have to inspect it first."

"They did, at least the outside of it, this morning." His mouth grimaced as he said it. "Jennifer said they responded to an anonymous phone tip. They found rats crawling all over some garbage that was lying just outside the back door."

She barely knew where to begin her tirade. "That's ridiculous! Your place is always clean. Besides, anyone living around here knows that garbage is an open invitation to bears. Garbage lying in the open is the *last* violation you'd find *anywhere* in Barringer's Pass."

"No kidding. I imagine that makes it even more horrifying for our customers."

The injustice was too blatant to overlook. "Some

petty bureaucrat is throwing his weight around. Or accepting bribes. That's the only way it could happen. You were set up."

He snorted in wry amusement. "Welcome to the other side, Miss Larkin. Yes, I was."

"How can you be so calm about it?"

His glance speared her, hot and dark. "Believe me, I'm far from calm. But I've been getting jerked around, warned, and set up for the past ten days. I knew those two were up to something with their staged accusations, and I should have seen this coming, done something to head it off."

She wanted to reassure him that a brief fight with the health department wouldn't be a permanent black mark against him. That rumors weren't impossible to overcome. But it wasn't true. She should know.

"I'm done taking this shit."

The low words jerked her wandering attention back. He hadn't said it forcefully, or pounded the table, but something in his dead-flat tone made the little hairs on her neck stand up. His stare had become distant, his mind suddenly somewhere else, and she knew she was seeing a different Jase, a more determined one. The Jase who had focused on the lofty goal of Olympic gold, and achieved it.

"How can I help?"

His gaze snapped back to her. "I appreciate the offer, but you can't."

"Jase, I've dealt with these people, too. If this inspector's trying to throw his weight around, it'll help if he knows you're not in this alone."

"I'm not. He'll come back once we open this afternoon, and Russ and Jennifer will be there. I may invite a reporter, too, to get a firsthand account of our passing grade. The Rusty Wire always passes. But you can't be there." He held up a hand when she started to protest. "Zoe, I don't want you caught in the middle. Matt might be willing to let you become an accessory in his schemes, but I'm not. I want you far away from this."

She sulked, knowing he wouldn't budge. It bothered her that he thought Matt had used her, but she had no way to refute it. It bothered her even more that he could be right. She wanted to place the blame on David and Ruth Ann Flemming, manipulating behind the scenes, but couldn't shake the memory of Matt's confidence in the face of outright rejection. As if he *knew* Jase would change his mind.

As if he knew how to make him change it.

Mentally she made a note to track Matt's activities the same way she intended to track David's and Ruth Ann's. And felt a small tug of guilt.

Working against her own employer was unethical, another step across that line of right and wrong behavior she'd been following so rigidly.

She winced. *Rigid* was a word she was beginning to hate. It put blinders on her, made her predictable, and allowed people to use her. She was done with rigid.

Jase was right, she had to choose sides. If the side she'd been on was wrong, then she'd just have to bend. She could do that, even if it did make her feel a bit queasy. The last time she'd thrown the rule book aside, she'd taken a header straight into the mud. This time she hoped it got her *out* of the mud.

"I need to get home and find some clean clothes before I have to go back to work."

"With Matt?" A muscle jumped beside his eye and

his mouth flattened as he digested the disturbing news. "I don't trust him. I don't like to think of you being anywhere around Matt Flemming."

"I probably won't be. I have plenty to keep me busy besides Matt." Except for one thing she needed to tell him. But she didn't want to argue with Jase. "I know you want to get to the Rusty Wire, make sure everything is perfect if inspectors will be there later today."

"You're right."

She saw that determined look again and almost felt sorry for whoever drew this job at the state health department. Jase was fighting for his saloon, and right now the health department owned the front lines. He'd be all over that inspector.

The coming battle had stiffened his back and touched his eyes with a cold, dangerous look. It all fell away as he pulled her into his arms, holding her close and kissing the top of her head. "I'm sorry this came up. Bad timing."

"It was time for me to go, anyway."

He pulled back, the hint of a smile touching his mouth. "Are we still pretending you're going to get tired of me?"

He smiled as if it was a harmless joke, but it hit her right in the gut. She'd barely admitted to herself that getting him out of her system had been an excuse to sleep with him, and a weak one at that. He'd never been fooled. He wasn't only perceptive, he was bold. And a bit too cocky.

She put on a cool look. "Is it so hard to believe that a woman might get her fill of you?"

"I think plenty of women have had their fill of me. It's different with you and me."

How could he figure that out so easily, so painlessly? She ignored the sudden racing in her pulse, more ready than ever to deny any feelings for him. "That remains to be seen."

"Okay. You're leading this dance. I'll follow, as long as you take us in the right direction."

She wanted to demand what the hell he meant by that, but she was afraid of the answer. Afraid he would get that determined gleam in his eye, the one that meant he'd stop at nothing to win. Afraid he was ready to have a relationship with her.

She had a big problem with that.

The only good thing about his saloon being on the verge of failing inspection was that it took his mind off Zoe. Sleeping with her had packed a bigger wallop than he'd expected, and he'd been expecting plenty. He didn't need anything fuzzing up his thinking right now.

They already had enough to close him down. The rats and the garbage within inches of his back door pretty much sealed the deal. He figured he had one chance to turn it around. A clean inspection inside might help him convince the inspector that he'd been set up, that the garbage and rats were so out of line with the rest of what he'd found he could consider it a mean practical joke.

And so far, so good. The few infractions in the kitchen were minor, and typical of any restaurant. Tongs placed on a counter that hadn't been disinfected. A container of chopped green peppers in the refrigerator without a lid. Infractions they'd fixed on the spot. He'd asked the inspector how often he saw those things, not because he didn't know but because the reporter from the *Echo* was taking detailed notes and he wanted it in her story. He even obliged her with a few quotes as they followed the inspector to the storage room, boasting about how they'd always passed previous inspections with good scores, and how confident he was about this one.

Gloria from the *Echo* nodded as she took notes, then pulled out a digital camera. "How about a picture? Can I get you by the pizza ovens?"

"Sure." He posed with arms folded confidently, flashing the grin that he knew darn well made him look both likable and competent. It had worked on the cover of *Time* magazine, it would work on the front page of the *Echo*.

"Perfect. One more," she said, angling for a different view.

At the back of the kitchen he heard the inspector ask, "Where's the light switch?"

"Got it," Russ said, just as the camera flashed in Jase's eyes. A second of silence followed.

His smile was still in place when Russ exclaimed, "Holy crap! Jase! What the fuck?"

Bile was already rising in his throat as he rushed the few steps to the storage room. He pushed past the inspector in time to see two mice scurry behind a case of canned mushrooms. One shelf above it, three more mice sat placidly atop a bag of sugar, nibbling on the contents that flowed from a mangled corner.

Below him, a camera flashed. He looked down to see Gloria wedged between him and Russ at thigh level, kneeling as she framed another shot.

He stepped in front of her, backing her out as he closed the door. Not that it mattered. They'd just blown their inspection score to hell. As Russ had so concisely put it, *What the fuck?*

Behind that panicked realization, questions began forming. He needed to think.

Russ grabbed his arm. "There must have been a dozen of 'em," he whispered hoarsely. As if it was a secret. "Maybe more." He turned a stunned expression on the inspector, who was busy writing. "The Rusty Wire doesn't have mice. Ever."

The guy looked up. "Those weren't elephants."

Russ glared at the man so hard Jase stepped between them. Arguing was useless. His mind sorted through possibilities, automatically narrowing it down. Defining the problem to find the solution. Competitive mode.

The inspector didn't matter, that ship had sailed. "We know they weren't in here before today," he told Russ.

"No shit! They were *never* in here before." He craned his neck to stare around Jase. "*Never*," he repeated. "Someone put them there to make us look bad."

"It worked," the inspector commented without looking up.

"You can't blame us!" He waved his arms in frustration, the most he could do since Jase had a hand on his chest, holding him back. "I run a clean place, damn it! I'm telling you, those mice weren't here yesterday."

The man stopped writing. "Look, I don't care if they've been living there for six months, or if Scotty beamed 'em in from Mars this morning. It doesn't matter. Either way, you got rodents in your food."

Russ looked like he was set to explode, and the

reporter looked poised to record the event. "Forget it," he ordered Russ, giving him a firm nudge backward.

Russ turned his anger on Jase. "What's the matter with you? Are you gonna just stand there and let him write us up for that?"

"There's nothing we can do about it now." He was a little surprised himself by how quickly his anger had turned into clear priorities. Discover how and who, then who put them up to it. Keep the goal in mind and don't get distracted. Compete. Win.

"Russ, listen. You're right, someone did this. I want to know who. If we figure out how, it'll narrow the possibilities. How did someone get back here? Who had access?"

Russ frowned. "Employees." He glanced at the three guys working in the kitchen who were now watching, openmouthed.

"Waitstaff, too," Jase said. "And you, me, and Jennifer." They couldn't leave anyone out.

"Hell, Jase, anyone could have slipped back here. Even a customer. You know how it is once it gets busy. There must be at least twenty customers out there, and more who already came and went."

"Not anymore." The inspector walked over and slapped a piece of paper in Jase's hands. "You're closed."

Chapter Sixteen

The Alpine Sky's annual Beer and Bratwurst Festival was an awkward place for a breakup. Or maybe it was a brush-off. She and Matt hadn't officially been a couple.

They hadn't officially been anything. That should have made it easier. But Zoe still felt jumpy standing next to Matt on the fringes of the crowd in the Alpine Village plaza. Surrounded by charming souvenir shops and clothing boutiques, the plaza was a picturesque setting for small outdoor events like ice carving in the winter and street concerts in the summer. Tonight it was a rollicking festival of oompah bands, lederhosen-clad dancers, and a hundred or so beer-drinking, brat-eating guests.

Streetlamps and decorative strings of lights held back the night, so Zoe had to blame the noise for not spotting Matt until he suddenly appeared at her elbow. Too late to avoid him.

"Bratwurst?" He held out a bun topped with sauerkraut, a fat sausage poking out at each end.

"No thanks." She smiled, as if her stomach hadn't developed a sudden case of nervous flips. Telling your boss you were no longer romantically interested in him was a delicate situation, especially when he was so obviously in a lighthearted mood.

"How about a beer?"

She shook her head.

He didn't seem interested in either one himself, setting the brat down on a sidewalk table. He stood beside her, watching the dancers lock arms and whirl in circles. "If I asked you for a date, would that also be a no?"

She looked at him, relieved he was so perceptive. "Yes. I'm sorry, Matt."

She expected a cross look, or at least a disappointed sigh. He nodded. "Okay."

For someone who'd tried to get her into bed on their last date, it was surprisingly offhand. She drew her brows together. "You're not mad?"

He flashed his combination magnetic smile and piercing gaze. "Why would I be mad? All's fair in love, right? You're entitled to your choice. I assume you've made it."

"Uh, thanks for understanding." She laughed self-consciously. "I've been afraid to say anything after you were so nice to me."

"Nice?"

"You know, the flowers, that lovely dinner, and . . ." She hesitated, then decided to say it because he deserved credit for being a decent guy. "And the things you said about not caring about my past. It meant something. It meant a lot."

He chuckled dismissively. "Whatever."

"Really, Matt. Don't blow it off. Not everyone is so forgiving."

He gave her a puzzled look. "Zoe, any guy would be happy to be seen with you. Face it, you're a hot chick. It doesn't hurt my reputation if people think I sleep with a sexually uninhibited woman."

Zoe blinked, momentarily stunned. He grabbed a beer from a passing waitress and gave her a wink. "Charge it to the resort, honey." The woman bit back a comment, then headed back to replace the beer he'd taken as he kept talking. "It's not going to hurt the next guy you go out with, or the one after that. I'd think you'd know that by now. Men aren't embarrassed by your history. That was your choice, and personally, I'm glad you made it. Or I was, until you decided to turn into a tease. Fortunately, I know a woman in Juniper who's available on short notice." He blew some foam off the beer and took a sip. "If you ever change your mind, let me know. This beer isn't bad, you should try it."

He made it his parting line. She stood staring at his back as he disappeared into the crowded sidewalk. Heat flooded her cheeks, a combination of humiliation and anger. "Bastard!" she muttered. "Goddamn son of a bitch bastard!"

She spun on her heel and marched back to the hotel. The five-minute walk was a good thing since she needed that and more to cool off. Needed time to wonder, too, if she'd responded to a subliminal suspicion when she'd rejected Matt, or just been incredibly lucky, in time to make up for being incredibly stupid for going out with him in the first place.

Now she had to find a way to keep working with

Matt without spitting in his face. But just until she found the evidence that tied David and Ruth Ann to the incidents at the Rusty Wire. After that, a new job would be in order. She made a mental note to talk to Tammy at the Greystone Lodge about an assistant manager position.

Zoe was online, scrolling through old phone records, when the phone rang. She huffed with annoyance and picked it up, hoping it wasn't another problem. She wasn't in the mood. "Zoe Larkin."

"Zoe, I want you to leave town."

The tension eased a bit. Interesting, because his voice used to have the opposite effect. "Hi, Jase."

"Did you hear me?"

"Yes. What happened with the inspection?"

"We're closed. There are mice in the food storage pantry."

"Oh, no! I'm sorry."

"Zoe, we don't have mice. Someone put them there."

A week ago she would have laughed in his face. Now she believed him. "I'm looking on this end. So far I can't find anything suspicious."

"Forget it. I don't need a name, except to know who they bribed to do their actual dirty work. If he works for me, he's fired. What I need is for you to get out of the war zone, because I'm going after your employer."

"No. We discussed this."

"We discussed it when they were playing dirty and I was stupidly waiting them out. Now I'm going to fight back, and I don't want you involved."

"Too late. I want to find out who's responsible, too, and I will."

"Zoe, you can't. You're right in the middle—"

"Jase, you're wasting your breath."

He exhaled, the sound laced with irritation. "This could end badly. It could ruin your reputation."

She gave a cynical snort. "Wouldn't be the first time. At least this time I'd be standing up for something more important than my right to throw a public tantrum. Do you know how you're going to do it?"

He paused, no doubt adjusting to the fact that he couldn't shake her. "I'm not sure yet. They want the Rusty Wire. All I can do is make them *not* want it."

"Jase, you could burn it down and they wouldn't care. It's the land they want."

"I know, and they have the zoning commission on their side. Probably city council, too. They're several steps ahead of me, and I don't know how to fight in that arena. I may need to see an attorney."

She bit her lip. "It's possible I know someone who could help."

"Who?"

"Can you go to the commune tomorrow?"

Jase tossed the two sleeping bags in the bed of Brandon's truck. They landed next to the nylon bag that held his tent. Stepping back, he dusted off his hands. "Okay, you're all set. You guys have a good time, and tell your nephew hello from me."

"I will. You have time to go get some breakfast?"

"Can't, sorry. I have to pick up Zoe in twenty minutes."

Brandon paused with his hand on the door handle.

"Isn't seven-thirty in the morning a bit early for a date?"

"It's not a date. We're going up to the People's Free Earth Commune."

His eyebrows went up. "That place where she grew up?"

"She thinks someone there might be able to help me fight the zoning board and town council. I doubt it, but I kinda wanted an excuse to talk with one of the old guys there I met in town. He does a lot of trout fishing."

"Old guy?"

"Older. Sort of a father figure for Zoe, I gather. Sounds like they all helped raise the kids together."

Brandon's mouth twitched up at the corner. "Oh."

"What are you smirking at?"

"At how fast that happened."

"What happened?"

"She's taking you home to meet the parents."

"It's not like that." When Brandon's smile grew bigger, Jase shook his head. "You're off base. She doesn't even want a relationship with me."

"Right. And what do *you* want?"

He opened his mouth to say, "Sex," just to shut Brandon up, but that sounded too crude and temporary. He considered saying, "A good time with an interesting girl," but that sounded too casual and impersonal for what he felt with Zoe. Good times came and went without affecting your heart, and it already felt like she'd moved into a sizable corner of his. If she walked away, he knew there'd be a loud ripping sound inside him.

Well, damn, what *did* he want?

Brandon laughed as he got in the truck. "You think about it, buddy."

Jase watched him drive off, still musing over the new realization. He wanted Zoe to stay. Not just overnight. He wanted it badly enough to work for it.

He could almost feel his center shift as it found a new balance. He would fight to keep the Rusty Wire. And he would fight to keep Zoe. It looked like his days of kicking back and doing nothing with his life were over.

He stood still, waiting to see if his stomach would knot or his brain start to throb. Nothing. Well, no, that wasn't true. He felt a spurt of adrenaline, the old, familiar jolt of his body jumping over the starting line, flying toward the goal.

It felt good.

Jase figured the trip to the commune was worth the time, even if it accomplished nothing. It was an opportunity to see Zoe in shorts and a stretchy tank top. As sexy as she was in business suits, less was better, and the nicely stretched top and those long, shapely legs were tough competition for the spectacular scenery.

The road snaked back and forth up Two Bears, alternately putting steep, wooded drop-offs on Zoe's side of the truck, then his. He was familiar with the route. Everyone who lived in B-Pass eventually got curious enough to take a drive past the hippie commune. Most were disappointed when they didn't see topless women cavorting among the trees to the accompaniment of blaring psychedelic rock, like some sort of perpetual Woodstock. They saw nothing but meadows and rocks and a long, twisting private road that led into a stand of trees.

Jase turned onto the dirt drive, following the switchback past outcroppings and boulders three times the size of his truck. When the trees closed in, he asked, "How do they keep curious kids from sneaking up here?"

"They don't. Anyone is welcome, but few actually bother to come, and *no one* sneaks up on them."

He glanced into the trees, remembering what she'd said about them being comfortable with technology. "Hidden electronic security?"

"Dogs."

He saw what she meant as he rounded the last corner. A pack of dogs of all sizes and no particular breed dashed toward the truck, providing an excited, barking escort for the final two hundred yards. Jase parked near the house and stared. The large wood and stone house looked more like one of the modern ski lodges than a family home.

"I was picturing a dilapidated old farmhouse."

"It's a prosperous commune. They have a pottery business and a jewelry line that they sell to the high-end retail market."

She'd mentioned the items. He'd been thinking braided leather bracelets and novelty coffee cups, but it looked like he might be wrong.

They waded through five dogs that became eight by the time they reached the large front porch. Before Zoe could knock, the door opened and she was swept into a hug by a woman in a long, lacy skirt and about a dozen silver bracelets, with a long, faded red braid. He guessed it had once been bright red before it was shot with gray. She held Zoe back. "Baby! You look great!"

"Thanks. Mom, this is Jase Garrett. Jase, this is my mom, Kate Larkin."

He held out his hand. "Ma'am. It's good to meet you."

Her blue eyes danced as she walked past his hand and wrapped him in her arms. "Welcome, Jase! We're so glad to have you here! Come in!" She ushered them through the door, deftly shutting the dogs outside. "Would you like something to eat? Drink? How about some iced green tea with mint?"

"Sounds great," Zoe said. "Is Amber here?"

"You just missed her. She went to Juniper with Marcy. They're working on getting another store to carry our pottery."

Jase knew Zoe was disappointed, but figured he'd meet Cal's sister another time. He was more interested in the airy great room they passed through, noting the upright piano, several guitars, and a modern stereo system. No computer, no TV; apparently they weren't too connected to the outside world. He was introduced to a woman named Feather who was dusting an overloaded bookshelf. She reminded him vaguely of his grandmother, if his grandmother had worn a feather in her hair, a tie-dyed blouse, blue jeans, and a pound of beads.

Kate led them into a large country kitchen and waved at a long, rectangular table. "I called Pete, he's on his way. Sit down. Tell me all the news."

"Everyone's fine," Zoe said, pulling out a chair next to Jase. "The usual—Sophie's playing with bugs. Maggie's playing with Cal."

Kate set three glasses on the table and sat down,

including them both in her bright smile. "Am I supposed to ask who you're playing with?"

Jase was amused to see a slight flush of pink on Zoe's cheeks. "I'm not playing. The Alpine Sky is trying to buy Jase's land, and things are getting nasty. I'm hoping Pete can help us figure out how to fight back."

"Us?" Kate asked, zeroing in on the part that had caught Jase's attention, too.

"Him," Zoe corrected. She flicked a look at Jase, and shrugged. "Us. I'm not taking my employer's side in this. They play dirty."

Kate nodded. "And you like to stick to the rules."

Zoe frowned. "Instead of sticking with vandalism, arson, and slander? Yeah, I'd rather stick to the rules."

Kate looked thoughtful and a little worried. Jase had a feeling he knew why. "It's okay, she's been bending a few other rules."

Kate beamed at him. "Thank you. I do worry."

"No need. I've pointed out her rigid qualities, and it turns out they're not set in stone."

"You must be a good influence."

Zoe shot him a what-the-hell look. "Yes, he's leading me down a path of sin and corruption," Zoe said. "You'd be so proud."

Kate patted her hand. "You needed a little sin in your life, honey." While Zoe rolled her eyes, Kate looked up with a smile. "Here's Pete."

They went through another round of greetings, with a bear hug for each of them. Jase was taken aback, but figured the hug meant he'd moved up to friend status.

"Hey, man, good to see you," Pete said. "Zoe said you had some questions for me."

"If you know anything about land use and zoning laws, I do."

Pete laughed, a deep, generous sound that made Jase think of Santa Claus, if Santa wore denim overalls and had a long ponytail. "Know more about them than those establishment fools running B-Pass. Good thing, too, 'cause they'd like to legislate our asses out of here. You gotta keep your eye on the Man, ya know?" He took a chair across from them. "So tell me the problem."

Jase did, leaning his arms on the table as he told Pete about the Alpine Sky's offer to buy the Rusty Wire, followed by the vandalism on his truck, the fire, and the accusations that led to closing the place down. "I think Matt Flemming is behind it, but I can't prove it. He'd buy me out if he could, but I'm not selling, so I need to find a way to make him forget about the land."

"Can you help us?" Zoe asked.

"Maybe. Hang loose a sec." Pete scraped his chair back and disappeared into the living room. He came back with a rolled-up map that he unfurled on the table, using salt and pepper shakers, a sugar bowl, and a bottle of hot sauce to hold the edges down. "Show me the piece we're talking about."

Jase leaned in to study the roads, orienting himself, then drew an imaginary circle around the Rusty Wire and his adjoining fifty acres. "Here. From Evans Road to the eastern end of the resort."

Pete considered it for several seconds. "No developed land around it, so no impact on adjacent neighborhoods. Makes it harder. Flat or rugged?"

"As flat as it gets around here."

"So no geologic hazards like falling rocks." He

rubbed his chin through his gray beard. "Any wetlands?"

Jase shook his head. "Mostly trees."

"Hmm." Pete tugged absently at his beard. "I'll have Feather look at this later, see if she knows of any endangered wildlife or plants that might be there. If you can show this parcel is the habitat of an endangered species, Mother Nature wins. They can't do a thing with the land."

He hadn't even thought of that. "I'll take her there if she wants to see it."

"Not necessary. She's probably already been there and taken notes. She monitors all the flora and fauna around B-Pass so she can raise hell if anyone tries to mess with irreplaceable resources." He moved his improvised paperweights and rolled up the map. "Let us think about it for a few days, see if we can come up with something."

It didn't sit comfortably. "I didn't mean to give you a project. I'm sure Feather has other things to do than tramp around my land looking for endangered daisies or marmots or whatever."

Pete laughed. "I guarantee Feather has already covered every inch of your fifty acres, and taken notes. She keeps a file, and she doesn't ask permission—Feather's not cool with obeying laws, especially when it comes to private property. She says no one can own the land, it's here for everyone."

"Oh." He didn't know what else to say to news that an old hippie woman was sneaking around B-Pass, taking notes and keeping files.

Zoe smiled. "Thanks, Pete. If anyone can help, it's you and Feather."

"Hope we can. We'll go over it tonight. For now, I think Jase and I have some fishing lures to look at."

Jase grinned, more confident of getting valuable tips on lures than advice on saving his saloon. "I'm looking forward to stealing all your secrets."

Pete did his Santa laugh again. "The only secret is a strong magnifying glass and jeweler's tools. That's why we're going to my shop. You too, Zoe. There's something I want you to see."

"Oh, boy, jewelry." She jumped up. "Did you come up with a new design? I volunteer to be the first on my block to wear it."

"Not exactly new, but there has been a change." He winked at her, making it sound mysterious, which only made her smile more.

"Great! Jase, you gotta see the stuff he and my mom make. Maggie carries some of it in her store."

He let her pull him along after Pete, walking hand in hand with her as they left the house and crossed the compound. They took their time as she threw sticks for their canine escort while pointing out the goat barn, pastures, and pottery shop. As they approached the jewelry workshop she explained that it was housed in the commune's original farmhouse, where she'd been born.

He looked at everything, but looked more at Zoe. Her bright exuberance was in sharp contrast to the stiff, suit-wearing woman he'd first met. He'd known there was heat beneath that straightlaced facade, but hadn't guessed at the easy, carefree side of her, the one without checklists and rules. The one who romped with dogs and giggled over the antics of kid goats. He figured it must take a lot of effort to hide the real Zoe.

Or a lot of fear. Distancing herself from the wild Larkin girls had taken her too far in the other direction. She might not like it, but he was going to have something to say about that.

Pete ushered them into his workshop, and back to a table where a young man was bent over a magnifying glass, doing something with a length of silver wire. "I'd like you to meet my new apprentice."

The man raised his head, expectant smile already in place. A second later it slipped into a surprised stare.

Zoe had the same expression. "Eli?"

"Twinkie!" he blurted out.

She grinned, then whipped around, giving Jase a stern look. "You did not hear that."

Eli came around the table to wrap her in an enthusiastic hug. When she came out of it, she said, "Jase, this is Pete's son, Eli. He and I grew up together here, and he left . . . what, about ten years ago?"

Eli nodded. "Princeton, then the Peace Corps, then some humanitarian work in Guatemala."

"Does this mean you're back here to stay?"

"Hope so. Brought my wife, Gwen. She fell in love with the place. We're expecting our first baby this fall, and hopefully it'll be born here, same as you and I were."

Zoe laughed. "The next generation of the People's Free Earth Commune! I want to meet Gwen. Is she here?"

"Probably somewhere around the barn. She's into weaving, and wants to start a herd of sheep so we can make clothing with the wool, maybe start a new business."

"I love her already. See you later, Jase."

"Hold on. You want to explain Twinkie, or do I ask Eli?"

"Oh." She smiled self-consciously. "You can probably guess. Junk food was nonexistent here. When I was about ten we visited some friends who had left the commune, and I discovered these little cream-filled pieces of heaven. I overindulged, and the result wasn't pretty. My friends at the commune, being sensitive, caring people, never let me forget it." All traces of embarrassment suddenly disappeared, replaced by a severe look. "But you will."

He smiled, making no promises. "Did you ever eat them again?"

The mischief flashed back into her eyes. "Are you kidding? Cream-filled heaven. They're my favorite dessert."

He spent two happy hours talking trout fishing and lures with Pete before he tracked Zoe down. He found her sitting on the ground running her hands through the wool of a placid black-faced sheep as it lay on the grass, chewing cud and ignoring her. She jumped up when she saw him.

"Come over here, Jase! Feel my hands. Aren't they smooth and silky? Lanolin, it's all over the wool. You can do so much with sheep!"

He rubbed his hand over the lotion slickness of hers, then kept it, twining their fingers together. "You sound dangerously like a kid with someone else's puppy who wants one of her very own."

She laughed. "I already have a job. But I have to tell Maggie because she could market the hell out of a commune clothing line."

The way happiness sparkled around her, he had to say it. "You love it here."

"I do."

"Did you ever think about coming back to stay, like Eli?"

She tilted her head as if considering it now. "Once. But it's not what I want for my life. Besides, give up Twinkies?"

"Right. The most important consideration."

"You'd better believe it."

Zoe thought the day couldn't have been more perfect, and it had a lot to do with sharing it with Jase. Taking him to the commune allowed him into the part of her life she held closest to her heart. If he'd been distant and polite, she would have been crushed. But he'd acted as if a family of gray-haired hippies was the most normal thing in the world. She'd been both pleased and proud of him.

They stopped by the house to say good-bye before starting back down the mountain, collecting more hugs and a bag of homemade granola that Kate thrust into Jase's hands. "All natural, grown without pesticides," she told him.

"Of course it is," he said, and kissed her cheek. Zoe's mom beamed. A wave of warmth spread through Zoe.

Jase looked in the rearview mirror as they drove off and shook his head. "I had this image of hippies lying around smoking dope and listening to old Hendrix records. Boy, was I wrong. That's the most ambitious, capitalistic group of people I've ever met."

She laughed. "I know. It takes work to make a

commune succeed. My family taught me to try hard at whatever I do, and I guess it stuck. I tried hard to be the best at rebelling. Then I tried hard to be good at hotel management."

He was supposed to smile. Or agree. Instead, he grew quiet, watching the road until she thought he'd forgotten the conversation. "Ever thought of being good at being Zoe?"

She frowned, because it sounded suspiciously like criticism. "What does that mean?"

"It means that teenage rebel and the supercompetent hotel manager . . . neither one is you, Zoe. And I wonder if you lost yourself somewhere in the middle."

If it wasn't criticism, it was at least presumptuous. She was pretty sure she knew herself better than he did, but she wanted to hear where this was going. "Really? If you know so much, then who am I?"

"Someone less extreme. Less controlled." It came out so quickly she knew he'd given it some thought. "Someone who doesn't gauge every move against a list of acceptable behavior. I caught a glimpse of that Zoe several times today, and she knocked me out."

The knocking-out part put a tiny jump in her pulse, which irritated her because she wanted to be mad at him. She wasn't *extreme* and *controlled*. "I'm happier up here because I'm not at work handling staffing and booking problems. So what? That's not extreme. In fact, I think that makes me pretty normal."

"I didn't say you were happier. I said today you weren't measuring yourself against some imaginary ideal. No checklist to make sure you did the proper thing. No plan, just you being you."

"Is that how you see me? Everything planned, nothing spontaneous?" The mad started edging back in, mostly because it sounded too true for comfort. "Is that what you think I did the night before last, put a big checkmark beside 'Sleep with Jase'?" She managed to say it without blushing, since she hadn't bothered to check that one off yet.

"No." Now *he* looked irritated. "That's not what that was. I know it, and so do you. There's something between us, something more than you're-hot-and-I-want-to-jump-your-bones. We acted on it." He took his eyes off the road long enough to give her a hard look. "Don't make that part of this, because I think that woman who let down her guard for one night was the real you, and I hope to hell I see her again."

Damn it, how could he flatter her and insult her at the same time? "What's wrong with having a plan? That's how people succeed. You can't tell me you didn't have a plan for reaching the Olympics—how much to practice, what races to enter, even what to eat and not eat."

"You're right, I had a strict plan. But not for my private life, not for who to date, where to be seen, where I could go. And I didn't worry about what anyone else thought of it."

Direct hit. She worried about what *everyone* thought. She had to.

"You know why I do it. I have to repair my image."

"Not if you lose yourself doing it." With a little force, it could have sounded judgmental and mean. It didn't. He reached out to close his hand over hers, squeezing gently, and his understanding gaze was so supportive her breath caught in her throat. "It's not worth it if the person everyone wants you to be isn't who you really are. If that's the plan, then screw it."

She settled into an uncomfortable silence. The problem was, she'd always had a plan. A plan when she rebelled and a plan when she decided to clean up her image. She didn't know how to act without one, or what to work toward.

Or who she'd be if she wasn't trying to fit someone else's ideals. That was the scariest part.

He was right, she'd lost herself.

Chapter Seventeen

Jase jerked to attention when he heard the back door of the Rusty Wire open. This late on a Monday night, with the place closed, the footsteps were loud on the wooden boards. Light, fast steps that indicated a shorter stride. A woman.

A thrill of excitement sliced through him, along with the memory of his last late night at the saloon. Scattered clothes, hot bodies pressed together, and Zoe's dazed look as he laid her on a table and blew her orderly world to pieces. He was still smug with satisfaction over that.

She'd put some major cracks in his world, too. That mental compartment where he put his sexual affairs, neatly separate from the rest of his life, wouldn't hold Zoe. She'd spilled into his life, occupying his thoughts when she wasn't occupying his bed. He'd barely thought of anything else since their first hot encounter six nights ago. He tried to keep his mind on other things, but it latched on to her and wouldn't let go, allowing the most insignificant

details to remind him of her. Details as small as footsteps in his deserted saloon.

It couldn't be Zoe, though; she didn't have a key.
He worked at getting the smoldering look off his face,
looking up with what he hoped was convincing surprise when Jennifer walked into the main room.

Her gaze took in the papers and open laptop covering the table he'd turned into a temporary office. He
closed the computer and leaned back in his chair. "Hi.
I didn't expect to see anyone here."

"I saw your truck. I thought I might be able to help
with something."

"I appreciate it, but there's nothing to do. The ex-
terminator verified that there are no mice living in the
storage room, and probably never were. No accumu-
lated droppings, no signs of chewing, no nests. It's all
paperwork from here out. Although I'll be asking that
reporter from the *Echo* to do another piece explaining
the situation."

"I can do that for you."

Like she'd taken on just about everything else since
they'd been closed. He shook his head, smiling. "Jennifer, I don't think you even know how to take time off.
Maybe I should take you fishing, get you interested in
something besides work."

Her brow creased. "Can't fish at night."

Jesus, the woman had a wide streak of serious. He
didn't want to insult her by laughing, so he merely
said, "You got me there."

She scanned the papers and ledgers that covered the
table. "What are you doing?"

A logical question, since he hardly ever cracked
a book or examined a file related to running the

business. "I'm taking advantage of our downtime to familiarize myself with income and payroll. Taxes, state regulations, all that stuff Russ takes care of."

"Why? Is he quitting?"

He snorted. "No, but the fact that you asked confirms it's about time I did this. I own the Rusty Wire, and aside from our net income and hourly wages, I don't even know the day-to-day details of running the place. So I'm educating myself about our licensing fees, liability coverage, the cost of employee health insurance, all that stuff. Russ handles it, but I should know it, too."

"Why?" Her brow furrowed slightly. "That's the manager's job. You don't need to bother, to have all those extra hassles in your life."

Maybe she thought he wanted a life with no responsibilities. If she did, it was his own fault. He'd never shown any other inclination since sinking into the cocoon he'd woven around himself.

"It's not a bother. I know I stayed out of it all this time, but I can't do that anymore. Not paying attention nearly allowed the Alpine Sky to steal this place out from under me."

"How? They can't make you sell if you don't want to."

"No, but they can make it impossible for me to do anything else. They're two steps ahead of me on priming the city council and the zoning board for a first-class golf course, and it didn't take them long to bring on the pressure tactics. They were hoping I'd accept their offer, but they were ready if I refused. They intend to win, and I know how single-minded that drive can be. They won't stop at anything. If I just sit back and watch, I lose."

"What can you do?"

His mouth twisted with distaste. "I don't know yet. It will have to be a legal answer, a way to block their plans, and right now I can't find any avenue they haven't already anticipated."

Jennifer absorbed the information, studying him. Her eyes were slitted dark pools he couldn't read. He'd *never* been able to read her, to follow her thinking; it was no wonder they had no real emotional connection. He hadn't even felt sympathetic warmth at her tentative advances. He called her a friend, but friendly stranger was more accurate.

She crossed her arms, the picture of stubborn resistance. "I just don't like to see you doing this. You were so content, and now you're changing your whole life because of this fight with the Alpine Sky."

"I don't have any choice, Jennifer."

"Yes, you do. Give them what they want. Sell the fifty acres and keep the Rusty Wire. They don't need it, and you do."

It was so unexpected, he simply stared.

"It's the best answer," she insisted. "You'd have your life back, no problems to deal with. Russ and I can handle the details. You'd be happy."

He felt off balance, hit with a double punch. The first one, suggesting he sell the land, had only grazed him. He'd never let Matt Flemming turn those fifty pristine acres into a golf course. But the second jab had stunned him like a blow to the head. She wanted him to hand over his problems, to escape back into his bland life. Let her handle everything. And it sounded frighteningly familiar.

Christ, was that what she'd been doing the past nine

years? Encouraging him to let everyone else deal with the problems?

The possibility repelled him, but at the same time he saw how easily it could have happened. She'd always taken on extra work, extra responsibilities. He thought she'd been bored. She could just as easily have been taking his life out of his hands.

And he'd let her.

He couldn't blame Jennifer for what he'd allowed her to do, but he didn't have to let it continue. He was a drowning man coming up for air, and he wasn't going under again.

"I *am* happy, Jennifer. I don't want to go back to the way I've been living for the past nine years. I was stagnating. You must have seen that."

She gave him her usual inscrutable look. "So?"

"So that's not living."

She tilted her head, pursing her lips as she thought it over. "You've changed."

"I suppose I have. About time, wouldn't you say?"

She gave no indication of having heard him. "It's because of her."

Zoe. Shit! He'd stumbled into that jealousy thing again.

It hit him in the gut, the same wrenching twist he felt every time he realized Jennifer wanted him. He'd hoped she'd pick up on his disinterest, but she obviously couldn't read him any better than he read her. Or else she misunderstood him completely. It made her interest all the more unexpected, and a little creepy.

It had to end.

"I guess Zoe is part of the reason I've changed." If you counted kicking him off his complacent ass with her persistent sales pitches. He'd have to remember to thank her for that. "I admire her determination and intelligence." True, although laughably incomplete when counting all the reasons he'd fallen for Zoe Larkin.

"You love her."

"What? No, I . . ." He hesitated, the automatic denial still on his lips. He wasn't sure what being in love felt like, but he'd experienced *not being in love* with numerous women, and it wasn't anything like what he felt for Zoe. What he felt for her had more warmth, more depth, more importance. What lay between like and love?

He finished his reply. "I don't know." Then waited to see how she'd take it.

Her reaction was so slow and deliberate that part of him wanted to shake her and say, "I'm not interested in you, there's someone else, move on." But he had to let her take it in, adjust, accept that he wasn't the one for her. He could at least offer a consolation. "You deserve to have someone special in your life, too, Jen. To *be* special to someone. There are probably a dozen guys you've turned down this year alone. Give them a chance."

That distracted her; a small scowl came and went across her face. "I'm not interested in them." Then, as if his feelings for Zoe had never mattered to her, she stuck her hands in her pockets and shrugged her shoulders. "I'm glad you have someone, Jase. I hope you and Zoe are very happy together."

He furrowed his forehead over her apparent sincerity. "Thanks."

"I'll see you around."

He nearly called her back just to make sure there

was no bitterness in her, no hurt, but hell, he didn't want to prolong it. Zoe or no Zoe, he and Jennifer were never going to have anything together, and the sooner she accepted it the better. For both of them.

He listened to the back door shut, and the faint sound of her car as she drove away. He should probably feel like shit for rejecting her, but he didn't. He felt lighter, energized. Telling Jennifer how he felt had made him realize how important Zoe was.

Love? He'd have to take that word out again, roll it around in his mind, see how it felt against his heart. It might be a good fit.

Zoe watched as the deliveryman pushed yet another handcart through her office door, unloading two more boxes in front of Matt and David, who beamed like kids at Christmas. "That's it," the guy told them, closing the door as he left.

Eight large boxes covered most of the floor space. "I can't get to the fax machine," she said.

"So move a box aside," David said, as if they didn't weigh seventy pounds each. He spoke without turning as he applied a box cutter to the cartons behind Matt's desk. Matt opened the flaps and reached inside as David moved to the next box.

She hadn't wanted to ask what was in them. They were cutting her out of the loop lately, not involving her in whatever they were planning. But she watched with interest as Matt pulled out plastic-wrapped items of clothing, passing one to David before ripping into another one. She watched him shake out a pair of men's pants in the Alpine Sky's official deep blue, examining the logo embroidered on the front pocket. The double *E* of Everton Equipment took on a silky sheen under the fluorescent lights.

"Subtle, but classy," he announced with satisfaction.

David opened a box and pulled out golf shoes in blue and white. "Good quality. This stuff is gonna sell like crazy."

She watched in disbelief as they pulled out more clothing, draping it over boxes to admire it before moving on. Shirts, sweaters, jogging apparel, caps, ladies' accessories—enough to open a store. Or, more accurately, a pro shop.

For a golf course that didn't exist.

"Were you looking for a big tax-loss item? You know Jase won't sell."

Matt gave her an indulgent smile. "You need to work on your confidence, Zoe."

It was *his* confidence that sent a chill skidding down her spine. He still expected Jase to change his mind, which meant more problems in store for the Rusty Wire.

David snickered. "If you can't look ahead, you'll never get ahead. That's Ruth Ann's motto, and she should know about getting ahead."

She narrowed her eyes and imagined punching him in the nose.

"Mr. Flemming?" The voice came from the phone on Matt's desk. "Your mother is on line two."

Matt half turned with an armful of sweatshirts. "Tell her I'll call her back, Diane."

"She said it's an emergency."

He pressed his lips together and eyed the two large boxes between him and his desk. He lifted a questioning brow at Zoe. "Would you mind hitting two and putting it on speaker?"

She was tempted to say no, but admitted to curiosity about what Ruth Ann had to say. Maybe her search for a new vacation resort location had been successful. Leaning over her desk, she hit the buttons on Matt's phone.

"Hi, Mom," Matt said. "Can this wait? I've got my hands full at the moment."

David chuckled as if Matt had said something incredibly clever. The little suck-up.

"No, this can't wait." Irritation put a razor's edge on Ruth Ann's voice, which was suddenly a lot sharper than Zoe remembered. "Kyle got prickly about his investment. He's been talking to his lawyer, or somebody, and they're telling him there're problems with the ownership. What the hell's holding up the papers?"

It took Zoe several seconds to connect the name to Kyle Russerman, the pro golfer who'd agreed to invest in the nonexistent golf course. There'd been no time lag for Matt, who froze in place. The mound of sweatshirts in his arms rose and fell visibly with each rapid breath as he edged toward hyperventilation.

"Put him on, I'll talk to him," Matt said.

"I'd love to," Ruth Ann said. "But I can't. He checked out of our suite an hour ago, bitching about fraud. The tight-assed little fucker."

Matt paled. David's color rose in contrast as he drew the same conclusion Zoe had—Ruth Ann had been getting cozy with Kyle Russerman in Aruba. Zoe wasn't above enjoying Matt's shock.

"Just fax him the papers on the land purchase, Matt."

Matt should take her off speaker. She figured it was a measure of his shock that he didn't think of it.

Behind his rapid blinking, she knew, his mind was racing. "There's been a delay on this end, Mom. A minor delay in the purchase. Tell me where you put Kyle's investment. I'll call the bank and have it refunded to him until we close the deal."

"Well, that would work, except the money's gone." Ruth Ann sounded personally offended, like money just up and disappeared if you didn't keep your eye on it. "A year's lease on a yacht and a tropical island aren't cheap, you know. Image costs, darling."

Matt's eyes met Zoe's. She saw panic and a half second's hope that she would turn off the speaker, which she met with placid disinterest.

He dropped the sweatshirts and threw himself over a large box, stumbling as he reached for his phone. David still stood frozen in shock as Zoe sat back and listened to Matt's verbal scramble.

"Give me the name of the company you signed with, Mom. Yes, the yacht, too." Zoe could no longer hear Ruth Ann's end of the conversation, but had no trouble imagining the petulant tone. "Are there any other toys you haven't told me about?" He was starting to sound more like a snotty little kid than an Ivy League–educated executive. "Well, you damn well better hope I can, or your accommodations will be a lot less pretty than your fancy new boat. What? When? Fuck! Hang on."

He glared at Zoe. "Get out."

She raised her eyebrows at his tone, but got up and left the office, figuring she should be applauded for not smiling. David hustled out behind her without being asked, yanking the door shut behind them. He swiped at the perspiration on his forehead. "I think the resort's in financial trouble."

"I'd say that's a safe bet."

"Ruth Ann likes to buy things." He wiped his palms on his hips, then repeated the motion as if the sweat wouldn't stop coming. "She doesn't have the best head for business, either. I'm not sure she stays within the letter of the law. This could be bad."

She'd be surprised if Ruth Ann gave the law any thought at all. "David, do you know anything about what they've been doing at the Rusty Wire to pressure Jase?"

"No." He wiped some more, darted a nervous look at her. "Not for sure."

She blew out a long breath and prepared for the worst. "Let's go have coffee."

Zoe figured she could have waited until the next day, but what would be the point? Nothing would change except her bright flare of anger, which might fade a bit, and what would be the fun in that? Matt was here now and her temper was hot. No time like the present.

She strode into her office, getting a vicious glare from Matt as he looked up from the fax machine. "I need some privacy."

"No problem." She flapped a sheet of paper so he'd hear the rustle, then set it on his desk. "There's your privacy."

He looked annoyed, then kicked a couple of boxes as he squeezed between them to retrieve the paper. It took three seconds for his head to jerk up and his brows to slam down. "What the fuck is this?"

"Exactly what it says. My resignation."

"You're required to give four weeks' notice, not two."

Two had seemed bad enough. There was no way she'd be able to take another month of working with Matt. "I guess I broke the rules. There's a lot of that going around."

He dropped the paper. "Are you implying the Alpine Sky did something illegal? If so, you'd better be able to back that up."

She dearly wished she could, but David had only known what Ruth Ann told him. "You were smart enough not to leave a paper trail, but we both know you're responsible for everything that's happened to the Rusty Wire. The ironic part is, if Jase agreed to sell you his land tomorrow, you probably couldn't buy it. Your spending got ahead of your greed, didn't it?"

"You don't know half of what you think you know." His lips smiled, but his eyes remained cold. "The financing for the golf course has been in place for a month. It's a no-brainer for the bank, a guaranteed win for everyone—Garrett, us, the town. So you go right ahead and tell Garrett to agree to our offer. He'll have his money tomorrow."

She couldn't tell if he was bluffing; his arrogance always came across as sincerity. Or maybe he sincerely believed his lies. Either way, she didn't want her name associated with his resort. And she knew Jase's answer without asking.

"Sorry, it's a moot point. He's not selling."

He raked her with a cool look. "I see where your loyalties lie. Are you fucking him, too?"

She glared. "Go to hell."

Tension crackled between them, prickling her skin

like the heavy air before a thunderstorm. "Pack up your things," he ordered. "You're leaving now."

She smiled, baring gritted teeth. "Maintenance is already on its way with a box." She hadn't expected him to wait out the two weeks. Her only regret was losing two weeks' pay. The money would have come in handy while she looked for another job.

He hit a button on his phone. "Diane, call security to escort Ms. Larkin out." His eyes narrowed and his mouth set in a hard line. "Don't expect to get a good recommendation from the Alpine Sky."

"A recommendation from you won't mean much pretty soon. I'm better off without one." It felt good to toss it in his face.

She just hoped it was true. Otherwise she was throwing away her dream career based on nothing more than suspicion and hearsay.

At least she was protecting her reputation. When all Matt's shaky financial deals collapsed, her name wouldn't be part of it.

Jase spotted the headlights through the trees from the elevated vantage point of his porch, and watched her pull up to the house. Building on a steep rise had put his front door a full story above the driveway at the top of a curving stone stairway. Small ground-level lights lit the way. He figured by the time he was seventy he probably wouldn't want to climb all those steps, but for now the effort was worth the view. Looking over treetops into the vast mountain sky always made him sigh with contentment.

It was a good place to wait for Zoe. The lights were on in the house behind him, but he'd left the front porch in darkness to better see the stars and feel part of the night. She probably couldn't see him on the glider.

For a moment she was visible in the light of her open car door, then she slammed it shut and became little more than a shadow. He wouldn't have needed that moment of light to recognize her. The outline of her body, the way she moved were imprinted on his mind. At some subconscious level he knew her walk, recognized the smooth curve of her back from shoulders to waist, the sway of her hips, the tilt of her head. They were as familiar to him as if he'd known her for years.

Shoes clicked softly on stone. A quick gait, energetic and light, not the trudging step someone might have at the end of a workday. He doubted Zoe ever trudged.

She reached the porch but hadn't seen him off to the side on the glider. "Hey," he called softly. "You're home early."

She turned, already smiling. Setting down a box and her purse, she came to him, settling onto the cushion beside him. "By a couple of hours. Should I have called first?"

"Don't be ridiculous." She hadn't moved in with him, but only because it seemed too soon to ask her. She'd been there every night, anyway, an island of happiness in a frustrating week.

He slipped his arm around her and tilted her chin up for a kiss. She curled her hand around his neck, let her lips linger on his, then cuddled against him with a sigh.

"Tough night at the office?"

"It probably should feel like it, but no. More like

satisfying." She toed off her shoes and curled her legs onto the glider. "I quit my job."

He pulled back so he could see her face. "You what?"

"Quit. I gave two weeks' notice, but Matt chose to kick me out on the spot. All my stuff's in that box. He was probably right to do it. If I'd stayed I would have been searching for evidence to use against him. Now all I have is David's accusation that Ruth Ann said Matt was behind it all."

That wasn't news to him. "That's why you quit?"

"He made me a part of it, using me as a dupe to make him look innocent."

"He never looked innocent to me."

She smiled. "You just didn't like him because he was coming on to me."

"Sweetheart, I wanted to *kill him* because he was coming on to you. I didn't trust him because he's the kind of guy who will say what you want to hear, and steamroll over you if you get in his way."

"You're right, and I wish I'd seen it sooner."

He didn't say anything because he wished she'd seen it sooner, too, and didn't like to think of her being with Matt.

Dancing with him.

Kissing him.

And when they were alone, maybe doing more than that. He wouldn't blame her for falling for a slick come-on from a guy who fit every requirement on that stupid list of hers. But he could blame Matt. The thought of him putting his hands on her, undressing her, making love to her . . . His body went rigid with anger and he imagined tearing the guy limb from limb. For a start.

Zoe stroked her hand over the bunched muscles in his arm. "I never slept with him."

He closed his eyes and released a long breath before saying, "I'm not judging."

"I know, but I'm saying. I didn't."

"Okay." He figured it was the enlightened response. It didn't stop a smug, fist-pumping "Yes!" in his mind.

"There's something else." She tilted her face up to look at him. "Jase, I think Matt is pushing this golf course harder than we knew. I heard part of a conversation between him and his mother today. It sounds like they might have falsified documents or bribed people, something that made it look like they already owned your land, and got Kyle Russerman to put a chunk of money into the golf course. He must have become suspicious and now he wants his money back, but Ruth Ann has already spent it."

"Christ, what arrogant asses. I hope to hell he sues them. But, babe," he said, and waited for her to look at him, "this is why I wanted you far away from the Alpine Sky."

"I know. But I was never involved in the financial side, so they can't hurt me."

He squeezed her tighter, hoping to hell she was right. "Good."

They sat quietly, listening to the whisper of aspen leaves in the breeze. Zoe snuggled against him, warm and soft, smelling vaguely of the sunscreen she'd applied earlier that day. Sunscreen *he'd* applied, taking it out of her hands so he could stroke lotion over her neck and rub it inside the V-neck of her knit top. He'd taken his time, feeling the need to kiss various parts of her first, until her purring, arching response led to the need to shed his own clothes and carry her to bed. The sunscreen had been abandoned in favor of massage oil that was applied with maddeningly slow strokes in intimate places. When neither could take any more, they tossed the oil to the floor and plunged into a slick, desperate finish.

The memory, tripped by nothing more than scent, had him burying his face against her neck, inhaling deeply. The smell of sunscreen made him hard, a reaction that might have disadvantages in the future, but that he couldn't find any problem with at the moment.

Reaching down, he flipped the lever that locked the glider in place, then shifted so she was reclining next to him. A tight fit, but workable. He slid his hand up to cup her breast, and she arched into it. Rubbing his thumb over the tip, he nuzzled her ear. "Do you realize that until the Rusty Wire reopens we're both unemployed?"

"Mmm. I guess we are. I like the way you do that."

"We'll have to find a way to fill our time."

Her hand slipped down to his zipper, finding the hard ridge beneath it and rubbing along its length. "We could get together. Work on some ideas."

"I like the one you're working on right now."

She kissed him, lips soft and mobile, tongue sliding sensuously over his. "It has variations. I could make a list."

"You do that." He eased his hand beneath her skirt and up her thigh, watching her eyes.

"We should . . ." Her playful smile went slack and her eyes lost focus. "That feels so good . . ." A small groan escaped her throat. "Oh, God . . ." Her voice died on a whimper.

Right there, he thought. That was the moment he waited for each time they made love, when the part of her that made plans and lists was swamped by a tidal wave of pure *feeling*. Seeing her lost in bliss, knowing he was the cause, was as arousing as the hand that opened his zipper and gripped him inside his jeans.

More. Giving a woman pleasure had never outweighed taking his own, until Zoe. The blurry, dazed look he put in her eyes touched something deep inside him. Driving her up, watching her come apart, was nearly enough to send him over the edge with her. Slipping inside her to do it again took every ounce of control he had to keep from ending too soon.

The shuddering breath she took told him she was nearly there. She reached for him blindly, grabbed his shoulder, bunching his shirt in a desperate grip. "Oh my God, Jase . . ." She ended in a gasp as her body clamped around his fingers. He moved his hand, letting her ride it out until her muscles relaxed and she gave a long sigh.

He kissed her, then pulled down the panties he'd been pushing aside, sliding them all the way off. She sat halfway up as he did, leaning on one elbow while working his pants open enough to pull his erection free. He groaned as she fondled the tip, then slid her hand up and down. The desire to bury himself inside her became a whole lot more urgent.

"Jase," she murmured as she lowered her head. The warm, wet feel of her mouth was an erotic punch to the gut. "This glider isn't going to work."

She was right, but the building pressure in his groin meant he wasn't about to walk all the way to the bedroom. There might be better alternatives, but he wasn't up for pondering them. The hell with it. He slid onto the floor and took her hand.

She grinned at him slowly as she got up. Straddling his hips, she raised her skirt as she lowered her body, until the skirt was bunched at her waist and her body locked tightly to his. She rocked gently, closing her eyes and humming with satisfaction.

Pure lust shot through him. Only one thing kept it short of perfection, and he reached for the buttons on her blouse to remedy it. "Sweetheart, I've got a thing for you in a suit, but this feels too much like a desk clerk providing naughty room service."

"Not your kind of fantasy?" She stripped off her blazer, then tossed the blouse after it. One click and the bra was gone, too. "Better?"

He grinned. "A naked woman—the classic fantasy."

She leaned forward, her hair making a curtain around them as she kissed him. "Just a simple man with simple needs, aren't you?"

"Nothing simple about you, babe. And you're what I need." She pushed up, changing the angle, and he put his hands on her breasts. Heat flared in her eyes and she threw her head back, moving faster.

He let her set the pace, drinking in the vision of her moving above him. She closed her eyes, reaching for that peak again and he concentrated on holding back his own. Rapid breathing filled the night, and the slap of skin against skin. Cool air skimmed their bodies, but Zoe's skin stayed hot beneath his hands, a sheen of sweat glistening in the light from the window.

If he'd ever had a juvenile fantasy about this, it couldn't come near the reality. He might have imagined the adrenaline shot to his libido, because there'd never been anything lacking in his fantasies. But he'd never imagined the delicious ache that went with it. Never experienced it with another woman, either. Watching Zoe lose herself in bliss, there was no mistaking the powerful tug on his heart.

It nearly pushed him over the edge. He was almost relieved when she panted out a helpless cry and braced herself on his shoulders. He gave a couple of hard thrusts and sent them both rocketing, riding the spasms until they faded and died. Drained, he closed his eyes and wrapped his arms around her as she collapsed on top of him.

He held her for a minute until he felt her skin go cool and dry in the rising wind. The feel of rain came with it, the building storm sucking up the last of the day's heat. He rubbed his hand over her back. "Cold?"

"Mmm."

He supposed that passed as coherent conversation after the energetic end she'd just tacked on to an exhausting day. "Tired? Hungry?"

"All of the above," she mumbled into his shoulder. She lifted her head, gave him a leisurely kiss, then blinked at her surroundings. "Jase, I'm naked on your front porch."

"I noticed." If he'd thought anyone could see, she wouldn't be. It was dark, and his neighbors were several hundred feet away through the trees.

She looked worried. "This would go a long way toward shattering my carefully constructed good-girl image."

"I think your image is safe, honey. No one can see us." But something tightened inside him at the loaded words. It meant he was part of her bad-girl side, the part she didn't want others to see. He wished she didn't feel the need to be one or the other, since both were part of who she was. But he couldn't make those choices for her. If he was going to continue being part of her life, he'd have to be content to be the part she kept hidden.

He could do it. But not forever.

Chapter Eighteen

As much as she loved being with Jase, they couldn't be together all the time. She had her own life.

That's what Zoe told herself as she had lunch with Sophie, talking about her sister's research on mutant bugs while trying not to think about Jase. Then hanging out at Maggie's store, helping uncrate the strange fossils Maggie sold to her high-end customers, again trying not to think about Jase. She was only partially successful.

The trouble was, she no longer had her own life. Without a job, she had no idea how to fill her days. The past four days since she'd quit had nearly driven her crazy.

Jase had other things to do. He hadn't been specific, but had been excited enough about some new project he worked on in his garage that she knew she had to find something to do on her own. It probably had to do with trout lures; she didn't care to ask for fear that she'd actually have to listen to the answer. Besides, it gave her a good opportunity to spend a few hours researching lanolin and how to extract it from sheep wool. The commune's sheep had sparked her interest, and even if she didn't have time to develop the project herself, she could pass the information on to Gwen. She almost envied Eli's wife the opportunities ahead of her.

Finally, having exhausted all other possibilities, she resorted to housework. Cleaning bathroom grout was one of her least favorite chores, and doing it required a desperate lack of options. Resigned, she got out the cleanser and a couple of old toothbrushes for the stubborn spots.

Kneeling in the bathtub, she sprayed a line of cleanser along the base of the tile where the wall met the tub. Fifteen minutes later, with the toothbrush bristles worn to stubs, the ring of her cell phone cut through the music from the radio beside the sink. She looked up, blew a loose strand of hair out of her eyes, and considered letting it go to voice mail. It probably wasn't Jase or her sisters. But it was an excuse to stop scrubbing grout, and that was enough. Stripping off her latex gloves, she stepped out of the tub, turned off the radio, and looked at the display on her phone: the Greystone Lodge.

"Hi, Tammy."

"Okay, girlfriend, give me the scoop."

She sighed, knowing all the other resort managers and assistant managers would have heard the news. "Sounds like you already know it. I quit my job."

"That's not what I heard. I heard you were fired."

It hadn't taken long for the story to get distorted. The Larkin name probably made a scandal more believable. She set her jaw and tamped down her irritation. "No, I wasn't fired. I gave notice, and Matt Flemming showed me the door. I wouldn't mind if you cleared that up with whoever gave you the news."

"Um, I don't think I can do that. I heard it from my general manager, who just got back from a long lunch with Matt."

Her muscles went slack with shock and she met her own wide-eyed stare in the mirror. He'd twisted the story. Was he that threatened by the thought of her talking, or did he merely hate her?

Clamping her mouth shut, she got a tighter grip on the phone. "He's spinning it, Tammy. I swear. I found out he was involved in some stuff that was unethical. Hell, it's illegal. I couldn't be part of it."

"I figured it must have been something bad on his part if he was running you down like that."

She gripped the counter edge and swallowed. "Like what?"

"He told Jerry you'd been assigned to some special project, something about them trying to buy out the Rusty Wire."

"That's true."

"He said things started going wrong. You couldn't close the deal and stuff happened." Tammy paused. "Illegal stuff."

"Also true, on the surface. But it was Matt who was involved with the illegal things, not me."

"I didn't think you'd do it," Tammy said. "Especially when he claimed you were sleeping with the owner of the Rusty Wire and plotting against the Alpine Sky. I *knew* you'd never do either of those things."

Oh, no. Oh, shit.

The edge of the tub was two steps away—too far.

She sank to the floor and leaned against the vanity drawers. In her chest, her heart jumped to marathon speed, banging against her ribs. "Tammy, I . . ." Shit, this wasn't going to sound good, but since it was going to get out anyway, she might as well see how it was accepted by a friend first. "I swear I wasn't involved in any of the things that happened to the Rusty Wire. But . . ." She drew in a deep breath, let it out. "I *am* seeing the owner. It has nothing to do with Matt trying to buy his land."

She could feel Tammy's disbelief in the long pause. "You're involved with some guy who runs a low-class honky-tonk? *You?*" Her voice rose at the end, as if it was too incredible to believe.

She made an effort not to bristle. "It's not low class. And his name's Jase Garrett. He's a good guy. The thing is, I kind of ditched Matt to be with him, so now he's pissed." And vindictive—she wished she'd seen that part coming. "He hates me, and he knows the things that have been happening at the saloon are going to get ugly and involve the police. He's probably trying to make me look guilty so they won't take a closer look at him."

"He said the police already took you in for questioning."

The caution in Tammy's voice was more upsetting than what she said. She clearly didn't want to believe Matt, but Zoe could already hear the skepticism. The facts were lining up with everything he'd said, making his accusations sound true.

"Zoe, he said you were the number one suspect in the fire at the Rusty Wire, that you and the owner conspired to burn it down to get the insurance money.

I didn't believe it, but . . ." But obviously her opinion had changed. "He said he was just going to tear it down anyway, so you and the owner came up with a scheme to get a little extra money out of the deal."

"No," she said around the tightness in her throat.

"You're saying the fire was just a coincidence?"

There it was—disbelief, coming through loud and clear. Zoe squeezed her eyes shut, letting the back of her head fall against the vanity. Matt's spin was masterful. The only question was whether he'd come up with it on the spot, or had planned all along to let her take the fall if things went bad. No wonder he wasn't upset that she chose Jase over him. It made his story even more believable.

The rumors would be swirling already. She knew how it would snowball, and the exact form it would take. Matt did, too. They'd say the Larkin girl had reverted to form, screwing up a promising career because she couldn't stay out of some man's bed, and couldn't stay on the right side of the law.

Anyone left in Barringer's Pass who believed she was a decent person would have to question it in the face of so many damaging facts. Including people like Tammy who worked at the other resorts. The places where she might try to get a job.

"Tammy, he's lying." She tried not to sound weak, but Matt's offense was going to be pretty damn effective, and she had little defense against it. "He *needs* to get the Rusty Wire and its land, and Jase won't sell, so Matt's trying to pressure him into it. He has a big financial mess brewing over this scheme. When I found out, I quit. I haven't done a thing to hurt the Alpine Sky. I never would." Even though she hoped its owner rotted in hell.

"Well, Jerry believed him. He told me that if you approached us about a job, we weren't interested. And, uh . . ." She hesitated, then spit it out. "I'd rather you didn't use me as a personal reference."

Shit, shit, shit. Anger burned in her chest, and the need to defend herself, but hopelessness was even stronger. It settled over her, smothering her anger under the knowledge that she could never win against an attack on her reputation. All those years of being seen in the right places, associating with the right people, trying to make *the Larkin girls* stand for something good . . . it all meant nothing. If people she considered friends doubted her this easily, she'd already lost.

The silence from the other end went on for too long. "There are other resorts, Zoe."

In other words, cut and run. And never be able to hold her head up in Barringer's Pass again.

A word of support would have been nice, some indication that Zoe's side of it might be true. Apparently she wasn't even going to get that much. "Thanks, Tammy. I'll talk to you later." They both knew it was unlikely. She ended the call.

Zoe stared at the wall three feet away, not seeing the nicked paint and plastic stick-on towel hook. Letting the knowledge sink in. It was happening again.

Curling up in a ball was tempting, but she'd never accepted defeat without a fight. She wouldn't start now, even if all she had was her word against Matt's. Even if people listened with poorly disguised doubt. She would at least deny his accusations.

But that was it. With surprise, she realized she had no desire to mount a campaign in her own defense and plan ways to win back people's trust. Matt had just proved how useless that would be. Her past would always be held against her whenever it was convenient.

So she'd do what Jase had suggested and be herself . . . whoever that turned out to be. She had no checklist for it. All she knew was that she couldn't stay in Barringer's Pass. She had no job, and no hope of getting one now that her name was once again mud. Wild behavior might be forgiven; arson and fraud would not. She'd have to go someplace where they'd never heard of the Larkin girls.

There was one glaring problem with that: Jase lived in B-Pass. He had a business here, a business he loved and was willing to fight to keep. She couldn't expect him to leave it.

And she'd fallen for him so hard she wasn't sure she'd ever get over it.

She sat on the floor, blinking at nothing. Trying to accept what she'd just realized. She loved Jase, and she couldn't stay in Barringer's Pass. No matter what plans she made for the future, they couldn't include him.

Jase grinned when he saw Zoe. The day had gone well, and with her there, the evening promised to be even better.

"Zoe, over here." He waved from the garage as he locked the side door. She turned and met him at the door.

"What are you doing out here?"

For a moment he considered taking her back inside to show her, to share his excitement and let her see that he still had a passion for accomplishing something, and that he was no longer locked inside his self-imposed prison. But the new design was still on paper and there wasn't anything to show yet except the work he'd done ten years ago. That didn't say anything impressive, and he realized he *wanted* her to be impressed. In a few more days, when he finished the prototype, he might have something that qualified.

He took her hand and guided her toward the back door. "Just fooling around in my workshop. Tell me about your day."

"There's not much to tell. I saw my sisters and cleaned my house; just a normal day."

Her disinterested tone made him take a closer look, noting the bored shrug and the way she evaded his gaze. Normal, his ass. That vague response might have been normal for Jennifer, but for Zoe it was downright depressed.

"What else happened?"

"Nothing important."

"Uh-huh." He held the kitchen door for her, then steered her toward the table. "Sit. I'll pour us some iced tea, and you tell me whatever it is that happened that you're not telling me."

She shot a look at him, a little rebellious spark he was glad to see, then gave in with a distasteful curl of her mouth. "I got a call from a friend who works at the Greystone Lodge. I guess it took the shine off my day."

It was as good a description as any for how she looked. He set two glasses on the table and pulled up a chair. "Why?"

"Because she told me her boss had lunch with my boss. My former boss. Matt's spreading rumors about me, implying that I was fired for mishandling the offer to buy your land. He's blaming me for the things that happened at the Rusty Wire."

"That son of a bitch!" He jumped to his feet, ready to take Matt down on the spot, then paced the kitchen in frustration. He couldn't shake the bastard out of his life, and now it seemed Zoe couldn't, either. He wondered how she could be so calm. "He's gone too far, Zoe. At the very least it's illegal for him to say things like that about an ex-employee."

"Oh, I'm sure he'd deny it. And Jerry, the manager at the Greystone, would back him up. But Matt knew exactly who to talk to. He's good at that, reading people and knowing just how far they'll go. Jerry will see that word gets around. Resort managers are an incestuous group—employees often advance by bouncing from one resort to the next, wherever there's an opening at the time. It'll be off the record, but true or not, rumors that I was fired will spread fast. No one in this town will hire me. Probably not in Juniper, either."

"Shit!" Impotent rage ripped through him, leaving every muscle taut and ready for action. He needed to punch something, preferably Matt's face. He damned the little prick to hell several times before realizing that Zoe wasn't equally agitated. She sat there, withdrawn and thoughtful, making wet rings on the table with the condensation from her glass.

"Zoe, I won't let him get away with this. I can refute everything he says about you hurting the Rusty Wire."

"But you're sleeping with me and supposedly trying to scam your insurance company, according to Matt. Who'd believe you? Besides, people like to believe the worst about someone, especially the Larkin girls. They say they don't, but they'll always hold on to that doubt: *She seems nice, but I heard she sets fires and sells out her employer. Probably eats puppies for breakfast.*" Her mouth pulled into something less than a smile. "I know how it goes, Jase. I can't win this one."

"You aren't even going to try?"

"Oh, I'll deny it." She pressed another watery circle onto the table. "But it won't make a difference. I just don't know if I care anymore."

Concern halted his pacing and pulled at his brow. This was not the Zoe he knew. "I don't believe you. Your reputation is important to you, more important than your job. Christ, Zoe, everything you do, your whole plan for how to live your life, is about presenting a perfect image to the world. Now suddenly you don't care?"

Her gaze flicked up to his, then away again. "I've fought this battle before, Jase, and I lost. It doesn't matter how conservatively I live and how rigidly I stick to the rules. People want to remember me as that wild Larkin girl, and nothing I do will make them forget. They'll ignore years of good behavior and embrace one juicy morsel of gossip that confirms their previous opinion. I can't fight human nature. So I'll deny the rumors to anyone who asks, but I won't ever again change who I am just to be accepted." She lifted an eyebrow. "I thought you'd be happy to hear that. You're the one who told me I need to be myself."

"Yes, so that no one else defines who you are. That's what Matt's trying to do to you. You can't let him."

"I can't stop him. All I can do is not let it change

me." She showed a tiny smile. "I also need to make a new plan, because the old one's shot to hell."

He frowned, unsure how to counter his own argument, but certain that he should. Zoe being herself was fine. But this emotionally beaten woman wasn't her. If she made any choices in this depressed state they would most likely be the wrong ones.

It must be shock. When it wore off a couple of days from now, she'd remember how much her hopes and plans depended on repairing her image in Barringer's Pass. Her fighting spirit would come back. Until then, he'd do whatever he could to protect her reputation, and to reveal Matt Flemming as the scum he was.

"Don't decide anything yet, Zoe. Give it some time."

Her smile was strangely wistful. "I intend to. As much time as I can."

Chapter Nineteen

Jase tipped his chair back and tried unsuccessfully to peer over Gloria's shoulder. Watching her take notes for her next article in the *Echo* made him nervous.

He walked around the empty bar and filled a whiskey tumbler with water, knocking it back in one gulp. "You sure I can't get you something to drink?" he asked.

She didn't raise her gray head from the notepad. "No thank you."

He walked back to sit at the table. She was writing her "impressions," she said. That had to be good. She'd followed the inspector, seen everything he'd seen, and heard him approve their reopening before he left. But Jase wanted to make sure her impressions included speculating on the reason the violations had happened in the first place. The public should know the Rusty Wire had been unfairly accused.

More than accused; they'd been targeted. He couldn't prove it, but hinting at that angle might swing some support his way. He'd need it if he was going to influence future zoning and development in B-Pass, which was rapidly becoming a new priority.

Seeing her pen stop, he jumped in. "My concern is that what happened here could happen to anyone in this town. Closing down a business like mine is easy; getting it reopened is far more difficult, and expensive."

He paused while she scribbled. Why didn't the woman use a recorder, for God's sake? When she looked up, he continued.

"I can't say for sure who targeted the Rusty Wire, whether it was a prank or a serious attempt to ruin me." Couldn't say it for the record. Off the record, he'd be glad to instill some fear about the big resorts throwing their weight around, trying to shape the future of Barringer's Pass. "But you have to wonder who will be next."

Too ominous? He considered toning it down it as Gloria scribbled away, then rejected the idea. He'd stand by that statement. If the resorts ever decided they didn't like their shops or restaurants having to compete with the independent ones in Barringer's Pass, the same thing could happen to any small business owner in town.

Gloria looked up. "So you attribute these incidents to the Alpine's Sky's attempt to buy the Rusty Wire?"

"I didn't say that."

"No, you didn't." She smiled.

"I just noted the coincidence in timing. I understand if the paper is afraid to stir up controversy."

One eyebrow disappeared under an artful swoop of gray hair. "Are you at all familiar with the *Echo*, Mr. Garrett?"

He smiled. The *Echo* loved a good scandal or, barring that, a messy, controversial issue. Life in small towns could get boring without a little social drama now and then.

"There's talk of your situation around town, you know. People have noticed those coincidences you spoke of, how problems began at the Rusty Wire after you rejected a buy-out offer."

Take that, Flemming! He rocked his chair onto its back legs, getting comfortable but keeping his expression sober. "Small businessmen *should* be concerned."

"Mr. Garrett, you aren't accusing the Alpine Sky of any wrongdoing, but you've made it obvious that they are the ones who stand to gain. Are you worried that bringing this up will anger the owners?"

"Not at all. If they aren't involved, then I'm sure they're just as upset about it as I am." Better practice those sympathetic expressions, Matt.

"One particular connection to the Alpine Sky has been noted by several people I talked to. Is it true Zoe Larkin is a close friend of yours?"

"What?"

"She was recently fired from her job at the Alpine Sky."

Hell. The chair legs hit the floor. Goddamnit. "She wasn't fired. She quit."

"Really? That's not what the owner says."

He set his teeth, holding on to his temper. "Talk to some other employees. Just promise to quote them anonymously, since they might want to keep their jobs."

"So you got the story of how she left the resort directly from Miss Larkin?"

"Yes, I did."

She poised her pen over the tablet. "I understand you're good friends." Gloria emphasized *good*, smiling to let him know she didn't mean a fishing buddy.

He opened his mouth to assure her that they were indeed very close, that this information was correct. Then stopped.

Caution buzzed in his brain. Zoe was already depressed about what Matt had done to her reputation. Or more precisely, what he'd undone. With one well-placed rumor, he'd trashed her carefully reconstructed image. How much grief would it add if Jase confirmed they were close, that she had literally been sleeping with the enemy? It would be as good as saying she had betrayed her employer.

And there was that little matter of appearing socially correct. He didn't fit the bill. Despite what she said, he knew how important image was to her. No way in hell would he say anything to imply she had a close relationship with a lazy saloon owner who had no life and no apparent ambitions.

He put on a surprised look for Gloria and chuckled. "We're supposed to be good friends, huh? Well now, I guess that's flattering, since she's a pretty woman and all, but Zoe's hardly my type. A bit stiff and overachieving for my taste. We met when the Alpine Sky sent her to make an offer for my land, so naturally when she left her job she told me because I wouldn't be dealing with her anymore." He shrugged. "That's hardly good friends. I'd say we're more like acquaintances."

"I see."

Gloria looked disappointed, so he assumed he'd done a good job of separating Zoe's reputation from his. If he got nothing but that from Gloria's article, he'd still be happy.

Correction, he'd be satisfied. Not happy.

He couldn't feel good about putting a barrier between them when his impulse was to keep Zoe close. The way she made him feel, the way she meshed with his life amazed him more every time he was with her. He'd thought her ambitious, type-A personality would drive him up the wall, but he had to admit she hadn't once tried to tell him what to do with his life. And making love with a woman who believed in bringing her full attention to everything she did . . . well, the benefits could not be overstated.

He wanted to keep her in his life, and he didn't intend to hide it from the world. But with Matt trying to make her look bad, she didn't need to worry about a low-class boyfriend dragging her down. They could keep their relationship quiet for now.

If Gloria clarified their connection in the *Echo*, he couldn't possibly hurt Zoe. The town would believe they were acquaintances, no more.

Zoe pulled up beneath the Alpine Sky's big portico, right at the front doors. She waved at the surprised doorman as she strode in. "I'll only be a minute, Joe."

She'd just find Janice in Payroll, get her final check, and be out before David or Matt saw her. No disdainful looks from Matt, no juvenile sneers from David.

Unfortunately, David was walking from his office toward the front desk as she slipped past it.

"What are you doing here?"

"Are you the watchdog now?" She tried to pass him, but he blocked her way.

"You don't work here, you can't just walk in like you own the place."

"Fine. I was going to see Janice, but if you want to play errand boy, then you do it. Tell her I came for my paycheck."

He gave her his best condescending look. "Look in your bank account. It's direct deposit, like always."

"I did. It's not there. Checks get deposited every Friday, and today's Monday, and still no check. They must be holding it."

The smug sneer made an appearance. "Maybe because you were fired."

"Oh, for God's sake, I wasn't fired, and that would have nothing to do with me getting paid if I was. Would you just check with Janice? Or let me do it myself."

He sighed, as if she'd just caused him a pile of work he didn't have time for. Turning, he walked back to his office. She followed, standing impatiently as he placed the call.

"Janice, do you have a check there for Zoe Larkin?"

He had it on speaker, and Zoe heard a hesitant "No."

David added a frown to his expression of weary tolerance. "Was it mailed to her?"

"No," Janice said, her voice getting more timid. Nervous?

David rolled his eyes to the ceiling. "Well, did you submit her name with Payroll or didn't you?"

"Yes, of course."

"Then where did the check go?"

A long pause followed. "There isn't a check. There aren't *any* checks."

"What do you mean, no checks?" David dropped

into his chair and began typing on his desk computer. Zoe looked over his shoulder and caught the bright blue and white logo of a local bank as he put in his password. "Are you saying no one got paid?"

"No. I mean yes, that's what I'm saying." Her desperation verged on tears.

David peered at the screen, scanning up and down his recent activity, with pending credits and debits. "What the fuck? Janice, why didn't you tell me the checks were delayed?"

"I thought they'd get here today. I don't understand what's wrong," she whined. "I tried to ask Mr. Flemming, but I couldn't reach him."

Zoe felt cold prickles dance across the back of her neck. "Call him," she told David.

David hung up on Janice without saying good-bye and hit Matt's extension. The call bounced directly to voice mail. "Goddamnit," he muttered, and dialed another number, which she assumed was the line for Matt's private secretary at the small corporate office of Alpine Resorts, Inc.

A harried woman's voice demanded, "Yes?"

"Alice, this is David Brand. I'm trying to reach Matt. Do you know where he is?"

"No. But if you find him, I'd appreciate it if you'd tell him to call his office immediately."

The prickle spread down Zoe's spine. Matt's personal secretary *always* knew where he was, even when he was out of the country.

"Alice," she spoke up. "When did you last see him?"

"Last Friday. He stopped by before going to the Alpine Sky." Papers rustled and a desk drawer banged shut as she spoke. "Damn it," she muttered. "I know

I had the legal papers for the land deal around here somewhere. Did Matt take the file over there?"

David's mouth went slack as his worried eyes met Zoe's.

"Alice." Zoe spoke loudly to get the secretary's attention. "We'll look for it. Why do you need it?"

"I don't, his lawyer does. Could you let me know if it turns up? Or if you hear from Matt? I've got several people asking for him from First National and from Price Accounting."

"Sure, Alice, we'll let you know."

David ended the call, still staring. "He skipped."

"My guess is someplace in the Caribbean that doesn't extradite to the U.S. Or cruising international waters on a big yacht."

"Shit," he groaned. He looked at his bank account, still glowing on the computer screen. "Oh, fuck. Oh, shit."

Zoe made a pained sound in sympathy. Her bank balance wasn't quite that ominous, but it wouldn't pay the bills for long. She'd have to move and find another job sooner than she wanted to.

She didn't bother saying good-bye. David wouldn't have heard anyway. It was too soon for him to see the irony of the situation, but it prompted a bitter laugh from her after she left. If he could wait it out, he'd get the manager position by default. She was glad to let him have it.

Jase blinked at his cell phone as it rang again Monday afternoon. *The People's Free* it said, obviously unable to print the entire name of the commune. "Hello?"

"Jase, it's Feather. Zoe gave me your number. I

wanted to give you an update on our research into your land."

He perked up. Feather and Pete had had a week and a half to work on it. "What did you find?"

"Nothing good," she said, and his brief hope plummeted. "I'm sorry, Jase, but I wanted you to know. We chased down every exception to the zoning ordinances and looked for legal precedents, but they've got you in a tight spot. The current zoning board is high on growth, and the plan for a golf course has them practically tripping out. They'll push it through no matter what you want."

He cursed under his breath. "I was afraid of that."

"Me, too. So after that, I hoped we could find an endangered or protected species on your land. All it would take is one protected butterfly or flower. The federal Endangered Species Act would keep them from destroying the habitat. Most of the protected species are in Hawaii, like fifty percent of them, but Colorado has a few, maybe two percent."

"You must know a lot about endangered species."

Her mild tone was suddenly gone. "*Someone* has to watch out for the plants and animals. They're the helpless ones. We're responsible for what we do on this planet."

He nodded and barely resisted saying, *Yes, ma'am.* It seemed there was an iron core beneath Feather's soft exterior.

"Now," she went on, slipping back into teaching mode. "I surveyed most of the land around B-Pass myself years ago. Logged all the endemic species and migrating birds. But I'm sorry to say none of the federally protected species are anywhere near B-Pass."

He swore under his breath; he was out of ideas. "You went above and beyond, Feather. Thanks for trying, and tell Pete thanks, too."

She paused, obviously not ready to give up. "You could just refuse to sell," she suggested.

"I have. But that's only a temporary solution. The Alpine Sky will never stop harassing me, even if they get new owners someday. I've realized how vulnerable that land is to development, and I want to know it's protected for a long time to come, no matter who owns it. The resorts have taken a lot of the wilderness around here. I don't begrudge them some, but they have enough. It's a small valley."

"Wait, back up. You said 'no matter who owns it.' Does that mean you'd consider selling it?"

"I don't see that happening. I'd need a guarantee that the land was safe from development."

"No matter who owns it."

"Yes."

Feather snorted. "Why didn't you say so?"

"Because I don't see what difference it makes."

"You gotta keep the faith, brother." The line went dead.

He smiled at the phone, and shook his head. The old hippies were a little odd, but he liked them.

Jase's truck was already in the Rusty Wire lot when Zoe pulled in. No other cars were there.

She shivered with pleasure, remembering a similar situation two weeks ago. Alone in the saloon with Jase, no customers, the end of a long, hot day . . . the memory still aroused her. Except for the rays of sunlight slicing low through the pines in the west, the scene was the same.

She figured the sexual tension was just as high this time, maybe higher. It was no longer about the mystery of what he looked like beneath his clothes, or how he might touch her and how he'd feel moving inside her. She knew all those things now. It was the knowing that increased the tension, that made her want him at every opportunity. At this rate she would never get him out of her system.

But she had trained for a career, and become good at it. You didn't just throw that away.

Steeling herself against that reality, she concentrated on remembering their first encounter. If Jase wanted one more memorable session of table sex in his saloon, she was more than willing to participate.

The visual that went with that thought had her smiling as she rapped on the new back door. She hadn't finished knocking when something slapped beside her against the door. She squinted at the brown mark against the creamy white metal of the door, wondering if someone had thrown a stone. At the same moment, a distant crack echoed off the mountains, sending overlapping echoes rolling through the air.

A rifle shot. She heard them enough during hunting season to recognize the distinctive crack. But they shouldn't be on Jase's land, which is where she assumed the sound had come from. And what animal was in season in August?

She took another look at the brown mark on the door. As she did, a second bullet popped against the door, tearing a hole inches from her shoulder. The echoing report rolled after it. Shit! She ducked, one hand on the doorknob, jiggling frantically. "Jase! Jase, open the door!"

A third bullet slammed into the door, a foot below the last one. Too close to her head. Any thought that it was accidental fled from her mind. She was the target.

What was she thinking, calling Jase? If he opened the door, he'd be in the line of fire. She dropped her hand. She should run for cover.

The Dumpster. It was the closest thing, and big enough to protect her.

She crouched low, ready to run.

The door opened and Jase looked down with surprise. "Zoe, what are you . . ."

A fourth bullet hit the door at the same moment she threw herself against his lower body, tumbling them both inside. "Close the door! Fast!"

She wasn't sure if Jase recognized the slap of the bullet, but he couldn't miss the booming echo. He didn't hesitate. He dove against the door, slamming it shut. She wondered belatedly if it would really protect them, or if the bullets would pierce the metal panels. She rose on shaky legs to look, but Jase grabbed her arm and whirled her around.

"The bar! Go!" He shoved against her back, leaving his hand there as she stumbled, then ran full out to the front of the saloon. Dodging behind the bar, she searched for a hiding place, finding none. She huddled against a wooden keg. It was little protection against a rifle if the shooter followed them inside. Nothing would be. Running straight through the saloon and out the front door made more sense. She'd rather take her chances in the open than be a sitting duck.

She turned to tell Jase and saw him cradling a

shotgun in his lap as he opened the safe. She hadn't seen him pull it out, but it looked like he meant to use it.

His plan might be better.

He pulled out a box of shells, slipping five into the barrel. Pulling his cell phone from his pocket, he thrust it at her. "Call 911."

She did, starting over once because her shaking hand hit the eight along with the nine. She waited through a slow connection and one ring, telling herself to be concise and not babble incoherently.

"Nine-one-one operator."

"Someone is shooting at us. The Rusty Wire saloon. They're outside, west of the saloon, in the trees."

"Where are you, miss?" The voice was admirably calm compared to Zoe's, which was quivering. Of course, no one was trying to kill the operator at the moment.

"We're inside, behind the bar."

"Stay there, someone is on the way. How many people are in the building?"

"Just Jase and me. He's the owner." She watched him pump the shotgun and take a position facing the back hall. "I think we're okay. He has a gun."

"Tell him not to go outside," the operator said quickly. "Or anyplace else in the building. Tell him he needs to stay right where he is."

He wasn't going to leave her, she knew it, but she told him anyway. "The lady says not to go anywhere."

"The lady's not here," he growled, jaw set so hard she saw the cords in his neck. "If someone comes through that door, I'm not going to wait for him to shoot us. You tell her to tell the police they'd better announce themselves and show some ID before they come in here."

Zoe relayed the message, feeling suddenly calmer and safer with the knowledge that Jase was willing to shoot first and ask questions later. That shouldn't be comforting, but right now she preferred it to being a helpless victim.

"Ma'am? Did you see the shooter?"

"No. Tell the police he was shooting at the back door. The front probably isn't in his line of sight."

"Are you sure there's only one shooter?"

Damn, she hadn't thought of that.

The sound of sirens reached her, increasing rapidly. Within seconds the wailing was right outside the saloon, then abruptly silenced. Another siren in the distance grew closer. Jase had risen to his feet when pounding shook the front door. A man's muffled voice yelled, "Jase! You in there?"

Relief washed through her as she disconnected the call. She stood, yelling back, "Cal! We're okay."

"Zoe?"

Jase strode to the door, fishing keys from his pocket. "Stay back," he ordered her.

Huddling behind the bar didn't feel as safe as standing beside two armed men. She hurried to follow Jase.

Unlocking both sets of doors, he opened the outside one a few inches, blocking her. Cal stood, gun held at his side, scanning the surrounding trees. She saw the large white letters spelling POLICE on the back of his bulletproof vest before he turned to glance inside. "Anyone hurt?" His attention was already back on the tree line, even though Zoe doubted he could see the right area from here.

"No," Jase said.

"Did you see the shooter?"

"No," Zoe answered. She tried shoving Jase aside, but he didn't budge, so she settled for peeking over his arm. "I think the shots came from the trees around the other side. I knocked on the back door, and four bullets hit it, right next to me."

Another black police SUV pulled in, lights flashing, and Cal gestured with his gun for them to go around the building. "Stay inside," he ordered, then trotted after the SUV.

Jase looked at her. She expected anger for not following his orders to stay behind the bar, but worry lines wrinkled the corners of his eyes. He stroked a hand over her hair, cupping her face. "You're really okay?" he asked, his voice gravelly with emotion.

She nodded. "Just shook up."

He ran his hand up and down her arm, looking pretty shaken himself before setting his mouth in a grim line. "He's gone too far this time."

She didn't have to ask who he meant. "He's gone, period. Jase, no one at the Alpine Sky knows where Matt is. Even his personal secretary can't reach him. He left. I think he skipped the country."

A furrow creased his brow in an irritated twitch. "Why?"

"His financial problems are snowballing. Bankers and lawyers are trying to reach him."

His mouth curled with disgust. "A real stand-up guy. But what makes you think he left the country?"

She hesitated. "Ruth Ann is in the Caribbean, throwing money around, and I assumed he'd join her. Maybe hide out someplace where the FBI can't find them."

"Or maybe just disappear into the trees and take some revenge. He might even convince me to sell at the same time. That sounds like a better solution than running for the rest of his life."

She stared. He was right. Matt would save himself. She simply hadn't considered he'd do it by killing her. It was an extreme move for someone who'd seemed so organized and rational.

But emotionally detached. The memory of how easily he'd accepted her relationship with Jase sent a cold chill down her arms. She didn't want to believe he'd resort to murder, yet couldn't say it was beyond him.

Attempted murder was bad enough, but she'd kissed this guy. Envisioned how he'd fit into her life. Considered sleeping with him, for God's sake. She pulled a chair off one of the tables and sat down. Jase didn't say anything, but laid the shotgun on the table and stood behind her, massaging her shoulders.

It took a full hour before Cal told them the woods were clear. They'd found the shooter's position easily enough by figuring out the highest point with the best line of sight. No shell casings had been left, but recent scuffs in the dirt showed where he'd knelt. Unfortunately, scuff marks didn't provide clues to the shooter's identity.

It didn't matter. She didn't need the police to tell her who had taken those shots. Neither did Jase.

They remained at the table after the police had gone, too drained to move. Elbows propped on the table, she rubbed her fingers over her forehead, trying to massage away the tension. It wasn't working.

"I'm not safe here," she finally said.

"No, you aren't."

"I need to leave town."

He looked relieved. "I was afraid I'd have to argue the point."

"I'm not stupid. I don't want to get shot, and I don't want you shot because of me. You're probably still in danger."

"Agreed—this won't end until Matt's caught. If his company is in as much trouble as you think, threatening me is the only reason he's sticking around. If I leave, he'll disappear, too, and we'll never know when he might show up again. I'm staying until it's over. But I can look out for myself better if I'm not worrying about you. Once we catch him and this is over, you can come back." He stood, picking up the shotgun.

That was the hard part. She swallowed the tightness in her throat, speaking to his back as he carried the gun back to the bar. "I can't come back. I need a job, and none of the resorts here will talk to me. Maybe someday they will, when the whole story comes out, but for now they'll believe Matt."

He stopped, and pivoted toward her with a frown. "So find some other kind of work."

"Resort management is all I know, Jase. I've worked at the Alpine Sky since I was twenty-one. I can't go back to waiting tables to pay the bills."

An intense look came over his face. He set the gun on the bar, striding back to her. "Why not?"

"Because it's not enough money." She would have thought that was obvious.

"It's not just about money."

"Of course it is." She shook her head over his

apparent disinterest in money. She'd never understood it. "Maybe you can turn down a few million dollars, but I have a car payment."

"That's not what I meant." He brushed off her reasonable concern for income. Apparently she'd never learn his secret to living without money.

Squatting in front of her, he took her hands in his own. "Zoe, why did you choose to go into hotel management? I'm betting it wasn't something you'd always wanted to do."

She lifted a shoulder. "Not really."

"It was part of your plan to repair your image in this town, wasn't it? Because the resorts have all the power and prestige in B-Pass, and managing them might allow a little of that to rub off on you."

She wondered if she was that transparent to everyone. "What's wrong with that?"

"Nothing, if your goal is to repair your reputation. Is it?" His gaze held her in place. "Is that what you still want most in life?"

She'd already told him it wasn't. Getting respect from the residents of Barringer's Pass shouldn't be more important than respecting herself, than doing what she wanted to do. But she'd let it be, for ten years. And it hadn't gotten her anyplace.

Sucking in a deep breath, she let it out slowly as she shook her head. "You're right, hotel management was never what I *wanted,* it was just what I needed to do. But, Jase . . ." She worked to keep desperation out of her voice. "I don't know what I want most in life. Between doing what I had to do to shock my family, then what I had to do to repair the damage, I never thought about what I *wanted* to do."

He smiled. "Didn't make a list for that, huh?"

"Maybe I should have." And she was starting to think that if she made one, Jase belonged near the top.

"This is your chance to change direction if you want to, Zoe. Don't lose it."

The sketchy outlines of an idea teased her mind, a product line and marketing plan for wool items made from the commune's sheep. With enough time, she was sure it would work. It sounded tempting, but . . . "I can't afford to, Jase. I need an income, *now*."

"So work for me."

"What?"

"As soon as this is over and you come back. Wait tables, tend bar, balance the books, whatever. You're hired. It's not as much money as you made before, but it'll keep you going for a few months while you figure out what you really want to do."

"That's nice of you, really. But I can't. I need medical benefits—"

"The Rusty Wire offers a health care package."

"It does?"

"Hey, I'm a responsible employer."

And she'd be sleeping with the boss, which goes over so well with fellow employees. "I don't know . . ."

"Please." He brushed a stray hair off her face, stroking her cheek as he did, turning her insides quivery with longing. "Once this mess with Matt is over, stay in Barringer's Pass while you figure out what you want to do with the rest of your life. If you need a day off, take it, anytime. Work as few or as many days as you need to."

"That's a ridiculously generous offer."

His fingers trailed over her cheek again, his thumb

smoothing along her lips. He leaned in, kissing her where he stroked. "I want you to stay, Zoe."

She wasn't made of stone. Her heart pounded crazily against her ribs, and she barely managed to keep her smile calm. "I guess you've got yourself a waitress."

He smiled back.

For several seconds she absorbed the warm feeling, saying nothing, with a dopey smile stuck on her face.

"Touching."

Jase jerked to his feet. Zoe turned a startled glance toward the back hall.

Jennifer stood watching them, a cardboard box in her arms.

"God, Jennifer, you scared me to death," Jase said. "I didn't hear you come in."

"I was quiet."

Zoe thought she looked a little annoyed as she set the box on the bar. If she'd been there long enough to hear Jase offer Zoe a job, it might account for her bad mood.

Jase paused, as if unsure of what to say to her simple statement. "So what are you doing here? Did you bring supplies for the bar?"

"That?" Jennifer looked at the box. "It's just some old newspapers soaked in whiskey. But I guess you could say it's for the bar."

The casual statement fell like lead in the sudden silence. Zoe could think of only one purpose for spilling alcohol over newspaper.

Chills crept over her. Jennifer showed no emotion either way about setting fire to the saloon. She simply didn't care. A new crop of goose bumps broke out along Zoe's spine.

Jase was very still, but she saw his muscles tense. "I'd feel better if you took that box outside."

"I'm sure you would." She reached for the gun Jase had left on the bar. "But I no longer care what you think."

The sharp edge in her voice left no doubt about her intentions. Zoe rose cautiously, standing on weak legs beside Jase. She felt slightly less vulnerable than when she was sitting, even though there was no chance she could outrun a blast from the shotgun. She hadn't asked Jase what the shells were loaded with, but it didn't matter. At this range, even a slug would be deadly in experienced hands. More likely, it was loaded with bird shot, which meant Jennifer's aim wouldn't have to be nearly as accurate for the scatter pattern to kill.

Jennifer competently slid the bolt back to see if it was loaded. Jase eased in front of Zoe as he spoke. "I was about to put it away."

"That's okay, I would just have to get it out again." She eyed him casually. "I didn't expect you to hang around here after your girlfriend was nearly killed."

The words sank in as everything else seemed to slow down. Jennifer knew about the shooting. Knew Zoe had been the target. Zoe doubted Jennifer spent her time listening to a police scanner.

She glanced at Jase, fighting a sense of unreality, not wanting to believe what her brain was telling her. He didn't move, but standing so close she saw what Jennifer probably missed, the momentary flinch, as if he'd absorbed a hard blow. The pain of betrayal.

"*You* shot at Zoe?"

"God, you're slow." Holding the gun at her waist, she steadied the barrel with her other hand. "But you caught up just in time to appreciate the ending." She smiled with satisfaction at her own words as she thumbed the safety, then raised the shotgun and leveled it at Jase.

Chapter Twenty

He didn't care about the saloon. All Jase could think of was protecting Zoe.

He angled his body to shield her better, but stopped at Jennifer's oddly melodic "Uh-uh-uh." She shook her head in warning. "In case you were thinking of moving, don't. Obviously, my aim is rusty, but at this range I can't miss."

He didn't doubt it. It was the only thing he was sure of. "What are you planning to do, Jennifer?"

"Put things right." She glanced at the box. "And burn down the Rusty Wire."

He didn't try to hide his confusion. "Why?"

"Because it's important to you. That means it has to go, along with anything else you care about." She gave Zoe a significant look.

The panic that shot through him made him want to leap at her, wrestle away the gun—a suicide move that would only get them both killed. He tried to override his fear. To think. Her detached attitude confused him. Murder generally sprang from hatred, but Jennifer seemed oddly unmoved. An ugly possibility came to mind. "Did Matt Flemming put you up to this?"

"No. Really clinging to preconceptions, aren't you?" She rolled her eyes. "You're so dense, Jase. But you make a good point—I'm sure Matt won't mind. He was disappointed when the first fire didn't do more damage. It was just dumb luck the fire truck was already on the road, coming back from a run, when I called."

"He asked you to set the fire?"

"He *paid* me." She laughed. "Fuckin' idiot. I would have done it for a lot less than he gave me, too. He must want this place real bad. He'll be glad to see it burn down."

"He won't know about it," Zoe said. He heard a slight quiver in her voice that stabbed his heart. "Matt's gone. The authorities are already looking for him. Looking at his financial dealings. They'll follow the money trail right back to you."

Jase thought it was a good try, but Jennifer laughed it off. "You think I'm stupid? He gave me cash."

The new bedroom furniture. The realization barely had time to flash through his mind before she motioned at him with the shotgun barrel. "Would you like to start the fire yourself before I shoot you? Just set the box under the bar, knock over a couple bottles, and strike a match. It'll be ironic, burning down your own bar just like some people thought you tried to do for insurance money. Want to do it?"

Not a chance in hell. He had to figure out how to prevent it, and all he could think to do was to keep her talking. "How can you do this? You love the Rusty Wire."

She sneered. "I don't give a damn about the Rusty Wire."

"But you put in so many hours here." He was honestly surprised by her response. "You were here even when you didn't have to be. You did whatever needed to be done."

"To keep you from doing it." She shook her head with a pitying look. "You still don't get it, do you?"

"No, I don't."

"Because you're so self-centered. You only saw what you wanted to see—a cozy saloon where you could put your feet up, have a beer, and watch the bar babes."

He winced; the description was too accurate for comfort. "You're right, Jennifer." He'd heard somewhere that using a person's name made them more sympathetic toward you. "That was my life for nine years." Not entirely, but it seemed important to agree with her. To placate her. "But I'm not doing that anymore. I wasn't fulfilled, wasn't accomplishing anything."

Jennifer's fingers turned white on the shotgun. "Figured that out, did you?"

"Someone pointed it out, and they were right. What I had wasn't a life."

"No shit!" She yelled it, startling him with the sudden change. Rage sped through her, stiffening her back, burning from her eyes. "You didn't *deserve* a life! Not after taking Adam's. And I made sure you didn't have one. For nine fucking years!"

He'd obviously flipped a switch in her brain, and he wished he knew how to turn it off again. A crazy person with a gun was bad enough; a crazy person with a gun and a grudge was miles worse.

"I babysat you," she said, getting into her rant. "Made sure you remembered what you'd done, kept your guilt alive. What you'd taken from me. It was a daily dose of revenge. But then *she* came along and ruined it all." Jennifer's heated gaze burned into Zoe before shifting back to him. "It would have been okay if she'd just jiggled her tits in your face like the others, but she pushed you to do something, and you started getting all sorts of fucking *ideas* in your head, getting interested in the business and making plans. And you *fell in love* with her." Her scowl deepened, anger twisting her features into something ugly. "Like you had some right to be happy. Well, you don't!" she screamed, her voice rising with a hysterical edge. "You goddamn fucking don't! It's your fault I'll never be happy again, so you damn well won't be happy, either!" A drop of spit clung to her lip, and her chest rose and fell rapidly as she regained her breath. "And I'm going to make sure of it. I can set the fucking fire myself." She lifted the gun.

"It won't work," he said, thinking fast. "Even with the fire, they'll be able to tell we were shot."

The gun dropped a bit as she glared over it. "Who the hell cares? Let 'em pin it on Matt. They will, you know. Everyone knows he wants to get rid of the saloon, and to do that he needs to get rid of you. And he's conveniently on the run, already suspected of crimes." She pursed her lips thoughtfully. "Yeah, I like it. I bet I can even fake a few sniffles on your behalf."

A chill spread through him. She was right. Matt would get blamed, and she would get away with murder.

Beside him, Zoe tensed and her breathing quickened,

but she wisely didn't move. He reached for her hand, wishing he'd told her what Jennifer had realized. That he loved her. Instead, he gave her hand a reassuring squeeze. He'd get her out of this so he could say it himself.

She gripped his hand in return, and hung on. He hated to do it, but he pulled his hand away. He had to be ready to move fast if he could catch Jennifer off guard.

If he couldn't . . . well, a gunshot didn't kill right away, despite what TV and movies would have you believe. He'd have time to reach Jennifer and overpower her, enough time for Zoe to get out of here.

"I'm sorry, I didn't know you felt that way about me," he said. Still trying to soothe her. To stall her.

"Of course not." She spit it back at him, as if the words left a bitter taste in her mouth. "Everything's all about you, isn't it?"

He hoped her perceptions about that were as skewed as her logic, but couldn't think about it now. He needed to get her off the topic of Adam's death.

"Jase didn't kill Adam," Zoe said.

Shit! He shot a frown at Zoe, a desperate message to drop the subject, but she wasn't looking at him. Her steady gaze was on Jennifer as she defended him.

Jennifer glared. "Shut up! You don't know anything about Adam."

Listen to her! he thought.

Unfortunately, Zoe seemed bent on defending him. "I know what happened. Adam took a dare and ended up dead."

"Because of Jase!"

"Adam was an adult, wasn't he?"

"He was my husband!"

"He was capable of making his own decisions. He chose to do something stupid. It's not Jase's fault he died."

Jennifer's vicious stare slowly changed to one of perverse satisfaction mingled with hate. Chills shot down Jase's back as she raised the shotgun to her shoulder.

"Pay attention, Jase," she said, sighting down the barrel at Zoe. "This is what it feels like to lose someone you love."

Chapter
Twenty-one

Z oe froze. She'd planned to duck, but apparently gazing down the barrel of a gun induced paralysis. She stared.

Jase didn't freeze. A blur of motion beside her made her blink. The next second a chair hurtled through the air, coming between her and the deadly black hole of the shotgun.

"Run!" Jase yelled. It was enough to break her stare, to get her muscles moving.

She dove sideways at the same instant a blast broke the air. Above her, tiny pellets crashed into a hanging light, dinging into metal and shattering glass. Glass and spent pellets clattered to the wooden floor in front of her.

Zoe hit the ground moving, scrambling for cover. She'd already thought it out, knew the only protection would be a table, if it wasn't too heavy to tip. But she wouldn't be able to do it before Jennifer took a second shot. Zoe got to her knees, glancing over her shoulder to see which way to dodge. Hoping Jase had already found cover.

He hadn't. His long strides ate up the distance between him and Jennifer.

But not fast enough.

Jennifer's expression was contorted with hate as she swung the shotgun toward him. Not bothering to aim. She didn't need to; Jase was too close to miss.

The second it took for the gun to arc down and around stalled into an eternity. Zoe screamed his name, dreading what was coming, and knowing she was too late to change it. Already seeing the result. Hundreds of tiny lead pellets would rip into him, tearing a hole so big he wouldn't stand a chance.

"Jase!" The name ripped out of her the same instant he dropped. The same instant the gunshot exploded.

Jase fell on Jennifer in a flailing tangle of arms and legs, with the gun poking out to the side, held in two fierce grips. Zoe was up without thinking, racing toward them. Jase was still alive, still struggling for the gun, and she had to help. Blood already smeared Jennifer's shoulder and face. His blood.

He rose with a violent movement just as Zoe reached him. Half-kneeling above Jennifer, he tore the gun from her grasp. Beneath him, she uttered a feral sound, half growl, half scream, reaching to yank it back. In one swift motion, he turned the stock down, gripped the barrel, and swung it at her head. She fell back, motionless.

"Jase!" Zoe touched him, wanting to see his wound, but afraid to hurt him.

He sucked in a heavy breath and fell hard on his ass. "Tie her up," he managed, raspy and breathless.

Her eyes were on the blood covering his shoulder, spreading as she watched. She reached for him, fear squeezing her chest. "Let me see."

He twisted weakly, possibly the best he could do, but enough to fend her off. "No! Tie her first!" He panted for breath, met her eyes. "I'm okay. Do it."

She didn't want to fight him, but knew he wouldn't give in. Knew, too, that he was right. If Jennifer regained consciousness, she was a threat. She had to secure her so she could look after Jase.

"How?" She said it aloud as she stood, her mind racing. "Do you have an electrical cord?"

His brow furrowed as he sat on the floor. "In the office. Desk lamp."

She ran. The lamp was small, and stubbornly attached to its cord. She didn't care. She turned Jennifer over, tied her hands behind her back, leaving the lamp, minus its shade, dangling from her wrists.

She turned to Jase. He was lying on the floor, blood spreading across the wood planks. Her stomach flipped, but a reassuring thought kept her focused. There was no gaping hole. He must have been grazed by the edge of the shot. Not hundreds of pellets. Maybe fifty? Please, God, maybe a lot less.

The amount of blood dimmed that hope.

She knelt by his head, fingers frantically running over his shoulder, looking for the worst source of bleeding. Blood seeped onto her hand, obscuring everything. She swiped at his neck and as much of his shoulder as she could expose beneath the shirt.

And found the source. Red holes and lines dotted his neck, oozing blood as she watched, running in rivulets to his shoulder and the floor. Covering his neck in red.

"You're not okay!" she accused. Raw fear kept the threatening tears at bay. "This is not okay!" She met his eyes, not caring if he saw her terror, because he was scaring her to death and it made her angry.

His eyes looked back, unfocused. As she watched, they closed. His head fell to the side.

"Jase!" Panic turned into a ball of sickness, rising in her throat.

No time for it. Think! Stop the bleeding.

She raced to the bar, tearing through cupboards, knowing towels would be there somewhere. The stack of folded white cloths caught her eye. She grabbed a handful, and ran back to kneel beside Jase, pressing the whole mass of them to his neck.

"Don't die," she ordered, even though he couldn't hear. She repeated it, "Don't die, don't die, don't die," becoming a chant as she pressed with one hand and reached into her pocket with the other.

Pulling out her phone, she called 911 for the second time that day.

Chapter Twenty-two

J ase was gone. The doctor at the urgent care clinic had taken one look at his wound and had him medevaced to the hospital in Juniper. Their surgery team was better able to handle the delicate repair on his nicked artery. Cal had kept her calm with updates, but it was hours before the police were done with her and she could make the drive to Juniper.

They wouldn't let her see him. His sister, brother-in-law, and niece were with him, and three visitors at a time was the limit.

She sighed and found a seat in the waiting room where all she could do was remember the blood and imagine the damage. He was alive, that was all that mattered. She cringed at the thought of what he'd suffered, and trembled over how close she'd come to losing him. She could almost understand Jennifer's pain at losing her husband, even if she couldn't forgive the twisted way she'd made Jase feel responsible for it. She couldn't imagine losing Jase.

After more than four hours of frantic worrying, she

couldn't relax. She needed a distraction. Scanning the waiting room, she spotted an abandoned copy of the Barringer's Pass *Echo*.

It was the latest issue, the one with the story about Jase reopening the Rusty Wire. She read with a satisfied smile as the reporter cast suspicion for the harassing incidents on Matt and Ruth Ann Flemming. The scandal brewing there was going to keep the *Echo* busy for months to come. Jase had some nice, diplomatically worded quotes about their possible involvement, and a few other things to say about—

She sat up straighter as she spotted her name. Then went cold at what followed:

Garrett denied any personal involvement with Zoe Larkin, the woman who had been representing the Alpine Sky in the negotiations. Ms. Larkin recently left her job at the resort under questionable circumstances, with her boss hinting of a romantic involvement with Garrett. "I'd say we're more like acquaintances," Garrett scoffed when asked about it. Emphasizing their strictly business relationship, he added, "Zoe's hardly my type . . ."

The rest of the story blurred as her eyes lost focus. She lowered the paper, staring at nothing, replaying the lines in her mind. Imagined Jase smiling condescendingly as he spoke. "*Zoe's hardly my type.*"

An ache began deep in her chest. It hadn't taken him long to distance himself from her questionable circumstances. Right there, on the same page with that snarky innuendo from Matt, he'd let everyone know he had nothing to do with her. Any questionable actions were all hers.

It had been bad enough to find out that Matt was

only looking for a good time. But Jase had liked her family, understood the side of her she barely knew herself. She'd *trusted* him. But when scandal once again hovered around her, he'd backed off fast enough to burn rubber.

It was the one thing she couldn't forgive.

She wanted to be furious, but right now it hurt too much. She pressed a fist to her chest, rocking slightly, riding out the pain.

"Zoe Larkin?"

She jerked her head up and found a cute blonde standing in front of her with a questioning look. Jase's niece, Hailey. She nodded.

"They said to let you know you can go in now."

"Thanks."

"I'm Hailey Watson. Jase is my uncle."

"I know." She dug deep to find a polite smile.

Hailey tilted her head, friendly but curious. "He was asking if you were here. I think he wanted to see you more than us."

The girl was obviously fishing, and Zoe wasn't about to take the bait. She got to her feet. "It was nice to have met you, Hailey. Room 238, wasn't it?" She hurried down the hall.

He was propped up in bed, hooked up to an IV, and looking better than someone should an hour after emergency surgery. The bandages around his neck and shoulder were a pristine white, a strange contrast to the memory of all that blood. The image was too fresh in her mind, and concern swamped the mixture of anger and hurt brewing in her chest.

She stood nervously beside his bed. "Are you really okay?"

"Yes." He reached for her hand, and she let him keep it. Pulling it away would be mean, and she couldn't be mean to someone who'd just survived a brush with death. Someone stitched and bandaged and weak from blood loss. Someone she loved despite his betrayal and the fact that she was leaving him.

Realizing how deep the love went was depressing. It would take a long time to go away.

He squeezed her fingers. "They said you saved my life."

"You saved mine, throwing that chair and jumping between us."

"We can spend a long time thanking each other." He tugged her closer. "Zoe, I *want* to spend a long time thanking you. Being with you."

Panic jumped in her chest. As emotionally exhausted as she was, she recognized another heart-wrenching moment rushing at her, one she couldn't deal with right now. She tugged her hand away and stepped back. "Don't!"

He smiled through a puzzled look. "Don't what? Zoe, I'm just trying to tell you that I love you."

Tears filled her eyes so fast everything went blurry. She blinked hard. "Don't say that!"

The smile disappeared. He took a long, careful look at her. "Why?"

She waved a hand at the bandages. "Because you're hurt. Because you just went through something traumatic." She winced, knowing what she was doing was just as traumatic. To both of them. "I can't talk about this right now."

He studied her even as he became more withdrawn. "I can. Getting shot hasn't changed how I feel about you." He frowned as she chewed her lip. "But maybe it's changed how you feel. Unless I was wrong and you never cared as much as I hoped you did."

Oh, God, she cared. She didn't want to, but she did. Too much. So much she could hardly breathe. She started to lift her hand to her chest and realized she still held the newspaper. She thrust it at him, letting it fall onto his lap when he didn't take it. "Here. Before you tell me how you feel about me, maybe you'd better review what you told everyone else."

He glanced down at the front-page picture of the Rusty Wire and the headline "Was Restaurant Closing Intentional?" "What are you talking about? I kept you out of it."

"Yes, you did." He didn't even see what was wrong in leaving her to deal with the fallout of more rumors. Just like Matt. The comparison put her in touch with the anger bubbling beneath the surface. "You completely disassociated yourself from anything I may have done to hurt my employer. And why wouldn't you? I'm not even your type."

He frowned. "I never said that."

Denial, that was his defense? "Oh, you said it. Either that, or the *Echo* is making up its own quotes, and I've never known Gloria to do that. I suggest you refresh your memory." The tears she'd held back were burning her eyes. She had to get out of there. "Whatever you have to say you can tell me later," she said as she turned.

"Zoe, wait, damn it!"

She didn't. The door closed behind her as the first tear slipped down her cheek.

They kept him at the hospital for two days. She knew because Cal told Maggie, who told Zoe when she picked her up to drive to the commune four days after the shooting.

"I don't want to know," she said. "Today was supposed to be an escape from stress. I don't want to think about him."

Maggie gave her a worried look as she drove. "Are you sure that's the right thing to do? Shouldn't you two talk it out?"

"So I can hear his excuses?"

"So you can hear his reasons. I can't believe Jase would throw you to the wolves."

"But he did. He wants nothing to do with the rumors flying around about me. Don't tell me no one in town has mentioned that the Justice Department is including me in their investigation of the Alpine Sky. That they haven't whispered about how you never could trust Zoe Larkin to do the right thing."

Maggie pressed her lips into a grim line. "Not to me, they haven't."

Zoe couldn't help a fleeting smile at the ferocious loyalty of both her sisters. "I know I'm being stubborn about this, Maggie, but it's the one thing I expect in a man when it comes to my past. Support. Plenty of people in this town will always believe the worst of me, and I need a partner who will stand by me, and take my side. If *he* won't, why would anyone else?"

"I thought what people said didn't matter. Wasn't that your new philosophy?"

"It still is. But not talking about me would be even better. Then I might be able to find a job."

"No job openings for someone with negative press, huh?"

"Or for someone who will leave as soon as a better

offer comes along. I didn't realize underemployment would be so hard to achieve."

Maggie pondered it for a few seconds. "I could put you on for a couple of days a week at my store."

And divert all her net income to another employee she didn't need. Zoe shook her head, even though the gesture touched her deeply. "No, you couldn't, Mags. You don't need another employee. But thanks." She'd find something, somewhere. She had to.

Maggie didn't comment and they each sank into silence as she negotiated the twisting roads up the mountain to the People's Free Earth Commune.

They pulled up to the house, escorted by the usual pack of barking dogs. Maggie looked off to the side as she put the car in park. "Did they buy a new truck?"

"Not that I heard." Zoe followed her sister's gaze, and her stomach hit her toes. "That's Jase's truck."

"Huh. What a coincidence."

She shot Maggie an evil look. "I don't believe that. Mom called you."

"Be a big girl and go in the house, Zoe."

Zoe got out and slammed the door, scowling at Maggie across the roof. "You'll pay for this."

"I'll apologize later." She stooped to dog level, ruffling furry heads and thumping shoulders, completely ignoring Zoe.

Zoe turned a dark look on the house. "Aw, hell," she mumbled, and started toward it.

Her entrance through the front door interrupted gales of laughter from the group in the living room. Smiling faces turned her way, and her heart gave a painful jerk to see Jase at the center of the group.

Fitting in, charming her family. It felt like another betrayal.

His smile faded into a surprised look as the others invited her over. Well, that was something. At least he hadn't been in on the setup.

"Zoe! What a nice surprise!" her mother said. Zoe narrowed her eyes at her.

"Come on over here," Pete called with expansive arm gestures. "Look what Feather and I figured out for Jase."

Curiosity overcame resentment when she saw an unfamiliar face in the group, an obvious townie in a suit and tie, with a leather briefcase that screamed lawyer. "What are you all up to?" she asked. Her eyes flicked to Jase's neck. A patch that seemed much too small to cover a wound that had nearly taken his life was there. The memory brought cold shivers, and she looked away.

Pete jumped up and pulled her over to the sofa, nudging her into his seat. Next to Jase.

Jase's mouth twitched at the obvious ploy. It was the same look he would get from Zoe just before pulling her into his lap and sliding his hands under her shirt. Her stomach did little flips. She tried to ignore him, looking instead at the documents on the coffee table.

"What's this?"

"I just gave away my fifty acres," Jase told her.

"Gave away?"

"Donated," Feather corrected him. "To the Julius and Miriam Wallace Land Trust."

"What's that?"

"It's a conservation group," Jase told her. "Their goal is to keep large areas of the Rockies in their natural state, which is exactly what I wanted for that parcel. And the town can't rezone it or legislate it into development."

"The trust owns it outright? What if they decide to sell it?"

"They can't. They can't do anything with it." He smiled happily.

"I assure you, Mr. Garrett, they don't want to," the lawyer said.

She ignored him, caught by Jase's smile. "It sounds wonderful. And generous." And suspiciously like something Feather would lobby for. "Are you sure you want to do that? That land might not be worth three million, but you could get one million, easy. If you wait you might find someone who won't want to cut down most of the trees for fairways."

"I might. And then maybe they'll change their mind and decide that what Barringer's Pass needs is a mega shopping center, and I won't have any say in the matter. No, this is the best solution. The money's not important, and this way I know my great-great-grand-children will still be able to enjoy the natural beauty of the mountains."

Her extended family beamed and nodded at this wisdom—giving away assets had never fazed them if the cause was right. It seemed Jase was equally lacking in material concerns. "I'm happy for you, Jase. And I'm glad you turned down my offer to buy."

"It wasn't your offer, it was the Alpine Sky's."

Making the distinction was oddly touching, and she blinked at his serious gaze.

Kate jumped up. "This calls for a celebration! Vegetable smoothies for everyone!"

The group chorused agreement. Jase gave her a doubtful look and leaned closer. "Do I want a vegetable smoothie?" he asked in a low voice.

It was an acquired taste, at best. "Definitely not."

He stood, smiling at Kate. "I'll pass, but you all go ahead. Zoe and I have something to talk about." Without warning, he took her hand, pulling her to her feet.

She hung back. "Jase . . ."

He leaned close. "We're going to do this sooner or later. You really want a vegetable smoothie first?"

She knew when she was beat. She followed him out the back door to a large rock that had served as a meditation bench for decades.

"Sit," he ordered. "I get to talk first."

She crossed her arms, tired of being manipulated by everyone. "Why?"

"Because I want to apologize."

"Oh. Good reason." She sat.

He looked down at her as if contemplating where to start. "I didn't know you'd be here today," he said.

"I know you didn't."

"I was going to wait another day or two in the hope that you'd realize you were wrong."

She narrowed her eyes. "*That's* your apology?"

"No. Hang on, I'm getting there." He paused to look her over thoughtfully. "You care about me, don't you?"

She drew her eyebrows together in a what-the-hell expression. "How is that relevant?"

"Just answer the question."

She sighed. "Of course I care. Why do you think I was sleeping with you?"

"To get me out of your system so you could move on to the right guy."

She *had* said that. Faulting him for believing her probably wasn't fair. She shifted uncomfortably. "Things changed," she muttered.

"They did. I wasn't expecting it, either. I didn't even realize it until Jennifer tried to kill you, and then I realized what was on the line. Things changed." He nodded. "I fell in love with you."

He simply watched her. She squirmed under his gaze, hating him for making this even harder than it had to be. It could have been a neat, clean break, but no, he wanted her to spill her guts all over the place.

She jumped to her feet and stalked the three steps to reach him, hands fisted, arms stiff at her sides. "You want me to say I fell in love with you, too? Okay, fine, I did." She rushed on as a smile played at the corner of his mouth. "But it doesn't change anything. It doesn't change what happened, or the fact that you treated me like shit. I'm still waiting for my apology so we can part on halfway civilized terms."

His face softened as he took her by the shoulders, drawing her close. "One thing at a time." His hands moved up to frame her face.

Her stomach fluttered nervously. "Are you even listening?"

He closed the distance between them and she went perfectly still, blinking at the intensity in his blue eyes.

"Damn it, Jase, don't you dare—"

His lips met hers, confident and sure of her response. She resisted for one second, then gave in because her heart wouldn't let her do anything else, melting into his kiss as she always did. Holding nothing back. It didn't matter that loving him would make leaving harder. Once his hands slid into her hair and his tongue licked into her, she was gone. She kissed him fully, matching his passion, until he finally set her back, each of them breathing hard.

He stroked her hair, letting his hand trail down her arm. "I want to do a whole lot of that later."

Her throat closed around the sudden sense of loss, and she shook her head.

"I know," he told her. "I hurt you, and I'm sorry."

If he thought it was that simple, he didn't really know her after all. She took a couple of deep breaths, blinking back the threatening tears, letting her anger flow back in. "Sorry's not enough," she told him.

He winced. "No, it's not. But it's all I have. I tried to protect you, and you probably thought I was hanging you out to dry."

"Because you were. Why else would you publicly disavow any connection with me?"

"Because I was too dense to realize you didn't mean what you said. You told me you wanted to repair your image in this town, and I knew being associated with me wouldn't help, so I said we weren't together."

A cold hand gripped her heart, knowing he had every reason to believe that. She'd believed it herself in the beginning. That seemed like a long time ago now. "I'm not embarrassed to be with you."

"If you think it would help, I'll call that reporter back and tell her we're having a torrid affair and that I've totally compromised your high standards when it comes to men."

"No, of course I don't want you to . . ." She

frowned. "You don't believe that, do you? About compromising my standards?"

"You *did* point out my lack of ambition and achievements."

"I didn't know you then."

"But you were right."

"I was narrow-minded. God, Jase, did you really believe I didn't think you were good enough for me?" She put a hand to her forehead. "Okay, maybe I did think that at first, but not when . . . not later. Oh, shit." She rubbed her temples, realizing how much they'd underestimated each other. "I'm sorry."

He didn't look upset. In fact, his lips twitched at the corner. "You're apologizing?"

She narrowed one eye in warning. "Don't ruin it. Jase, I don't care if you're a saloon owner with no other means of support. That was my own prejudice, and I was wrong. You're a good man, and that's far more important."

"Thanks, but I'm not just a saloon owner."

"No, you aren't, and that's my point. You're the one who said it—your job shouldn't define you. There were a lot of things I got wrong about image and reputation, but . . ." She drew in a deep breath. "I think I've got it right now. And I like you just the way you are."

"Even if I don't care about making a lot of money."

"Right."

"But if I found a way to make money, a lot of it, say by using my experience in sports to start a business, it wouldn't change how you feel about me?"

"Of course not. Why, were you thinking of trying it?"

He smiled. "Maybe. I'll tell you later." He ran his fingers through her hair, and she decided she was never again wearing it pinned up in a prissy bun. "Zoe, are we good about that article? I really am sorry."

She sighed. "Yes. I should have trusted you more, Jase."

"I'll let you make it up to me. Come back to my house."

The hunger in his voice stirred something low in her stomach, causing heat to settle between her thighs. "Now?"

He dipped his head, kissing her neck and sending shivers over her whole body. "There's something I want to show you in my garage. It's about that business idea."

She was sure it wasn't as important as what she'd show him in his bedroom, but it did remind her of another uncomfortable fact. She put her arms around his neck. "Jase, I have to ask a favor first."

He raised his head. "Anything."

"Remember when you said I could take a part-time job at the Rusty Wire until I find another job?"

"Yes."

"Well, I've been asking around the past couple of days, and it seems no one is interested in talking to me at the moment. I think that'll change once the facts get out about Matt, and his side of the story is discredited. Or I might decide to do something else—I've been thinking about those sheep here at the commune. There's a business just begging to be started if I have the time to do it. Anyway . . . can I still have a job at the Rusty Wire?"

His good humor slowly faded. "I've been doing some thinking, too. I'm sorry, Zoe, but I have to withdraw my offer."

"I can't have a job?" She dropped her arms. "Why not?"

"Because you'll just stay until you find something better, then leave."

"So? That was always the idea. You were fine with it."

"Well, I'm not anymore. I have to look out for my own best interests, you know."

She squinted, looking closely to see if he was kidding. He wasn't. She imagined she was going to be furious as soon as she stopped being numb.

He nodded to himself, as if approving his own decision. "You've already said you won't stay long. That's not an attractive proposition for an employer."

She ground her teeth. "I thought you wanted to help."

"I think it should benefit both of us. If you want a job, you'll have to marry me."

"I . . ." Her mind stumbled and went blank. "What?"

"Then I'll know you won't leave. And if you still want to work at the Rusty Wire, you can, since you'll be a part owner."

She fought against the spreading numbness in her mind. "You're asking me to *marry* you?" she said. But no, that wasn't exactly right. "You're *blackmailing me* into marrying you?"

"Ugly word. Nevertheless, I'm not willing to take a chance on you leaving me."

The numbness slowly faded. He was serious. Ten years of sensible planning, waiting to meet the right man vanished in a flash. She'd broken her own rules, and fallen in love with the wrong man. And this was the result.

She waited for the crazy fluttering in her chest to stop, marveling at her own reaction. Pure excitement, without a drop of fear. That list was history.

She chewed her lip, pretending to consider it. "I suppose I'd have to sleep with the boss."

"I'm afraid that's mandatory."

"Figures. Would I have to take up fishing?"

"That's negotiable," he allowed.

She crossed her arms, stalling for time. Every impulsive decision she'd made about Jase had been right, and her impulse here was the strongest one she'd ever had. Still, she knew that years from now she'd want to say she'd given it at least a half minute's thought. "Any benefits?"

He arched an eyebrow.

She bit back a smile, thinking she wouldn't mind taking advantage of the benefits very soon. "Pension plan?"

Slowly, he shook his head, showing the first hesitation she'd seen. He almost looked nervous. "I'm afraid not. The position doesn't allow for retirement. It lasts forever."

Rockets started going off in her mind, bursting into sparkling showers. "Hmm." She rocked on the balls of her feet, pretending to ponder his offer, amazed he couldn't see that it was a done deal. "When do you need my decision?"

His gaze was steady on hers, serious, and just the slightest bit worried. She bit her cheek hard, using the pain to hold back the threatening grin.

"I'm not interviewing other applicants. I'm willing to wait until you're available," he said.

She let him worry for a few seconds longer, then

nodded decisively and held out her hand. "I'll take the job."

His face broke into a grin as he shook her hand, then drew her into a long, bone-melting kiss that left her seriously overheated. She wouldn't have minded if it went on for another fifteen or twenty minutes, but he set her back suddenly. "Let's go." Pulling her by the hand, he skirted the house, walking fast toward his truck.

She trotted to keep up with his long strides. "Where are we going?"

He glanced at her, his smile touched by a predatory gleam that stirred a wild pulse of excitement in her. "I neglected to mention the job training program." His smile turned downright feral. "It starts immediately."

Fantasy.
Temptation.
Adventure.

**Visit PocketAfterDark.com,
an all-new website just for Urban
Fantasy and Romance Readers!**

- Exclusive access to the hottest
urban fantasy and romance titles!

- Read and share reviews on
the latest books!

- Live chats with your favorite
romance authors!

- Vote in online polls!

 www.PocketAfterDark.com

26119

More Bestselling Romance
Books from Pocket!

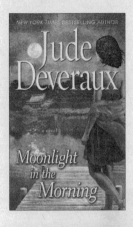

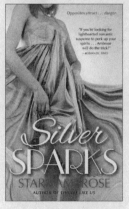